BLOOMS
OF CONSEQUENCE

BREEANA PUTTROFF

FIRST EDITION
ISBN 13: 9781940481104

~~~~~~~~~~~

Cover Design: Mallory Rock

Formatting & Layout: Mallory Rock

~~~~~~~~~~~

Thirteen Pages Press
P.O. BOX 350944
DENVER, CO 80035

Blooms of Consequence: The Dusk Gate Chronicles Book 4 is a work of fiction. Names, characters, places and incidents are products of the author's imagination, or the author has used them fictitiously.

DANGER

"ARE YOU OKAY, WILL?" Quinn asked quietly, still holding William's hand as Nathaniel finally pulled away, finished with raising the tattoo.

After a long moment, he opened his eyes and nodded, although the gesture was unconvincing. "Are you?" he asked, wincing as he struggled to lift his head enough to get a look at the new artwork on his chest. "Please tell me you're not still hurting."

She gave him a half-smile, rubbing her thumb against the back of his hand, but she didn't answer.

His eyes widened, and he glanced up at the bandage that now covered her new tattoo.

She tried to shrug, but only her right shoulder rose, and a searing stab of pain rippled through the left one. "Ow... Okay, that was a mistake."

"It will be sore for a few days," Nathaniel said, setting aside the tools he had been using and digging into his more-familiar leather medical bag.

Quinn looked at William's tattoo. The blue ink stood in sharp contrast to the rest of his skin, forming the formidable symbol that represented the Friends of Philip, and she was suddenly acutely aware of the permanent mark under her own bandage. "Did we really just do that?" she asked, as a sudden wave of reality hit. Being here in Eirentheos sometimes felt so disconnected from her real…her other…life that it was easy to believe the things she did here wouldn't truly matter.

And maybe during her first journeys here, that had been true. But now…

"Yes, you really just did." Nathaniel leaned in again, and Quinn tightened her grip on William's hand as her uncle spread a healing salve over the design, and then taped a thick piece of white gauze over it. William squeezed his eyes shut while he was being touched. "It took me awhile to get used to it at first, too," Nathaniel said. "But you have a long time to adjust. That tattoo isn't going anywhere."

Her stomach tightened with a strange feeling as she thought about that…it was permanent, what she'd done. Even if she did walk away from all of this and go back to her life in her world, she would always have this reminder. And other people would be able to see it. "I wonder what my mom would say," she wondered aloud.

Nathaniel's gray eyes met hers, and she wasn't sure how to read the expression in them. "I don't know what Megan would say, Quinn. But I think Samuel would be proud."

Beside her, William struggled to sit up. Once he'd managed it, he put his arm around her shoulder, careful not to touch either of their bandages.

"Would he?" Quinn asked. "He's the one who left…the one who chose to get married and to have a baby in my world instead of here. Did he really want me here?"

Nathaniel sighed, his expression serious now. "His situation was complicated, and the choices he made were his own. He kept you there because he wanted you safe. If he were here now, that's probably still what he would want…for you to be safe…but he still would have been proud of your making a decision for yourself…once he adjusted to the fact that you're grown up enough to make it. I'm not sure I'm ready for that part myself."

She swallowed; she'd thought that she'd long ago accepted the death of her biological father, but the things that had happened lately brought his absence into sharp focus sometimes. It didn't help that she wouldn't be facing the choices she was now if he was still alive.

"In any case," Nathaniel added, keeping his eyes on hers, "I'm proud of you."

She didn't know how to answer. William's arm tightened around her as she struggled to think. It was only recently that she'd found out that Nathaniel was actually her uncle, her father's brother, and not just the small-town doctor she'd known her whole life.

Nathaniel looked as awkward as she felt as he finished putting things away inside several leather cases, but he smiled reassuringly at her, and she realized he didn't expect a response. He pulled a small glass bottle out of his medical pouch. The little round pills inside rattled as he set it on the table in front of them. "Both of you should take two of them every six hours for the next day or so. I'm going to go speak with Stephen and see if we can figure out what's going on here."

At almost the same time Nathaniel was going out of the room, Thomas reappeared in the doorway. "More ice, anyone?" he asked, grinning and holding up two small cloth bags.

"Yes, please," William said, but his hands didn't move. Quinn, still reeling from the conversation with Nathaniel, held both of her hands out, though the right one made it further than the left. Smiling, Thomas crossed the room and set one ice pack in each of her hands.

Maybe she was wrong, and she had recovered at least a little bit, because her hands cooperated now as she lifted the first bag to her chest. After a tense moment of adjusting to the cold, the ice felt good against her flaming skin.

"Okay, Will," she said, raising the other, "this is going to feel awful for a minute, but then it'll help."

He nodded again, the only gesture he seemed capable of at the moment, and she thought about how strange it felt to be talking him through something. Usually it was William, the healer, who was speaking to her in soothing tones, right before he applied a stinging ointment or stuck a needle in her.

"Crap!" He sucked in a breath, squeezing his eyes shut as she pressed the little blue bag to his chest.

"That's usually my line," she said, inching closer to him while holding both ice packs in place.

After a moment, he relaxed slightly and replaced her hand with his, holding the ice against the bandage himself. "Why did we do this again?"

"Because you could get it over with *now*. Imagine watching *that* and then thinking about it for a couple of moons before doing it to yourself." Thomas said. He was teasing, but there was an edge to his voice.

Quinn knew he was upset about not being allowed to join the Friends of Philip with them now. Stephen had agreed that Thomas could join before he was officially of age, but he had to wait until his sixteenth birthday, when his twin sister, Linnea, would be of age.

In some ways, she thought, it was more important to him than it was to her and William. He was the one who had been held hostage and tortured in Philotheum, the one who had been rescued by guards brave enough to be members of the secret resistance. Those guards were now facing a likely execution for that bravery.

Yes, Thomas very much had a stake in joining the Friends of Philip.

Looking at Thomas's face, thinking about what he'd been through, made the pain she was in seem worth it somehow and eased her doubts about what her real father would have wanted. He was gone, and it was up to her now.

Beside her, William straightened, matching her posture, and tried to smooth his expression. "Help me out?" he asked Thomas, holding up his shirt, which had been folded over the back of the couch.

"Not being allowed to officially join yet doesn't change how you feel about it, Thomas," William said as Thomas helped him ease the fabric over his head. Quinn held the ice pack until the shirt was on, and then she pulled back his unbuttoned collar and pressed the bag against his bandage again. William shuddered, but kept talking as he reached to hold it himself. "And you never know; Father may yet change his mind now that we're not going to Bristlecone."

"Maybe," Thomas said. "But you're right; it doesn't really matter if I'm allowed to officially join or not. I know which side I'm on. Speaking of not going to Bristlecone, though…Quinn, are you all right with that?"

She had never noticed before just how ingrained a habit shrugging was, but the memory of the sharp pain a moment ago managed to stop her. Was she all right? She hadn't even thought about that yet…what it might mean if they couldn't get to the gate. "I don't know, Thomas. Before yesterday, I wasn't even planning on going back home yet. We were going to be leaving for a trip through the kingdom, remember? I wonder if we can do that now?"

Thomas frowned. "No, I don't think so, Quinn. It would be too dangerous for any of us to be traveling away from the castle. There was a reason my father was sending us to Bristlecone, remember?"

"Right, that was stupid of me to even mention." Quinn swallowed, remembering that they weren't sure how much Tolliver knew, remembering the missing guard and the strangers camped around the gate. Everything had changed so quickly since yesterday, so many big things had happened, that she hadn't even had time to think about any of it. One moment they'd been planning the traditional kingdom tour to commemorate William's coming of age, and the next they'd been going to Bristlecone; and then, just a little while ago, it had all changed again.

All day, she'd had gnawing anxiety about seeing her mother again. It was only now she realized that she'd been looking forward to it, too.

"It wasn't stupid, Quinn. None of us has any idea what's really going on right now," William said, rubbing his thumb against the back of her hand.

Something about the gesture, or maybe his words, set off an unexpected reaction inside her. Her stomach clenched, and hot moisture appeared in the corners of her eyes. She blinked furiously, trying to make them go away, but more kept building. A second later, she was mortified when drops started running down her cheeks. She yanked her hand out of William's and tried rubbing them away.

"Yeah, Quinn," Thomas said kindly. "Hey, are you okay?" his voice changed, and she knew he'd seen what she was trying to hide.

She was fine. She tried to tell him so, tried to tell both of them as they leaned in close, but her voice wouldn't work. When she opened her mouth, all that came out was a shuddering sob, and the tears flowed faster. It was suddenly hard to breathe. Thomas retrieved the ice pack from where it had fallen into her lap and held it back against her chest, and William rubbed her back, but she couldn't stop crying.

She didn't know why, didn't understand why she couldn't make herself stop, but the third time she tried to speak to explain that she was just fine, William looked up at Thomas. "Go," he said. "Give her some space, please."

She hadn't known that she didn't want him there, but when Thomas pulled the door closed behind him, she felt an overpowering sense of relief. Still, though, the tears didn't stop. William set his ice pack down as he scooted so close to her that she was practically in his lap. He pulled her head against the side of his chest that wasn't hurting and held her there.

At first, she sobbed harder, still not understanding where the tears were coming from. He just held her tighter, not saying anything.

Eventually, the torrent slowed into a steady stream, and finally she could almost put words to the emotion that had overtaken her. "What if I can never go home again?"

In the next moment, she knew exactly why, the other night when he'd told her he loved her for the first time, she'd had her answer for him right away. He didn't speak immediately, didn't shrug off her concerns or tell her it was going to be okay, when neither of them knew if that was true. He looked at her thoughtfully for a long moment before he finally answered. "I don't know."

It was enough that she was able to finally stop crying. She took a deep breath and composed herself, nodding at his answer…the only truthful answer there could be. William reached into his pocket, but when he pulled his hand back out, it was empty.

"I already went through all of your handkerchiefs, remember?" she said, glancing down at the bandage on her chest.

"It's been a long day already, hasn't it?" He cupped her chin in his hand, brushing away the remnants of her tears with his thumb.

His touch brought with it a new thought, one that made her shiver, and she took his other hand in hers. "I'm glad I'm stuck on the same side of the gate as you."

The way his eyes widened gave her hope that the idea of being separated like that alarmed him as much as it did her. She didn't get the chance to ask him, though, before he brought his lips to hers.

His lips were feather-light as they brushed against hers, sending a flood of warmth all the way to her toes, before he moved on, planting soft kisses along her chin and her cheekbones, kissing everywhere the tears had been, replacing her doubts with the one thing she was certain of right now…him.

By the time he finally pulled away, her thoughts had cleared, and her resolve was back where it belonged. "Sorry about that."

William didn't answer; he just leaned in again, kissing her softly on the nose before leaning back against the couch cushion. "I wonder where Linnea went."

Linnea found her mother outside, sitting comfortably on one of the polished wooden benches, baby Hannah nestled in her lap while most of the rest of Linnea's youngest siblings played nearby.

"Where are Emma and Alex?" she asked, coming to sit next to her.

Charlotte smiled and adjusted Hannah on her lap so that she could turn and look at Linnea. "Mud fight." She nodded toward a recently watered patch of flowers. "Mia took them upstairs to change."

"That sounds about right." Linnea chuckled. "They didn't cause too much damage," she said, glancing over at a wide circle of gravel littered with shovels and other digging toys. That space had once been a flowerbed, too.

Her mother laughed aloud. "I think I could have *another* thirteen children and none of them would be as destructive as you and Thomas were. Of course, I had three other small boys *and* Rebecca when you and Thomas were little. I'm not sure why we didn't stop having children after you." Charlotte's criticism rang hollow, though, as she kissed the top of Hannah's head, taking a deep sniff of her neck before leaning over and kissing Linnea on the head, too.

"I wish I could tell you I'm sorry you're not getting to go on your trip," Charlotte said, "but right now I'm really just glad you're going to be somewhere I can find you."

She nodded, reaching to take her little sister from her mother's arms. Hannah squealed as Linnea blew bubbles on her tummy, trying to figure out how to ask the questions she so desperately needed the answers to. Finally, she decided on point-blank. "How much danger am I in?"

The dark shadow that passed over Charlotte's eyes gave her the answer that no words could, and she curled up under her mother's outstretched arm. She stayed there for a long moment, feeling the smooth silk of her mother's burgundy blouse against her cheek while Hannah's tiny fingers picked at her thumbnail.

"Is Quinn the reason you've been sending William to Bristlecone all these years?" Something William had said a while ago had made her wonder about this, but it seemed like it might be too touchy a subject to ask him or Quinn about directly.

Charlotte closed her eyes, her dark eyelashes a sharp contrast against her pale cheeks. "I'm ashamed to admit it, Linnea, but yes, that was a big consideration when your father and I decided to allow that."

"Why?" But she knew the answer before her mother answered. "You were hoping that Quinn would find her way back here."

"Of course we were hoping that. We were never happy that Samuel's heir was born there in the first place. We always felt that she belonged here."

There was something unspoken in her mother's response that made Linnea's breath catch in her throat. "You can't have expected that she and William would actually end up together. Unless you're an oracle and I don't know about it."

"My great-grandfather was, you know."

Linnea's eyes widened. "Was what? An oracle? No, I didn't know that."

"I'll tell you the story sometime, but no... Although it was always a hope at the back of our minds that it would be that easy…that William and Quinn would find each other and choose to... We didn't dare to dream that it would actually happen, or at least we never expected it to."

"But now it has." Quinn and William had officially announced their courtship at William's birthday party a couple of nights ago, and from the way those two looked when they were together, Linnea was certain things between them went deeper than that. "So now all of your problems are solved?"

"Your tone is quite unbecoming, Linnea."

"I'm not feeling very *becoming* at the moment."

Charlotte sighed. "I know." She ran her hand softly down Linnea's dark, curly hair, twisting the end of a strand around her finger. "We don't know exactly how much danger you're in…how much danger any of you are in. Your father and I plan on speaking to everyone tonight, after he's had a chance to meet with Marcus and the rest of the head guards to make a decision. For right now, we're thinking that we will be keeping the castle locked down completely. None of you are to be allowed off the grounds until further notice. Rebecca and Howard are staying here now, as well. Someone has been sent to collect their belongings."

"What? What about the seekers? What about William's clinics?"

"I don't know. I'm sure things will change as we get more information and more things sorted out. Our biggest concerns, of course, are the four of you. When I think of what could have happened… If Paul hadn't…"

Linnea shivered. She'd had plenty of time last night when she wasn't sleeping to imagine what might have happened if Paul Moran, a guard who had worked for her family for years hadn't disappeared yesterday morning, alerting everyone to a secret plan to kidnap Linnea. "Is the castle secure now?" she asked, with a sick feeling in her stomach. The abduction had originally been planned for today. She still fought nightmares from when Thomas had been captured in Philotheum, and she hadn't even been there to see it.

"Of course it is," Charlotte said, tightening her grip around Linnea's shoulders. "Do you think I would be out here with the children if it weren't?" She tipped her head casually toward the western corner of the playground, and Linnea followed with her eyes. Now that she was looking, she could make out the outline of Ben Westbrook, standing near a little grove of trees, keeping an eye on the children as they played and on Charlotte and Linnea as they talked. She relaxed slightly. Ben she trusted.

"Seriously, though, Mother. Do you really think that William and Quinn courting is going to solve anything? That's putting an awful lot of pressure on them, isn't it?"

"No, it doesn't solve anything. It won't solve anything even if they…if Quinn decides to try and make a bid for her throne. There are still a lot of obstacles. And your father and I don't *want* to put pressure on them. We owe them that much…letting them make those decisions on their own."

"But it's what you want, isn't it? The two of them to take their relationship past courting? For Quinn to decide to take the throne and for her and William to marry…unite the kingdoms and all that?"

Deep lines appeared on Charlotte's forehead. "From where we're sitting right now, Linnea, *yes*. That seems like the quickest route to a solution that would be good for everyone. It could potentially restore peace to Philotheum, restore the relations between our kingdoms, bring happiness to William and hopefully to Quinn as well."

"Except for the part where she has to become the monarch of a kingdom she knows nothing about, in a world she didn't grow up in, leave her family and get married at seventeen…which is not exactly the norm in the world where she's from."

"Yes, except for that part."

"And you're just leaving that bit out when you talk to them."

"Regardless of what we feel would be best, it isn't our place to demand that of them. We're hoping that we don't reach the point where we have to force the issue…that they have time to come to a decision on their own. Your father and I would ask you to respect that, Linnea."

"You don't think they've figured all of this out?"

Her mother sat up, meeting Linnea's eyes with a hard, set gaze. "I'm quite certain they've both figured out some of it. Your father and I are not so sure they've reached all of the same conclusions, or that they understand all of the possible implications of their relationship."

"Or they've thought about it, but are in denial."

"Leave them be, Linnea. That's not a request."

"It's not fair to them, Mother. All of this plotting behind their backs."

"You're right, it isn't. Which is exactly why you need to stay as far out of it as you can. Especially you, with your gift for influence. Enough damage has been done to them already. The last thing we want is for Quinn to make a decision that she can't really own. It has to be her choice."

"What if she makes the wrong one?"

"I don't know."

NINETEEN DAYS LATER

WILLIAM FOLLOWED THE GARDEN path behind the castle all the way to where it ended in a large gravel circle, surrounded by benches and flower patches. Past the circle was an expansive lawn. Another path began here, leading well past the lawns and out to the crumple pitch, but he wasn't interested in following it. He'd already found what he was looking for.

Quinn sat in the middle of one of the lawns, her bare feet poking out from under the hem of her long, simple linen skirt, her long, wavy auburn hair loose down her back, reflecting the warm rays of the afternoon sunlight. One hand was at her forehead, shielding her eyes as she looked up, watching a bird as it swooped out of the sky toward her, landing not-quite gracefully a few feet away from her.

William chuckled as he watched the bird – still a fledgling, though it was growing quickly – walk toward its master. Quinn held out a treat, and the bird gobbled it up before allowing her to stroke its head.

Warmth filled his chest at the sight, and he quickly crossed the lawn to reach them. "Hey, beautiful," he said, leaning down to kiss the top of her head. It was warm from the sun and smelled of her rich, flowery shampoo. He lingered there for a moment, breathing it in before he sat down beside her.

"Hi." She turned to face him, her dark gray eyes lighting up with her smile. "Did you finish figuring out whatever it was you were working on?"

"No," he said. "But I was getting frustrated and bored with it, and I was missing you."

She raised an eyebrow. "You, bored in your lab? I didn't think that was possible."

He chuckled. "It didn't used to be." Reaching into his pocket, he retrieved a cloth-wrapped bundle. Opening it, he withdrew a small chunk of dried meat, and held it out to the young bird. Raeyan snatched it up. "Of course, I didn't used to have anything I'd rather be doing."

He stretched out one finger and used it to trace her arm, from her wrist all the way up to her shoulder, before looking up at her face. Her cheeks turned a light shade of pink, a sight that made his heart flutter and.

Raeyan, the bird, annoyed at being ignored, butted his head into William's hand, looking for another treat.

"No, you don't," Quinn chided, reaching over to press one finger gently down on Raeyan's light gray head. "No more until you've carried this to Thomas for me." She held up a small square of purple cloth and tucked it inside the little silver cylinder that was attached to Raeyan's leg. The bird made several clicking sounds at her, but she stared him down with a firm glare. "Go."

William chuckled as the bird took flight. "Takes after his mother, that one."

Raeyan's mother was William's seeker bird, Aelwyn, who was no doubt perching nearby in the trees, supervising the training of her one offspring that had been chosen as a human companion. Her mate, Sirian, wouldn't be far off, either.

"Is it just you and Thomas, or is Linnea out here somewhere too?" William asked.

"Thomas is out by the crumple field, and Linnea's on the front lawn. We've been running him in different patterns. He's actually getting good."

"They learn quickly. They're smart birds. He could probably go a lot further if there was anywhere safe to send him."

Quinn sighed. "Being cooped up in the castle is bad for everyone."

"I know. I was half tempted to push the issue the other day and insist on going to Cloud Valley with Nathaniel."

Her eyes widened. "And leave me here to worry about you? It's not worth the risk, Will. It bothers me enough that Nathaniel is gone. I don't understand what's so important that he needs to be traveling right now, either."

"He's never been much for staying close to the castle. It's easier to avoid questions about his real identity if he's never in one place for too long. And Eli needs the supplies and help out there."

"Are they still getting the reports of shadeweed?"

He nodded. Patches of the extremely poisonous plant had been showing up all over certain areas of the kingdom, in places it had never been found growing before. And in two towns, they were still getting occasional cases of citizens…mostly children…who showed up in clinics with symptoms of shadeweed poisoning, but no idea when they might have come into contact with the plant.

"Is that what you were still working on in the lab? A better remedy?"

"Yes."

"And you haven't had any luck? I thought it was going well."

"I did make a pretty big breakthrough for the early stages, actually. Nathaniel took a sample to Eli."

"A way to make that awful stuff taste better?"

"No. This one you don't have to drink at all."

She raised an eyebrow. "I think drinking it might be a little more popular with the kids than more needles, Will."

"Not that stuff. Especially when, most of the time, they turn around and throw up half of it. If this works, and I think it will, we'll be able to cure shadeweed poisoning with one or two doses of medicine that will work better and not make them sick."

She smiled. "That's a good thing, then."

"I'm boring you to death, aren't I?"

"I don't understand half of what you tell me, but I like when you talk to me anyway. I think the stuff you do is kind of awesome."

He reached up to touch her face, running his index finger down the side of her face and along her chin before leaning in to kiss her. "I am a lucky man."

She shook her head. "I think I'm the lucky one."

He kissed her again, this time taking a little longer before he finally pulled back. "Are you doing all right, Quinn?"

She studied him, an intense look in her eyes. "I'm just as good as anyone else. We're all stuck here."

He closed his eyes for a minute, silently reminding himself that he wasn't going to press her about this. It had to be hard on her, stranded in his world, no idea of when, or if…no, he wasn't going to think like that…*when* she would be able to see her family again.

It had to be on her mind today, though. The gate would be opening again tomorrow, and although they were hoping they might be able to try to go through, more strange refugees kept showing up in the area, making it unsafe to attempt to get to the bridge without the chance of being seen.

If they couldn't go through, that would be twice. Another whole day missed in her world, another ten days stuck in his with no answers.

Keeping his promise not to push it, he leaned in, meaning only to kiss her gently again, but it quickly turned into something more. Whatever emotions she thought she was keeping inside about the uncertainty of her life came pouring out as soon as his lips touched hers.

It was several minutes before they were able to separate, breathless and lying down in the grass, their hands still entwined. For a long moment, he stared up at the bright blue sky above them, watching the few clouds that were gathered there. Back behind them there was an approaching line of ominous gray, and he hoped, as he had been hoping every afternoon, that the clouds would actually arrive before they dispersed in the dry air. It hadn't rained in weeks.

While he stared up into the endless sky, he contemplated his feelings. As tense as the last few weeks with Quinn had been, they'd also been, without question, the best weeks of his life. He still couldn't believe that she'd said yes when he'd asked her if he could court her, that he'd actually managed to find this girl and begin a relationship with her…that she was here beside him now.

He rolled up onto his side, propping his head on his hand, so that he could look down at her. With his free hand, he reached for the delicate silver chain around her wrist, running it between his fingers for a moment before he turned his eyes to her face. "I love you, Quinn."

She smiled. "I love you, too." Her fingers found the chain on his wrist, the courtship bracelet that matched hers.

Getting used to the striking new tattoo on his chest was a simple task compared to getting used to this…to being able to just tell her how he felt, to have her return his smile and say it back to him. He'd always worried that he was never going to find someone who would really understand him, who would be able to deal with his need to hide away and study, or especially someone to whom he could talk about his travels and experiences in the other world.

Finding Quinn had exceeded even his wildest imaginings. And when he'd learned that she was really from this world, that they had even that in common... well, he must have done something right for the Maker to smile down on him like this.

Of course, it complicated things, too. Whatever Quinn decided to do was going to have a big impact on him. One thing the last couple of weeks had given him was time to think, and he knew, now, that he was prepared to follow her whatever she ended up doing, whether she went back to her own world, or…and in some ways this thought scared him even more…to the castle in Philotheum. He wasn't sure what he thought about the distinct possibility that she might become a queen, but he had decided it didn't matter.

Lately, he'd actually been considering proposing to her.

He wouldn't do it yet, of course. She had enough big decisions to make in the near future…he wasn't going to add to that. And he especially didn't want her to make any rash decisions *because* of him. He wasn't planning on going anywhere she didn't go…he'd show her that before asking her.

A flutter of wings overhead interrupted his reverie. He glanced up, expecting to see Raeyan returning from his practice run, and was startled when, instead, it was Linnea's bird, Zylia, that swooped gracefully down onto the grass in front of them.

Quinn sat up, frowning and reached to open Zylia's cylinder.

"What is it?" William asked, not liking the expression on her face as she read the note.

"I don't know. Linnea says we should meet her in the front hall immediately."

In the next instant, he was on his feet, reaching for her hand. "Let's go."

Thomas and Linnea were both standing in the main entrance when they arrived. They didn't look upset…maybe she'd jumped to conclusions when she'd read Linnea's note, Quinn thought. Lately they'd all been looking for disaster around every corner.

"What's wrong?" William demanded.

"Nothing's *wrong*," Linnea said. "But Rebecca's water broke."

"Oh." William looked a little pale. "And Nathaniel's not here."

"No, he's not. And Lilly and Graeme are still at his sister's house." Linnea reminded him…though Quinn thought it was a little unlikely he'd forget that he was the only trained healer in the castle right now.

"And there's that whole thing where we're not allowing anyone except family and trusted friends and servants inside the castle…" Thomas added. "So…"

"I've only delivered one baby by myself!" William said. "And that wasn't on purpose."

"Well, this is your chance to increase that total," Thomas said.

"I'm not sure I should be practicing this on my *sister*."

Linnea shrugged. "It's pretty much you or Howard…and I don't think Howard is up for quite that much."

"All right. Where is she?" William still didn't look comfortable with the idea, but Quinn saw him shift into what she called his "healer mode".

"Come on," Linnea said, grabbing him by the hand and dragging him toward the stairs.

Quinn looked at Thomas.

"Some days I'm glad I wasn't born to be a healer," he said.

"There's never a day when I wish *I* was." She looked up the stairs. Linnea and William had already disappeared. "Poor Will."

"Are you kidding? He'll be freaked out for approximately five minutes, and then he'll be over the moon that he got to do something medical for the first time in weeks."

She frowned. "Yeah, maybe if 'something medical' wasn't the possibility of having to deliver his sister's baby."

"You think you know my brother better than I do now, huh?" He bumped her arm with his elbow.

"That's sort of the point, isn't it? You're not courting him."

He smiled, studying her. "You're protective of him. Even with me."

"And?"

"And nothing, Princess. I approve." He leaned over and kissed her on the cheek. "If you're going to be stealing him away from me, I'm going to expect you to look after him."

"I am not stealing anyone away from anything."

He chuckled. "You're right, that was a bad choice of words. This is a purchase you are paying for in full, to be sure. But you are going to take him home with you, I think. Wherever you decide that is."

She stared at him for several seconds, unsure how to answer that…not ready to discuss that with anyone yet. Finally, she settled for changing the subject. "Nathaniel is supposed to be coming back this evening, isn't he?"

Thomas grinned. "Yes, he is."

"I think maybe we should go and send Sirian with a message…see if we can get him to speed it up."

"You know, Quinn, just because I already have a lot of sisters, doesn't mean I'm not excited about getting a new one."

"How is she?" Thomas asked when Will came into the common room a little while later.

"She's good. Not really in serious labor yet. It's going to be a long day, I think. Maybe a long night. Right now, she's playing Choice with Mother, Linnea, and Howard. You can go in if you want."

"Can I go?" Emma asked, jumping up from the little table.

"Sure," Thomas said, standing and taking her hand. "Alex, do you want to?"

Alex's emphatic "No!" made William chuckle, he knew exactly how his little brother felt. He loved Rebecca, but this was a little too much for him. He was hoping desperately that Nathaniel would get back before he actually had to do anything.

"Can I go play?"

William glanced down at the page of math problems Alex had been working. Alex had finished more than Emma had, so he figured it was only fair, and he nodded.

"You can sure clear a room fast," Quinn said, once everyone had gone.

"We could go, too," he told her.

She frowned. "There're a lot of people in there already. I don't want to overwhelm her. She's really doing okay?"

William smiled, relieved. "She's good. Excited, I think. If someone other than me was here to help her, I'd be excited, too. It's hard to believe I'm going to be an uncle." He sat down next to Quinn on the couch, and she took his hand.

"Not how you wanted to spend your day is it?"

"I like the *idea* of delivering babies…but not like this."

"I know. I can't imagine Rebecca is thrilled about it, either. I love my little brother to pieces, but I wouldn't want him anywhere near me if I was in labor."

He chuckled. "Exactly."

"Thomas and I sent a message to Nathaniel, hoping he'll hurry back."

"Thank you."

"No problem. Hey, I have a question."

"What?"

"It's just... It doesn't seem like Rebecca's been pregnant for what would be nine months in my world."

"Oh. Right. I never thought about explaining that to you. She hasn't been. For whatever reason, pregnancy in our world is exactly the same as it is in yours. Somewhere around two hundred and eighty days."

"How is *that* possible, when everything else is so different?"

He shrugged. "I don't know how any of it is possible. My best theory is that something about the atmosphere in each world dictates how people age, but it doesn't affect pregnancy, which is regulated by something else."

"By what?"

"I don't know. Whatever it is that regulates a woman's body, I suppose. Anyway, it's probably a good thing. I mean, I'm not the girl here, but if I was *you*, and I was trying to choose between the two worlds, I think the one where you'd have to be pregnant for ten times as long would be a deal breaker."

She giggled. "I suppose it might…if I was pregnant."

"Well, someday you will be."

Her eyes grew much too wide, and heat rushed up his neck as he realized he'd been making a very big assumption. "You do want to have children someday, don't you?" It had never crossed his mind before that she'd grown up in a world that was different from his in this way, too…in her world it wasn't just a given that people would have children when they got married.

"Yeah… I mean, yes, I do. *That* is just way far ahead of where my mind is right now."

He laughed, more from relief than anything. "Well, I wasn't thinking it would be tomorrow."

"William?" The voice from the doorway startled them both.

"What, Simon?"

"Have you seen Maxwell?"

"No. Not since breakfast, I don't think." He turned to Quinn, and she shook her head.

Simon sighed. "He's probably off with Catherine again somewhere. He's never around when we need him."

"What's going on?"

"The last patrol of the bridge saw some more refugees in the area, after it had just been clear again the day before yesterday." He looked meaningfully at William. "I don't think there's going to be any chance we can try the gate again tomorrow."

William stole a glance at Quinn, but she only nodded. It was news she'd been expecting.

"Let me know if you see Maxwell," Simon said, before he disappeared down the hall.

FIRE

"I KNOW, GIRL, a ride around the paddock is not the same as a real one, I'm sorry," Quinn said, holding out an apple to Dusk. The horse snuffed at it, but then snatched it out of her hand. "It could be worse, you know," she admonished. "I haven't *left*."

William was standing in the stall next to her, brushing out Skittles. She didn't have to look at him to know that sentence had gotten his attention. The gate had opened again the night before last, and she knew he was worried about her, but he hadn't asked her about it. Maybe he was afraid of upsetting her.

"I had a dream the other night," she told him.

He stopped brushing. "A nightmare?"

"No, not really. It was very vivid; I felt like I was really there."

"Where?"

"Bristlecone."

He set down the brush and walked over to the wooden half-wall that separated the two stalls. "Tell me."

"It was like it was normal. You and I both went to the gate and went through. It must have been a Sunday night, I think, because I got up and went to school the next morning. You were there, too."

"Not avoiding you, I hope."

She looked into his eyes. "I'm not even sure I could imagine that even in a dream anymore. It's hard to believe you ever used to do that."

"That's probably the biggest regret I have, you know…that I treated you that way."

"You didn't know."

His gaze was intense. "Does that matter? I mean, when you first came here, you didn't know anyone; this wasn't your life, and still you were nice to everyone. I do realize now that I could have acted like a decent human being, even if I was keeping a secret."

She ran her hand down the side of his face. "Well, in my dream, you did. You walked me to my first class, and we sat together at lunch."

He smiled. "I would have liked that."

"Zander was mad. So was Abigail. Nobody else was talking to me."

His face dropped. "I thought you said it wasn't a nightmare."

"It wasn't really. It was hard at first, but you were there. After school, I went over to your house, and we did our homework together. And then… it was a dream, you know, so it wasn't just one day. Eventually, Zander moved on. Maybe he started dating someone else, or something, I don't know. And Abigail could only be mad for so long before she was just dying to know more about the elusive William Rose."

He chuckled. "Yeah, my anonymity would be in deep trouble in about thirty seconds, wouldn't it?"

"I don't think I'd give it that long."

He reached for her hand. "It would be kind of fun…to walk around Bristlecone High School, holding your hand."

"It was good in my dream." Her stomach gave a little flip at his answering smile.

"So what else happened?"

She shrugged. "The details are mostly vague, but I think there were lots of things. You having dinner with my family, helping Owen with his math the way you do with Alex sometimes..."

He squeezed her hand. "I'd love to know Owen like that."

Her cheeks warmed a little at the next part. "You asked me to prom."

"Well, that's a given," he said, sliding his finger under her chin to lift her gaze back to his face. What kind of dress did you wear?"

She rolled her eyes. "I wasn't really looking at me."

"*I* would have been."

"Anyway, it was all just stuff like that... maybe just an idea of what it would be like if we were normal teenagers in Bristlecone." She'd stopped short of telling him about the part of her dream where he'd proposed to her shortly before graduation, not knowing how he'd feel about *that*. Not knowing how she felt about it.

He pulled her hand to his lips; his breath was warm against her knuckles. "We could do that, you know, if that's what you want. At some point, we're going to be able to get back to the gate again, and we could go back to Bristlecone and have all of that. We could still get back there long before spring break is over."

"You would do that?"

"Yes, I would. I'm in this, Quinn. Please don't make your decision based on *me*. In some ways, it would be a lot less complicated, wouldn't it? If we just had a simple life there...graduation, college..."

"Would it really be less complicated, do you think?"

He shrugged. "It *sounds* less complicated."

She nodded, and stretched across the wall to kiss him on the cheek. "Everything sounds less complicated when you're not in the middle of it." She picked up Dusk's brush and was about to walk back toward the horse when William grabbed her hand again.

"Are you feeling okay?" he asked.

She frowned. "Yeah, I'm fine. A little tired maybe, but what else is new?"

He ran his hand over the back of her arm for a minute, and then reached to brush across her forehead. "You just feel like you might be a tiny bit warm."

"It's hot in here," she said. "And we're working."

"If you're sure you're okay."

"I'm sure." She headed back to Dusk. She could feel him watch her for a minute, but then he returned to what he'd been doing.

The thing was... the other parts of her dream that she *hadn't* told him about, weren't really less complicated. They were just different. In her dream, William had proposed to her before graduation…before *his* graduation, which was coming up in just three short months in her world. And her mother had been furious, refusing to let her see William anymore.

There'd been a summer of balancing on eggshells…dividing their time between his world and hers, and then the prospect of another long school year before *her* graduation. She'd been left to deal with a year at school without him, with William far away at college somewhere while she navigated her senior year with friends who were okay, but who no longer meant to her what they once had. Friends she'd be leaving behind permanently in a year, anyway.

Sure, life in her world wouldn't involve making a choice about whether to try to take a crown in a kingdom on the verge of war. Her family and friends there weren't in constant danger, weren't battling someone like Tolliver. But that didn't mean life there would be easier.

"Everything okay?" he asked, again.

"Yeah, it really is, Will." The concerned look on his face made her reach up to feel her forehead for herself. It was damp, but she was sweating from the work. She was fine. "It's just… The dream gave me a lot to think about, that's all."

"Why didn't you tell me about it when you had it? I mean, not that I'm entitled to know everything you dream about, but you usually tell me about them when you remember them."

She smiled. "I usually like to tell you… it was just the other night, when the baby was born. You were a little preoccupied."

"I suppose that's true." Although Nathaniel, fortunately, had gotten the message, and made it back to the castle well before Rebecca delivered the beautiful little boy, William had still been up pacing the hallway in nervousness and excitement, ready…if a little hesitant…to lend a hand if needed.

"Did you hear that?"

"What?" The hand with the brush fell to her side, and she cocked her ear toward the door. "Is someone yelling?"

"I think so."

She listened again for a second. There were definitely several voices…men's voices; the yelling was coming from the direction of the castle.

William was already outside Skittles' stall, latching the gate.

Quinn and William were running across the lawn toward the castle when she first noticed the clouds.

At first, they looked like rain clouds…the kind they'd been seeing every afternoon, always promising a storm that never materialized…but something wasn't quite right. They were moving in too quickly, for one thing…a solid line of thick clouds was advancing from the east, even though the sky was perfectly clear and blue from every other direction.

Although there was a strong breeze blowing, it was hot, carrying no hint of the cool air an approaching storm would bring.

Just before they ducked into one of the service entrances, she caught the barest hint of a smell that made her heart sink all the way to her stomach.

By the time they reached the main hall and found Linnea standing just inside of the massive front doors, Quinn knew her expression matched the stricken one on Linnea's face.

"Where's the fire?" she asked.

"I saw the smoke, just to the south," Linnea said. "In the woods…it looked like it might be near the bridge. A couple of soldiers just came rushing in…they were headed toward my father's office."

Near the bridge. A shudder ripped through her body. From the other end of the hallway, Thomas was approaching, looking as worried as she felt, and she could sense that someone was close behind her. She didn't even have to look to know it was Ben Westbrook, who had lately taken it upon himself to be her personal guard. He'd probably been out near the stables somewhere, too, keeping a respectful distance so as not to interfere with her privacy, but also keeping a watchful eye.

William's hand found hers, cold and clammy, but comforting all the same.

Not knowing what to say, she just nodded.

The procession to Stephen's private office was silent. The heavy door was closed when they arrived, but Quinn didn't even stop to knock; she just opened the door and went in. Behind her, she saw William hesitate for only a fraction of a second before he followed, leading the rest of them into the room.

Nathaniel was there, standing huddled in a circle with King Stephen and two soldiers. Dark gray circles underneath her uncle's eyes told her more than she wanted to know. Simon and Maxwell were in the room, too, sitting in two of the armchairs, quietly discussing something.

The soldiers' uniforms were both soaked in sweat; they'd clearly been riding as hard as they could to get here. When he saw Quinn enter the room, Stephen said something in low tones to the two men, and they quickly excused themselves from the room, closing the door behind them.

Quinn stopped before she reached Stephen and Nathaniel and just stood there, unable to make herself go one step further. She didn't want to hear this.

Linnea, of course, needed to hear it for herself. "It's the bridge, isn't it?"

Stephen nodded. "We have some sources telling us that the fire may have started near where the refugees were camping. We can't get anyone into the area. I don't know if the bridge is affected."

Quinn's knees felt wobbly. William took hold of her hand and squeezed.

"Our biggest concern right now," Stephen continued, making his way over to a couch across from her, "is that the fire is spreading quickly through the area. It's a remote wooded area, but it isn't going to take much for it to reach some of the outlying homes. I'm told there are already reports of heavy smoke on some of the farms that aren't far from there."

"I'm going," William said.

"Of course," Stephen answered. "You can go to the emergency camp. Nathaniel and I were already discussing what kinds of supplies we need to be gathering, and making sure that our standard preparations are enough to care for our own people, as well as any refugees who were camping there. We need to look at what we can provide to anyone who may have lost their shelters and food supplies with the fire as well."

Maxwell's head snapped up. "These are the same people we've been worrying about for how long now? We still don't know who they are or where they keep coming from. We don't know if there's someone who's behind all of this, or how compromised that gate may have already been."

Stephen's gaze was level as he looked at his second-born son. "I may not know who those people are, Maxwell, but I do know who I am. They're in my kingdom, and if they've suffered a loss, we will help them."

"I'm going too," Quinn said.

"It's too dangerous," Nathaniel answered. "You're the biggest thing we're trying to protect."

"I don't care. There's no sense protecting someone who does nothing but sit uselessly inside a castle doing nothing when there's an emergency. I'll help set up the clinic and stay there. I'll pass out supplies. I'm not staying here by myself."

Ben, who had been standing silently by the door, stepped forward now. "I'll go with her."

Stephen closed his eyes for several seconds, appearing deep in thought.

"I'm sure we'll need the help, Father," Simon said. "There are so many in our kingdom right now who are fed up with having so many refugees and living with the uncertainty of not knowing what is going to happen. Many of them are going to be unwilling to help foreigners right now. And if any of our own people's homes are destroyed, everyone will be that much angrier. We need to set the example we want to see."

Stephen opened his eyes and nodded. "You may go into the emergency camp or other areas we set up to help, Quinn. As much as we all want to know what's happened to the gate, though, nobody is going anywhere near that area until the fire is fully contained. Understood?"

"Stephen!" Nathaniel protested, but Stephen turned a steely gaze on him. "She's an adult, Nathaniel. I don't actually have the authority to even ask what I'm asking of her. I can't stop her from making her own choices. The most I can do is request, and, honestly, I see Simon's point. What good does it do anyone to keep her hidden away here in the castle?"

"You don't know that someone didn't set that fire."

"No, I don't." He looked over at Thomas and Linnea. "The two of you, on the other hand, are still underage. For now, you will stay at the castle and help here."

From the look on Stephen's face, Quinn knew that the request for Thomas and Linnea to stay here had little to do with their ages. Linnea would officially be of age in less than two more moons. Thomas and Linnea were in more danger than Quinn was. Nobody really knew who Quinn was, but Linnea…Tolliver would still like nothing better than to find some way to force Linnea to marry him, thus "uniting the kingdoms" and fulfilling the prophecy he believed in.

As for Thomas…the ordeal he'd been through, and the time the family had spent searching for him, worrying about him, was just too recent. Nobody was prepared to deal with the idea of Thomas in any danger right now.

THE STRANGER

NATHANIEL, WILLIAM, AND QUINN went directly to the castle clinic from Stephen's office. Within minutes, they were digging through the supply closets, and putting together packets of things they would likely need when they got to the emergency encampment.

Ben showed up outside a few minutes later with a wagon, and he began carrying loads out from the clinic. Thomas and Linnea made several trips out from the kitchen with baskets of sandwiches, fruit, and jugs of water.

Quinn was more nervous than she wanted to admit. Growing up in the dry mountain forests of Colorado, forest fires had always been a potential threat, and one that terrified her. A few years ago, a fire had devastated most of a small town only half an hour away from Bristlecone. The first whiff of smoke she'd caught from the fire today had taken her right back to the stress and worry of that time.

More than the fire itself, she was worried about the people they were going to encounter. For nearly two weeks now, they'd been wondering and worrying about how these new batches of Philothean refugees kept finding their way to the base of the bridge Stephen so fiercely protected.

Refugees had been entering the kingdom for many moons now, but most of them had been Friends of Philip…people with families they wanted to get safely out of Tolliver's reach before returning to Philotheum to continue working to keep their kingdom loyal to its history and traditions.

Nobody knew what might be going on in Philotheum to make those who *weren't* Friends of Philip want to escape, but the biggest concern was *where* they kept ending up. Stephen's soldiers had been working tirelessly to gently encourage the refugees to settle elsewhere…even though most of them had no idea why the gate was such a sensitive area, but somehow the refugees never quite seemed to disappear. There were always more.

Marcus Westbrook, who was Stephen's most trusted guard, had confided the other day that he was beginning to suspect it was the *same* people who kept returning to the area.

Stephen was convinced that there was someone behind it, and was especially worried that someone might know the truth about that bridge…the fact that once every ten days, at dusk, the center of the bridge opened as a gate into another world…the world where Quinn had been born. It was why they hadn't dared to try to use the gate, and the possible security leaks were why they had all been confined to the castle for the past couple of weeks, ever since they'd discovered that not even all of the castle guards could be trusted.

Quinn agreed with Stephen. There was something else going on here that they just couldn't see. She hadn't told anyone yet about the *other* dreams she'd been having lately…the ones that had nothing to do with Bristlecone. Although she was used to having disconcerting dreams, lately they had grown frightening and vivid again.

There had been a lot of dreams about the decision she was facing…the one that she was beginning to suspect that she'd already made…there had been other dreams, too, even stranger ones. She'd been dreaming a lot about the gate itself…not just about going home, but about traveling between the worlds. Most of the time, she couldn't remember exactly what had happened in the dreams, but there was an ominous feeling to them. More than once, she'd woken up crying.

Finally, the wagon and the horses were loaded and ready to go. Dusk was looking at her almost smugly. Being walked around the castle paddock a few times a day wasn't her idea of good exercise. She whined excitedly as Quinn double-checked all of the buckles and fastenings of the saddle and bridle, and carefully secured the very-full saddlebags.

"You're sure about this?" William's voice, close to her ear, startled her. They'd all been pretty quiet while getting ready…concentrating intently on the task at hand. "Because it honestly makes me a little nervous to think of you out there."

"I'm sure. What I really wouldn't be able to handle is sitting in the castle by myself while you're all out actually doing something. You can't keep me locked up forever."

He opened his mouth, and then closed it again. Instead, he leaned in to kiss her on the forehead before he turned away to mount Skittles. She stared after him for a moment, appreciation for him washing over her. He tried so hard to understand what she was dealing with. She appreciated his thoughtfulness in remaining silent on certain things almost as much as his ability to really listen and understand the things she did want to talk about.

She only hoped that she managed to do the same for him.

"You still feel a little warm to me," he muttered as they started walking. "Tell me if you start feeling bad or something."

And, then, sometimes he was a bit overprotective, too.

Smoke was thick in the sky as William, Nathaniel, and Quinn rode away from the castle, with Ben following closely behind with the wagon.

Thomas, Linnea, and some of William's other siblings were there to see them off. Even Howard took a few minutes away from caring for Rebecca and their new baby to make sure they had everything they needed.

They hadn't even had a chance to have a Naming Ceremony for the baby, yet. William had confided that the ceremony would probably end up being something small and private, just for family, given everything that was going on. Hardly fitting for the first royal grandchild, but they'd make it nice somehow.

Quinn knew her own Naming Ceremony had been *very* private, even though she was technically the heir to the Philothean throne.

The air smelled strongly of fire…similar, in a way, to the smell of a campfire, which Quinn loved, but with a darker, mustier overtone that made her skin crawl.

The roads were busy. People were heading back and forth between the castle and the capitol city, and even more were heading out past the city to help with the firefighting efforts. She knew that Maxwell and Simon both had been out near where crews were working to dig a fire line between the forest and the first houses outside the city.

It was a short ride to the temporary emergency camp just outside of town. Quinn was pleased to see more people than she had expected working together to set up an enormous tent, and various other shelters. There were crates of vegetables and lots of supplies already, and someone had pounded stakes in the ground for tying up the horses.

"This was fast," Quinn said, a little taken aback at how much had already been done and how organized it was.

"It's not the first time," Ben said, coming to help William remove Dusk's saddle bags. "It's been a mostly dry season so far. Everyone's been watchful for fires. There was a small one outside of Cloud Valley a moon ago."

Quinn nodded. It made sense. So the fact that they had an elaborate system already set up wasn't surprising. But what was surprising to her was the number of refugees in the camp. There weren't any. Ben helped her and William unload all of their supplies and carry them into the tent that would serve as a clinic, but aside from the crates, boxes, and a couple of cots, it was empty. "Where is everyone?" she wondered.

William shrugged. "No news is good news."

And no news it was. After all of the stress of getting there, the afternoon passed slowly. The only people who came into the camp for supplies and information were those fighting the fire. Jacob arrived from Mistle Village, though he brought nothing with him. The clinic in Mistle Village was still being rebuilt after it had been destroyed when someone set fire to it. Quinn wondered if fire was always this big a part of life here in Eirentheos.

Jacob and William tended a few patients, but they were mostly blisters from digging fire lines, and a couple of cases of smoke inhalation. The only people who came into the camp, though, were citizens. The refugees seemed to have disappeared.

Most of the reports they heard were good…the fire was still small and staying in the unpopulated wilderness. The main worry was that the refugees were trapped somewhere, but so far nobody had seen any signs of people in the danger zone.

At one point, Quinn actually dozed off on one of the cots in the clinic. She woke with a start at the sound of William and Jacob whispering across the tent from her.

"Oh my gosh, I'm so sorry," she said, sitting up so fast that it made her a little dizzy.

"It's okay," William said. "You can rest if you need to. I know you said you were tired."

Nathaniel was chuckling. "We only just noticed that you'd fallen asleep. I think you would have kept sleeping if we hadn't been trying so hard not to wake you."

"I came to help," she said. "Not to take a nap."

William sighed, but he didn't argue.

She knew she was probably just being stubborn. There was little to do for the next hour…she could have napped.

Then, just before dusk, everything exploded.

Quinn and William were standing outside, watching the plume of smoke on the distant hill as they filled jars of drinking water from large containers volunteers had hauled over from the nearby wells. The wind, which had been blowing steadily toward the east all day, suddenly stopped and then picked up again, blowing to the northwest.

Although the fire was still much too far away to reach them, the smoke that filled the camp was overwhelming. She watched, terrified, as flames suddenly appeared just at the top of the ridge that separated the river valley from the slope down toward an area where she knew there were houses.

Everything happened very quickly. "The fire might have jumped the line. Those homes haven't been evacuated!" Maxwell called, running past them on the way to his horse.

Quinn was reaching for Dusk's saddle when she felt a hand on her shoulder. Startled, she looked up and saw Ben standing there. "No, Lady Quinn. You must stay here."

"We have to get those people out of there!" She knew how unpredictable fires were. They might only have minutes before the fire raced down the hill toward those homes. All around them, people were mounting horses, and taking off on foot, hurrying to warn those families toward safety. She had never missed telephones as much as she did right now.

"You putting yourself in danger won't help anybody."

"He's right." William came up next to them. "Besides, we'll need people here, too. You have to stay where you're safe, Quinn."

"Are you going?" she asked him.

He shook his head. "It's always best for healers to stay where we know we'll be needed. And anyway, I wouldn't leave you."

The feeling that she wouldn't be helping if she stayed passed quickly. Within twenty minutes, the camp was flooded with newcomers. A new tent was quickly set up to accommodate those who'd had to leave their homes, and Quinn was busy with carrying cots, unfolding blankets, and directing frightened and upset people to the areas that were set up to feed them.

Full darkness had settled over the kingdom when Simon rode slowly into the camp with a wagon she didn't recognize. "We have an injury here!" he yelled.

Quinn barely had time to wonder what had happened before Nathaniel, Jacob, and William were at the wagon, unloading a man and carrying him gently into the tent clinic. She started to walk that way to see if she could assist, but Simon stopped her before she reached the tent. "He fell off his horse trying to get his family out of the area. His wife and children need help."

She followed Simon over to the wagon. Inside, a woman and three small children were huddled under blankets.

"Hello," she said. "Are you all okay?"

"We're not hurt," the woman said. "Just worried. The children are frightened."

Quinn looked over at the oldest child, a boy who was maybe seven cycles. "I'm Quinn," she said. "What's your name?"

"Lewis."

"It's nice to meet you, Lewis. Can you help me get your brother and sister out of the wagon and then we can go get you all something to eat?"

He nodded slowly. "Where's my father?"

"He's in that tent right there," Quinn pointed. "Good healers are taking care of him. Once we have you guys settled, I'll go find out what's going on, okay?"

She lifted the three children down to the ground, and then extended her hand to help the woman.

"Thank you," the woman said. "My name is Celia Maywood. Are you the Lady Quinn, Prince William's companion?"

When she nodded, Celia's eyes widened for just a second, before she allowed Quinn to lead her across the camp to the shelter tent.

She didn't say anything, but something in the woman's expression caused a tight feeling in Quinn's stomach. It was enough to make her wonder just what rumors were circulating in the kingdom about her. Was it a good thing that people knew she was courting William?

The night didn't get any easier. More and more families flooded the camp. Though the man who had fallen from his horse was the most serious injury, the healers inside the tent were kept extremely busy with minor injuries and breathing problems from the smoke.

Well into the evening, Quinn found herself returning once again to a community well a little way away from the camp. Ben had been following her back there all evening, helping to carry more buckets of water, but when she'd left he had been helping organize some new crates of fruit and vegetables volunteers had brought in for breakfast in the morning. She thought he was working hard enough without asking him to carry more water.

She was way past exhausted herself; she actually had to stop halfway to the well to set the buckets down for a minute while she waited for a wave of dizziness to pass. For a second, she felt hot, and then she shivered.

Should have listened to William and taken that nap while I could, she thought. Then she realized that her lips were very dry, and when she thought about it, she couldn't remember when she'd last stopped to take a drink. She promised herself she'd remedy that as soon as she got to the well, and she picked the buckets back up again.

The only light was the just-past full moon, but she was familiar enough with the route and the well that she'd left her lantern back at the camp so that she could carry two buckets.

The voice startled her so badly that she nearly dropped the first bucket down into the well.

"Lady Quinn?"

She didn't recognize the voice, and she spun around to see who it was. An unfamiliar man was standing there, almost too close. There were a lot of people she didn't know at the camp, but something about his proximity sent a shiver running down her spine. She took a deep breath, trying to stay composed. "Can I help you with something?"

She took a small step backwards, pressing her back against the stone wall of the well, but the man stepped closer. Her heart began to pound furiously.

"I'm here to ask you to come with me, please."

Definitely not. She stood up as tall as she could, and stepped deftly to the side. "Who are you?"

The man was unfazed; he shadowed her movement, boxing her in, trapping her. "I need you to come with me."

She watched, in horrified slow motion, as he extended his hand toward her. She opened her mouth, ready to scream. Surely someone would hear her.

"I wouldn't do that if I were you," the man said, in a low, warning tone. His hand stopped a couple of inches from her face, and opened. There was a small object resting on his palm that made her heart stop completely. She recognized the object instantly, though she couldn't wrap her mind around what it could possibly be doing here.

It was a small carving of a wooden horse, half the size of the man's palm. She knew that if she examined the details carefully, she would make out a perfect representation of Dusk's profile. William had carved it himself, sometime after her very first visit to Eirentheos. He'd brought it back to her world to give it to her, as a present for Annie. It had quickly become the little girl's most prized possession.

It shouldn't be here. It should be where it belonged…back in her own world, in her little sister's pocket…Annie had been known to change coats to make sure she had a pocket to put it in…or in the special place on her dresser where Annie kept it while she was sleeping.

She stared at the horse for several long seconds, before the man closed his hand and withdrew it.

"Come on, Lady Quinn."

MIISSING

WILLIAM WAS EXHAUSTED. The line of patients coming into the clinic was endless. Fortunately, there hadn't been many serious injuries yet, and the reports he'd heard seemed to indicate that everyone had been evacuated safely, and that so far no homes had been destroyed by the approaching blazes. But still, the work for him…and Jacob and Nathaniel…kept accruing.

He couldn't remember there ever having been a wildfire so close to the Eirenthean capitol city. After the evacuation of the homes on the hill, their temporary camp had filled to overflowing, both with evacuees, and with friends and relatives desperately searching for their loved ones.

"William, have you eaten yet?" Nathaniel asked, just as William sent another patient outside after a breathing treatment. "I never saw you go for dinner."

"Um…" Quinn had said something earlier about getting him a plate, but he'd gotten busy and forgotten quite a while ago. "No." Now that he thought about it, he'd never eaten lunch, either. *Had Quinn?* She'd worried him today. She kept telling him that she was fine, but something just wasn't quite right.

"You should go," Jacob said. But just as he spoke, there was a loud wail a short distance from their tent.

A minute later, a woman appeared in the doorway, carrying a disheveled, screaming toddler. She was covered in dirt, and her short blond hair was in stringy knots. It had been a long, difficult day for all of the families here.

"What happened?" William asked, walking over to them.

"She fell. Her elbow is bleeding."

"I'll take care of it," Nathaniel said, stepping in front of him and leading the mother over to one of the cots. "Just get me a wet towel so we can get her cleaned up, and then go eat. You and Quinn should go back to the castle for the night soon anyway."

William nodded, and headed for the stack of towels on the table where they were keeping the buckets of clean water. But when he went to dip the towel in the bucket, he realized it was empty. He looked down to the floor for another bucket, but there were only two, and they were both empty as well. The other buckets were missing. He frowned. Quinn had said she was leaving to get more water quite a while ago. *How long had it been?* Surely she and Ben should have been back by now?

"Nathaniel, have you seen Quinn?"

"Not for half an hour or so. Maybe she's out helping with the food?"

"Maybe." But she wouldn't have forgotten the water for the clinic, would she? An uneasy feeling settled in William's stomach, though he tried to brush it off. They were all tired. She could have set the buckets down thinking it would only be for a minute, and then gotten caught up in some other task.

He stepped outside the tent, looking for them. Would Ben have forgotten to bring in his water, too?

Looking around as he went, he walked over to the canopy they'd set up as a kitchen and food-serving area. He didn't see her anywhere.

"There's still plenty of food, Prince William," someone said, but he wasn't hungry now. Without even acknowledging the young man who'd spoken to him, he walked past the food tables, to where people were stacking empty crates. He was just about to leave and start really searching the camp for her, when he saw Ben.

"Ben!" he called. "Where's Quinn?"

Ben looked up at him, and his eyebrows knitted together. "Last I knew, she was in the clinic tent with you."

An icy feeling gripped William's insides. "She said she was going to find you and go get some more water."

"When?"

"I don't know. At least half an hour ago. I haven't seen her since."

Ben went rigid, and William's heart began beating at an erratic pace. "Quinn!" he yelled, following Ben as the guard took off running in the direction of the well.

It took Quinn only a few minutes of walking with the man to realize exactly how stupid she had been. Even if he did somehow have Annie somewhere, which, frankly, was impossible, she would have had much better luck getting to her safely if she had guards.

The sight of that little horse had sent all her logic flying out the window. Of course, as she'd walked, she had realized that it probably didn't mean anything. Any number of people could have known that William made a horse like that to give to Quinn. Will's cousin Gavin…the traitor…might easily have known enough about it to fake a replica of it. For what reason, she didn't know, but it didn't matter. It couldn't have been real. In the black night, there was no way she would have been able to tell the difference.

Annie was safe at home in a different world. There was no chance she was here. And now Quinn had gone and gotten captured, putting herself and probably everyone else in danger. It was possible Tolliver had sent this man after her…the thought of what he might do to her made her insides begin to twist in nausea, and she forced herself to not think about that right now. Maybe she could still get out of here.

"Don't even think about screaming," the man said, flashing a glint of steel at his belt, and she bit back the one she'd been about to let loose. They were too far away now. Someone might hear her, but they wouldn't be able to get to her in time. She wondered what her chances were of getting the knife away from him.

"Is my little sister all right?" she asked.

The man didn't respond; he just kept walking, but the shadow that slid over his face, even in the moonlight, sent a chill down her spine. Crap. She'd told him something he hadn't known. She was relieved, though, at what his face hadn't shown. She was pretty sure he didn't know anything about Annie; if she was here, she was probably okay.

"Who sent you?" she demanded.

Again, he didn't respond; this time it was as if he hadn't even heard her, though he might have started walking even faster through the thick woods. Quinn found herself struggling to keep up as they made their way in the darkness. There was no trail; they dodged rocks and branches in the dark night. They were headed northeast of the city, a direction she had never traveled before. She had no idea what this part of Eirentheos held. From everything she could tell, it was utter, unpopulated wilderness.

The man didn't touch her; he was, in fact, maintaining a careful distance between them, which she thought was odd, but she was grateful. More than once, she thought about ducking away from him, making a run for it back through the trees, but something told her he would be more than capable of stopping her if she tried.

And what if Annie was out here somewhere? Could someone have gone into her world and kidnapped her little sister? If Tolliver was armed with the right information, she certainly wouldn't put something like that past him. The question was: did he have enough information to be able to do that?

After several more questions that failed to yield any acknowledgement from him at all, she determined not to speak to him again. It was probably best, anyway. She'd already given him more information than she'd meant to with her question about Annie; it wouldn't be wise to let more slip.

By the time they'd been walking for what must have been over an hour, keeping up a conversation would have been nearly impossible for her anyway; she wasn't dressed or equipped for this kind of hiking, and she'd already been exhausted and thirsty before they'd started. She started having trouble keeping up, and a new wave of dizziness was hitting her every few minutes now.

When a slow, sickening wave of heat rolled over her and stayed, making her suddenly sweaty and sticky, she nearly started crying.

The man didn't even glance back at her when he opened the leather water pouch that hung from his belt, taking a long drink as he walked.

He finally slowed his frantic pace just a little when they hit a particularly dense, forested area. She couldn't see anything except the outlines of trees everywhere. He was slow enough now that she was only a few steps behind him.

When they reached an area where they had no choice but to climb up a small, rocky ridge, she saw her opportunity. As he crouched close to the rocks, beginning to climb from the first small ledge to the top of the ridge, she reached for the knife at his belt.

Just as her hand closed around the hilt, his weight shifted, bumping her arm against his leg. In nearly the same instant, his hand was around her wrist, holding it tight.

"Try it again, and I'll take your hand off," he spat. "I don't care if I am supposed to bring you back in one piece. You can live with one hand." With that, he shoved her away from him.

The motion disrupted her equilibrium on the small ledge, and every muscle in her body contracted as she struggled to maintain her balance. But in the next second, another wave of the dizziness hit, and she lost it. Her foot slipped from the ledge, skidding and sliding down the rocks, taking her whole body with it. As she was scrambling to right herself, her leg scraped hard against the rocks just before she landed with a violent thud on the uneven ground below.

The man, who had finished his climb up the ridge, stared down at her impassively as she took an inventory of the damage.

Her hands were skinned, but not too badly. Her ribs were going to be bruised, for sure, and maybe her back, too, but she didn't think it was serious. There was an abrasion on her left arm that was painful and damp to the touch, slowly oozing blood…so much for William's careful effort at putting that arm back together after the last time she'd gotten hurt. She'd probably just scarred it permanently.

The real damage, though, was to her left leg. She must have slammed her leg against one of the rocks really hard to cause the deep, ragged cut that was there now, filled with dirt and pebbles.

"A little help?" she called up to the man.

"So you can try to grab my knife again? I don't think so."

"What about bringing me back in one piece?"

"You are." He didn't seem particularly worried. Of course, if it was Tolliver who'd given those orders, she supposed he wouldn't be upset so long as she was alive and able to talk…not that she'd ever answer Tolliver's questions.

"Fine," she muttered under her breath. The gash on her leg needed pressure to stop the bleeding, and she didn't have anything. She inspected her pants, and found one of the new tears. Pushing her fingers through the hole, she was preparing to rip off a section of the material when, unexpectedly, something soft landed on the ground by her feet.

"Use that," the man grumbled.

She reached for the object, and was surprised when she unfolded a large square of cloth. Sighing, she glanced up at the man, who was now more a mystery than he had been. He certainly seemed not to like her…she wondered who had given him orders not to harm her.

She wrapped the bandage tightly around the wound on her leg and then struggled to stand up. The man was silent and unmoving as she worked her way up the ridge, the palms of her hands stinging each time she touched the rocks.

She was desperately thirsty now and more than a little lightheaded. And hot. Even though the night was cool, she was pouring sweat. Her lips were more parched than they'd ever been, and the skin on her face felt tight.

"Scary looking, isn't it?" Linnea said, coming to stand next to Thomas on one of the third-story balconies of the castle.

He nodded, still staring off at the reddish-orange glow on the hill to the west of them. The plume of smoke was visible even in the darkness, obscuring the light from the stars. "Father said that it sounds like they're getting some of it contained, though, and they may have a fire line established before the homes again. How are the little ones?"

"Asleep. Alice was hard to get down, though. She's really upset about the fire. Mother's still sitting with her, I think. Mia said she was going to try to come and find you once Mother comes and takes Hannah from her."

Thomas nodded, and she could see deep lines in his forehead. "Alice worries a lot for such a little girl."

"She's so much like William."

He nodded again.

"Are you going to come inside soon?"

He stared out at the fire again for a long moment before he answered. "It's hard to be the one at home waiting, isn't it?"

She reached up to squeeze her twin's shoulder, hearing his answer in the question. He'd be out here until Ben, William, and Quinn came riding up the road and into the courtyard, safe back at the castle for the night. He placed his hand over hers, and patted it gently. "Do you want me to bring you anything?" she asked.

He shook his head, not taking his eyes away from the scene in front of him.

"Do you want me to go inside and leave you alone?"

After a short pause, he shook his head.

Linnea leaned her elbows on the top of the high wall of the balcony, and looked out at the horizon. The flickering of the flames really was mesmerizing. If it hadn't been so frightening, it would have been interesting to watch the orange and red glow spread slowly back over the hillsides, making tiny jumps…probably as it moved from one tree to the next. She shuddered at the thought of what the rolling hills would look like once this was over. Already today there had been more birds than usual in the skies, more small animals roaming the trees behind the castle.

"You and Mia seem to be getting pretty serious lately," she said.

He didn't answer for just long enough to raise her suspicions.

"How serious are you?"

Thomas sighed, and reached into his pocket. "Before all this happened, today was supposed to be Mia's day off, you know?"

Linnea nodded. Charlotte had actually tried to get her to still take the day, but Mia, being Mia, had refused, and spent the day helping with the children anyway.

"Anyway, I was going to take her out for a picnic tonight and give her this." He held a thin silver chain up in the air.

Linnea didn't have to look closer to know what it was…a courtship bracelet. She reached over and patted Thomas on the shoulder. "Are you still going to do it tonight?"

"Of course not." He frowned. "I only get to do this once, Linnea. I'm not going to just throw it on her after a long day of working, while we watch to see if the kingdom's going to burn down. That wouldn't be very charming of me."

She rolled her eyes. "I think Mia would probably find you charming however you did it."

"That's true. I am irresistible."

"To some people, I guess."

He bumped his shoulder lightly against hers. "What about you? I haven't seen Jared around much lately."

"That's probably because he hasn't been."

"You're going to leave a trail of broken hearts longer than the Philotheos River, aren't you? *Ow!*" He grabbed her elbow and pushed it away from his ribcage.

"You're one to talk." She grinned and then turned to stare out at the fire again. "Jared's nice enough, but he just didn't get it. He expected me to be able to just go and spend time with him whenever he wasn't busy for a little while in the stables. Like I wasn't doing anything except sitting around and waiting for him to be free."

Thomas sighed and reached over to rub her back.

She was actually starting to get sleepy, resting her head on her arms as she leaned against the wall of the balcony, when the sudden pounding of horses' hooves below her made her stand up straight. Stretching up on her tiptoes, she leaned over the wall so she could see the road leading up to the main gate of the castle.

"Is that William?" she asked.

"Yes…and Jacob, I think. Where's Quinn?"

Linnea strained to see as far as possible, but there were only the two riders. "I don't know. Maybe he's just coming back to get something?" But that didn't seem right. William was riding too frantically. He didn't even stop at the gate. If it hadn't been William, the guards down there would have never let him tear through so quickly, even though Jacob stopped to dismount and talk to them.

"Let's go," she said, pulling at Thomas's arm.

They got to the top of the stairs that led to the family's private wing at the same time William reached the bottom.

"Where's Father?" he yelled, as he came running toward them. The tone in his voice sent Linnea's heart flying into her throat; something was *wrong*.

He didn't wait for an answer. Linnea and Thomas both moved out of the way to let William pass and followed him down the hallway. Even in the middle of an emergency, they all knew they could count on finding their father in one of his children's rooms at this time in the evening. It never mattered what else was going on…he took turns with them each night, tucking in the little ones, or sitting and chatting for a while with those who were older.

Sure enough, they caught him just as he stepped out of Josh and Daniel's room and into the hallway.

"Will …"

"Quinn is missing," William interrupted. "We can't find her anywhere."

Linnea was afraid her legs were going to give out under her. "What do you mean? Where's Ben?"

"He's still back at the camp, searching for her. Jacob made me come back here to tell you." William was obviously distraught. His cheeks were sunken and gray, his hair disheveled, and his voice was scratchy.

"Come, all of you, out of the hallway," her father said, taking the few steps to open the door of Linnea's room.

Once inside, Stephen extended his hand toward Linnea's couch, but none of them made it more than a couple of feet inside the door that Stephen didn't even bother to close. "What's going on?" he asked. "What do you mean you can't find Quinn?"

Moisture appeared in the corners of William's eyes, and he blinked furiously. "I don't know, Father. She said she was going to ask Ben to take her to go and get water at the well, but she never asked him. We found two of the buckets up by the well, but not her. We searched the entire encampment three times. Dusk is still there, still tied up where she was, but Quinn isn't anywhere."

All of the color had drained from his father's face. "Ben is still searching the camp?"

"Ben and Nathaniel both. Jacob ..."

"He needed to get out of there, Stephen." Linnea turned to see Jacob standing in the doorway. Sweat covered his brow and soaked the front of his shirt.

Her father nodded. "All right. William, is there anything else you can tell me that Jacob doesn't know?"

"I don't think so. I don't know *anything*." One of the tears he was clearly working so hard to control rolled down William's cheek, and he brushed it away with the back of his hand in a harsh motion.

Linnea couldn't swallow the hard lump that formed in her throat as she watched her father gently reach over to squeeze William's shoulder. Her brother jumped at the touch, taking a step backwards.

"Can I go back now?" William asked.

"No." Stephen's voice was firm. "Jacob is going to go with me to find Marcus and get some more people looking for her. You are going to stay here tonight and sleep. Thomas and Linnea?"

"We've got him, Father," Thomas said.

"We'll find her, William. I promise to come and get you if anything changes, but we *will* find her."

Jacob and her father disappeared without another word. As soon as they were gone, Linnea turned to William. "Wha..."

The look that Thomas shot her stopped the words cold. He stepped right in front of William, moving so that he was making eye contact. "When is the last time you ate, Will?"

His lips were a tight, straight line as he shrugged.

"I'll go get someone to fix a plate," Linnea said quickly. As much as she preferred to be in the center of things, she could see that she needed to leave her brothers alone right now. Thomas was the only one in the family who really *got* Will, who knew how to deal with him when he was upset.

"You need a shower, Will," Thomas said, after Linnea had disappeared.

William shook his head. "I need to find her."

"What are you going to do? Go riding off in the dark by yourself?"

"She's probably scared."

Thomas felt his own chest tighten at that thought. He took a deep breath, willing himself to stay calm for his brother's sake. "She's probably just off helping somebody with something, Will. You know how she is. If there's a kitten up a tree, Quinn will go. Ben and Nathaniel have probably already found her, and they'll be riding up here any minute. You're going to want to hug her, and you stink. Go take a shower."

He didn't get a chuckle out of his brother, but at least William followed him across the hall, into the room where they usually both slept. Thomas walked him all the way into the bathroom, even turning on the water and setting the little bottle of calming lavender-and-vanilla oil on the ledge next to the soap.

"Take your time, Will. She's going to need you to be calm and put together."

Outside the bathroom, Thomas had to stop for a second to take a few deep breaths of his own. Today, for the first time, it had struck him just how difficult it must have been for everyone when he had been the one missing. He hadn't realized, when he'd taken off on his own, what he might be doing to the people he loved at home, the ordeal they'd been through. Surely after that, Quinn wouldn't be so stupid as to wander off on her own, would she?

Fear for her clenched his stomach and he sank to the floor.

A soft knock at the door had him up again almost immediately. He tried to compose his expression as he went to answer it.

"Thomas? Is everything okay? I heard your father went rushing downstairs..." Mia's green eyes were filled with concern.

He shook his head. "No, Mia, I don't think so."

Mia's expression changed from concerned to fearful as he led her over to the couch and told her what was going on. He knew Mia was particularly fond of Quinn. "What can I do?" she asked.

"I don't know. I guess right now we need to try and stay calm until the morning…try and keep William calm, especially."

"He's really in love with her, isn't he?"

"More than he even realizes, I think. I don't know how she puts up with him, but she's definitely the best thing that's ever happened to him."

Mia punched him playfully on the shoulder. "You know you love him."

He smiled. "I do, Mia." He stretched out his hand to take hers, playing with her fingers for a minute before looking back up at her. "I kind of like you, too, you know?"

She leaned in and rested her head on his shoulder. "I 'kind of' like you too, Thomas." They sat there like that for a few minutes before she turned back to him. "You should probably go and talk to your mother. I don't think she knows what's going on yet."

Although he had to fight the urge to just bolt out the door several times, William forced himself to stay in the shower until most of the muscles in his back and chest had loosened at least a little bit. He went through several washcloths scented with the calming oil, trying very hard not to think anything negative about where Quinn might be right now.

What Thomas had said was true. If she'd run across someone who appeared to need some kind of help, she wouldn't have hesitated. She could still show up tonight and act like they were all crazy for being so worried. He was going to have a major conversation with her about this...

When he finally walked back out into the room, he was relieved to find that he was alone. A covered silver tray was sitting on the low table in front of the couch, and he felt a wave of appreciation for Thomas, who knew him well enough that he'd probably convinced Linnea to leave it there and give him some space.

He didn't feel hungry, but he lifted the lid anyway, and found a smoked ruska and cream cheese sandwich on his favorite soft bread and a small bowl of glasberries…Quinn's secret favorite. Exhausted as he was, he just couldn't bring himself to sit down, so he carried the sandwich with him and paced the room, trying to work off some of his nervous energy. The fruit remained untouched. He just couldn't, not right now.

Finally, he realized that his efforts were useless. Nothing was going to calm him down. Nothing except Quinn, safe in front of him, wrapped in his arms. Without even realizing how he got there, he found himself in her room, staring down at her neatly made bed, the deafening silence echoing in his head.

The quiet sound of the door closing woke him. He didn't know how long he'd been asleep, lying there on Quinn's bed, his face buried in her pillow. He was so grateful that it hadn't been a washing day; the pillowcase smelled of her.

He rubbed his eyes, squinting to make out the silhouette making its way across Quinn's dim room, lit only by a few small nightlights along the wall, close to the floor.

"I didn't mean to wake you," his mother said quietly, setting something down on the night table…a glass of water.

"It's okay."

The bed shifted as Charlotte climbed up beside him. "We'll find her, William," she said, softly combing her fingers through his hair. "We'll find her, and everything will be all right."

Her words weren't convincing, especially not in her slightly raspy voice which told him that she'd been crying, but he decided to believe her anyway, and buried his face back in the Quinn-scented pillow, closing his eyes once more.

MORNING

QUINN STARED DOWN AT the plume of smoke from her seat on the hillside. Dandelions quivered in the grass at her feet, their shadows dancing in the sunlight.

"Interesting view, isn't it, milady?"

She frowned, staring up at the white-haired man who had appeared beside her. He sat down in the grass next to her, and smiled kindly.

"I don't know if I'd call it interesting," she said. "Terrifying, maybe. Ugly." She pointed up at the thick, black clouds in the sky, just in time for a small piece of ash to come drifting down at her feet.

Aivin reached down and picked up the charred flake. At one point, it might have been a leaf. It crumbled in his hand.

"Ugly," she reiterated.

He looked at the black flakes…contemplating them, it looked like. "I suppose it is a bit ugly right now. It won't always be. Much of what the fire is burning away is old, dead wood and debris. Once it's gone, new plants will be able to grow, stronger and healthier."

"What about the trees and plants that are being destroyed now?"

He turned to look at her, his ice-blue eyes piercing into her. "You can't have both. You can try to hold on to the part of the forest that's filled with dry, rotting *wood, knowing that at any minute it could burst into flame, or you can let it go, suffer through the fire, and then let the new, good stuff grow in."*

"We're not talking about a forest fire anymore, are we?"

"Were we ever?" His gaze never shifted from hers.

"What are we talking about, then?"

He raised an eyebrow. "Coy doesn't suit you, Lady Quinn."

She blinked.

"It rarely befits those who are born to be leaders, when it comes right down to it."

"So this is about me making my decision. Dandelions or roses. Old wood or new. Take my throne, or pack it in and go home."

"When are you going to stop pretending…to yourself and to everyone else…that you haven't made the decision already?" His blue eyes fell now on the tattoo on her chest, visible through the thin strap of her camisole…she didn't remember coming out here wearing only that. But then again, she didn't remember coming out here at all…

"When are you going to stop accusing me of pretending things I don't mean to be pretending?" she asked, still remembering the last uncomfortable conversation she'd had with him.

"Beloved, perhaps I'll be able to stop asking such questions when you stop doing the things you don't mean to be doing, and start doing the things you mean to." He leaned down then, and kissed the top of her head, with such absolute gentleness that she could never be certain that it had actually happened.

"The choice, milady, is, as ever, yours."

The room was still dark when William awakened. Although there was no way he could have slept for more than a few hours, he was wide awake. He lifted his head from Quinn's pillow, squinting to find the source of the noise that had roused him.

"How long have you two been in here?" he asked. Thomas and Linnea were both sitting on Quinn's couch, their outlines just visible in the low light coming from the floorboards.

"Not long," Thomas said, standing and walking over to him. He carried something in his hands, and when he reached the edge of the bed, he held it out to William.

"Thanks," William said, accepting the still-hot mug of tea. He closed his eyes and breathed in the comforting steam before taking a sip. He studied his brother for a moment, noticing that he was fully dressed, in different clothes than yesterday. "Is there news?" he asked.

"Nothing," Thomas answered. "Father sent several more guards to search the entire camp, and they haven't turned up anything. Nobody has seen her. They're going to search again at first light and then decide what to do."

"So what are you two doing in here?"

"We're going to search, too. We're ready to leave right now."

"Father's all right with that?"

Thomas shrugged. "We dealt with staying here yesterday without complaining. We were needed at the castle with the children. We'd probably have gotten in the way down at your clinic. But this is different. I'm not sitting around in the castle when Quinn is missing. We're going to find her and bring her back today. I don't care where she is."

Fifteen minutes later, the three of them were down at the stables saddling their horses.

"Where is Ben, anyway?" Linnea asked as she climbed up on Snow, her white mare. "Did he ever come back from the camp last night? He's the one who was supposed to be guarding Quinn."

"I don't know." Thomas was mounting his own horse, Storm.

"He was distraught," William said. "Nearly as much as I was. Quinn was supposed to ask him to go get water with her at the well. I don't know why she didn't." His throat was suddenly tight again, and moisture was threatening behind his eyes.

"Are you sure she didn't?" Linnea asked, a strange sound in her voice.

"What do you mean?"

"I mean…what if we can't trust Ben as much as we thought we could? What if he knows more than he's telling? We trusted Paul once, too, you know."

A sick feeling ripped through William's insides. "He's a Friend of Philip! He's Marcus' son."

"I know," Linnea said, closing her eyes. "I'm sorry. I shouldn't have said that…it's just hard to trust anything right now, you know?"

William didn't know. Right now, he didn't know anything.

"Oh, stop, Linnea," Thomas said, a sound in his voice that William didn't understand, but that he didn't have the energy to wonder about.

"Has Ben ever done one thing…even one…to deserve to have you saying that?"

She looked down at the ground. "No. He hasn't."

"You need to deal with your feelings some other way than *that*, Nay."

William had no idea what they were talking about, and he didn't care. He rode away from the stable without another word.

In the pale light of the morning, the emergency camp was even more depressing than it had been the night before. Well before they even reached it, as they approached from a hill, William could see that it was much calmer and quieter than the night before. There hadn't been any additional evacuations during the night. He scanned the sky, breathing a sigh of relief when he saw that the plume of smoke had moved…the fire was drifting back into the deep woods, away from homes.

Slowly, William brought Skittles to a stop.

"What are you doing?" Thomas asked, riding up and stopping next to him. On his other side, Linnea stopped, too.

"I don't want to go in there."

"Into the camp? Why? What's wrong?" Thomas's brow furrowed in concern.

William closed his eyes for a moment, remembering the night before. "If we go talk to everyone there, we're not going to be able to leave and go searching for her. Someone will stop us, try to calm us down, tell us something stupid like everything's going to be okay, or they've got it under control. I'm not going to do that. I'm going to go and find her. Now."

Thomas was silent for a long moment. William could see him deliberating what he was going to say.

"I'm not sure it's a good idea to go off completely on our own," he finally said.

"What, Thomas? Since when are you afraid of jumping into the action?" William was surprised at the twinge of irritation that tightened his chest.

Thomas looked over at Linnea for several seconds before he turned back to face William. Linnea didn't look nearly as shocked at her brother's departure from his usual adventurous spirit as he would have expected her to. In fact, she stared intently down at her hands as Thomas spoke.

"You're right, Will. Half a cycle ago, I wouldn't have given it a second thought. Really, I probably wouldn't have even waited until it was light out…I'd have talked you into sneaking out of the castle in the middle of the night to go searching for her. Half a cycle ago I didn't know better. I wouldn't have stopped to think about how that would affect everyone else…to wake up this morning, not only worrying about Quinn, but then finding us missing too."

William's heart sank guiltily. "Sure, Thomas. Get all mature on me now." Linnea and Thomas followed him in silence as he turned Skittles and headed down the hill toward the camp.

With Quinn missing, security in the camp was intense now. Several guards patrolled the area; one was just heading back down from a trip to the well. None of them spoke to William as he led his siblings over to the clinic.

It should have been a relief that when he walked into the clinic and there were no patients…only Jacob, sound asleep on a cot, and Nathaniel who opened his eyes and sat up at the slight noise of them walking in.

He should have been very grateful that the empty clinic meant that there were no serious injuries, that the citizens of his kingdom were healthy and well. But he couldn't bring himself to be happy about that. Instead, he felt stupid for having insisted that he come out here, for bringing Quinn with him where she wasn't safe. They would have managed just fine without him, and she would be in the castle right now, with him.

Nathaniel clearly hadn't slept at all. He looked even more exhausted and distraught than William felt…it even appeared that he had been crying.

William looked down at the floor. "I'm sorry," he said softly, as moisture pooled in his own eyes. "I should have listened to you…should have made her listen."

He heard Linnea swallow loudly behind him.

Nathaniel didn't answer, he just stood and walked over to William and put his arms around him, hugging him tight to his chest.

"We're going to find her," Thomas said, after several minutes when Nathaniel had finally released his hold. "We're going to find her today. Right now. What's going on with the search?"

Quinn woke up drenched in sweat from the morning sun hitting the eastern wall of the tent where she'd been sleeping. She could tell from the angle of the light that it was still early, but she was surprised that she'd slept so long…that she'd slept at all actually.

And, somehow, she'd not only slept, but had actually managed to dream.

Of course, she'd been exhausted. They hadn't walked too much farther after she'd hurt herself…maybe only twenty minutes or so, but it had felt like forever.

By the time they reached some kind of camp, tents gathered around a clearing, her entire body was aching, and she felt like she might collapse at any moment.

The man led her to the first tent they encountered, a large canvas affair that could easily sleep ten people, maybe more. It was completely dark. "Here," he said, pulling open a flap in the heavy material, and pointing inside.

Her stomach dropped at the idea. She had no idea who or what might be in the huge tent. In the clearing, she could see the faint glow of lanterns inside other tents, but they were several yards away from her. This tent was completely dark. She thought about calling out, but then realized she could be putting herself in more danger if she did that. The man hadn't touched her, at least; for all his lack of concern, he hadn't actually harmed her. He didn't even follow her into the tent. He closed the flap behind her, and she could hear him shuffling around just outside, settling down onto the ground right in front of the entrance.

Inside the tent, it was silent. Using her feet, she felt around near the door. At first, she thought it might be completely empty, but as she fumbled around in the darkness, her hands fell on a bedroll, still rolled, and, even better, a leather pouch filled with water. Not knowing what else to do in the darkness, she sat down on top of the bedroll, taking in her surroundings.

She unscrewed the top of the pouch, desperate for the water inside, and was just lifting it to her lips when she heard a shuffling sound on the other side of the tent. Her heart nearly stopped. Someone was in here with her.

Growing completely still, she listened. She could hear breathing…there was more than one person in the tent, though at least one of them was asleep, maybe two. Slow, deep breaths came from the corner opposite of where she was sitting.

Someone was awake, though…had just awakened, probably from the noise of Quinn entering. Her heart pounded so loudly in her ears that she was surprised she could hear anything at all, but she could. Whoever was across the tent was trying to be quiet…was managing it fairly well, even. She had to strain to hear the soft movements.

The sloshing of water inside the leather pouch alerted her to the fact that her hands were shaking violently.

"Hello?" The whisper from across the tent turned her insides into ice. It was at once terrifying, and achingly, comfortingly, familiar.

"Mom?"

"Quinn?" The voice was no longer a whisper, but a low rasp.

"Yes, it's me."

And then there was the sound of shuffling against the ground as her mother nearly ran across the tent to her, pulling her into her arms.

"Ow, Mom. Careful," she said, loosening her mother's grip from her aching shoulder.

"Why? What's wrong?" Megan's voice took on an edge of panic.

"I just fell and hurt myself on the way here…I'm okay," she added quickly, although the sudden lightheadedness that overtook her when her mom let go made her think that might not be entirely true. "I'm just going to sit down. I need a drink."

Megan sank onto the ground beside her as she sat back down on the rolled blankets, and reached for the water pouch.

She drank quickly, nearly draining it before she finally stopped.

"Better?" her mom asked.

"A little." This was definitely not the truth. She was no longer thirsty, but she had drunk the water much too quickly, and now nausea rolled through her. "Who else is here?" she asked, more to change the subject than from any ability to feel curious at the moment.

"Annie and Owen are both asleep over there."

She should have been able to process immediately just how bad that was…just what this could mean, especially if Tolliver was in one of these other tents, but right then, she felt too sick to even understand what was going on.

"Is there any more water?" she asked.

"Yes. I'll get you some," Megan whispered, walking away from her.

Quinn used the momentary distraction to reach for the cloth around her leg. It was too dark to see what she was doing, but she did what she could by touch. Removing the bandage, she soaked it with what was left of the cool water in the pouch.

Wincing, she cleaned up her injuries as best she could. Megan returned a few seconds later with another full pouch of water.

"What are you doing here?"

"It's a long story," Megan whispered, and Quinn heard, more than saw, her head turn back toward where the two children were sleeping.

"Are you okay?" Her voice was so low that she almost had trouble hearing it herself.

"Yes, we all are."

"Was it…" she could barely bring herself to say the name, "was it Tolliver who brought you here?"

"I don't know who that is."

Her whole body sank into the bedroll with the relief of that sentence, although the tension started returning only a few seconds later as she struggled to figure out what that might mean. "Then who did?"

"Some man named Jonathan."

Jonathan? She could only think of one person named Jonathan…one person who was still alive, anyway.

"Prince Jonathan?"

"I don't know, Quinn. Why? Do you think it's William's brother or something?"

"No. If he's a prince, it's not of this kingdom." Jonathan was the name of the youngest prince of Philotheum…her father's youngest brother. But why would he be here, and why would he kidnap her family and now her?

As she tried to process that, she realized that the nausea she'd been feeling was growing stronger. Beads of cold sweat broke out on her forehead, and her mouth started watering in a very unwelcome way.

She didn't even have time to warn her mother before she dashed away, to the farthest, hopefully empty, corner of the tent, and vomited in the dirt. Megan rushed to her side, pulling her braid back out of the way, and rubbing her back while she was sick. When it was finally over, her legs felt like jelly, and she was almost too exhausted to follow her mother back across the tent.

Megan helped her sit down, and she waited, only a few feet from the blankets where Annie and Owen slept, their quiet breathing filling the air in a way that would have been relaxing and peaceful in any other circumstance.

Part of her brain wanted to keep going, to figure out what could possibly be going on here, how her family had gotten here, and why Jonathan…if it was Prince Jonathan…would have taken all of them. But her body would have none of it. As soon as Megan pulled the blankets over to her and unrolled them, Quinn collapsed into them, sucking in a breath at the pain in her leg as she made the mistake of trying to put weight on it while she adjusted herself.

"Quinn, baby, are you all right? Maybe we should get someone to help us."

"Mom, no!" She didn't know who these people were, but they obviously knew too much about her already. The last thing they needed to know was how weak she was right now. "I'm fine. I'll be fine. I think I just need to get some sleep."

"Okay," Megan said, still sounding unsure, but she covered Quinn, and kissed her forehead. "Wake me if you need anything."

Quinn nodded, though right then she couldn't think about anything except how much her leg was hurting. She lay there, trying her best not to think about how much she wished William was there, knowing that if she allowed her thoughts to even drift in that direction, she would start crying and be unable to stop.

Somehow, though, she'd fallen asleep.

Now, in the early morning light, she tried to get a grasp on her surroundings. Her mother and her siblings were still asleep. Owen was curled up on his side in his blankets, his hand over Annie's arm. She was sprawled out everywhere, out of the covers, her arms and legs in four different directions, brown hair spread around her head like a tangled crown, completely passed out, her little face reflecting contented dreams.

Quinn was still partially distracted by the memories of her own dream from the night. She couldn't yet remember all the details of the dream, but parts of it kept coming to her in flashes.

Sitting completely still, she strained to listen for any noises outside the tent that would give her information about their situation, but other than a few birds chattering in the nearby trees, it was silent. No…if she strained there was a low, grumbling sound just outside her tent. Snoring. Someone must be guarding them, perhaps the man who had brought her here, and he was asleep right outside the entrance.

Not wanting to wake him…or anyone else, for that matter, she looked around the tent. It was completely empty, other than the bedroll and the canteen. The tent was made of a heavy, dusty brown material; it was probably something like canvas, if they had canvas in this world. As she'd noted, somewhat gratefully, last night, it had no floor. Although it had been swept clean of rocks and other debris, she was on bare ground.

Bare ground. That gave her an idea.

Quietly, she crawled to the back wall of the tent, well, limp-crawled…when she tried to put weight on her knee, she was rewarded with a sharp pain that radiated all the way up her leg. Sliding her fingers under the edge of the heavy material, she tried to lift it up far enough to peer underneath, but it was stretched too tightly. She managed to get her fingers underneath, could feel the cooler air outside, but she couldn't lift it more than about a quarter of an inch. Sighing, she retreated to the bedroll.

It might have only been a few minutes, but the time seemed to stretch interminably, and the tent grew hotter as the sun began to rise. She sat on the blankets, trying to keep herself calm, trying not to think about the pain in her leg. At least her shoulder didn't seem to be as badly injured as she'd first thought. It was definitely bruised, and it hurt if she lifted her arm too far, but it hadn't bled very much, and was probably going to be all right.

Just as she was about to get antsy enough to actually try peeking out the flap of the tent, she heard a noise that stopped her cold.

A small voice, one she would have recognized anywhere, no matter what world she was in, rang out clear next to her. "I need to go potty!"

The sound of Annie's voice woke everyone up. Megan bolted upright. Owen was a little slower, but once his eyes fell on Quinn, he was instantly wide awake. In one swift motion, he was out of the blankets and in her lap. She tried not to cry out from the pain of him touching her leg as she shifted his weight to the side, wrapping her arms around him tightly.

"Quinn!" Annie yelled. "Yay! Mama said we were going to see you today!" And then Annie's arms were around her neck, too.

Her sister's characteristically loud announcement apparently had an effect outside the tent, too. There were voices now, and shuffling noises in the dirt, although Quinn couldn't make out anything anyone was saying.

"Mama, I really need to go potty now!" Annie yelled, practically in Quinn's ear.

"Ow, Annie. Too loud," Quinn said, wincing and backing her head away from the little girl.

Suddenly, there was a motion at the opening of the tent, and the man who'd brought her here last night poked his head in, making her jump.

Annie, on the other hand, was unaffected. "Levan, I need to go potty."

The man cleared his throat, looking at Quinn's mother. "You can take the children out," he said, "but this one," he nodded toward Quinn, "needs to stay. Jonathan would like to speak with her."

Megan opened her mouth, discomfort twisting her face. "You'll bring us right back to her?"

"I'm to bring all of you to Jonathan."

He held the flap open while Megan, Annie, and Owen quickly put their shoes on, and then followed him out, leaving Quinn alone.

Her heart pounded erratically, and a sudden pain in her hands made her realize that she'd balled them so tightly into fists that her fingers were turning white. She carefully released them, and the blood rushed back in, making her fingers tingle sharply. As painful as that was, though, her leg was worse; the pain above her knee was steadily growing stronger, throbbing with every quick beat of her heart.

But it didn't matter. She couldn't just sit here and wait; she knew that…she needed to know what was going on outside that tent. Desperately, she searched the inside of the tent with her eyes. This time she saw it. An extra flap of material halfway down the side wall, secured with a button the same color as the tent's material.

Standing up made her wince again, but she pushed through the stabbing pain in her leg, and made it over to the side of the tent. Carefully unfastening the button, she pulled the material just barely to the side, revealing the corner of a small square window.

Without opening it any further than she had to, she peeled the corner up enough that she could get a look outside.

There wasn't much to see. This side of the tent faced the forest, not the rest of the tents she'd seen last night, or to wherever Levan had taken her family. If she stuck her hand out, she'd be able to touch two different trees. Taking a deep breath, she pulled the flap the rest of the way open.

Suddenly, there was a soft fluttering sound, and then a whoosh that nearly knocked her over as something came flying through the window. She had to clamp her hands over her mouth to keep from crying out.

After a few panicked seconds, the flapping object landed neatly on the ground in the middle of the tent. It was Raeyan.

The bird stood primly in the center of the tent now, blinking up at her with his bright black eyes, looking awfully pleased with himself. Not that he hadn't earned it. Quinn had never been so happy to see a bird in her entire life.

"Where did you come from?" She whispered, so quietly she almost couldn't hear herself.

Raeyan turned his head to the side, giving her a look that was almost disapproving, and she actually had to stifle a giggle. "Okay, then. I guess I have been underestimating you." Though she was only mouthing the words, he strutted toward her, and pushed his head gently against her leg, in a way that made her almost certain he understood.

Suddenly, there was a stirring outside the tent, and a noise that made all of the blood drain into her toes…quiet footsteps approaching the tent.

What would they do if they found Raeyan inside the tent? There wasn't time to do anything. All of her muscles were frozen as she waited for the tent flap to open.

William paced agitatedly in the grass a few yards past the outer boundary of the emergency camp. Skittles, standing next to him, saddled and ready, seemed almost as antsy as he was…every few minutes the horse would tap at the ground with his front hoof and whine.

Logically, he knew Thomas and Linnea had been right. It would have been foolish and inconsiderate to go running off all on their own to look for Quinn. But every minute they spent here at the camp, every moment of listening to reports from guards who were actively searching, mapping out the places where she might have been taken…she had to have been taken by someone, there was no other explanation…every moment of sitting here and not *finding* her, was killing him.

He couldn't even listen to it. All of the talking, and the theories, and the possibilities… *No.* There was no possibility other than she was okay somewhere nearby, and he was going to find her today. Five minutes ago at the latest.

Nathaniel had seen it on his face…the fact that at any moment, William was going to lose it, and when he'd stormed out of the clinic, he'd heard his uncle caution his siblings to leave him alone. Or Linnea, anyway. Thomas knew enough to keep his distance when he was like this.

He knew that if Quinn was here, she'd handle it…probably she'd be in there *organizing* the search for him. If he was the one missing, she'd have found him by now. But that was the problem; she wasn't here. A shudder shook his body as he tried, unsuccessfully, to banish the thought that she might not come back.

Glancing up at the sky, he offered up a prayer to the Maker, begging for help…for a sign of where they could look, for her to just come walking back into the camp like nothing had happened, for anything that would bring Quinn back.

It was then that he noticed the two birds circling overhead. Aelwyn and Sirian. The sight of them startled him for a moment…it had been quite a while since he'd seen either of them flying freely like that; they'd taken their nesting seriously, both always hovering near the nest rearing their hatchlings. He knew they'd been out more frequently lately, since most of their brood had launched, but with being confined to the castle, William hadn't seen them. He'd seen more of Raeyan than either of them lately.

Raeyan. He scanned the sky and the tops of the nearby trees quickly, knowing that they would still be taking their one remaining offspring out on longer and longer flights, helping with the training process, but the younger bird was nowhere to be seen. *Was it possible?*

He whistled to the birds, calling Aelwyn to him. His companion dipped lower, winding in an elaborate motion over his head, but she didn't land. She circled twice and then darted toward the north for several hundred feet before turning back and flying overhead for a moment, before turning to repeat the pattern.

William didn't hesitate; didn't think twice about going back into the camp and alerting anyone. Completely ignoring the earlier admonitions from his younger brother, he climbed into the saddle and took off after his bird.

Quinn really hoped she wasn't going to have a heart attack. Her heart was pounding so heavily that she was beginning to feel nauseous and hot, even though nobody had entered the tent…not *yet*, anyway. The footsteps had stopped, and then headed in a different direction, but she was sure she didn't have much time.

Her fingers were shaking so badly that she could barely work them to open the little silver canister on Raeyan's leg, but she managed it. She didn't think she'd ever been this relieved to see a charcoal pencil and rolled up paper as she was right then.

She didn't have any idea where she was or who she was with, and between the hurry she was in and the way her hands shook, her message was probably going to be both useless and indecipherable, but she hastily scribbled that she was okay and in a tent somewhere northwest of the camp…an hour or so on foot, and shoved the roll of paper back into the cylinder.

"I'm sorry I don't have anything for you, Raeyan," she whispered, leaning down and kissing him on the head, "but please, take this to William or Thomas or Nathaniel, or somebody, okay?" Then she pulled the edge of the window open again, and shoved him out. As she sat back onto the bedroll, pain shot through the cut on her leg, making her suck in a breath.

Squeezing her eyes shut, and concentrating on breathing through the pain, she listened to Raeyan's escape. She could still hear the rustling in the trees as he hopped up, hopefully trying to find a spot where he could take to the air, when the footsteps sounded again, crunching in the dirt back to the tent.

Suddenly, she wasn't so sure that her nausea was just from the anxiety. A sickly wave of heat rolled from down her neck and chest, settling heavily in her stomach just as the flap finally opened, and the man, a new one she didn't recognize, poked his head inside. "Lady Quinn?"

Bile rose in her throat, but she choked it back…she wasn't going to give him the satisfaction. Instead, she stared at him, blinking.

His eyes swept her still form, and she saw them widen slightly as he took in the bloody cloth wrapped around her thigh.

"Are you all right?"

There was genuine concern in his voice, which caught her off guard for a second…only a second though. Remembering that she was being held hostage, and that these people had her family, too, brought her composure…and anger…back quickly. Narrowing her eyes, she shrugged; she wasn't okay, not at all. Her leg was throbbing, and just thinking about speaking aloud made her worry that she would vomit again right there in front of him.

"Did this happen on your way here?"

She kept her stoic expression firmly in place, but she nodded. Did it really matter when it had happened? Where did he get off with the concerned act? If he really cared about her well-being, she wouldn't be here.

"Do you need help standing?"

"No." She spit the word through her teeth and forced herself up, squeezing her eyes shut for a moment against the searing heat that flowed through her leg, and the fresh bout of dizziness that made her immediately want to lie down again.

The man seemed not to notice…either her acting was better than she thought it was, or he was extraordinarily polite for a kidnapper. He took a step backward, holding the flap of the tent open wide.

She followed him out. Now that she could see the sun, she realized it was still earlier than she'd thought. For as much heat as it had been pouring into the tent, she'd expected the sun to be higher in the sky. The morning air was cool and helped her nausea subside a little, even though it was still heavily scented with smoke.

"There's a stream just through those trees," the man said, pointing. "If you need a few minutes to yourself…"

She frowned at him for a minute, studying his face. He was probably in his late thirties, with dark brown hair and eyes. Nothing about his clothing…rough woven pants, and a white short-sleeved shirt that tied around the neck…gave away anything about whom he might be or where he was from. A quick glance at his soft, smooth hands, though, suggested that a tent in the wilderness wasn't his usual habitat.

He looked sincere. After a few seconds, she decided that she wasn't immediately threatened by him, and that his offer of time to herself was genuine. He waited silently while Quinn appraised him, and while she turned and walked in the direction he was pointing, concentrating with everything she had in her to not limp.

Obviously he wasn't worried about her running off, she thought, as she ducked through the trees, hearing the flow of the promised stream before she actually saw it.

Of course, she *wasn't* going to run off. Her family was here. Remembering the sound of her sister's voice, here, where it didn't belong, brought the nausea roaring back with an intensity she could no longer fight. She vomited fiercely several times, unable to stop until there was nothing left and she collapsed, exhausted on the bank of the stream.

For several minutes, she couldn't move, couldn't even lift her head, but finally the worst of it passed, and she struggled to sit up and clean herself up in the water.

She didn't know how much time she had before someone came looking for her, but she wanted to get herself together as best she could before facing whatever the rest of this situation was going to bring. She didn't want Annie and Owen seeing her this way.

What did it mean that her family was here? Had they come through the gate on their own? Maybe, but why? Or had someone with too much knowledge actually managed to breach the gate and gone into Quinn's world and kidnapped them?

Quinn shook her head and dipped her hands into the stream, bringing a handful of the cold water up to her face. She couldn't think that way yet…that thought was too terrifying. It wasn't worth wondering about right now. As soon as she was finished here, she would be getting the answers anyway. It wasn't worth getting worked up about now.

When her face and mouth were clean, she turned her attention to the part she was dreading. Her leg.

Ignoring her injury wasn't going to be a choice. The bulky cloth she was using as a bandage was in the way of her being able to lower her pants to relieve herself – and she wasn't going to be able to put that off any longer.

The whole cloth was stained red, and the bottom layer of it was stuck to her skin…she tried sliding her finger underneath it to loosen it, but the resulting stab of pain made her abandon that idea immediately.

Tears threatened, along with a warning in her stomach that the nausea was only taking a break.

She took a deep, shaky breath, and then, grateful for the shallow, sloping bank, she removed her shoe and sock, stretched her leg out, and slid it into the water.

The cold water made her gasp at first, but she gritted her teeth and kept at it. It only took a minute or so to adjust. Slowly, she slid her leg further and further into the stream, turning her body sideways as far as she could so that she didn't get completely wet. Finally, the water reached the bottom of the bandage. She used her hands to scoop more of the clean stream water over the bandage. The jolt of pain as the water hit her cut made her cry out. She stopped scooping for a minute, taking several deep breaths before forcing herself to continue.

Blinking back tears, she pushed herself to get the bandage all the way wet, and then carefully untied the cloth and loosened it.

The wound was worse than she'd guessed. Deep and raw, with edges that were angry and starting to turn red. The wet cloth the night before had been a bad idea. She couldn't bring herself to look at it for more than a few seconds. Without looking again, she carefully edged her leg all the way into the stream, where the water could flow over the injury.

Ignoring the pain as best she could, though every muscle in her body was tight, and she was definitely nauseous again, she concentrated on washing every trace of blood out of the cloth, until it was as clean as she could get it. She knew that she should really be keeping her wound clean and dry, but at the moment it looked like clean was going to have to do.

Setting the bandage to the side on the cleanest-looking rock she could find, she pulled her leg back out of the water, and somehow managed to get back to a standing position.

She had just finished taking care of her personal needs behind a tree, when she heard heavy footsteps in the foliage, and then the man's voice again.

"Lady Quinn? Are you in need of assistance?"

"No." Her anger hadn't abated at all…if anything, she'd crossed from furious to livid. There were footsteps again, moving a little further away, but stopping still nearby.

She finished adjusting her clothes, and then took the clean, dripping bandage from where she'd set it on a rock. Pulling back up on the leg of her woven pants, she hazarded one more glance at the injury, nearly vomiting again in the process, and then covered it with the bandage. She wrapped it as tightly as she could stand, hoping that keeping tight pressure on it would help when she tried to walk again.

Sweat was dripping down her face from the effort by the time she emerged from the trees to face her new guard again, but she was on her own two feet and walking, and she wasn't in immediate danger of vomiting again.

"I want to see my family," she said. "Now."

The man nodded and began walking up the path toward the campsite.

 THE LAST PRINCE

TRACKING AELWYN WAS EASY and familiar. She would fly ahead of William for several hundred yards, but then circle back and dip down low, right in front of him, almost as if she was checking up on him.

The bird had been his companion since he was thirteen, and the bond between the two of them had been strong since the very beginning. Aelwyn had even been tolerant of his frequent absences from this world; she would always be waiting in the trees near the gate when he returned, ready to pick up right where they'd left off…so long as William brought her back a treat.

He didn't know where she was leading him now. They traveled northwest from the emergency camp, heading the opposite direction of the fire. The area was all wilderness…thick with shady trees and lush vegetation. He crossed several small streams, but only once did he and Skittles stop to drink and refill his canteen. Even the horse seemed to understand the urgency of the situation, and took only a short drink before stomping his feet impatiently for William to remount.

If they were in Quinn's world, the terrain here would probably be popular for hiking and camping, he thought ironically. But as those were not popular pastimes in Eirentheos, William didn't see any signs of other people as Aelwyn led him deep into the woods. There were no trails here; he had to ride slowly and calculate their path carefully, avoiding trees and rocks. Skittles didn't seem to mind, though.

After nearly an hour of riding, the bird dropped down into the trees in front of him, out of sight, before popping back up again, and coming to land several feet in front of Skittles. William brought the horse to a stop and looked around, listening.

Then, several things happened at once. He heard a loud crunching noise behind him, Aelwyn squawked loudly and took to the air again, and William realized, with a sickening thud that resonated down into the deepest part of his insides, exactly how stupid he had been.

He turned to face the noise, and found himself looking down at two men he didn't recognize. Though they were dressed simply, in clothes that didn't identify them at all, and the horses carried no identifying blankets or banners, either, both of them were large and muscular…the build typical of soldiers and castle guards.

"Nice of you to come, Prince William," the taller one said.

Quinn followed the guard up the path and back toward the campsite. Part of her wondered where the man who'd brought her here last night had gone, but she didn't really care. She'd allowed herself to be kidnapped…that was done. Now she just wanted to get back to her family and then figure out what was going on here and how she was going to get them out of it.

She didn't dare hope that Raeyan would be successful in getting her message to someone…and even if he did manage it, her scribbled note wasn't exactly informative. No, she was going to have to try to get them out of here herself. Of course, she didn't have any idea how to do that.

They passed the tent where they'd slept last night, and headed toward the other tents. She was surprised at how small and empty the campsite seemed. In the daylight, she could see that there were fewer tents than she'd guessed…only four were huddled around a small fire circle. The fire was extinguished. There were no people here.

The man led her past those tents, and toward a thick wall of trees. Quinn was beginning to get very anxious. Where was he taking her? Where was her family? But as soon as they stepped through an opening that had been cleared in the underbrush, she had her answer.

They were in another small clearing. Here, there were two large tents and an even larger canopy, with drapes covering at least the two sides she was facing. A man stood on the opposite side of the canopy from her, right by the corner. He held a sword, and appeared to be guarding the clearing. He nodded toward the man Quinn was following.

"Look at these flowers, Mommy!" Annie's sudden voice shot through Quinn like an arrow, making her blood run cold. She hadn't realized that in the short time she'd been away from them that she'd become terrified they'd be separated again.

Suddenly, she was no longer following the man, no longer walking carefully to hide her limp. She dashed for the front of the canopy as quickly as she could.

No drape covered the west-facing side of the canopy. It was open, letting in the sunlight and air, though it was shaded from the increasing morning heat. Annie was standing just inside the entrance, proudly holding up a handful of pretty pink flowers towards her mother, who was sitting on a rug at the back of the canopy with Owen curled up next to her.

None of them saw Quinn right away, although the man who was in the tent with them did.

"Ah, the *Lady* Quinn," he said, taking a step toward her.

She could almost hear her mother's eyes lock onto her, and she could definitely hear her little sister's excited shriek, but Quinn held out her hand to her mother…asking her to stay seated for a moment, and she kept her eyes on the man.

She'd never seen him before, but she knew immediately who he had to be…that the mysterious *Jonathan* would turn out to be who she'd been afraid of seeing here. He had the same square chin, straight nose, and high cheekbones as Nathaniel, but his wide gray eyes were just like the ones that had stared back at her from the picture on her bedside table at home her whole life.

Even though he'd dressed in very ordinary, rugged clothes…probably to disguise his identity…as he stepped toward her, she could see his well-trained bearing.

"*Prince* Jonathan."

Surprise widened his eyes. Behind him, her mother watched with interest, though she looked ready to stand and run between them at a moment's notice.

Her own eyes narrowed as she scrutinized Jonathan, trying to assess the situation. He looked a little shocked at her easy identification of him, and she was suddenly quite sure that she knew more about him than he did about her. But why had he brought her here, then? And what was he doing with her family?

Annie, seemingly unaffected by the seriousness of the situation, ran up to her. Quinn sucked in a breath as the little girl wrapped her arms around her legs, and Jonathan's eyes flicked down to her leg, and then back over her shoulder.

"Was I not clear that she was to be brought here unharmed, Clarence?"

"I spoke to Levan about it. He says she fell…he didn't touch her."

"Is that true?" Jonathan asked, turning back to her.

"Come over here, Annie." The sound of her mother's voice nearly brought tears to her eyes. She blinked hard several times, and deliberately focused her attention back onto the man in front of her…her real father's youngest brother…knowing that if she looked too much at her mom and her siblings, she was going to lose her composure completely, and if she did that, she might miss her chance to figure out what was going on here in time to gain an advantage.

"No, not exactly," she said.

"Then what happened?"

Her eyes flicked to her mother, and then back to him. "It's not important right now."

His eyes narrowed, but he nodded. "Are you all right?" he asked, studying the cloth on her leg. She followed his gaze, noting that the cloth was stained again, this time with pink and yellow streaks. Bringing her eyes quickly back up to him, she took a deep breath and promised herself she wouldn't look again.

Her first instinct was to tell him defiantly that she was just fine, but then she saw a hint of what might have been genuine concern in his eyes, and she shook her head once. "I don't think so." Truthfully, her leg was blazing, and the nausea had returned, tightening her stomach in sickening waves. She felt warmer than she should have, too, even considering the heat of the morning. Twice, on the walk here, she'd felt a shuddering chill, followed a few seconds later by a flash of heat.

"Shall I send for a healer?"

So he had a healer here. His set-up might be more elaborate than it appeared to be. She was starting to think that Jonathan's presence here might have something to do with all of the "refugees" who had been camping in the area near the gate lately.

"Not yet," she answered. "I want to know what you're doing with my family here, first." Besides, she didn't want anyone touching her…anyone besides William, anyway. Maybe Nathaniel or Jacob. Definitely not someone who was aiding and abetting in the abductions of her and her family.

Jonathan frowned. "Maybe first you could tell me what Stephen's son could possibly be doing, courting someone from another world. Is this Stephen's plan, then? To take over both kingdoms entirely, with help from your world?"

Quinn's eyebrows shot up so far that she thought she might have to go searching for them later. "Stephen doesn't want to take over Philotheum. Is that the story Tolliver is telling you? Is that how he's getting your support? *You*, of all people? King Jonathan's youngest son?"

He narrowed his eyes, contemplating her. "What makes you think I support Tolliver?"

Quinn raised an eyebrow again, and he suddenly looked wary, as though he might have slipped and said something he shouldn't. Of course, considering the circumstances, what had just come out of his mouth was fairly dangerous.

"What are you doing here in Eirentheos, then, if Tolliver didn't send you?"

He sighed, and something in his expression shifted. "How do you know so much about our political situation?"

She stared at him, studying him carefully, frowning. She was now certain that he didn't know who she really was. Her eyes flicked to her family in the corner. They looked all right. She still didn't know how they'd gotten here, but Jonathan obviously already knew that they were from another world…that she was. *Had he gone there and gotten them?* That didn't seem likely.

"Who do you believe I am?" she asked.

"I'm trying to figure that out. Tolliver believes you're some kind of spy, possibly from another world, where Stephen has allies who are going to help him in his takeover of Philotheum."

"And he sent you here to prove it."

"Yes."

His quick, honest answer surprised her. "What do you believe?"

He sighed again. "I never believed that Stephen wanted to take over our kingdom. But then, I never believed there really was a gate connecting this world to another one, either."

"What changed your mind about that?"

He glanced back at her mother and her siblings. "When I watched your family appear out of nowhere onto a bridge the night before last."

Well, that answered that question, although she couldn't figure out what would have possessed her mother to bring her siblings and come looking for her here. There were still several days left of spring break, and she hadn't made any promises about when she would return.

"And my mother told you about the big conspiracy Stephen has to take over the kingdom using a woman and two small children?"

He met her gaze. He'd been raised a prince in a castle with Hector and Tolliver…he would rise to whatever challenge she set. "It actually appeared to be news to her that you are courting Prince William."

Her own expression was guilty as she finally glanced back at her mom. Quinn had somehow come to have an entire life here in this world that her own mother knew nothing about. The last time she had been home, she had told her mom a little about her relationship with William, but it hadn't been so serious then.

Nausea bubbled up in her stomach again, and she swayed, but managed to stay on her feet and keep herself from vomiting.

"Are you all right?"

"I need to sit down." She wasn't going to let this stop her from having this conversation. Every instinct she had was screaming how important this was.

He picked up a wooden folding chair and set it on the ground next to her. As she sank down into it, in the most dignified way she could manage, he pulled up another chair across from her, and sat down.

His action put her strangely at ease…that he sat down to stay level with her, rather than towering over her. "Better?" he asked, in a gentle voice that caught her even more off guard.

"Sort of," she said.

In the corner, her mother twitched, again as if she was about to dash across the tent to her, but Quinn shook her head once, silently begging her mother not to, not yet.

Taking a deep breath, she mustered up the strength to look him in the eyes. "What is your goal here, Jonathan? Not what you're telling me Tolliver sent you for…I don't believe for a minute that you're actually doing his bidding the way he surely thinks you are. Why did you really come? What do you want?"

He paused for a long moment, clearly weighing his next words. "When I came here, I wanted to know if it was really true…the rumors. If Stephen really does want to see the kingdoms united again. If he's willing to stand up and help me remove my half-brother, and somehow return our crown to the rightful line."

"But now?"

"Now I don't know what to believe. Why is Stephen in contact with another world? I didn't believe Tolliver…thought it was all just more of his nonsense and bluster. I really thought Stephen would never do something like that. But here you are, courting William. And you are from another world, are you not *Lady* Quinn?" His sarcasm on the word *lady* was thick and mocking.

"Sort of," she answered.

"What do you mean? Either you are or you aren't."

"All right. I was born and raised in a different world than this one, yes."

"Then what are you doing here? Why do you know as much as you do? Because *I* don't 'believe for one minute' that Stephen – or any of his sons – would just share that level of information with some little girl from *anywhere* unless they had a reason for doing so."

Although she knew his words had been carefully selected to elicit a reaction from her, she still bristled at his tone. She had to close her eyes and pull two long breaths in through her nose to keep herself from spitting out a response that she would regret.

"What does Stephen want with you?"

She opened her eyes and stared at him, her expression hard and even. "You're the one who has kidnapped me and my family. You think I trust you enough to give you *any* answers about Stephen when you can't even tell me why you're here? You could get your information and then just kill us all anyway."

The glance toward her family then was involuntary. Annie was sitting in her mother's lap, wide-eyed. Quinn struggled to read her mother's expression. It was a strange combination of fear and...*pride?* Owen's face surprised her the most, though. He was perfectly calm, watching her with interest. As she looked at him, he glanced once at Jonathan, and then nodded back at her. His meaning was clear. *Owen trusted Jonathan.*

Jonathan stood from his chair and paced back and forth along the length of the canopy, watching Quinn intently as he did.

Finally, he returned to the chair across from her, though he leaned across the back of it, rather than sitting.

"Tolliver sent me here to gather more information about you…the mysterious girl from nowhere, who is suddenly courting the enigmatic Prince William. Tolliver is, shall we say, somewhat excessively interested in you, Quinn."

She nodded. "I've met him."

"What did you *do* to him?"

"I believe my biggest offense was rejecting his...*advances.*"

Jonathan coughed, but nodded. "That sounds about right."

"At the time, he accused me of being a conquest of Thomas's, and thought that Thomas was simply having difficulty sharing his toys."

"So you've come by your misgivings about my half-brother honestly, then."

"Quite. I'm not overly fond of his feelings of entitlement to a throne that doesn't belong to him, either."

Once again, Jonathan's eyes widened in surprise.

"Why do you care, Lady Quinn? What difference does it make to you who sits on the throne of my kingdom?"

Her heart was fluttering like a hummingbird's wings, and the waves of nausea were so strong that she was having difficulty remaining on her chair. This was it. Somehow she knew that whatever she told Jonathan here was going to determine the course of her future. Alvin's voice from her dream resounded in her head. *"The choice is yours."*

Her decision wasn't going to come quietly in the privacy and safety of Stephen's office. It would come now.

She stole one more glance at Owen. He smiled encouragingly up at her, and suddenly she was surer of herself than she'd ever been. She could do this…so long as she didn't first vomit on the ground.

Slowly, she reached into her pocket and loosened the pin that held the small cloth pouch in place. Setting the pouch in her hand, she untied the drawstring, opened the bag, and reached inside.

Jonathan watched in awed silence as she removed the two pendants, both made of Philothean gold. She picked up the older of the two, and held it in the air in front of him.

"Samuel didn't die in Philotheum," she said.

Jonathan leaned closer, and reached for the pendant, though he didn't take it from her. He simply held it between his fingers, closely examining both sides. He glanced down at the pendant that still sat on her other hand. When he spoke, his voice was so quiet she had to strain to hear him. "You are his child."

She nodded, but could no longer form words. The nausea was so bad now that she couldn't help it. Dropping to the ground in front of her chair, the motion sending searing waves of pain shooting through her leg, down toward her toes, and up through her hip, she leaned down and threw up.

WILLIAM'S QUESTION

FEAR CHURNED IN WILLIAM'S stomach as he followed one of the men…the other was right behind him, making sure he didn't go anywhere.

Stupid and reckless…that's what he'd been. Quinn was going to have his head for this…if he ever saw her again. Even Thomas had apparently grown more sense than to take off alone the way William had.

The two men gave off the distinct demeanor of castle guards. Though they didn't speak much as they led him through the woods, the few words they did utter carried the subtle hint of a Philothean accent. William had no idea what he was riding into, but he was sure it wasn't good.

Eventually, they rode into a small clearing with a few tents. It appeared to be mostly empty, except for one man sitting outside one of the tents. They rode through the clearing and between some trees to a place where four horses were tied. Here, they dismounted, tied their own horses, and turned to William.

Swallowing hard, he climbed down from his saddle and handed his lead to the man standing nearest him.

He tried to pay attention to his surroundings as he followed his two captors back through the clearing, but he just couldn't seem to focus. His heart was pounding so hard that the sound pounded in his ears.

When he found himself in another clearing, walking up to a large canopy, he had no idea how he had gotten there.

What he saw when they reached the open side of the canopy, made him forget where he was completely. Quinn was curled on her side on a mat near the entrance. A woman who looked a lot like Quinn's mother…although that was impossible…had Quinn's head in her lap, while a man crouched in front of her. Over in the corner, two children huddled together, looking worried.

As he watched, Quinn lunged forward, coughed, and then threw up on the ground.

The man who was crouched in front of her leapt backward out of the way, although the amount of vomit was very small. William didn't hesitate; he dashed across the short distance, edging the man the rest of the way away from Quinn, and pulled her into his arms.

"Quinn! What's wrong?"

She stared at him, and blinked several times, as if she couldn't believe what she was seeing.

"It's really me, sweetheart, I'm here. What's going on?"

She was hot, too hot. Her hair was matted to her forehead with sweat, and her eyes were shiny and bloodshot. She shrugged, glancing down at her leg.

"What did you do to her?" He demanded, fury rising in his voice as he turned to the man next to him, but before the man could answer, he felt Quinn's flaming hand on his arm.

"It wasn't him," she said quietly, her voice rough from retching. "I fell last night, on my way here."

"You mean as you were being kidnapped in the dark?" William had never been so angry in his life. He stood, and the man did, too, facing him. "This is your fault. What is wrong with her?"

"Prince Jonathan? Do you want us to take him out of here?" One of the guards who had brought him here took a step toward William.

Prince Jonathan? William looked up at the man again. It had been many cycles since he had seen Tolliver's older half-brother. For a long time now, Hector had sent only Tolliver to visit for official events…probably because he'd only been concerned with trying to marry Tolliver into Stephen's family. And William had been young the last time he'd traveled to the castle in Philotheum.

Now that he was looking, though, he could see it, could recognize the prince.

He never did get to hear Jonathan's response to the guard's question. At that moment, there was a rustling in the brush at the edge of the clearing, and then the sounds of several horses as they walked through the foliage, and surrounded the canopy.

The riders were all wearing the purple and silver livery of his father's guard, and the first one to dismount and walk up to the canopy, sword drawn, was Ben.

⁂

Everything happened so quickly then that afterwards, William could never remember how it happened at all.

The next thing he knew, he was mounted back on Skittles, a very ill Quinn nestled in his arms. She protested at being carried, but he ignored her. Ben and another guard, Nolan, followed behind him on their horses as he rushed back toward the castle. After only a few minutes, she fell asleep against him.

He didn't know what was wrong…how bad her injury was, or why she was so sick…but he didn't want to take the time to find out while they were out here in the woods. He didn't have anything to treat her with out here, anyway. He wanted her back at the castle in his clinic, where he would have everything he needed.

Just as he finally emerged from the woods onto an actual road, Quinn woke up, and looked around in alarm. "Where are we?"

William slowed down just a little, afraid she'd woken because the jostling was hurting her. "Shh... sweetheart, you're safe now. We're going back to the castle right now."

Her eyes widened. "Where are my mom and Annie and Owen?"

William's jaw dropped. "That really was your mom? How did she...? What is she doing here?"

"I don't know! Will! Did you just leave them there? Stop! We have to go get them!" She pushed weakly at his arms, trying to take control of Skittles.

"Hey," he said, bringing the horse to a stop, and allowing Ben and Nolan to ride up beside them. "Calm down. We didn't just leave them there. There were other guards. They'll be bringing everyone back to the castle."

"Are you sure?" She looked panicked, and William wrapped his arms tightly around her.

"I'm sure," he said softly into her ear.

"Everything is under control, Lady Quinn," Ben said, leaning close and making eye contact with her. "I spoke to your mother for a few minutes while William was with you. She was only concerned with you getting back to the castle as soon as possible, but she and your siblings are following right behind. If it makes you feel any better, Nolan here will go back and check. He'll have them brought to you immediately." He nodded toward the other guard. "Right, Nolan?"

"Yes, of course." A moment later, Nolan was halfway down the road in the opposite direction.

"Okay, love? Let's just get you back, please?"

Quinn only woke once more on the rest of the trip to the castle, and that was only because her stomach was heaving again. William held her on the side of the road, supporting her as she retched, but all that came up was the little bit of water he'd forced into her before they'd started riding.

He didn't think he'd ever been so happy to see the castle in his life. Ben rode ahead of him, speaking to the guard at the gate, and everyone got out of the way as William rushed her back to the clinic. Ben followed him, and helped him carry her inside.

"Everyone's going to be in an uproar," Ben said, as they carefully laid the girl onto a cot.

"I know they will. But could you keep them out of here for at least a little bit? Give her a few minutes to relax and let us figure out what's going on? Unless it's Nathaniel?"

"Sure." Ben patted William on the shoulder. "Just take care of her, okay?"

William nodded.

Although he'd never seen her so sick or exhausted, Quinn's eyes were open as he approached her, pulling with him a cart of supplies. Her cheeks were bright red, and her skin was dry and hot.

"Hey, love," he said softly, reaching for her wrist and using his fingers to find her pulse.

"Hi."

"Feeling pretty rotten, huh?" Her heartbeat was a little too rapid for his liking, but it was strong.

She nodded slightly.

He pressed down gently on her fingernails, and watched as the color refilled too slowly. "How's your stomach?"

"It's been better."

"Do you need to throw up again?"

"Not right now."

"Good." He leaned over and kissed her too-hot forehead. "Can I feel?" he asked, setting his hand gently on her abdomen.

She nodded.

"I need to open some buttons, okay? Just a couple."

She nodded, and he had a feeling she'd have been blushing if her face wasn't already as red as it could get from the fever.

"It's a little awkward, isn't it? I've never courted a patient before."

"I consider that a good thing."

"Me too." He unbuttoned the bottom two buttons of her shirt and then froze. A bright red lacy rash snaked over her entire abdomen. "Oh."

"What?" she asked, alarmed.

"I think you have redrash."

"What? I have a rash? From what?" She tried to pull her head up to look, but he put his hand on her shoulder and gently pushed her back down.

"Yes, you have a rash. I think it's something called redrash…that would explain the fever, too. I knew something was up with you yesterday."

"What is redrash?"

"It's a childhood illness. It's usually not serious. *Everyone* gets it here…actually, we thought that Sarah might have had it last week. But, of course, *you* wouldn't have had it when you were little."

"But it's not serious?"

"Not usually. Not for little kids, anyway. The older you are, though, the worse it can be. It's probably why you have such a high fever and you're throwing up."

"Can you treat it?"

"We almost never have to, but I have an anti-viral remedy I can try, after I get some blood and make sure that's what it is."

"Okay."

"Why is this damp?" he asked, tapping lightly on her leg, just below where the bandage peeked out from a tear in her tattered and bloody pants.

"I tried to clean it out in a stream earlier…I didn't have anything dry to wrap it back up in." She was starting to go a little green at the edges again.

"Okay." He leaned up and kissed her again on the forehead, lingering for a second to bask in her scent. She was sweaty and dirty, but it was still her, here and real in front of him, and breathing her in calmed him enough to remember what he needed to do next. Sitting back down on the stool next to her, he pulled several packets out of a drawer and ripped them open.

"I'm going to give you some medicine that will get rid of the nausea, all right?"

She nodded.

"But I need to start an IV first."

She closed her eyes for a long second before nodding again. "I think I knew that was coming," she whispered.

"Have you ever had one before?" He kept his voice intentionally light as he picked up her arm and started running his fingers up and down, searching for a vein. This wasn't going to be easy; she was really dehydrated.

"No."

"It won't be as bad as you think."

She shrugged. "I think I kind of got over my fear of needles after the tattoo raising. It can't be as bad as that, can it?"

"No." He smiled and reached for the bottle of antiseptic and a cotton swab. "Not nearly as bad as that. It'll just pinch for a minute."

"Okay."

William applied the tourniquet and carefully cleaned the back of her hand. She'd closed her eyes again, but she wasn't asleep.

It only took him a few seconds. She winced when the needle went in, but relaxed again almost immediately. He drew some blood first, saving her a second poke, and then prepared the syringe of anti-nausea medication and a bag of fluids.

"Better?" he asked, after letting her rest for a few minutes.

"Is that stuff magic?" Already her breathing was steadier, and her heart rate had slowed a little.

"It seems like it sometimes."

"Is that the medicine you invented?"

"Yes. But I think the fluids are going to help you the most. Once you get dehydrated like that... Yesterday was already a long day, and you really weren't drinking enough even then."

"It's okay to take credit for things sometimes, you know."

"I know." He blushed, turning her hand over so he could kiss her palm. "Truth is, I don't care who invented what so long as you feel better."

She smiled, but then her expression changed to serious…sad. "Will," she whispered, grabbing hold of his hand, and pulling it toward her chest. "I was so scared."

Hot moisture pricked at the corners of his eyes, and he had a hard time swallowing. "I know, love. So was I." He climbed up on the cot and lay down next to her, pulling her as close as he could without jostling her, resting his head near hers. "I was afraid I was never going to see you again."

"But then you rescued me."

He leaned back just far enough to be able to look at her face. "No, not exactly. You rescued yourself. I got all hot-headed and ran off by myself to go looking for you and got captured myself…don't freak out, we're safe, remember? But apparently Raeyan found Ben with your note."

"Really? I didn't think he would ever manage that."

"Well, he did."

"Wow. I'm going to have to find him a really good treat."

"I think we can figure something out." He'd been quite proud of the little bird after hearing that story from Ben.

She was quiet for a long moment, studying his face, and he scooted himself closer to her, watching her, too, unable to tear his eyes away. There were smudges of dirt and blood all over her face and neck, but it didn't matter. Nobody…nothing…had ever looked as beautiful to him as she did right then.

"I love you so much Quinn."

"I love you, Will. So much."

"I don't ever want to be separated from you like that again."

She found his hand again and squeezed it tightly. "I'm not going anywhere."

"Marry me, Quinn."

Whoa. Where had that come from?

Her eyes widened in surprise, but she didn't look quite as shocked as he felt. "Are you serious?"

Was he? Until that moment he had never let his thoughts drift that far into the future, but now that he was thinking about it, he realized that he couldn't imagine anything else. "Yes, I am."

She took a deep breath, and he saw her throat move as she swallowed.

His palms started sweating as he waited to hear the refusal that he knew was coming.

But when she spoke again, it wasn't to say no. "Any chance we could talk about this when you're done sticking needles in me and after my toothbrush and I have been reunited?"

He chuckled and smiled sheepishly, both relieved and shocked that she hadn't just come out and told him to get out of here. "That was a little inappropriate of me, wasn't it?" Although his heart was beating much more quickly than normal, he was surprised to discover that he wasn't mortified by what he had just done. He was even more surprised to realize that his question had, in fact, been serious.

She shrugged. "Maybe a little." But she smiled, and somehow the moment wasn't awkward the way it seemed like it should have been…like him blurting out a proposal to her was the most natural thing in the world.

The atmosphere between them was easy and relaxed…well, as much as it could be, with her still in pain…as he scooted down onto the stool next to her. "So… do you want to tell me what happened to this leg?" he asked, digging in a drawer for scissors.

"You really don't want to know, Will." She grimaced as he touched her.

He stopped. "Oh, yes I do."

"I was following that guard…I think his name is Levan…up a little ridge, and I thought I might be able to get his knife, but I missed, and he pushed me away. I knew I was taking a risk."

Anger gripped his stomach. "It's not your fault, Quinn. You weren't out there walking through the woods for fun. I wish you'd gotten the knife."

"What would I have done with it anyway? Gotten away, maybe. But then I'd be wandering in the woods by myself, and we wouldn't know my family is here. It *is* my fault. I went with him in the first place. So stupid."

"What happened?" He started cutting away the leg of her pants to expose the whole bandage.

She closed her eyes. "I was getting water from the well by myself…I know I should have asked Ben to go with me, but he was busy, and I thought it would be okay…"

He stopped cutting for a second and squeezed her fingers gently.

"This guard came up behind me, and he had Annie's horse…the little wooden one you carved for her." Her eyes widened again suddenly. "Are you sure they're bringing my family back here?"

At that moment, the door of the clinic opened, and Nathaniel came inside, but he was immediately followed by two more figures.

"William! Quinn!" Charlotte and Stephen both rushed across the room.

"Sorry, Will," Ben called from the doorway.

William shook his head. "I didn't expect you to be able to keep my parents out, Ben."

"What were you thinking?" Charlotte shrieked in William's ear. "You could have been killed! Or worse!"

"Worse?"

"You know what I mean, William." She was hugging him so tightly, though, that her anger was unconvincing.

His father, though…he wasn't sure he'd ever seen his father looking this upset. There were dark purple shadows under Stephen's eyes, and his cheeks were pale as he looked back and forth between William and Quinn.

"Is she all right?" he asked, eyeing the IV and the stained bandage on Quinn's leg. Nathaniel had already taken William's place with the scissors.

"I'm okay," Quinn answered, and William almost risked a smile at her determination to speak for herself. "Or I will be. What's going on out there? Is my family here?"

"Yes. They've just brought your mother and your little brother and sister to the castle. I spoke with your mother briefly. She very much wants to see you, but I held her off for a little while. I wanted to know how you want to handle it. Simon is taking them upstairs."

"Good. I don't want them to see me like this."

"Quinn, love, you were worse when we left the camp. She's probably worried," William said, stroking her hair back.

"I know, but I can't, Will. I just…I need to be fixed up and clean and dressed, okay?"

"Okay."

She turned back to Stephen. "Do you know what they're doing here?"

"I don't. I only talked to her briefly, and our only topic of conversation was you. You've had us scared half to death, Quinn. I don't know what Jonathan is doing here, either."

"Can't you just ask him? He was arrested, wasn't he?"

"No, William. The guards who found you were more concerned with getting you two and Quinn's family back here to safety. And it isn't like they have a protocol for arresting another kingdom's prince, so they erred on the side of diplomacy."

"Because Tolliver was being diplomatic when he captured Thomas?"

"Jonathan is not Tolliver," Quinn said quietly.

Stephen sighed. "We can discuss this later when you're feeling better. Is she really okay, Will?"

"Her injuries are not terrible, but I think she has redrash."

"What?" Nathaniel said, taking her arm in his hands and examining it.

"It's on her abdomen," William said. "It hasn't spread to her arms yet, and I haven't looked at her back. She was already getting sick yesterday, I think…I just didn't realize it."

"How are you feeling, sweetheart?" Charlotte asked, sitting down on the edge of the bed.

"I've been better, but I'm already not as bad as I was." Her eyes widened. "Did I just expose my whole family to this?"

"Annie and Owen, maybe," Nathaniel said. "But they probably won't get very sick if they do get it. In little kids, half the time we don't even know they have it. It's like Fifth Disease in your world."

"What is Fifth Disease?"

"Exactly. It's a childhood rash illness that doesn't even warrant a real name…like redrash. Most of the time, it's not even worth missing school over. You had it when you were little, though. You were maybe five, I think."

"What about my mom? Will I get her sick?"

"No. But I'm sure she won't be happy about this. She caught it the one time she came here…from William, if I remember correctly. Spent the last two days she was here in bed, throwing up." Nathaniel sighed. "It didn't help her like this world any better."

William's heart sank. He knew, logically, that it wasn't his fault, but of course he would have been the one who got Megan sick.

"Do we have to tell her?"

"I'm not comfortable lying to your mother, Quinn," Stephen said.

"I'm not talking about lying," she said. "But what if it just doesn't come up?"

Stephen looked at Quinn, his eyes serious. "I won't say anything. But if she asks me, I will tell her the truth."

"Me too."

"Then how you handle it is your choice, Quinn."

"What's going on with the fire?"

He studied her for another moment before he answered. "They've got it fully contained on all fronts that impact people. The rest will come in time. We should be able to lift the evacuations by tomorrow or the next day. There are no serious injuries, so nothing for any of you to worry about. William and Nathaniel…are you up to taking care of her, or shall I send for some help?"

"I'm fine, Stephen," Nathaniel said. "William can finish if he'd like, or I can take over for him."

"Will?" Nathaniel said, after Charlotte and Stephen had left again, leaving Ben still watching the door. "What do you want me to do here?" He had finished cutting away the rest of the material on the leg of Quinn's pants, and was now working on loosening the bandage without hurting her, but as soon as he gave the gentlest of tugs, she wrinkled her nose, and her chest stopped moving for a second.

"Do you want some pain medication, love?" William reached for the supply cart again.

"Will it make me sleepy?"

"Yes. But that might be a good thing. You're going to need stitches again."

He could see her processing that, weighing her options, but in the end she shook her head. "I don't want to be groggy when I see my mom in a while."

"It will wear off, you know."

"I just…I need my head to be clear. Please let me try it without."

"Okay." He looked over at Nathaniel. "Can you do this, then, please? I think this time I want to be the one who just gets to sit with her and hold her hand."

MEGAN

"I COULD KILL YOU both with my bare hands right now."

"Hello to you, too, Linnea." Quinn said, leaning heavily on William's arm as he walked her into her bedroom.

"What in the Maker's name were you thinking?" she flew across the room toward William. "You just introduced us all to a completely new level of stupid."

"I think they've figured that out, Nay." Thomas rose from the couch, and walked over to assist her. "Are you okay, Quinn?"

"I will be," she said as the two boys helped her walk to the couch and sit down. "Right now, I'm really sore and tired, and my leg is numb."

Fortunately, the medicine William had given her for the nausea and the fever was still holding out, and she didn't feel really sick. Her stomach and back were starting to itch, though.

Linnea still looked furious, but she didn't say anything else as she went to sit down across from her.

"She really wants to get cleaned up, Linnea," William said. "I was hoping you could help her get a shower. I've got her leg wrapped up nice and tight so she can get it wet. And this is some lotion for when she gets out…she has redrash."

Quinn shot him a look for talking about her like she wasn't even here…like she was a child, but he was too far in his zone to notice.

He had removed her IV drip, and just capped the port and left it in her hand so she could walk upstairs and get cleaned up. She knew he was anxious to get another bag of fluids in her when she was done, though.

"Of course. You two get out of here," Linnea commanded.

Alone in the shower, with Linnea just outside and the door propped open in case she needed her, the stress of the day finally got to her. Under the hot water, the tears gushed out in an unstoppable flow. She wasn't quiet, but Linnea left her alone, and for that she was grateful.

After twenty minutes or so, she was finally drained and calm again, and Linnea helped her turn the water off and get into her robe.

Linnea dressed her in silence, helping her rub the soothing lotion on her back and then getting her into a simple, soft cotton blouse and a long flowing skirt that would hide her injury, but allow for easy access when William or Nathaniel came to check on her.

"I'm sorry," she finally said, as Linnea helped her up onto the bed and began combing her hair.

Linnea rolled her eyes. "You I'm not so mad at. I'm a little peeved that you went up to that well without a guard…and you really don't want to know what you put William through last night…but *him?* Will's not supposed to be the idiot in the family."

"I think I have a pretty good idea of what that was like." Whatever he'd spent the night thinking about had led to that proposal down in the clinic. And her own night…alone and injured in that tent without him…had her seriously considering it. "I think he's pretty upset about what he did already. He knows how stupid it was. But it's not like anybody saw any of this coming."

Linnea nodded. "How long are you going to avoid seeing your mother?"

"I'm not avoiding her. I just wanted to get myself put back together before she saw me in a million pieces."

"She's your mother. Do you think she cares about that?"

Quinn took a deep breath. "She needs to see me okay, Linnea. She needs to see me handling this, and even happy here. It's important."

"Oh," Linnea said, setting down the comb and coming around to face Quinn. "You've made a decision, haven't you?"

"I told Prince Jonathan who I really am. In front of my mother."

It only took Linnea a second to regain her composure and remove the look of shock from her face. "That will do it."

"Pretty much."

"All right, then. You need to be on the couch, and not the bed, and I'll do something nicer with your hair. Maybe a little blush and lipstick too? You're awfully pale."

By the time Linnea and Thomas left her room to go and retrieve her mother, Quinn felt much more human, if not entirely better. She was clean, and her hair was done…she'd even allowed Linnea to talk her into the makeup.

William had re-attached the IV drip, and given her another dose of the anti-nausea medicine, along with some pain medication that was less effective, but at least wouldn't put her to sleep, now that some of the numbness in her leg was beginning to fade.

He was next to her on the couch, holding her hand as she waited, anxiously staring at her open doorway.

"You can do this, love. It's just your mom."

She nodded. She hadn't yet told William what she'd told Linnea. "I know."

All of the careful mental preparation she'd been doing for the last few hours was for naught, though, the moment Megan walked in, and dashed across the room to her.

She thought she'd gotten all of her tears out when she was in the shower, thought that all of the hours of deciding how she was going to handle this, would keep any extras at bay, but she was wrong.

The moment her mother's arms were around her, a torrent of saltwater poured from her eyes, and great heaving sobs wracked her chest.

She wasn't alone, though, her mother was crying, too.

"Come on Will," Linnea said from the doorway, and a minute later she shut the door as everyone else disappeared, and it was just Quinn and her mom.

"Are you really all right?" Megan asked when they were both finally calm again. She was looking at Quinn's IV suspiciously.

"I'm fine, Mom. Nathaniel and William are just very cautious."

"I saw you earlier. I've been so worried about you, and nobody would tell me where you were."

"I know. I'm sorry…that was my fault. I didn't want you to see me like that."

"You didn't want me to *see* you like that?" Megan's voice rose. "You're my child, Quinn! I want to be there for you, especially when you're sick or hurt."

She squeezed her eyes shut and took a deep breath, trying to hold back the flood of emotion that came at her mother's words. "I know you do."

"Then why wouldn't you let me? Did I really mess things up between the two of us so badly that you don't even want your mom when you're hurt?"

It felt like she'd been punched in the stomach. "No, Mom! It isn't like that."

"Then tell me what it's like."

"First of all, what are you even doing here? Why would you bring the kids here?"

"I was worried about you. I didn't ever plan on doing anything like that, but the other night, the kids and I were just on our way out to dinner, when my cell phone rings. It was the hospital, calling because Nathaniel hasn't shown up for two shifts in a row, and they're worried about him."

Quinn's mouth fell open. "Why would they call *you*?"

"I've always been his special emergency contact…it was something we worked out years ago, just in case something like this ever happened, in case one day he just stopped showing up at work. Who else could they call? I'm sure they tried his house first, but William isn't there, either."

"I guess that makes sense, but still…"

"I know you said you might not come home until the end of the break, but when I got that call…I just knew something was wrong. I couldn't just sit there, knowing so much more time was passing for you here…"

"But what would possess you to bring the kids? If you were so sure something was wrong, why would you bring Annie and Owen?"

"It was a very last minute decision. It was just starting to get dark. I could either take the kids into the restaurant and sit and worry about you, or drive to the bridge. I didn't even really think about it."

Quinn sighed. "I know how those decisions are. I thought people maybe grew out of that."

Megan chuckled softly. "Growing up isn't a one-time thing. There's no magic point where you're just grown up and you make the right decisions all the time."

"Well that stinks."

Her mom actually smiled. "Anyway, the important thing now I guess is that we're all safe, and you're going to be okay, and we can all go home together when the gate opens again."

A weight dropped into Quinn's stomach so suddenly that she was very glad for the medicine William had given her…without it, she might have thrown up again right then.

She stared down at her hands, remembering the conversation she'd had with Linnea while she was finishing getting ready.

"Your mother isn't going to like what you have to say, Quinn," Linnea had said. "You have to understand that and be ready for it. There's nothing you can do, no amount of explaining that's going to change that. In time, she might learn how to be okay with it, but not tonight. You still have to tell her. You can't dance around the issue, or try to soften the blow, or any of those things that ultimately fall into the category of not being honest with her. She deserves the truth, and she needs to hear it from you."

She knew Linnea was right, knew that it was why she was in here alone with her mom. William would have stayed with her, to make it easier. Linnea and Thomas would have, too. But that wasn't fair. This was between Quinn and Megan, and her mom did deserve to hear the truth from her.

"I'm not going home, Mom." Her voice was barely above a whisper, but she knew her mom heard, because suddenly she grew completely still.

"What do you mean?"

"I mean… I might go back there sometimes, temporarily…to visit, to see you, but I'm going to live here."

"Don't be ridiculous, Quinn! You're sixteen. You can't just move out!"

"I'm almost seventeen. And it doesn't matter, anyway. Sixteen is of age here. I'm an adult."

"Well, in our world that's still called kidnapping."

She took a deep breath. "So call the police, then, Mom. Tell them I've been kidnapped and I'm being held in a castle in a kingdom in another world."

"You're not even finished with high school!"

"I know. But that doesn't matter here, either."

"Why, Quinn? Why are you doing this? Is your life with me and Jeff and Annie and Owen really so terrible that you feel the need to run off and live like a fairy tale princess? Is that it? Is it because we don't live in a castle with servants running around, catering to your every whim?"

Her jaw dropped. "Really, Mom? That's what you think of me?" Tears threatened behind her eyes again, but she wasn't going to let them win.

"Is this about William, then? You're going to leave your family and run off after a boy at seventeen?"

Quinn bit her tongue, fighting back the rising anger that would only make things worse if she allowed it to get hold of her. Her mother was upset. Very upset, and she had a good reason to be. She was going to say things she might not mean.

She waited for her mother to get it out of her system, to finish yelling, finish what she needed to say. And then she allowed silence to settle between them for a long moment before she spoke.

Her hand drifted up to the necklace that Linnea had helped her put on...her gold birth pendant. She held it, rubbing the etched surfaces between her thumb and forefinger.

"My father lied to you."

"No kidding. He told me his family was loving and supportive and that they would never do something like come and try to take my child away."

The tears almost won this time, she had to look away for a second while she blinked and wiped under her eyes with her sleeve. "Look, Mom... I know you're upset, and that you have every right to be. But I'm trying to talk to you here. You aren't going to like this conversation. I can't change that…and neither can you. But we could try to talk and understand each other without saying mean things that we'll regret later. Please?"

Megan's eyes were red and damp again, too, but after a moment, she nodded. "I'm sorry. I'll try. But I don't think it's a given yet that I'm going to lose this argument."

She nodded. That was okay. Her mother didn't have to accept everything tonight. "So long as you let me be honest with you about what my intentions are."

"Fine. So Samuel lied to me about what, exactly?"

"Who he was. Who his family is. Because Stephen and Charlotte are not his family."

"I know Stephen is only his cousin or something, Quinn. He never told me much about his real parents. He told me he went to live with Stephen's parents when he was a teenager…they were his aunt and uncle, I think."

"Well, they might have been very distantly related, but they were not his actual aunt and uncle."

"No, you're right. He did say they were more distantly related…otherwise William would be *your* cousin. I know all of this. He didn't lie about it. I don't know why you think he did. I know he wasn't really a prince or anything special. And that was fine with me. It was bad enough I was marrying someone from another planet."

Quinn rolled her eyes at the planet remark, but decided not to comment. "That's the part he lied about, Mom…the part about not really being a prince."

Megan raised an eyebrow.

"He was a prince. Not of Eirentheos…the kingdom we're in now, Stephen's kingdom. He was the prince of another kingdom. Philotheum. And he wasn't just any prince. He was the firstborn. The heir to the throne. He was supposed to be the king."

There was a long pause.

"And what? So you're the long-lost princess or something?"

Quinn closed her eyes, pulling a deep breath in through her nose. "Something like that."

"Did you ever think that maybe the reason your father didn't ever tell us those things is because that's not what he wanted for you? Maybe he didn't want to be the king. Nathaniel's his brother…that makes him a prince, too, right? Why doesn't he go be the king?"

"It doesn't work that way. Look, Mom… I don't want to do this right now. It's been a really horrible couple of days; I'm not feeling that well, and we don't have to figure this all out tonight. You're here now, and so we have time. Can we just… I've missed you, and it would be nice to spend some time with you and I don't want us to argue the whole time. And I really, really, want to see Annie and Owen."

And a nap. More than anything, she wanted a nap. Preferably with her head against William's chest, listening to his heartbeat. Not questioning her every sentence, just listening, the way he always did.

"Please, Mom?"

Megan took a deep breath, and Quinn could see that she was trying to calm herself. Finally, she nodded. "I've missed you too, sweetheart. So much."

"I know, Mom."

"You know the other reason I came…I think part of me was just looking for any excuse to come to you…I couldn't handle the thought of not seeing you on your birthday."

She frowned. "My birthday's not for…" But she stopped, because she hadn't even thought about it, didn't even know what the date was back in her world.

"Your birthday is tomorrow, Quinn. Or today, or whatever. I don't know what day it is in our world now."

"I didn't even realize that. I had forgotten all about it. I don't even know how it works here…what day my birthday is on, here."

Her mom scooted closer and put her arms carefully around Quinn's shoulders, hugging her gently, and stroking her hair. "Well, I didn't want to miss it. I wanted you to be home for it. I love you."

"I love you, too, Mom." She ignored the "home" part of her mother's words, but she could tell from the tone that this conversation was far from over.

They stayed like that for several moments before Quinn finally pulled back. "Where are Annie and Owen?"

"Last I knew they were in a big playroom with a bunch of little kids. Annie was having the time of her life. That brother of William's…Thomas? He was in there playing with them…really had them all going. He's a nice kid."

Quinn smiled. "Yes, he is."

"If you were going to date one of them, why didn't you pick him?"

She rolled her eyes. "William's a nice guy too, Mom, once you get to know him."

Walking into the common room was a strange experience. Quinn had only been gone from the castle for one night, but the room fell silent when she appeared in the doorway with William and her mother.

William had his hand under her elbow, helping her walk, which was clearly bugging her mother, but she didn't really know what to do about it. With half her leg still numb, she kind of needed the support.

Most of the family was in the common room, though many of the youngest children were across the hall in the playroom…Quinn could hear the shrieking. Stephen wasn't there, and neither were Simon and Maxwell…Quinn suspected they were busy with everything that was going on…but everyone else was. Charlotte sat at the far end of the room, chatting with Rebecca, who was nursing the new baby.

Charlotte looked up immediately when Quinn entered, and she almost stood, but then settled back, restraining herself…probably trying to be respectful of Megan.

Thomas and Linnea were there, and so were William's next-youngest brothers, Joshua and Daniel.

Everyone looked concerned, and Quinn knew she would have to deal with…and hug…every one of them in turn, but the instant focus of her attention in the room was the little boy who stood up from the low table where he was working a complicated puzzle, and bolted toward her.

"Owen!"

He carefully wrapped himself around her right side, somehow knowing just how to avoid her injury, and she squeezed him as tightly as she could, leaning down and kissing his head. *Oh...* He'd had a bath, and he smelled of the soap the children in the castle used. It was such a strange combination of scents…both of her homes mixed together in the soft brown hair of the little boy she loved.

Blinking back tears, she cleared her throat. "Hey, buddy. How are you doing?"

He looked up at her. "I was worried about you."

"I know you were. I was worried about you, too. Are you okay?"

He nodded. "I've never been in a castle before. Did you know they really do have a gate on the front door?"

"They have them on all of the entrances. I'll take you and show you soon, okay?"

His eyes lit up, and Quinn knew he was all right. "You should sit down," he said, nodding toward her leg, even though her bandage was hidden by her long skirt. He studied William for a second, and then put her arm over his shoulder, and helped lead her over to one of the overstuffed armchairs.

William chuckled quietly, but didn't say anything as he helped Quinn ease herself down, and Owen pulled more pillows from the other chairs. A warm feeling filled her chest as she watched William's careful interaction with her little brother. He showed Owen how to adjust the pillows, somehow making the little boy feel instantly important and included.

Owen noticed, she could tell, even though he hadn't yet spoken to William…probably wouldn't for a while, even. It took Owen time to get comfortable with new people. But he allowed William to stand close to him, and in the end, when Quinn was settled in the chair, he gave her a small smile before retreating back to his puzzle.

Charlotte couldn't wait any longer. As soon as Quinn was sitting down, she hurried across the room.

Several emotions warred in the queen's eyes as she knelt by the chair, pulling Quinn into her arms. Anger and fear and relief were all there, but the only one she immediately poured onto her was love.

"Thank the Maker," she whispered into her ear. "I'm so glad you're here. Are you really all right?"

"I'm fine."

"Not too itchy or hot?"

She shook her head. "William gave me some medicine and some lotion to help."

"Okay," Charlotte said, kissing her on the head before turning her attention to William, and wrapping him in an enormous hug.

For the second time in the few minutes she'd been in the common room, Quinn had to swallow back the lump in her throat. Why couldn't it have been that easy with her own mother?

BIG DECISIONS

THE SUN HAD BARELY dipped below the horizon when William insisted on taking Quinn back to her room. He could see that she was trying to stay awake, but she could barely keep her eyes open, and she'd started wincing just holding baby Hannah on her lap and had to hand her off to Thomas.

"Isn't it a little early for bed?" she asked, as he opened her door.

"Are you honestly telling me that you could stay awake and keep visiting with everyone?"

"Good point," she answered, unable to hold back a yawn. Her protest rang hollow anyway, since she hadn't objected at all when he'd suggested it in front of everyone.

"Besides, you really have been off the IV long enough." He walked her over to her couch, where they'd left his supplies when he disconnected her earlier so she could go to the common room and have dinner with her family.

"I ate. And drank water, too."

He smiled…she was so determined not to seem helpless. Was she worried she was bothering him? He hoped not…while he wished, for her sake, that she didn't need him to, he liked taking care of her. "You're going to have to keep down more than six bites of vegetable stew and half a cup of water before I take you off this thing for good, love."

"Were you counting?"

"I am a doctor…it's kind of my job. Anyway, even if you didn't need the fluids, you do still need another dose of the anti-viral…and some real pain meds now."

She sighed, but, thankfully, didn't object this time.

"Can you get yourself into your pajamas, or do you want me to get Linnea or Mia to help you?"

"I'll do it. I'm actually kind of glad you dragged me out of the common room. I'm a little peopled out right now."

"Do you want me to leave you alone?"

"No!" The intensity of her answer surprised him, and made his breath catch in his throat. "Sorry. I mean, no, I don't want you to leave right now."

He smiled, reaching to tuck a strand of hair behind her ear. "I'm not a people?"

"You're the only person I want right now, that's all."

He didn't have the words to describe how that sentence made him feel, all he could do was pull her into his arms and hold her tight against him, feeling the reassuring weight of her against his chest, and her warm breath on his shoulder.

Her leg brushed against his, and she made a face.

He pulled back immediately. "Is your leg hurting again?"

"I'm fine." She started walking toward her armoire.

He sighed at her stubbornness. "Where are your pajamas?"

"Third drawer, but I'll get them. I need to go brush my teeth and stuff anyway."

But he was faster than she was. He was already at the armoire digging in her drawer by the time she had finished her sentence. He pulled out a nightgown, and crossed back to her, putting his arm under hers, and helping her to the bathroom door without putting weight on her leg.

"How long are you going to treat me like an invalid?" she asked, when he was waiting outside the bathroom door to half-carry her to her bed.

"As long as I can get away with having an excuse to touch you more than usual," he said, grinning as he lifted her onto the sheets.

"You're in an awfully good mood considering the crappy day we've had."

"It wasn't all crappy." He took her hand and started re-connecting the tubing. "And I thought it ended pretty well. I had fun spending time with Owen and Annie."

"Owen really likes you," she said.

He liked Owen, too. The little boy had kept to himself in a corner most of the evening, drawing and playing with blocks, but he was watchful. More than once he'd run over to retrieve something for Quinn that she hadn't even asked for yet.

He and William's little sister Alice would probably get along really well – after they'd had a couple of days to work up the courage to actually talk to each other. "He's a really great kid. You can tell how much he loves you. He notices everything you do, Quinn. Annie's pretty precious too, though." That one had fit in with the rest of the boisterous crew immediately.

"She loves your little sisters."

"I know." He chuckled. "I heard her asking your mom if she could sleep with Emma tonight."

"I'm sure *that* thrilled my mom. Now she's going to be worried that Annie won't want to go back home with her."

He finished squeezing the syringe of pain medicine into her IV, and then sat down next to her on the mattress.

"It didn't go so well with your mom earlier, did it?"

She shrugged. "It probably went as well as it *could* go. But it was hard."

"I'm sorry." He kissed her forehead, and then lay down, sliding his arm underneath her.

She rested her head on his chest, moving her ear until it was right over his heart. "This is better," she said.

"Much," he agreed, pulling her hair back from her neck and running his fingers softly along the base of her scalp. "Do you want to talk about what happened with your mom?"

"Uh-uh," she mumbled. "Not right now. I'm starting to get really sleepy."

"It's probably the medicine. It works really fast. Want me to go so you can sleep?"

"No." Her eyes opened wide. "I don't want to be alone, Will. I need you." The fear in her voice hurt his heart.

"Okay, love." His answer was just as quick. "Shh, relax. I'm right here. I'm not going anywhere." Ever again, if he could help it. He settled further under her, and reached to pull her blanket over both of them.

When William woke in the morning, Quinn was sound asleep, her arm across his chest. It was still dark out, but they'd gone to bed so early that he knew he'd slept enough and wouldn't be able to go back to sleep.

Her arm was cool to the touch; the fever hadn't returned. He hoped that meant the anti-viral medication was working. It relieved him to see that the rash hadn't spread to her arms, either. She was having a hard enough time dealing with her mom's feelings about her being in Eirentheos; he didn't blame her for not wanting to share the fact that she'd gotten sick, too.

Afraid of waking her, he laid there for a long time, listening to her breathe in and out, thinking about just how much he liked this.

But eventually, he realized he wasn't going to have a choice. His body wouldn't allow him to stay there forever.

She didn't wake when he rose, although even in her sleep she grimaced when the motion of the bed jostled her leg. She seemed completely out; enough that he dared leaning down and kissing her forehead. That didn't disturb her…he thought maybe he could get away with getting some more meds into her.

For a brief moment, he contemplated putting some more morphine into her drip, but he had a feeling she might object to that if she were awake, and it didn't feel right, so instead he gave her something gentler and then left a note on her table telling her he was going to take a shower, in case she woke looking for him.

Thomas, who, it seemed, never slept, was sitting on a stool at the counter in the common room, sipping from a mug of tea when William came in.

"The change of clothes was a wise plan," Thomas said, nodding when he saw William. "It might not be the best idea to be sleeping in her room when her mother is here."

William was suddenly mortified. "Nothing happened, Thomas. It wasn't like that."

"Well, obviously. I imagine it would be hard to even kiss her without hurting her right now. But still, *really*, Will? Megan wanted to go in and say goodnight to her last night. I had to convince her that Quinn was already asleep and that it wouldn't be good to accidentally wake her."

William swallowed guiltily. "I didn't even think about that."

"Megan already thinks we're keeping Quinn from her, trying to sabotage their relationship or something. Can you imagine what she'd think if she walked in and found you in Quinn's bed? Mother and Father wouldn't exactly be pleased, either, you know."

William sat down at the counter and buried his face in his hands. "She just didn't want me to leave her last night, Thomas. And I couldn't do it."

The expression in Thomas's eyes softened. "I know. But you can't make a habit of it. Especially not while her mother is here."

"I know."

Thomas stood and got another mug, and then scooped tea out of a canister into a tea ball, placed it in the cup, and poured in water from a steaming kettle on the stove. He slid the mug across the counter to William.

"If you want to get away with sleeping with her, you're going to have to more than just court her."

"Yeah. I've kind of thought about that, Thomas."

Thomas's eyebrow arched into a *v* while he took a sip of his tea. "Thought about it how much?"

"I might have sort of asked her to marry me yesterday."

The mug slammed to the counter, splashing hot drops of the aromatic tea everywhere. "Sort of? Or you did?"

"I did."

Thomas's eyes were wide. "Now that is some fantastic timing."

"I know." William rolled his eyes. "I keep saying that they've pegged my gift all wrong. Mine should be romance, not healing, don't you think? After all, it takes a special kind of talent to propose to the girl you love while she's sick and halfway unconscious from pain after an injury sustained during her kidnapping." His voice broke on the last words.

"Oh, Will." Thomas came around the counter and sat down on the stool next to him, putting his hand on William's shoulder. "It's not as bad as that. I mean, she must not have told you to go fish in a different stream…you just slept in her room. What happened? What did she say?"

"She asked if we could talk about it later."

Thomas chuckled. "Sounds reasonable."

"Yeah." He still couldn't believe he'd actually done that…what would she think about that today?

"It also sounds distinctly different than a no."

That was true, he supposed. "It does, doesn't it?" He couldn't stop the sides of his mouth from edging into a grin.

"Yeah, it does. But it also sounds like you need to do a better job of it next time."

The soft sound of her door closing woke Quinn. Feeling disoriented, she lifted her head, scared for a second, until she saw the familiar line of light at the bottom of her curtains, and realized that she was in her room in the castle, and it was morning.

"Sorry," a familiar voice whispered from across the room. "I didn't mean to wake you. I was just coming to check on you."

"It's okay, Nathaniel. It's probably time for me to be getting up, anyway. How long did I sleep?" Asking that question suddenly made her remember *falling* asleep last night, and she looked around, panicked for a second, until a motion from across the room caught her eye.

William stood from the couch and walked over to the window, pulling back the curtains before returning to her bedside. "It's only just now breakfast-time, love."

She blinked in the bright light. "Is my mom up?"

"I haven't seen her yet," Nathaniel said, coming to stand next to the bed, and reaching for her wrist to check her pulse. "How are you feeling this morning?"

She shrugged, testing herself out. "Not so sick to my stomach anymore, I don't think. A little groggy, maybe."

"How's your leg?"

She thought about downplaying it, but realized she'd give herself away as soon as she tried to walk again. "It hurts." She pulled the covers off of her leg so he could check her dressing.

"Stephen wants the guard who did this to you arrested." Nathaniel looked pleased.

"I was trying to get his knife."

"Which is exactly what you *should* have been doing. You should have had one of your own to begin with. You've been practicing enough with them…it was stupid not to make sure you had one with you. Don't defend him, Quinn. He was kidnapping you."

"I know; I just wanted to be truthful about it."

Nathaniel shook his head. "No, you're feeling *guilty* about it. Stop. You didn't do anything wrong. He did. Jonathan did. I think Stephen should track *him* down and arrest him."

"He's your brother."

"Yeah, he is. Though he's made it awfully clear where his loyalties lie."

"Are you sure about that, Nathaniel? It's not like he knew who I was."

"Right. He just snuck into the kingdom and captured a prince and his girlfriend…oh, and the girlfriend's family. He's completely innocent."

"He was here trying to find out about the gate. He saw my family come through the gate. He thought I was some kind of spy or something for Stephen."

Nathaniel sighed. "You do realize all of this means we have a much bigger problem, right? Tolliver knows about the gate."

A chill ran down Quinn's spine, and she strained to remember her conversation with Jonathan yesterday. The memory was a little fuzzy. "I'm not sure he does yet. Or at least not any more than the rumors he'd heard already from the spies he's had here. He sent Jonathan here to see if he could find out if those rumors were true. But I don't think Jonathan reported anything back to him."

"What are you saying?"

"I don't know what I'm saying. I don't know enough about it yet, but I think we should talk to him, and not assume that we know for sure whose side he's on. I think we could give him the benefit of the doubt."

Nathaniel frowned, studying her closely. "What else aren't you telling us, Quinn?"

"I told him who I really am."

The room was completely silent for several moments as the impact of her statement sank in.

"So you've made a decision, then," Nathaniel said.

She closed her eyes, nodding slowly. "I also told my mother last night that I don't intend to go home again…at least not to stay."

William sank down onto the bed beside her, shock in his expression. "You really did that?"

"I really did."

"Are you sure, Quinn? Because you don't have to be."

Staring down at her lap for a minute, knotting and unknotting her fingers, she considered her answer carefully. Alvin's words from the dream she'd had yesterday morning in the tent came, unbidden, into her head.

"Beloved, perhaps I'll be able to stop asking such questions when you stop doing the things you don't mean to be doing, and start doing the things you mean to."

Finally, she looked back up at Nathaniel. "I know I don't *have* to. I could spend the rest of my life not *having to*. Nobody here is going to make me, are they? Everyone keeps telling me to just think about it, to wait until I've been home, to take my time. I could probably get away with *never* making a decision.

"But what would that accomplish? I could do what my father did…run away, and pretend I don't have to face this, but that won't really fix anything, will it? And it's all a show, anyway, isn't it? That I don't have to make a decision right now? Not deciding is a choice, too. Not deciding is making things worse, because nobody can *do* anything. I think I've known for a while now. I think I knew when I decided to join the Friends of Philip."

Nathaniel opened his mouth and then closed it again. Slowly, he nodded.

She took another deep breath before speaking again, looking at each of them in turn. "You two are the most protective of me…always ready to jump in and not make me do anything I don't want to do. And I appreciate that, and I love you both." She blushed, because she'd never told Nathaniel that before, but she realized that it was true.

"But right now…with this, I need you to *not* try to protect me from it. I need your support…need you to take my decision seriously, and stand behind me…not in my way."

Nathaniel stared at her for a long moment, but finally he nodded again. "Okay. Would you like me to go and speak with Stephen…set up a meeting with him?"

"Yes."

"Okay." Nathaniel finished re-taping her bandage, and packing some supplies back into the drawer on her nightstand. He took a couple of steps toward the door, and then hesitated, turning around and walking back to her.

"I loved you from the first moment your father handed you to me, Quinn…that's never changed, and it's never going to. I'm proud of you, baby girl, and I know, somewhere, he is, too."

He leaned down and kissed the top of her head, and she could see that his cheeks were flushed red, too. He straightened back up, looking a little embarrassed, which only softened her heart more, and then he left the room.

Once the door had closed behind Nathaniel, she turned to see William watching her intently.

"Can I just ask one thing?" He asked, as he took her hand in his.

She raised an eyebrow.

"This doesn't have anything to do with what I said yesterday, does it?"

"What? When you asked me to marry you?"

"Yeah." He was staring down at their intertwined hands.

She reached toward him, putting her finger under his chin, and tipping his face up so that he was looking at her. Her heart thumped in an erratic rhythm, but she took a deep breath. "No, it doesn't. I think I've been coming close to this decision for a long time…and yesterday morning, I realized that I'd already made it. I knew before I even said anything to Jonathan."

"Okay... so long as it's really your decision. I just wanted to make sure that you knew I'm not going anywhere whatever you decide." The last words were almost a whisper, and she studied him for a long moment before she spoke.

"Are we going to talk about that now?"

Now *he* was blushing. It was awfully early in the day for this amount of awkwardness. "I'm sorry," he said, his Adam's apple bobbing up and down. "My timing is awful, I know. I should have planned this…there should have been flowers... You'd probably even like a ring, the way people do it in your world."

"So... you *were* serious, then." Her stomach should have been twisting into knots, but it wasn't. There were a few butterflies, yes, but they were a completely different kind.

"Yes." His eyes met hers, and the depth of the emotion she saw there took her breath away. "Look…I know it's not good timing, that you're dealing with your mom coming here, that you're already making a huge decision..."

"That I'm only seventeen..."

"Yeah... I'm sorry. I shouldn't be doing this."

He was right…everything he was saying was true. It wasn't the right time, she was too young, she had too many other decisions to make... but she knew, somehow, that it didn't matter. It didn't matter when he asked, or where or how, or how old she was, or what was going on around them. None of it mattered, because whenever he asked, she would only ever have one answer to his question.

"Will..."

He looked up again, and she'd never seen him so nervous or embarrassed. His hand, inside hers, was sweating.

"Yes."

His eyes widened just a fraction. "What?"

"Yes, I am saying yes. I will marry you."

He looked confused for a couple of seconds, and then his mouth split open into the biggest grin she had ever seen. His sudden joy was so complete that it was contagious, and she couldn't help grinning too.

He pulled her into his arms and hugged her tightly before his mouth found hers, gently at first, but quickly turning more intense...

One sharp knock was all the warning they had before her bedroom door opened wide, and Thomas and Linnea walked right in, followed by Quinn's mother.

William stood up so fast it was almost comical. "Your leg is looking a lot better today."

She nodded, attempting to compose herself and failing miserably. She knew it was obvious to everyone...especially to her mom...what they'd been doing. Linnea, pretending not to notice, picked up the robe from the bench at the end of her bed and walked toward her with it.

"Thanks," she mumbled, as Linnea helped her hang it over her shoulders and put her free arm into the sleeve.

"You look like you're feeling better this morning," her mom said, and Quinn didn't think her face had *ever* felt this hot. Linnea moved behind her and started brushing out her disheveled hair.

The look on her mother's face made Quinn's heart sink into her stomach. She remembered her mother's accusation from yesterday,

130

and she realized that the idea of her and William getting married was not going to fly with her mother at all. Suddenly, she felt nauseous again.

"How's your leg?" Megan asked.

"It's okay." Grateful for the distraction, she almost stood up to demonstrate, but truthfully, it was hurting, and just the thought of putting weight on it made her nervous. "Sort of, anyway," she admitted.

"You never even told me what happened," Megan said. "How bad did you hurt it?"

"She cut it pretty badly," William said, the dark anger coming in again at the edges of his voice as Quinn lifted the edge of her nightgown to reveal the white bandage and the blossoming purple and red that covered her upper leg. "Twelve stitches."

"Oh, honey." Megan's whole demeanor changed, softening into concern. She sank down onto the bed, careful not to jostle anything. "Your first stitches... I'm so sorry."

From behind Megan, Thomas raised an eyebrow.

Quinn stomach tightened into a knot...yes, she was definitely nauseous again. "It wasn't the first time," she mumbled. "I'm okay, Mom."

Megan's eyes widened. "You've been hurt here before, and you never even bothered to tell me." It wasn't a question. "You get hurt while I'm here, and I'm not even allowed to be there for you. You just run away and hide from me...get everyone here to guard you. From *me.*" Her eyes flitted from Thomas to Linnea and William, both still hovering over Quinn. "I... I can't do this right now. Excuse me."

And with that, Megan stalked toward the door, slamming it behind her without ever looking back.

All of the blood in Quinn's body drained into her toes, and she was suddenly cold, even as tears pooled at the bottom of her eyes. What had she done? She didn't want to be fighting with her mom. Especially now...when she'd made a decision that meant that soon there would be a more permanent separation from her. *Holy crap*…was that actually what she had decided?

The room started spinning, and she felt an overpowering need to lie back down, though by the time she actually thought about it, her head was already on the pillow, and William was climbing onto the bed beside her.

"You look a little green," he said softly, easing her head onto his chest. "Did I take that thing out too soon? Are you going to throw up?"

She shook her head…she was pretty sure she wasn't. The tears weren't nearly as cooperative as her stomach, though, and despite her best efforts to hold them in, she could feel William's shirt getting damp underneath her cheeks.

"I'll get Mia to have some breakfast brought up in a little while," Thomas said. His voice came from over by the door. "We'll give you two some time, though."

She was relieved when the door clicked shut, and she was alone again with William.

"I'm s…orry," she choked, as the tears came in a flood now.

"Shh… love." He held her tighter. "I'm right here."

They lay there like that for several minutes, until Quinn's tears finally subsided, and she pulled herself back up again, yanking a handkerchief out of the drawer of her bedside table and wiping furiously at her eyes with it.

William sat up beside her, rubbing her back as he waited silently for her to finish. She took a couple of deep, shaky breaths, and then turned to look at him.

"I can't keep doing this," she finally said.

"What?" He wrinkled his brow, looking concerned.

"Freaking out. Crying over everything. It's stupid. I'm the one who made this decision. I have to figure out how to deal with it."

"Love, it's been a really challenging couple of days. You're allowed the occasional freak-out, you know."

"Yeah, I'm sure it makes me look like a real heir to the throne…crying because I had a fight with my mom."

He chuckled quietly, which for some odd reason calmed her a bit, rather than piquing her even more. "You're still human, Quinn. Kings and queens cry too, you know. My father one night when Thomas first came home after… You were just kidnapped and injured, and now your family has shown up unexpectedly, and they could have been hurt, too…I think a little upset is allowed. It's not like you were fighting with your mom over not getting home on time."

She closed her eyes and sighed. "No… I'm fighting with her over not going home at all." The lump was back in her throat, but she was *not* going to lose it again. She just wasn't.

William's arms closed around hers, and he pulled her closer so that her forehead was resting against his. "Yes, you are. And that isn't easy. Be patient with yourself, love. Let's take this one step at a time, okay?"

After a long pause, she nodded, pulling back a little to brace herself for his reaction to her next sentence. "We can't tell my mom about us yet, okay? I'm not ready for that."

His answering smile was gentler than she'd feared. "Well, I think she knows we're courting. But as for the rest of it…I think maybe we need to take some time for the two of us to get used to it ourselves before we bring the rest of the world in. Especially while you're fighting with your mom. I would like for our betrothal to be a happy thing."

"I'm not sure my mom will *ever* be happy about it, Will."

"Someday she will. Today's not that day, though. And that's okay."

"So you're really going to keep this a secret, and not tell anyone?" she asked.

"Well…" pink flooded his cheeks.

"You already said something to Thomas, didn't you?"

"I might have let it slip that I asked you. He won't tell anyone, though."

She sighed. "You know that means I'll have to tell Linnea."

He kissed her on the nose. "She would have gotten it out of you anyway."

"True enough."

He kissed her on the lips then, a gentle, chaste kiss, and then pulled back far enough to study her face. "You know, the important question is not whether your mother is happy about it, Quinn. Are you sure it's what you want?"

She closed her eyes and took a deep breath, searching herself. For just a moment, she imagined herself saying no, but that was a black thought, a physical pain inside her chest. She was sure. "Yes, Will." She opened her eyes again, and met his gaze, looking deep into his gray eyes. "I'm not sure about the timing, or my mom, or anything else that's going on. But I'm sure about one thing. I'm sure about you."

STEPHEN

THE DOOR TO STEPHEN'S office was closed as they approached, and Quinn was suddenly nervous…a feeling that grew stronger when she realized that she hadn't seen Stephen at all since she had returned. She wondered if he, too, was angry with her, and her heart started pounding as Nathaniel reached for the doorknob.

"Did you tell him?" she asked quietly.

He turned around and looked at her. "No, I didn't. This one is yours."

She swallowed hard, and then nodded.

Nathaniel reached for the door again, and William squeezed her hand. "You're sure you're ready for this?"

"Yeah." It wasn't exactly true, but she also knew that she was *never* going to be fully ready, and that waiting wasn't going to make it easier. The only thing that was going to settle her anxious nerves was just doing it.

When they stepped inside the room and she saw Stephen, though, her resolve almost faltered. He was alone, sitting behind his giant desk, and he didn't hear them enter at first. His head was resting on his hands, and he was pale.

She looked up at Nathaniel in alarm. He squeezed her shoulder gently, and then turned to close the door, but as he did so, a hand appeared around the edge, pushing the door back open. A second later, Alvin stepped into the room. "Mind if I join you?" he asked, looking at Quinn.

Stephen looked up at the sound and rose immediately to walk toward them.

"Um, no. Of course not, please come," Quinn said, a little flustered by Alvin's sudden appearance. She wanted to ask him what he was doing here, but was afraid that would sound rude.

"Somebody had to come and name the baby," he said, and it took her most of a minute to remember that Rebecca had just had the baby, and that she'd been wondering why he was here. *Could Alvin read her mind?* He smiled and winked at her, which, at that moment, didn't exactly make her feel better.

They met Stephen in the middle of the room, near the circle of couches and armchairs that surrounded a large, low table. He wrapped William in a hug that was so forceful it surprised her, and he didn't let go for several minutes. When he finally did let him go, he stepped back and gave him a severe look. "Don't ever do something like that again. Do you even begin to understand what could have happened? Do you?"

William stared at the floor. "Yes, Father. I know it was stupid, and I'm sorry."

"And you." He turned his attention to Quinn. "Are you all right?"

"Yes. I'm okay."

And then he hugged her, too, gently but tight, and her confidence returned. When he pulled away, she looked him in the eyes. "Are *you* all right, Stephen?"

He sighed. "Not very, Quinn. My kingdom is under attack. My *family* is under attack."

Her insides clenched down hard. "What do you mean?"

"Come and have a seat. We have a little while before I meet with my council."

William led her around to one of the armchairs before looking up at his father. "Do you want me in here?"

Stephen looked around, at Quinn, and then at Alvin and Nathaniel, who had taken seats on one of the couches. Nathaniel nodded slightly. Alvin shrugged visibly, smiling as usual, and Stephen turned back to William. "So long as Quinn wants you here, son, you're welcome to stay. Nothing I say is going to be private information for much longer. I will be sharing this with your mother later this afternoon. Simon knows already…he's discussing things with Marcus right now."

"Quinn?"

She nodded. Yes, she wanted him here. The decision they'd made this morning…whether they were ready to share it with anyone or not…meant that anything she did affected him, too. She was surprised to discover that thinking about that calmed her, rather than scared her.

William sat down in the chair next to her, and Stephen sat across from them.

"After you disappeared, Quinn, we were finally able to get some more information out of Gavin."

Quinn's hands balled into fists in her lap. Gavin was William's cousin who had been caught spying and passing information to Tolliver.

"He believes that Jonathan was sent here by Tolliver to gather information about certain things taking place here in our kingdom. Those "refugees" who've been appearing near the bridge for most of the last moon were not refugees at all, but a small group of forces under Jonathan's command."

Quinn took a deep breath and nodded…she'd sort of guessed that herself, after what Jonathan had told her in his tent. "Have they been planning an attack?"

"Not exactly…not this group of forces anyway. It appears they had two main objectives. Jonathan was to learn as much as he could about the possible existence of a gate to another world…which he has probably done…although Gavin thinks it's unlikely that more than a few of his men knew about that. That part is very secret."

"Then what's the other part? Why did the soldiers think they were here?"

Stephen's expression grew so dark that it made her shiver. "To accomplish what has always been Tolliver's objective…to return to Philotheum with Linnea."

The room was silent for several moments as the impact of that statement settled over all of them.

"He's never going to give up on that, is he?" Quinn finally asked.

"No. I can only guess that he really believes in the importance of the prophecy. Or someone does. Hector, perhaps. It may be that Tolliver is having a difficult time getting the support of his council to take the throne without fulfilling the prophecy. Certainly he's having a hard time holding the support of a good number of his people. If he just takes the throne, it's possible he could have a revolt on his hands, but if he had fulfilled the prophecy…"

"And they really think that kidnapping your daughter will unite the kingdoms?"

Stephen shook his head. "They don't see it that way, Quinn. What they see is a royal family on their side who has run out of options. There are no legitimate heirs, things are going wrong…but there's a simple solution. A prophecy that will unite them with a family that has produced an exceptional number of royal children. And we're blocking them, refusing them what they believe they're supposed to have."

"Linnea doesn't get a say in that?"

"I suppose they think she should be grateful…a sixth-born princess with the opportunity to be queen."

Quinn felt her nausea returning. "And so they're willing to go to war for it?"

"More than willing. One of our western villages was invaded late last night."

Yes…it was definitely nausea. "So we're at war."

Stephen's eyebrow went up just a little. "We? Yes, I suppose so. There's been no official declaration of anything. I suspect the invasion of Anwin is more a show of force and a distraction than anything else. But it certainly requires a response."

"*Anwin?* Isn't that where Charles is?"

"Yes, that's where Charles' home is, and where Ellen has also been staying. I'm sure it's some kind of message to them as well. Fortunately, they all left early yesterday morning to finally begin traveling here to the castle. Unfortunately, that means they're out there traveling, and they're not well-guarded."

Quinn suddenly felt guilty that she'd been glad that so far Ellen hadn't made her promised trip to the castle. She'd liked Ellen the one time she had met her, but her coming here felt like more pressure for Quinn to make a decision. She didn't know what Ellen's feelings were on Quinn being the rightful heir to the throne.

She was even more worried about meeting Charles for the first time. He had a daughter, Gianna, who, if Quinn didn't exist or choose the throne, would be the only rightful contender against Tolliver.

Worries notwithstanding, though, right now she only hoped they were all safe. Whether she knew them well or not…they were her family. More than that, now, she realized. They were her responsibility.

One more deep breath and she would be able to say what she came here to say. "How will it change things when they find out I'm the real heir, and that I intend to take my throne?"

Her words had the intended effect. Stephen's eyes widened and he grew very still. "I was wondering if that's what you had decided, when I learned that you told Jonathan who you are. That was very risky."

"I know. I'm not sure I meant to tell him…but I don't regret it. I've made the decision, Stephen, and I'm not going to change my mind."

"What about your mother?"

Quinn sighed. "I started to tell her last night, but she isn't ready to hear it."

William reached for her hand as Stephen nodded. She hadn't told him quite how badly that conversation with her mother had gone.

"This has to be very difficult for her," Stephen said. "It will take her some time to get used to the idea."

"I doubt she'll ever get used to it."

"She may never like it, but I think she'll accept it, eventually, if we take it slowly, Quinn."

"We don't have time to take this slowly."

"If I may interrupt, Lady…*Princess* Quinn," Alvin said, "I should think there's always time to do the important things right."

She turned to look at him, already feeling the stress of the conversation getting to her. "What is that even supposed to mean? We're about to be at war."

Alvin didn't appear to be fazed by her tone at all. His blue eyes sparkled as he answered her. "If you're going to be the queen of a kingdom, milady, this is something you need to learn. You must have your own affairs in order before you can hope to be successful at managing those of others."

She knew that the irritation that was rising inside of her was largely the result of the stress of the last few days, and she tried to keep herself calm. At the moment, she didn't trust herself to respond.

"So what do we do for now?" William asked.

"Right now, there isn't much to do," Stephen said. "We need to wait for Charles and Ellen to arrive here and discuss things with them. I've sent some forces to Anwin to see what we're dealing with there…and we're still dealing with the fire. Everything is as under control as it can be. Quinn, I think this might be a good time for you to recover, and to spend some time with your family. This is likely as calm as things will be for a while."

"And tonight, you'll celebrate," Alvin said. "There's a gorgeous new baby to name, and I believe I smelled a delicious roast on the way up here. I may just stop by the kitchens and make a request for that chocolate cake, too."

Quinn took a deep breath…wondering how her mother felt about Naming Ceremonies.

SHARING THE NEWS

"NICE ONE."

Quinn spun around, startled at the sound of William's voice. Behind her, a straw-filled dummy plopped to the ground, a small dagger embedded in the center of its chest. "Thanks."

He walked up to her and put his arms around her waist, kissing her on the tip of her nose. "I'm surprised you two are still in here doing this." She saw his eyes drift to her still-bandaged leg, but – wisely – he didn't comment.

"If she's out here, then she can avoid talking to her mother," Linnea said, pulling her arm back and letting her knife fly, neatly beheading another dummy.

Thomas shot a look at his sister, but Linnea didn't even notice.

Quinn rolled her eyes. "I'm not avoiding her. I talked to her at breakfast."

Linnea raised an eyebrow, and Quinn's heart sank. "Whatever, Nay. It's not like she's exactly talking a lot to me, either. I'm not going to hang out upstairs and just stare at the walls with her."

"It's true. Throwing knives is much more exciting." William was clearly trying to lighten her mood. Letting go of her, he reached down into a wooden box and withdrew a rough metal ball, slightly larger than a tennis ball. As Linnea crossed back over to them, he pulled back his arm and lobbed the ball at the dummy. It wobbled as the ball grazed the side, and then sailed past, landing about five feet back.

"You'd be deadly if you could aim," Thomas said.

William shrugged. "Not everyone can be you."

Quinn picked up another one of the balls. The first time she'd held one, she'd been surprised at how heavy it was. She took a step, and launched it overhand, connecting squarely with the dummy's head and sending it toppling over again.

William whistled appreciatively. "I'll stick to patching up the ones you two injure."

His tone was joking, but his words made her stomach flip. "I don't ever *want* to injure somebody."

"I know." He pulled her into his arms again. "Hopefully it will never come to that."

"Hopefully not." Right now, she didn't know what anything was going to come to. In the two days since she had informed Stephen of her decision, she had developed a new appreciation of an aspect of this world that she'd sort of been aware of, but had never really understood.

Things happened slowly here.

Last night, Ellen and Charles and the crew they were traveling with had finally arrived at the castle, but Quinn hadn't seen any of them yet. And if she was being totally honest with herself, she was out here mainly to work off her nervous energy at the prospect of encountering her aunt and uncle for the first time since finding out who they were. Actually, she would be meeting Charles, her father's oldest brother, for the very first time.

Avoiding her mother was only a secondary benefit.

Things hadn't improved much between her and her mom in the last two days. They'd tried talking several times, but anytime they went deeper than sharing niceties at mealtimes, the same main argument would break out over other small issues. Last night, when she'd tried to spend some time with her mom after dinner, it had become about her birthday.

"You really think you're just going to stay here?" her mom had said. "What about celebrating your birthday? Richard and Denise are planning on driving up from Denver this weekend."

Celebrating her birthday was the farthest thing from Quinn's mind. Nobody knew enough about how the time between the two worlds worked to be able to pinpoint what her exact birthday would be in this world. Charlotte had told her she could pick whatever day she liked, but she didn't think a birthday was all that important right now. Clearly, though, it was important to her mother. "I can have a birthday party here, mom. I can celebrate with you before you leave," she'd said, mostly to placate Megan.

It hadn't been what her mom wanted to hear, though, and Quinn had ended up retreating to her room well before bedtime.

"You know, Quinn, your mother is going to keep treating you like a child for as long as you're acting like one." Linnea's voice sliced into her reverie.

"How exactly am I doing that, Nay? If anyone is acting like a child here, *she* is."

"She's not out here hiding from you."

"I'm not hiding. She could ask anyone where I am…she could come out here if she wanted to."

Linnea shrugged. "She really doesn't know how serious you are. She's still using her anger to try to convince you to see things her way, where you'll be at home with her and you have time to work all of these things out. But you know better…and you're wasting it. You're letting the fact that she's not happy about it get in the way of this time you could be having together. It's hard for you, and you're acting on your emotions. If you want her to see you as an adult, then you need to act on your truth, no matter how hard it is."

Quinn sighed. William squeezed her shoulder gently, though he stayed silent beside her. Thomas started stacking the practice knives back into their crate. "How do I do that?"

"For starters, you could stop hiding things from her. Last time I checked, adults tell their families when they decide to get married."

"She is not ready to hear that, Linnea!"

"This is what I'm telling you. It's not about what you think she's ready to hear or not hear. It's about what the truth is, and what you're excluding her from. If you're enough of an adult to make that decision, then you're enough of one to tell your mother. And, honestly, William," she looked up at her brother, "that goes for you, too. This is not something that should be secret."

Without waiting for a response, Linnea turned and started walking back toward the castle.

Thomas stared, wide-eyed at her retreating form for several seconds. "I guess I'll go talk to her," he said, making his own awkward exit.

It took Quinn a long moment before she could compose herself enough to look at William. She knew her cheeks were pink.

He looked a little taken aback, too, but he managed a small smile. "I tried to warn you about her."

Her chest relaxed as she started breathing again. "She's your sister."

"I take *no* responsibility for that," he said, holding his hands up in the air.

Quinn chuckled. "I suppose I can't hold it against you."

He put his arms around her and pulled her close to his chest. "You okay?"

She nodded. "I'm fine…I'm just trying to wrap my mind around everything she said."

"Yeah."

"She's right, isn't she?"

William took a deep breath, and then he nodded. "I think she probably is."

Pulling away from him, Quinn paced back and forth for a few minutes, suddenly very nervous, though she didn't understand why. Finally, she went and sat down on one of the hay bales. William watched her for a long moment before coming to sit down beside her.

"Are you really sure it's what you want?" His voice wobbled, and she realized that he was just as nervous about this conversation as she was…maybe more. She sighed, Linnea was right…she wasn't acting like an adult…she wasn't really owning her decisions, and that was going to hurt everyone.

She took his hand in hers. "Yes, Will. I told you when I said yes that I was sure. And I'm sorry that I haven't been acting like I meant it. She's right. This shouldn't be a secret…this should be huge, happy news. That is…if you're sure it's what you want."

He didn't answer her right away. Instead, he stood up and took a step back, sending her heart plummeting into the depths of her stomach. *Oh no…*

But then she realized that he was fishing in his pocket, and before she had time to think about why, he was dropping down on one knee on the ground in front of her. Suddenly, her heart was back where it belonged, but racing like a hummingbird.

"Quinn Katriel Robbins Rose, I love you. I think I might have loved you the first moment I saw that you'd actually followed me through the gate, maybe even before that, I don't know. But whenever it started…I know where I want it to end. Somewhere on the other side of forever. And I promise I will love you, and stay with you, and support you in your decisions, and even make some of them with you… if only you will agree to be my wife. Will you marry me?"

It didn't matter that he'd already asked…that they'd already agreed. Tears streamed down her face, obstructing her view of the little purple silk drawstring bag he placed in her hand. Both of their fingers were shaking enough that they had to work together to untie the little ribbon at the top, which made her giggle enough to stop some of the tears, so that her eyes were clear when he turned the bag over and the little ring fell into her hand.

"Diamonds aren't really a thing here," he said apologetically as she held it up to examine it. "I didn't have any way to..."

"Shh..." she whispered. "It's beautiful." And it was. A delicate rope of gold braided around an identical line of silver...the colors of their kingdoms intertwined, making one precious whole. "It's perfect."

"This finger, right?" he asked, stroking the ring finger of her left hand, reminding her of just how much thought he'd put into this...into giving her a proposal and a ring the way it might have someday happened in her world, even though he didn't know much about it. Her *other* world she thought now. Somehow this world had come to feel just as much like home as Earth. Maybe even more so, since this was the one she'd chosen.

She nodded, and he slipped the ring onto her finger, kissing it gently before he stood again, pulling her up into his arms.

He kissed her mouth then, a long, slow, deep kiss that was filled with emotion from both of them. A kiss that made her feel safe and cherished and hopeful. One that let her know that no matter how difficult it was going to be to share their news, in the end, it would be worth it.

She wasn't sure how she was ever going to pull the rest of this off...fighting a war, taking a throne in a kingdom she knew nothing about...but this part with William she could do.

"So what do we do now?" she asked, when he finally pulled away.

"I guess we go and tell our families. I think we should probably tell your mother first...it's only right, since I didn't ask her. And I don't think it would be good if she found out from someone else."

She was nodding when she was startled by the sound of someone clearing his throat.

They both turned around to see Nathaniel standing there, looking uncomfortable. And he wasn't alone. Standing next to him, immediately familiar from the trip she'd taken to Philotheum, was Lady Ellen Fisher…her aunt. Quinn's face grew very hot again as she wondered how long they had been there.

"Sorry," he said, "I didn't mean to interrupt... I just... Quinn, you remember Ellen."

"Yeah. I mean, yes, of course I do." She walked up to them and extended her hand. It's lovely to see you again."

"And you as well, my dear."

"Did your journey go well?"

She saw Ellen steal a glance at Nathaniel before she answered, but her expression didn't change as she answered Quinn. "Yes, it was fine, thank you."

Nathaniel, though, never noticed his sister's hesitation. His eyes were locked on Quinn's left hand. She quickly hid it behind her back.

"Did I just... Sorry," Nathaniel was clearly flustered. "Quinn, we were looking for you. Charles would very much like to meet you. Also, Andrew and Natalie Gramble traveled here with them, and they're anxious to see both of you again."

"Oh!" William said. "How are they doing?"

"They're quite well," Ellen answered. "They would like to thank you again, William."

"Do they have the baby with them?" William asked.

"Yes, they do." Ellen gave Nathaniel another surreptitious glance, but this one was different... *Almost… pleasant?*

Andrew and Natalie had been with them the afternoon that William and Quinn had spent locked in Ellen's basement in Philotheum, and that was when Natalie had gone into labor. William had delivered their little girl…the first and only baby he'd delivered on his own. Quinn had often thought about the young couple and wondered how they were doing.

William had obviously wondered, too. She could tell he was intrigued, and happy at the idea of seeing them again.

"Are you ready, Quinn?" Nathaniel asked. "Is now a good time?"

No, she wasn't ready, but she wouldn't be ready later, either…would never be ready. She was just going to have to do it. She nodded.

As they all started walking back to the castle, Nathaniel hung back slightly, positioning himself just behind Quinn. She felt her face grow hot again as he studied her hand.

"Is that what I think it is?" he asked quietly, when he finally looked up to meet her eyes.

She looked down at her hand, running her finger along the braided silver and gold, unable to look at him as she answered. "Yes."

She heard him let out a breath, but she still couldn't bring herself to look and see his reaction. Her heart was pounding, and her hands had started shaking when she suddenly felt Nathaniel's hand on her shoulder, and then his mouth was near her ear. "I couldn't be happier, sweetheart."

She looked up at him in surprise.

"Does anyone else know?" he whispered.

She shook her head.

"I won't tell."

Just then, William looked back and frowned as he tried to decipher their quiet communication. Then he smiled and paused, falling into step with Quinn, and taking her hand. Nathaniel reached across Quinn and squeezed William's shoulder as they reached the back entrance of the castle.

Inside the castle, they followed Nathaniel up the stairs to the guest wing. William was a little surprised that they weren't going to his father's office or council room, but then he thought that this might go better in a less formal setting. He knew Quinn was nervous. Her hand was sweaty inside his, and it wasn't all from the fact that Nathaniel had just discovered their secret. As they reached the top of the stairs, her hand only grew colder and damper.

He squeezed her hand as they approached the door of one of the guest suites. She took a deep breath, and in the next instant, her whole demeanor changed. Although her hand trembled slightly now, the rest of her looked calm and collected. She almost looked taller to him as Nathaniel knocked on the door and then turned the knob.

William had been expecting to see everyone in the room, but only one man was in there with his father. He stood when they entered, looking like an older and more muscular version of Nathaniel.

"Quinn, William, I would like you to meet my brother, Charles," Nathaniel said.

"Hello Lady Quinn," Charles said.

Quinn sucked in a breath as soon as he spoke, but William didn't think anyone else noticed. She didn't hesitate with her response. "Hello, Prince Charles. It's nice to meet you."

"And you as well." Charles studied her face for a long moment before he held his hand out toward the couch. "Would you two like to come have a seat?" Charles was eyeing William warily, and he realized that it probably was a little odd that he was being included in this meeting, especially when nobody else knew just how serious his relationship with Quinn was.

Everyone was silent for what felt like a very long time as the rest of them took their seats, Nathaniel and Stephen in chairs that flanked one couch, and Charles and Ellen on a sofa facing them.

It was Ellen who spoke first. "So, Quinn, you've learned a lot about yourself since you and I first met."

"More than I could have imagined, yes."

"Nathaniel tells us you've decided to step in and take the throne. Are you sure you're prepared for that?" Charles broke in without hesitation.

William stiffened a little at Charles' tone, but Quinn didn't miss a beat. "I'm as prepared as it's possible to be, given the circumstances. It's not a decision I ever expected to have to make, and I didn't make it lightly, but it is what I have decided, yes."

"And you understand what we're up against?"

She shook her head. "Not all of it, no. That's something I'm going to need help and support with…I'd like to know that I have that from all of you."

Charles raised an eyebrow, glancing at Ellen.

Quinn's chest rose and fell as she inhaled deeply before she spoke. "I know we don't really know each other, and that this is hard for everyone. I want you to know that I didn't come here with the intention of undoing everything you've worked for, or to take over everything from you."

"Then what is your intention?" Charles asked. "Why should we trust you?"

"Maybe you shouldn't. I don't know what I could say to convince you. I know my father ran away and left you to deal with this instead of fighting to make things right. My intention is to stay and try to make things right, if I can."

"And how do we know you won't just run off and leave if things get too difficult?" Ellen asked.

Quinn's body tensed, but she maintained eye contact. "The only thing I can give you is my word. I can tell you that I fully intend to see this through." She pulled back the collar of her shirt to reveal her tattoo.

Charles' eyes widened just a little. He looked at Ellen, and she nodded, before turning back toward them.

"And what of you, Prince William? Are you prepared for all of this?"

He pulled back his own collar.

Ellen nodded again. "And to marry Quinn?"

William nearly choked on his spit. "Excuse me?"

"Surely you're both aware that the best chance we have at ousting Tolliver is for you to fulfill the prophecy yourselves…unite the kingdoms through marriage, and assume the Philothean throne. To do that, Quinn needs to marry one of you, and I assumed it was going to be you, since you're courting." She looked pointedly at William's courtship bracelet.

Beside him, Quinn had gone completely rigid, and he felt a little sick. Of course Ellen was right…but that wasn't why he'd asked Quinn to marry him. He honestly hadn't even considered the political aspect of it. So much for telling her mother first.

He turned to Quinn, searching her expression. She looked mortified, and there was some other emotion underneath that, too…*anger? fear, maybe?* But she gave him a single nod.

"Yes, Ellen. We hadn't shared the news with anyone yet, but Quinn and I are betrothed."

He felt his father's eyes boring into him, but he couldn't bring himself to look.

"Well, then, it sounds like congratulations are in order," Charles said. "I'm happy for you both."

"Yes," Nathaniel said, before William had the chance to respond. "It's very good news. Now, you've had your chance to meet with Quinn, and to voice your concerns. I'm sure it's been a long day for both of you already, and you'd like to have some time to settle in before dinner." He stood, and William immediately followed his lead. He extended his hand to Quinn in a way that he hoped looked like he was only being polite in helping her up, but really he was trying to whisk her out of the room as quickly as possible before they said something worse.

Stephen followed them into the hall. "Find Charlotte for me, please, Nathaniel? Ask her to meet us in Quinn's room."

Nathaniel nodded and disappeared down the hall. William held Quinn's hand tightly as they walked to her room.

Quinn was still in shock as she and William followed Stephen into her room, and he closed the door behind them. She couldn't tell if Stephen was upset. She was sort of upset herself. This wasn't why William had proposed to her now, was it? Just so they could fulfill the prophecy? She didn't think so, but an uneasy feeling had settled in the pit of her stomach. Was she really just a pawn in their political game?

"Sorry about that," Stephen said, turning to face them. "I wasn't expecting something like that to happen."

"Well, it did," William said. "That's not how we intended to tell you."

"So it's true, then?"

William's eyes widened. "Do you think I would do that to Quinn? Put her on the spot like that just to satisfy them?"

"No, I don't. I'm sorry, I just…I'm a little surprised right now, I guess."

"Good. Because I don't actually care what they think. I'm sure it does make things easier for them, and maybe it will make them take Quinn more seriously. But that's not why I asked her to marry me."

He pulled her closer to him, standing right in front of her, and used his finger to tip her chin up so she was looking at him. "Don't even think that, Quinn. I see it in your eyes…but stop, please. I don't care who you are, or what choice you make. I proposed to you because I want to be with *you*. Please believe that."

She hadn't even been aware that she was holding her breath until she nearly fell over with the relief of exhaling. "I believe you."

There was a knock on the door then, and Stephen pulled it open to reveal Charlotte…and right behind her was Megan. Suddenly, Quinn was having trouble breathing again.

"What's going on now?" Megan demanded. "I heard Nathaniel asking Charlotte to come here and speak to you. I'm done being left out of the loop on everything. Quinn is *my* daughter."

Everyone was looking at her.

"Come on in, Mom. Have a seat."

"Do I need to?"

"Yes, you probably do."

"All right, Quinn. What's going on?" Megan asked, as soon as she was sitting down in one of the chairs.

Quinn swallowed hard, searching desperately through her mind for the right words for this, but before she could, William began speaking.

"Megan, I'm so sorry. This is not how we intended to tell you this." He took Quinn's left hand in his, momentarily covering up the ring. "And, Mother and Father…this isn't how I pictured telling you, either."

Megan's eyes grew round. Charlotte's mouth opened slightly, but her eyes were sparkling.

"I have asked Quinn to marry me, and she has agreed. We are betrothed."

"No!" Megan shouted. "She is seventeen!"

"She's an adult in our world," Charlotte said quietly. "She has been for a full cycle already."

"Well it's not old enough in our world! She's a child!"

"Megan, I know this is difficult for you, all of this, and I'm sorry. But Quinn has already decided to live here in our world, and here she is old enough to make this choice as well." Stephen's voice was low and even.

There was no question about how furious Megan was as she looked at each of them in turn, and then stood and walked out of the room, nearly slamming the door behind her.

Everyone was silent for several seconds. Finally, Charlotte stood and walked over to Quinn, pulling her up and into her arms. "This is wonderful news, sweetheart! I can't think of anything that would make me happier right now."

Somehow, a minute later, she was wrapped in Stephen's arms, too. "We've always loved you like a daughter," he said. "It will be wonderful to make it official."

"We'll need to plan a betrothal ceremony," Charlotte said, her eyes shining. "I could pull it together quickly, I think, just in case your mother is planning on leaving right away when the gate next opens."

"I don't know that my mom will want to come anyway." Her heart was heavy as she thought about the way her mom had stormed out of the room. At this point, she wasn't sure her mother was ever going to talk to her again.

"Oh, sweetheart, you don't know that. Sometimes people need time. Especially mothers with their daughters." Charlotte reached to brush Quinn's hair off her forehead.

"Fathers are even worse," Stephen said. "It wasn't easy for me when Rebecca and Howard were first betrothed. Samuel might have been happy to find out you were going to marry William, but he'd have been upset that it happened this young…even if you aren't much younger than your mother was when he met her."

Quinn chuckled, although thinking about that made her sad, too. She'd never fully understood the term "bittersweet" until now.

"Anyway, whether your mother celebrates with us or not is going to be her choice, Quinn. All we can do is make sure we don't exclude her from it. We will hold the party while she's here, and leave the rest to her."

William squeezed her hand. "It will be okay."

She didn't fully believe him, but she nodded anyway. This wasn't how she'd pictured things going when she told her mom she was engaged…not that she'd really ever thought much about it. It had always been a vague idea of something that might happen far off in the future. Still, this wasn't how she *would* have pictured it. But then, everything about her life seemed to have changed the day she stepped off that bridge.

A loud knock on her bedroom door startled all of them. Stephen's eyes widened when he opened it. "What is it, Marcus?"

"Your Majesty, I'm so sorry for interrupting..." Marcus looked around at the four of them.

"I'm sure you wouldn't be here if it wasn't important. Do you need me to step out with you?"

"Well..." his eyes darted to Quinn and back, "We've just gotten some intelligence about where we might find Prince Jonathan."

"I'm really proud of you, you know," William said.

"Thanks," Quinn mumbled. Her eyes were still red and puffy, but she was getting calm now. "Not that that went very well."

He reached out and took her hand. "We knew it wasn't going to. But we got through it."

She nodded and he squeezed her hand, running his thumb against the braided gold and silver of her ring.

"I wanted to tell her first, Will. I wanted her to at least have that…not have to hear about it in front of your parents. She probably thinks we ganged up on her."

"I know. But that isn't your fault. She's the one who barged in here. And we didn't have any idea that Ellen was going to do that in front of my father, either."

He *was* proud of her. As hard as it must have been, she had even stayed calm, and she hadn't cried until the two of them were alone.

It had broken his heart, though, to watch her go through that. For the thousandth time, he wished it didn't all have to be so hard…that marrying him and choosing this world didn't also mean her having to say good-bye to the family that she loved.

At least his parents and Nathaniel had been happy…at least she'd gotten a taste of the joy that was *supposed* to go along with a betrothal announcement.

"Maybe someday we'll look back on this and be able to smile about it…when it's all in the past, and things are better, this will just be the crazy story of how we became betrothed."

"Maybe," she said. And he knew that it all depended on her being able to repair this relationship with her mother…on Megan somehow being able to accept this, and the two of them making it through. Otherwise, as happy as he knew their marriage was going to be…this would be a dark cloud that always hung over this memory.

Just then, there was a soft knock on the door, and her whole body stiffened. William stood and leaned over to kiss the top of her head before he went to answer it. "It will be okay, love."

When he opened the door, he was surprised to find Quinn's little brother, Owen, standing there.

"Hey buddy," he said.

"Hi." Owen didn't even look up at William as he passed by on his way to where Quinn was sitting on the couch. He immediately climbed up and curled himself against her.

William closed the door and went over to them. "Do you want me here?" he asked quietly.

She nodded, and so he sat down in one of the armchairs to let her and Owen have their space.

Owen didn't say anything for several minutes; he just snuggled up with his sister. But finally, he looked up at her. "You're not coming back with us, are you?"

Somehow, the tears that welled in her eyes stung at the bottom of William's eyes, too.

"No, I'm not." One of the tears spilled over and ran in a line down her cheek. Owen reached up and caught it before it fell.

"Don't cry, Quinn. It's how it's supposed to be."

A chill ran down William's spine.

"How do you know that?"

The little boy shrugged. "I just do. It's what you want, isn't it?"

"Some of it is what I want. I don't want to leave you or Annie, or Mom or Dad."

Owen cocked his head to the side. "Daddy left when he had a job to do."

"Yeah, he did. But he's coming back."

"But you're not."

"No. Not ever to stay, anyway. I'm going to live here. I'm going to get married to William, and I might even be a queen."

Owen smiled at her. "You will be a good one." Then he looked over at William. "Do you love my sister?"

William's heart swelled with tenderness for this sweet little boy. "Yes, I do, Owen. I love her very much."

"Then you should marry her. And I will love you, too."

The tears he'd been holding back finally betrayed him, and slipped from his eyes as he regarded the little boy. "I already love you, Owen."

William was halfway to the couch, wanting to sit closer to Owen and Quinn, when the bedroom door burst open and Megan walked in again. *Oh no.* She stopped cold when she saw Owen sitting on the couch.

"You did not just tell him this ridiculous idea."

The immediate change in Quinn's posture impressed him again. Suddenly, her back was straight, and she was looking right in her mother's eyes. "Yes, I did. Because it's the truth. It's what's going to happen, Mom, and I'm not going to lie to him or hide it from him."

Megan's face nearly turned purple with her rage, and William felt an overpowering urge to stand between her and Quinn, though he held himself back, knowing it would make things worse and not better.

For a long moment, Megan looked furious past the point of being able to speak. When she could finally form words, she said, "Let's go, Owen!" and escorted the little boy out of the room, slamming the door behind her.

RECONCILIATION

"AGAIN!"

"Again? Aren't you getting dizzy?" Of course, Thomas already knew the answer to that. Annie was just as rambunctious and fearless as Emma, even though she was quite a bit younger.

"No. Again!"

"All right." He picked up the little girl and spun her in a wide circle, letting go at just the right time for her to go sailing into the huge cushion in the corner of the playroom. She giggled wildly, her eyes sparkling in the way that reminded him so much of Quinn, except Annie's eyes were brown instead of Quinn's gray.

"My turn!" Emma called.

"No! Mine!" Little Sarah pushed her way in front of Emma. Even at two, she'd learned that she had to stand her ground to compete with her older siblings.

"Hey!"

"No, she's right, Em. You went just before Annie." Scooping Sarah up, he swung her in his arms three times before dropping her from his arms a couple of feet above the cushion.

He glanced across the room and saw that Alice and Alex were both still busy with puzzles, neither one of them seeming to notice the shrieking from this corner. As he turned back to the little girls, all three clamoring for his attention, a movement from the doorway caught his eye.

"Go on in, Owen," Quinn's mother was saying. "You could go do puzzles with Alex."

Thomas raised an eyebrow. Although they'd been here at the castle for a couple of days now, Megan had seemed preoccupied and distant for most of the time. He was surprised she'd picked up on the names of his younger siblings.

Owen shook his head slightly. It was obvious she was upset, and even more obvious that Owen was worried about her.

"Hey, buddy," he said, hurrying over to the door. "Alex and Emma had a new logic problem in their lessons today. Alex has been wondering if you would work on it with him."

Owen's eyes lit up.

Megan stood in the doorway for several more minutes watching as the children moved into other activities. "Thank you," she said as Thomas came to stand near her again. "You're very good with them."

Thomas shrugged. "They're fun. The biggest stress in their day is usually who gets to go first at something." He paused. "Are you okay?"

Megan frowned. He watched her expression change as she decided whether or not to answer, but then she shook her head. "Not really, no."

"Want a cup of tea?"

He could read that debate in her eyes, too, but she followed him across the hall to the common room. It was empty, which was normal for this time of day. The family usually gathered here in the early mornings or late evenings.

"So," he said, once they each had a mug, "are you going to stay mad at Quinn forever?"

"Not forever. Just until she starts listening."

"And by 'listening' you mean until she does what you want her to do."

"I'm still her mother. I'm still responsible for her."

Thomas rolled the little silver chain on the tea ball between his fingers before pulling it out of the mug and setting it on a plate. "Do you think Quinn is just being disobedient and petulant, and that if she just does what you want her to it will solve everything?"

"She's only seventeen!"

"And I'm only almost sixteen, but you're able to have a rational discussion about it with me."

Megan stared into her teacup for a long time. Thomas was afraid she was going to just get up and leave the room, but she didn't. Finally, she looked back up at him. "I don't want to lose her."

Thomas sighed, and looked across the counter at her. "Of course you don't. What I don't think you realize is that she doesn't want to lose you, either."

"She's the one doing all of this."

"Yes, Megan. She's growing up. It's what children do. Except me, of course…I don't plan on becoming more mature, just coming of age and then stopping."

Megan actually chuckled for a few seconds before she became serious again. "She wants to live in a different *world* than me. She wants to get married at seventeen!"

"How old were you when you got married?"

Tiny spots of pink appeared on Megan's cheekbones. "Nineteen. That's two whole years older!"

Thomas shrugged. "It's not the point, anyway. Think about it, Megan. Even in your world, she would have been starting to leave in just a year…and you wouldn't be ready then, either. You should have seen my mother when my oldest sister got married. There's no such thing as ready. She isn't doing this to hurt you or to get away from you. She's doing it because it's what she needs to do."

"But if she was going away to college in our world, she would come home in the summers, for holidays, for weekends..."

Thomas took a deep breath. "You knew Samuel wasn't from Earth when you married him."

Megan's mouth fell open. "I never thought..."

"Maybe you didn't. Maybe Samuel didn't tell you the truth about things, or maybe he did and you didn't believe him, I don't know. But that isn't Quinn's fault. She didn't ask to have parents from two different worlds; she didn't ask to grow up not knowing the truth about who she is. She's had to make some very difficult decisions, and it hasn't been easy for her."

He paused, taking a long sip of his tea before continuing.

"Honestly... this isn't usually me. I'm usually the fun guy who isn't much bothered about things, but I have to tell you...I've watched Quinn struggle with this. I've seen how hard it's been on her. And you're making it so much worse. I don't know if you think that you're going to somehow be mad enough at her to guilt her into going back to Bristlecone, but it isn't going to work. All you're going to accomplish is the real kind of losing her. The kind where she doesn't even *want* to go back and visit you when she can because it's too painful. Is that what you really want?"

Tears appeared at the bottom of Megan's eyes as she stared into her cup again.

"I didn't think so. You need to talk to her...not *at* her. *To* her. Don't mess this up, Megan. She's getting *married*...to a great guy, by the way. If you spent even an hour with the two of them, really watching and listening instead of being mad about it, you would see that. That's what you would want for your little girl...a man who loves her the way that William does.

"Don't miss it...don't throw away whatever amazing parts you could have, just because you can't have everything the way you want it."

"How do you know so much about this at fifteen?"

"It's natural. I'm just that talented." Thomas grinned. "Just try, okay? Because, I don't think I can pull off this much seriousness again anytime soon. I'm getting a headache already. Think I need to go throw some children and listen to them giggle again."

Megan gave him only a half-smile, but he figured it was progress. "I'll see you later," he said, walking toward the hallway, stopping just in front of the doorway to give Quinn a gentle squeeze on her shoulder.

Quinn had to blink several times to clear her eyes after Thomas left the room.

"You okay?" William whispered in her ear.

"I'd be better if everyone would quit asking me that every five minutes."

His eyes widened. "Fair enough." He squeezed her hand and followed her over to the counter.

"Hi," Megan said quietly. Was her mom blushing? Was that a good thing?

"Hi."

"How much of that did you hear?"

"I was there for a couple of minutes."

Her mom nodded, looking down at the floor. "I'm sorry, sweetheart. I don't know why I've been acting like this, I just..."

"I know." She reached for her mom's hand.

"This isn't going to be easy for me, Quinn. But I'm willing to try. I'm willing to listen, and I promise I'll try."

William shifted uncomfortably beside her. "Do you want me to give you two some time alone?"

There was a long pause, and then Megan shook her head. "No, William. You're going to marry my daughter, so we need to get to know each other, and apparently we don't have much time to waste."

"Speaking of time," Quinn said, "how much of it do we have? Are you going to want to leave when the gate opens again?"

"That's only a few days from now, isn't it?"

"It must be." Quinn looked at William; she'd lost track of the exact dates.

"Three days."

Megan nodded. "Stephen has actually been telling me that he's not sure we'll be able to leave that quickly. There's still fire in the area, and they don't know where that guy who kidnapped us is."

"Jonathan."

"Yes... I still don't understand what's going on with all of this. He's Samuel and Nathaniel's brother, right?"

"Right. He's the youngest one. He was born after their father died."

Megan rested her hand against her forehead. "I didn't even know he had siblings other than Nathaniel. I thought both of their parents died when they were young, and that's why they were living with their relatives."

"Their father did die, but their mother is still alive. She is still the queen of Philotheum."

"Bless you."

Quinn stared at her.

"I'm sorry. It's just that none of this makes any sense to me."

"I know." She sank down onto the stool beside her mother. "I'm still trying to make sense of a lot of it myself."

"So what you're telling me is that Samuel was really the heir to the throne in this other place, but since he's dead, now it's you?"

"Yes."

"And you're really going to do this?"

"Yes."

"Why? Is this really so much better than your life at home with us?"

She actually felt a crack open down the center of her heart. Now that the anger had faded, she realized, for the first time, just how much she'd been in denial about that part of it. Her hands were starting to tremble. Anger was easier than this. "No, Mom. It isn't about that. I love you. I love the life you gave me there. I don't want to leave there, not at all. It's not about *leaving* there, it's about staying here. I need to stay here. This is the right thing for me to do."

"I might not ever understand that, Quinn."

"I know. But do you think you could still love me, anyway?"

"Oh, baby girl." Tears ran down Megan's cheeks as she pulled Quinn into her arms. "I will love you always. Nothing could change that. Do you think I'd be mad about all of this if I didn't love you? I just don't want to lose you."

"I'll still visit. You can come here and visit, too. I know it won't be the same, but..."

"We'll just have to make it work. There are a lot of things we'll have to figure out, if you're really not coming back."

A thick feeling filled Quinn's throat as she sat back down on her stool. It had definitely been easier being mad. Maybe that's why her mom had been so angry. It didn't hurt as much.

William put his hands on her shoulders and rubbed gently. "It's going to be hard on everyone. But maybe right now we should enjoy the time we do have together. I know I'd like to know you better, Megan."

Megan studied the two of them for several seconds. "He is a pretty good guy, isn't he?"

"I think so," Quinn said, reaching up to cover one of his hands with hers. He leaned down and kissed her hair.

"You're going to take care of my girl?"

"Yes, Megan. There's nothing I wouldn't do for her. I love her. And I want you to know that I never wanted to take her away from you. Whatever I can do to make sure that you're as much a part of our lives as you can be...I promise you I'll do it."

"I guess we have a wedding to plan, then."

As sad as she still was, Quinn felt lighter…like a huge weight had been lifted from her. "Yeah, I guess we do."

"Are you ever going to show me the ring?"

Quinn felt William's breathing speed as she extended her hand toward her mom, the little silver and gold ring twinkling in the light from the window. She glanced up at him to see his face growing red.

"It's not much," he said quickly. "Rings are different here in our world…"

While her mom took her left hand, Quinn reached with her right one to grab William's wrist. "Don't," she said. "It's perfect. Don't you think so, Mom?"

"It's beautiful, honey."

As her mother stood and wrapped her arms around William's neck, Quinn felt the fissure in her heart begin to heal, just a little.

It wasn't until Linnea came to ask if she wanted help getting dressed and ready for dinner that Quinn realized she was going to have to deal with seeing Ellen and Charles again at the meal.

"Why would she need help getting ready? Are we supposed to dress up for dinner or something?" Megan asked.

Her mother's question made her forget about her nervousness at facing her aunt and uncle. It looked like her mom might actually try to participate with her in her life here…maybe, even though her family would soon be leaving, she would actually get to enjoy this time with them before that happened.

"Yes. We've just had some important guests arrive, so my mother will be throwing a big dinner." Linnea said. "There will be birthday cake for Quinn, too."

Quinn looked at her in surprise…she'd mostly forgotten about her birthday, let alone celebrating it.

"We'll find something for you, too, Megan. You and Annie come with us."

"I'll take care of Owen," William said, leaning to kiss Quinn's cheek. "Have fun," he whispered in her ear. He was smiling as they left, looking nearly as happy as she felt.

THE DINNER PARTY

"YOU AND THOMAS SHARE a room?" Owen asked, as William led him into the bedroom.

"Sort of," William said, smiling. "I actually have a room of my own, but I usually sleep in here with Thomas when I'm home. I always miss my family when I'm gone to your world, so I don't really want to be alone when I get back."

Owen looked up at him. "Is Quinn going to miss us?"

"She always misses you, buddy. She talks all the time about all of you, and how much she loves you all. I think she misses you especially, though."

He nodded. "Quinn understands me."

"Yeah, she does. She's good that way, isn't she?"

"Yes."

"I know you love her a lot, Owen. And she is always going to love you, even when you can't see each other all the time."

"Can I see your room?"

"Sure." William smiled as he walked Owen back into the hallway. Owen wasn't comfortable discussing his emotions with anyone, and William was aware of the trust the little boy had placed in him even getting as far as he just had.

"Wow," Owen said when William opened the door to his room. He headed straight for the long table that William had set up as a sort of mini-laboratory. "Is this real?" he asked, touching the base of one of the microscopes.

"Yes. They're all real."

"Where did you get them?"

"My uncle ordered them for me from catalogs in your world."

"Do you want to be a doctor like him when you grow up, too?"

"Well, here, in my world, I am mostly grown up, and I am already sort of a doctor."

"Can you fix people if they're sick?"

"Or hurt, yes, a lot of the time I can help them."

"Do you like helping them?"

"Very much."

"When you were my age, did you know that you wanted to be a doctor when you grew up?"

"I did. Actually, you see this microscope here?"

"Uh-huh."

"Nathaniel gave this one to me for my eighth birthday. I looked at everything with it."

"Can you see blood in it?"

"Blood cells?"

"Yeah."

"A little bit. But this microscope here is better for that."

"Could I see my blood?"

"You could if we had some. But I would have to poke your finger to get some, and I don't think you'd like that much."

"I don't care. I want to see it."

William frowned. "I don't know, Owen."

"I don't know anyone else who has a microscope."

"Your mom would probably buy you one. I can tell her where to look. Actually, I have some microscopes at my uncle's house in Bristlecone. You can have one. Just have your mom take you over there."

"She's not a doctor. She wouldn't let me look at my blood. Please?"

Something about it was important to the little boy…William got the feeling that Owen had thought about this before. He didn't know what it was, but he understood, very well, what it was like to have a curiosity about something that needed to be satisfied. He went to a drawer and found some rubbing alcohol, cotton balls, and a tiny lancet.

Owen didn't even wince when William pricked his finger. He was very interested in the process as William helped him squeeze a small drop of blood onto a slide, and then snap the slide onto the platform of the microscope. He showed Owen how to adjust the lenses and turn the dials until the blood cells came clearly into focus.

The little boy was fascinated, asking questions and listening intently to the answers as they found the different kinds of cells in the little drop.

"Is that what it's supposed to look like?" Owen asked.

"Yes. It's exactly what it's supposed to look like. It's perfect."

"Okay." Owen sighed, seeming almost…*disappointed?*

"Did you think it wouldn't be?"

Owen shrugged. "I just wondered if it would be different, somehow. But it isn't."

Oh. William swallowed hard.

"You know, Owen, *everyone* is different than other people in some way. Not in their blood, usually, but somewhere in their hearts and their minds. I wasn't much the same as my brothers and sisters, either. And I was very different than the kids at school. Sometimes that was kind of hard and lonely."

"Is it still hard?"

"Not usually. I'm older now, and I understand it better. And I know that the same things that make me different are the ones that make me good at what I want to do. They make me good at learning new things, and using those things to help people. There are plenty of people who love me just like I am, Owen…and there are just as many who love you how you are. You're perfect, already. Quinn loves you exactly how you are. So do Annie and your mom and your dad… and so do I."

"Will you still get to be a doctor when you marry my sister and she's the queen? Can a king be a doctor, too?"

William smiled at the quick change in subject…he'd gone a little too far again with Owen, but he hoped that what he'd managed to say would sink in over time. He really had fallen in love with the amazing little boy. It was going to be hard to say good-bye.

"I don't know how it will all work out, Owen. I'll still be a doctor, but I don't think it will be the same as I always figured it was going to be. That's okay, though. Sometimes you meet people, and you find out they're more important than whatever your first plans were, and so you make new ones."

"And my sister is more important than your old plans?"

"Very much more important. But speaking of your sister… Even though it usually takes the girls longer to get ready for dinner than us boys, if we don't get you into the bath soon, they're going to be waiting for us. And that's not good. So how about you pick which room you want to take a bath in, and then I'll go take a shower in the other one."

And also thinking of Quinn… Once William had gotten Owen in the bath, he remembered that they were going to be celebrating Quinn's birthday tonight, too. He hadn't really had a chance to get her anything…but last night he'd remembered something that he'd come across a couple of weeks ago as he'd been going through some of his old books.

Digging it back out of the drawer where he'd hidden it, he found a pretty cloth to wrap it in and tied it with a ribbon, leaving it on a table where he'd remember it.

As Linnea carefully finished lowering Quinn's dress over her head, Megan gasped.

"Oh, honey, you're so beautiful. So grown up."

A flash of heat hit her cheeks. "It's just a dress, Mom." She looked up to examine herself in the long bathroom mirror as Linnea and Megan both started buttoning up the back.

Linnea *had* outdone herself this evening. The floor-length gown she had picked out was a soft cream color, overlaid with dark green flowers down the short sleeves and the long skirt. She'd pulled up some of Quinn's hair into an intricate bun held in place with a gold barrette, but the rest of it flowed down past her shoulders. The image of herself in the mirror made her suck in a breath.

"Time to start looking like the heir to the throne," Linnea said, leaving Megan to finish the last few buttons while she fastened the pendant around Quinn's neck.

Looking in the mirror, seeing the dress, the way her auburn hair was swept up in an intricate design…the way the pendant lay against her neck like it belonged there…Quinn suddenly felt, for the first time, like she actually was the heir to a throne. For a second, anyway. After that, the sensation was so overwhelming that she had to look away and push it from her mind.

She turned to face her mother. "You look amazing, too." Linnea had managed to come up with a dress for Megan that complimented Quinn's.

"What about me?" Annie asked, running back into the bathroom and twirling so that her skirt flared out.

"You're always pretty," Quinn said, scooping her sister into her arms and hugging her tightly. "But especially right now."

"Can I have a necklace, too?" Annie asked.

"Uh..."

"Sure!" Linnea said. "Want to come with me to get one?"

"Yeah!" Annie practically leapt from Quinn's arms to follow Linnea out of the bathroom and toward the door.

Quinn was left standing there facing her mom, heavy emotion filling her chest.

"One thing," Megan said, and a tone in her voice made Quinn's stomach clench nervously. "What is *this?*" She pointed to her own chest, but Quinn knew exactly what she was asking, and heat flowed from the top of her head to her toes.

"It's a tattoo."

"Seriously, Quinn?"

She was never going to be able to explain that one in a way her mother was going to be happy about. Taking a second before she answered, she remembered her conversation with Linnea the other day – her mom wasn't going to treat her as an adult by this unless she acted like one, calm and decisive.

"It's a long story, Mom. I'll try and explain it later, but I really don't want us to get upset with each other tonight. For now, can you just trust me that I'm making the best decisions I know how to, and that all I want from you is for us to just love each other and have as many *good* memories together as we can, instead of fighting?"

Megan was silent for several seconds, but finally she took a deep breath and nodded.

"Thank you," Quinn said, feeling her hands relax out of their tight fists.

"I'm trying."

"I know. And I appreciate it more than I could ever tell you, Mom."

Megan blinked furiously for a few seconds, and then she cleared her throat. She walked toward one of the night tables, and picked up a little wrapped package that Quinn hadn't noticed before. "I wanted to give you your gift," she said. "I had it on me when I came, because I'd just picked it up from the shop that afternoon…whenever that was. I did ask Charlotte for help with wrapping it. I guess they don't have wrapping paper here?"

Quinn shook her head. "They do wrapped presents for some things now…I think they might have learned that from William or Nathaniel…but no, no wrapping paper."

The little gift was wrapped in soft, blue cloth tied with a ribbon. Quinn untied it, opened it, and looked up at her mom with tears in her eyes.

"I told you, Quinn… I think there was a part of me that knew this was going to happen, or that was trying to convince you not to do it."

It was a photo album. The pictures were all digital, or had been converted, but they were printed on the pages like a scrapbook. The first pictures were of Quinn as a baby, being held by Samuel or Megan, sometimes both of them. There was even one she'd never seen before…of Nathaniel staring at her in delight as she took a wobbly step.

Her mouth fell open, and the tears rolled down her cheeks. "Mom…"

The following pictures were in order, each of Quinn's school pictures, her in her flower girl dress at Megan and Jeff's wedding, her holding a tiny baby Owen, "helping" him learn to walk, kissing a newborn Annie…all the way up to the family photo that had been taken of all of them last summer.

"It's beautiful. I don't know how something can be so wonderful and so impossibly sad at the same time."

"Me neither, sweetheart."

They were still hugging when they were both startled by Thomas's voice. "Is everyone dressed in here?"

"Yes, we're ready," Quinn said.

Her heart gave a little flutter at the sight of Thomas and William standing by the doorway, dressed in their formalwear…crisply ironed black pants and white button-down shirts, covered with purple velvet capes fastened at the neck with the seal of Eirentheos. Between them stood Owen, his outfit matching theirs – they'd even found him a cape somewhere – freshly cleaned and combed. He smiled shyly up at Quinn and Megan, even as he fidgeted uncomfortably over the attention.

"Well, then," Megan said, clearing her throat. Quinn giggled a little at her mom's reaction.

William's eyes lit up as he stepped toward her. "Wow."

"I could say the same about you," she said, taking hold of his outstretched hand.

Thomas playfully wagged his eyebrows at Megan. "I thought you might like an escort downstairs."

"You're quite the gentleman, aren't you?"

"I do my best."

"Don't you have a girlfriend?" Megan asked. "I thought I saw you…"

"I do. I'm going to come back up here to get her in a little while. She had to finish helping get the younger children dressed and downstairs before she could get herself ready. In the meantime, she says she doesn't mind my escorting a lovely lady downstairs, so long as I keep my hands to myself. So, will you accept an elbow?"

"It's a tempting offer," Megan said, "but I believe there's a gentleman waiting for me already." She held her hand out toward Owen, who smiled as he took it.

Thomas sighed dramatically. "Watch out, Owen. That one will break your heart. Oh, well, at least Annie won't let me down, will you Princess?" he said, as Annie and Linnea reappeared.

"And, what? Leave me to fend for myself?" Linnea's eyes crinkled in laughter.

"I've got you covered, Nay." In one fluid motion, he scooped Annie off the floor and onto one arm, and then held out his other elbow toward Linnea. "Shall we?"

They approached the dining room just behind Charles and his wife, Thea. Quinn felt herself slowing down, and William looked down at her, squeezing her hand gently. "You can do this."

"Right." She nodded. She could do this. This was only the first test of many.

Just inside the door, she was distracted from her tension by the sight of a young couple. Andrew and Natalie Gramble were standing there, chatting animatedly with Charlotte. When they saw Quinn and William, both of them broke into huge smiles.

"Prince William! Lady Quinn! We've been so looking forward to seeing you again."

"It's good to see you, too," William said, returning Andrew's hug.

Quinn smiled at the beautiful baby girl nestled in Natalie's arms as she greeted the young woman. Natalie was only a year...*a cycle?*...older than Quinn. "How have you been?"

"Things have been difficult," Natalie said, "with everything that's going on. But the three of us have been well. We've wondered how *you* all have been. We never got the chance to properly thank both of you for being so calm and taking care of us that day."

"Anybody would have done that."

"No, Quinn. Not many girls who were scared and in the kind of situation you were in would have been able to put that aside and focus on a couple of strangers the way you did."

"I just wanted everything to be okay for you." Quinn shifted uncomfortably. "She's beautiful," she said, hoping to change the subject. "What did you name her?" Babies in this world weren't named immediately, and Quinn and William had been headed back to the castle with Thomas long before this child's Naming Ceremony.

Natalie's cheeks turned pink as she exchanged a shy smile with her husband.

"Her name is Quinn," Andrew said.

William's mouth fell open just as far as hers did.

"I... I don't know what to say. I'm honored of course," she stammered.

"Would you like to hold her?"

"Yes, please." She stretched out her arms to take the baby from Natalie. The tiny girl was soft and warm; Quinn couldn't help kissing her little head and taking a deep sniff of the sweet baby smell.

"We thought it would be fitting to name her after the kind girl who may turn out to be the queen we've all been working so hard to find."

Quinn had to pay attention to make sure she didn't lose her grip on the baby who was smiling up from her arms. "You knew?"

"We'd known for a while…Ellen and Henry, the two of us, and a very few other members of the Friends of Philip. What we didn't know was what you were like, or if we wanted *you* to know. Ellen hadn't even told Charles at that point. There are still many who have their concerns, but after that day, Lady Quinn... we knew."

"And now we hear that the news might be even better? That the two of you have an announcement to make?"

"It's true," William said, watching in delight as the baby in Quinn's arms wrapped her tiny hand around one of his index fingers, "I've asked her to marry me, and she's accepted…we're betrothed."

Although Quinn was still antsy as they approached the table for the meal, it wasn't as awkward as she'd been expecting. Ellen and Charles both seemed to have calmed down a bit after their earlier encounter. Maybe they'd been satisfied with her answer.

As the servants started bringing in the salad dishes, William led Quinn over to the table, pulling out chairs for her and her mother. Somehow in the last couple of days, even Owen had become comfortable in the crowd of children who were heading for the smaller table that had been set up just for them.

It wasn't a large crowd…just William's family and the guests from Philotheum, so Quinn easily spotted Thomas and Mia as they came through the doors. Mia's cheeks were flushed, and Thomas… well, if he'd looked any smugger, she'd have been checking his cape for feathers. Her eyes immediately went to Mia's wrist, and she was rewarded with the sight of the little silver bracelet.

She'd been about to sit down, but she straightened back up and nudged William with her elbow. "Did you know about this?"

"What?"

"That." She nodded toward Thomas and Mia.

He frowned. "That what? Oh." He finally saw what she'd seen. "No, I didn't. I mean, I'd kind of wondered…" A grin spread across his face and he took her hand before heading toward them.

"Mia!" Quinn exclaimed as soon as they reached them. "When were you going to tell me about this?"

Mia's cheeks turned from pink to a deep crimson. "Lady Quinn, I…"

"She was worried about upsetting you," Thomas interrupted. "She didn't want to take any attention away from your betrothal."

Mia flashed Thomas a withering look that made Quinn and William both chuckle quietly.

"Don't be silly, Mia. I couldn't be happier for you." She hugged Mia tightly, while William hugged Thomas, and then they traded places.

When they'd finished hugging, Quinn turned around to see that they'd drawn a small crowd. Linnea stood behind them, as well as Charlotte and Maxwell. She realized that she hadn't seen Stephen yet this evening. Or Simon…although his wife, Evelyn, was already seated at the table.

As soon as Quinn stepped back to let Linnea and Charlotte step in, she felt a tap on her shoulder. She turned around and found herself facing Maxwell. "Can I speak with you for a minute?"

Something about his expression made her mouth go dry. "Sure."

William followed her over to the corner by the door. For a second, Maxwell looked at him with what appeared to be exasperation, but then he closed his eyes, shook his head, and then turned his gaze back to Quinn.

"Earlier today, some of our guards found Jonathan and three of his men camping not far from here."

Quinn's heart started beating faster.

"When they confronted him, he asked to be brought here, to meet with my father."

"Oh?" She didn't know if this was good news or bad.

"He's asking to speak with you."

"Now?" She looked around the room, at the table being laid with food, at her family and William's.

"He was rather insistent. I've already spoken to my mother about taking care of things here."

"I'm coming, too." William said.

Max sighed, but nodded. "You might as well."

Quinn's stomach was tight as they followed Max down the hall to Stephen's private office. She was beginning to hate coming to this room; it seemed like she only found herself inside it when there was a crisis. Would her own office be like this when she ruled Philotheum? She shook that thought away…it wasn't helping her stomach.

The door was closed, but Max didn't bother to knock, he just opened it, and they followed him inside.

Simon and Stephen were both there, as was Nathaniel, who stood when they entered and came to stand next to Quinn. Jonathan was sitting alone on one of the tall armchairs near the fireplace.

"Max, thank you for bringing her. Please let your mother know I will come and find her as soon as I can."

Max's mouth opened partway, but he didn't say anything. He turned and left, closing the door behind him with a little more force than was strictly necessary.

"Thank you for joining us, Quinn," Stephen said, after he had gone. "I'm sorry to disrupt your dinner."

She looked into his clear, gray eyes, seeing immediately the kindness there and the strength, the raw power of a king who would never hesitate to make a sacrifice he felt was necessary.

"It's your dinner, too, isn't it? Besides, I have a feeling this is something I need to get used to."

Out of the corner of her eye, she saw Jonathan give a small nod. She turned to face him. "There's something you need to discuss with me that couldn't keep until after dinner?"

Jonathan's eyebrows moved higher on his forehead, and the corners of his mouth quirked up.

She moved closer, so that she was standing a few feet in front of him. "Do I amuse you?"

"Not at all, Princess. You're just... not what I expected, that's all."

"What did you expect?"

He shook his head. "It's really of no consequence to anyone what I expected. What *is* of consequence, however, is the news I've just heard about you and Prince William."

She glanced up at Stephen, who nodded.

"You know about my betrothal, then?"

"Yes. And while I can't begin to tell you what hope that news gives me, I asked to speak with you in order to ask you *please* for the time being, to keep it quiet."

It felt like someone had poured a glass of ice water down her back. "Excuse me?"

"I'm sorry. I know it doesn't sound like it makes very much sense."

"No, it doesn't make any sense at all."

"You're in more danger than you realize. Right now, you're of mostly passing interest to my half-brother. He wants to know why Stephen's sons are so interested in you, and he wants to understand your possible connection with a portal to the other world, if one exists. He's observing you, for those reasons, but not interfering. But if Tolliver were to find out who you really are, and then he found out that you have the very real potential to fulfill the prophecy yourself... he would use any means necessary to eliminate you, Quinn."

She had to remind herself to breathe.

"So what are you suggesting? We can't keep it quiet forever."

"I don't know how much you know about our laws and the situation in the Philothean castle."

"Practically nothing."

He chuckled. "That's very confidence-inspiring, milady."

"I'm working with what I have. Perhaps you can enlighten me."

"When my father died, because his heir was not yet of age, all of his power transferred to his wife, my mother, Sophia."

"But then she remarried."

"Yes, she married Hector. He was more than happy to step in and take control, to make decisions and to rule the kingdom as Prince Regent."

She could hear the catch in his tone. "But?"

"But, legally, the power still belongs to my mother. It can't be transferred to a new spouse, only to a successor."

"Which is why Hector wants so much for Tolliver to take the crown."

"Yes. But he doesn't have the power to give it to him, only she does."

Quinn thought about that for a long moment. "She's told him no…unless he fulfills the prophecy."

"I don't actually know how much my mother believes in the prophecy anymore. But certainly she's using it as an excuse. You have to understand, Quinn, my mother was broken apart when my father died. She was alone with four children, pregnant with a fifth, and unexpectedly in charge of an entire kingdom. A kingdom that was suddenly having political difficulties with one of its closest neighbors, Dovelnia.

"Hector was the answer to a lot of her problems. Charming, funny, willing to step in as a father to her children and help her take care of them…willing to bear much of the responsibilities of running the kingdom."

"Magically restore peace between Philotheum and Dovelnia…"

"It's easy to see these things from an outside perspective nearly thirty cycles later, Princess. At the time, there was no reason for her to suspect that he'd had anything to do with my father's death."

Her mouth fell open. "You know about that?"

"Yes. As does my mother, although by the time she realized what was really going on, too many things had been set into motion. It wasn't until after Nathaniel's so-called betrayal and subsequent… *death*," his eyes drifted toward Nathaniel, who was sitting there, very much alive, "that she finally began to understand what had been going on. By then, of course, so much of the damage was already done. She spent many cycles feeling guilty and stupid for having allowed it to happen. And she feels somewhat hopeless, too. She doesn't *want* to see Tolliver on the throne, but she doesn't see another viable option. At least he's her son, and if he did manage to marry into Stephen's family…"

"Then she would allow him to take the throne."

"Yes. She's secretly hoping that he doesn't manage it…that somehow she'll be able to hold him off until another heir, Charles' daughter, perhaps, if we could find her, could step up. She doesn't know that you exist. That would change everything. And the fact that you're actually going to fulfill the prophecy..."

"I'm surprised Hector hasn't just killed her."

"If he did that, the power to appoint a rightful heir to the throne would fall to Charles. Besides, Hector can only have so many people killed before the entire populace would be onto him, and he'd have an uprising. And of course, Hector doesn't *know* my mother has everything figured out. She's still playing the role of obedient, doting wife to him. It's a very difficult balance right now."

"And you're playing the act of obedient son?"

"Of course. Oh, and supportive older brother to Tolliver. I'm quite good at it."

He smiled with sincere charm. *Of course,* she thought, *he's a fifth-born.* "So what do we do?"

"We need to get you to Philotheum. To my mother. Preferably alive."

"Preferably."

"Can't we just send her a message or something?"

Jonathan chuckled. "No, Princess. It doesn't work like that. All communications into or out of the castle are strictly monitored. Hector has no idea that my mother has turned against him…or that I have, for that matter. Although that may have changed now… I'm sure I can't even trust all of my own personal guards who came here with me. My every step is noticed; for my whole life it's been this way. After Ellen and Charles left the castle, things grew even worse."

"Then how do you expect to get me to see her?"

"Very, very, carefully. I am hoping for help from my siblings," he looked meaningfully at Nathaniel, "as well as from the Friends of Philip."

"How do I know I can trust you?"

"You don't. I'm sorry for that. You're going to have to decide for yourself whether to take my advice or not. In the meantime, I hope you will at least consider what I've said, and keep your very presence in the kingdom as quiet as possible…especially your potential to fulfill the prophecy."

She was trying her best to hold on to her composure, but at his last words, she couldn't help burying her face in her hands.

"I am sorry, Quinn. And what I'm going to say next is only going to complicate your decision about me."

She moved her hands long enough to look at him while he spoke.

"I am the one who set the fire. I didn't intend for it to spread… Didn't even realize it could do what it did…I'd never built a fire before. It happened after I set fire to the bridge, hoping to destroy the gate to the other world."

Quinn was silent as they followed Stephen and Simon back down the hall to the dinner party. William reached for her hand. She allowed him to take it, but didn't look up at him. Her hand was cold and clammy; he pulled it closer to him and rubbed it with both of his.

He had not even begun to process what he had heard in that room tonight…didn't even want to think about it while they still had dinner to get through. He was glad he'd been there only because it meant she wouldn't have to explain all of it to him later.

Quinn paused when they reached the door, and he watched, amazed, as she pulled herself together. After a few deep breaths, she was standing taller, and her expression had changed from devastated to unaffected. She glanced up at him for a second, and gave him half a smile. "Ready?"

"If you are."

The meal was halfway over already when they entered the room. Charlotte stood as soon as she saw them and rushed over. Quinn shot her an apologetic look, but left her to talk with Stephen, and William followed her over to the table.

"Sorry about that," she said, sliding into the seat beside her mother. "Did I miss any good gossip here?"

Confusion flickered in Megan's eyes for a second, and then it was replaced by a decisive look. "Mia and Thomas were just showing us their courtship bracelets," she finally said. "And I realized I never even asked you about yours."

Up until that moment, William's feelings about Quinn's mother had been conflicted. He'd felt sort of bad for her, that everything with her daughter seemed to be falling apart, but his bigger concern had been for Quinn. He'd been angry with Megan for lying to her, for not telling her who she really was, or letting her have a relationship with Nathaniel…and angrier still at the way Megan had been treating Quinn, that her petulant reactions were making everything so much harder for the girl he loved.

Now, though, he realized that Megan really did love Quinn, too. That her behavior before had all come from fear…maybe deep down she'd always known that this day was coming…that she was going to lose her daughter. And who would handle that with grace?

He unbuckled the clasp on his bracelet and handed it over for Megan to examine along with Quinn's.

A CHANGE OF PLANS

EVERYONE RETREATED UPSTAIRS FAR earlier than usual after a formal dinner. There had been music after the meal, but nobody really seemed to feel like dancing. The cake had been delicious, as always, but it didn't really feel like a party.

At some point, Stephen and Charlotte had disappeared, along with Ellen and Charles, but Quinn hadn't felt like following after them. She would track them down tomorrow. For tonight, she needed some time to process everything she had learned, and to talk with William.

She walked upstairs with her mom and her siblings, to the guest suite where they were staying. After kissing Annie and Owen goodnight and telling them to go and brush their teeth, she turned to her mom.

"Thank you for tonight, Mom."

"I didn't do anything except eat with you, honey."

"Yeah, you did. And I want you to know that I noticed, and that I see that you're trying, and it means more to me than I know how to tell you."

"I love you, sweetheart."

After all the weeks of fighting and avoiding each other, her mom's tight hug was almost too much, and she had to struggle to maintain her grip on her composure. "I love you, too, Mom."

When Megan finally pulled away, she looked at Quinn in concern, brushing her long hair back behind her shoulders. "Is everything okay?"

"Yeah. Everything's fine."

"It's just... I thought Charlotte and Stephen were going to say something about your engagement tonight..."

Of course her mom would have noticed that. Instead of being annoyed by that, though, she was just grateful that her mom was acknowledging the reality, and, in keeping with what she'd promised, was trying her best to be okay with it. "Everyone who was there already knows, I think. Nothing has changed."

It was obvious that her mom didn't fully believe her, but she didn't press the issue either, which made Quinn want to hug her again. So she did.

"You're sure you're all right?"

"I'm sure. I'll see you in the morning, okay?"

William was waiting for her back in her room, but he wasn't alone. Although she'd sort of forgotten about anything except how much she wanted to have a few minutes to process and talk things through with William, she realized that she was grateful that Linnea and Thomas were there, too. William was already telling them what Jonathan had said.

"So how much do you trust Jonathan?" Linnea asked, as Quinn came in and sat down at the end of the couch, next to William.

She was silent as she thought about that, playing absently with the edge of the embroidered pillow. "Would it sound crazy if I said that I trust him?"

"A little." Linnea nodded. "He did just admit to trying to burn down the kingdom."

"I think that's part of what makes me trust him, though. He didn't have to admit that."

"And if he has managed to destroy the gate?" Thomas asked.

"Can he do that? Would burning it down destroy it?"

"I don't know," William said. "We won't know until it's supposed to open again and we try to use it."

"We'd all be stuck here. Forever." Knots formed in Quinn's stomach. She hadn't allowed herself to think about that part of Jonathan's confession.

"Possibly. You still trust him?"

She closed her eyes, trying to make some kind of sense out of her wildly raging thoughts. "I don't know." Unbidden, an image came to her from the first day she'd met Jonathan in the tent, of Owen nodding at her, at her understanding of what that nod had meant. "Yeah, I still kind of do. I can even see why he would want the gate destroyed. It's caused nothing but problems for his kingdom…and he didn't even know about Nathaniel and my father using it to escape. And can you imagine if Tolliver found it and figured out how to use it?"

"If he has destroyed it, you'll never be able to go home again, Quinn. Your mom, and Owen and Annie won't, either."

"I know." It was hard to speak around the hard lump that had formed in her throat and the swirling nausea that was gripping her stomach. "I know that. But just because it would be a huge tragedy for me, personally, does that mean he's wrong? Does the fact that the home I grew up in…the fact that Jeff is still there," her voice broke on her adopted father's name, and she had to take a break before continuing, "does that mean using the gate the way we have been is actually the right thing to do?"

Nobody spoke for several minutes. Quinn used the silence to take several deep breaths, to try to calm down her racing heart. She was trying her hardest not to think about the implications of what she had just said. It didn't feel real…it felt more like one of the fun late-night conversations they'd all had before, filled with what-ifs and speculations about the connection between the worlds that they didn't understand. She *needed* it to keep feeling like that, or she would never get through this conversation. As it was, she knew there was no chance she'd be sleeping tonight.

"Well," Linnea finally said, "it *is* a stone bridge. I don't know if a fire would actually destroy it. And anyway, we won't know about that until we try to use it. We'll know in a couple of days."

"Is it only a couple more days already?"

"Three, I think," William said, rubbing her knee softly.

"Okay." She nodded.

The knock on the door startled them all. Quinn was even more surprised when Thomas pulled the door open to reveal Ben.

"I'm sorry to interrupt," he said, "but I've been asked to bring you to a meeting with some of the members of the Friends of Philip."

"Tonight?"

"Yes. I know it's late, but your presence has been requested Lady Quinn, and yours as well, Master William."

"All right."

Quinn, William, and Ben were nearly to the council room when she suddenly heard footsteps behind her. She spun around and nearly fell over when she found herself nose-to-nose with Alvin.

"It's nice to see you again too, Milady," he said, putting a hand under her elbow to steady her. "And might I say you look especially lovely this evening. Quite fancy for a political strategy meeting."

Heat flowed up her neck and into her cheeks as she realized she was still dressed for dinner. She wasn't actually sure how she was supposed to dress for a "political strategy meeting", but she supposed an evening gown was a bit over the top.

They'd now reached the heavy, double wooden doors to the council room. Alvin breezed ahead of them, and let himself in, leaving Quinn standing there, suddenly self-conscious about her clothes. William had at least managed to shed his cape.

Ben turned to her, looking for a moment as if he was deciding something. "I know it's none of my business, Lady Quinn," he said quietly, "but if you are to be a queen, then I would think that you're entitled to wear what you like to whatever occasion you wish. And you *do* look lovely…how I'd picture a queen in any case. I have a feeling Alvin may just be testing you…to see if you'll rise to the challenge."

"Thank you, Ben."

Ben stepped into the room, and Quinn took a last glance up at William.

"Ben's right," he whispered in her ear. "You're beautiful, and nobody is going to be worried about what you're *wearing*. I've seen my father dash off to meetings in his pajamas."

"So you and Ben are telling me I should own it."

He chuckled. "Own it?" Is that some kind of phrase from your world?"

She shrugged, starting to smile, too.

"I've never heard that before, but yes, it's fitting. It's yours, Quinn. Go in there and 'own it'."

So she did. She straightened her shoulders, and walked into the room, straight to the empty chair next to Stephen, at the head of the table. She looked around at the other people who were gathered there. Simon was on the other side of Stephen; to her right were Marcus, Nathaniel, Charles, and Ellen. Ben and William took seats at the other end of the table.

Alvin, who was sitting on the other side of Simon, winked at her when she glanced his direction, and she knew Ben was right. It had been a test to see if he could rattle her…*why?* To teach her something? Maybe to focus on things that were important, instead of unimportant details. She wondered if he'd stick around long enough for her to ask him.

Whatever the reason…it really *didn't* matter. If she really was going to rule a kingdom, then she needed to be prepared to run to a meeting however she was dressed. Everyone else could deal.

"What's going on? I assume this has to do with what Jonathan said earlier?"

Stephen cleared his throat. "Yes, that's part of it. In addition to the things you heard from Jonathan today, Quinn, he told us something terrible this evening. Dorian and James Blackwelder have been convicted, and are scheduled to be executed."

Oh no. The room started spinning around her. The Blackwelders were the Philothean guards who had rescued Thomas from his imprisonment. Thomas literally owed his life to the two men.

"Aside from that, earlier today, another regiment of Tolliver's forces attempted to cross the border. Our troops were able to stop them, but there is still some fighting in Anwin and things are escalating faster than we were anticipating."

"So, time's up."

"Yes. We need to do whatever we can to get you on that throne as quickly as possible…to end this."

"I still don't trust Jonathan," Charles said. "How do we know he's not just trying to trick us, to make us more vulnerable?"

"Do you have to trust him to know that he's right?" Everyone looked at Alvin. "Whether he gave you some of that information for his own purposes, or not, he is right in that Sophia is the one who can put a successor on that throne."

"So can a unanimous vote of the council."

"Ah, Charles. That would be true only if Sophia were dead, and the council was acting on the authority of a proper member of the royal line. Do you really think you could ever get that council to vote unanimously on anyone except Tolliver? You're lucky as it is that he hasn't managed to replace enough members to achieve that goal already. Luckier still that there would be consequences for him if your mother…your *mother*, Charles…died unexpectedly. Take a step back and remember what your father would have really wanted for your kingdom…what you really want, when you don't let the whisper of an idea get in the way."

Charles sat all the way back in his chair. Quinn frowned, trying to figure out what that had been about, though she thought she had an idea.

"I think what we really need from all of you," Stephen said, "is to know whether Quinn has your support moving forward. For the record, she has the support of Eirentheos. Now we need to know about you."

"How do we know she really is who she claims to be?" There was still a defiant gleam in Charles' eye, and Quinn was almost sure her guess was correct. He had been hoping to put his own daughter on the throne. But when she looked up at Alvin, he shook his head once at her.

"They could be making all of this up." Charles' voice was louder now.

She shifted uncomfortably in her chair; she didn't have any idea how she could *prove* to anyone who she was. Her fingers closed around the pendant on her neck.

"She is Samuel's daughter, Charles. You know that…you didn't doubt that from the moment you laid eyes on her. She has his hair, his eyes, and his pendant. That isn't what this is about." Ellen said, surprising Quinn with her fierce tone. "I had my hesitations about whether she was serious, whether she was up to this, but we got our answers. Quinn, you have my support."

"You all know where I stand," Nathaniel said. "So it's just you, Charles."

"If you're all so certain that we should hand over our kingdom to a young girl who knows nothing about us, then fine. I'm not going to fight with you about it. If this is what we're going to do, then I say we move on it now. And I don't think we should tell Jonathan everything, just in case we *can't* trust him."

Quinn's hands were still shaking as William led her back to her bedroom after the meeting. He closed the door behind them before putting his arms around her. He didn't ask if she was okay…he'd taken her admonition the other day…*earlier today?* he couldn't keep track any more…seriously. He could understand that. It was a challenging time, but she didn't need people constantly asking her if she was okay with it.

Really, she was handling it all remarkably well…at least in public. He wondered if he would ever stop being impressed at the way she could instantly transform herself from a scared girl to a self-assured leader when she had to.

"This is all happening so fast."

"Five days." That's what they'd decided at the meeting. Enough time to make plans and say their goodbyes. Enough time to see Quinn's family through the gate in three days…provided the gate *wasn't* destroyed. Ellen and Charles didn't know all the details about the gate. "Five days until we leave, anyway. The trip will take much longer."

"That should be interesting," she said with a wry expression. "I don't think Charles likes me very much."

"That has nothing to do with you…he obviously had his own agenda before he came here."

"So it wasn't just me who noticed that?"

"Definitely not. Alvin had him pegged, too." Just as he always had everyone pegged…it hadn't escaped his notice that Alvin had pulled Quinn to the side for a moment as everyone was saying goodnight. He'd decided not to ask her about it, though, figuring she would tell him about that when she was ready.

She sighed, and he went to her, putting his arms around her, kissing her on the forehead. "You did great in there."

"It doesn't feel like it."

"You did, though. Hey," he said, suddenly remembering, "I have something for you."

She frowned.

"Well, we were supposed to be celebrating your birthday tonight."

"That doesn't seem like the most important thing right now."

"Anything that celebrates you is important to me, Quinn. Besides, you should take it while you can get it. Birthdays are sort of rare here…it's a few thousand days until your next one."

Her eyes widened, and he smiled. "Yeah… that was one of the few things I really liked about going to Bristlecone when I was little. I didn't have to wait as long for things as my brothers and sisters did. And then there… people have birthdays all the time. If there were twenty-four kids in your class, that was like two birthdays a month. And people brought cupcakes…" As he talked, he walked over to the chair where he'd laid down his cape, and picked it up, retrieving the little package from the pocket.

"It's not much," he said. "But, I found it a couple of weeks ago when I was going through some old books, and…I really couldn't believe it. I had no idea I'd done this. I wish I remembered it, but I don't. I guess another downside of spending time here is that my childhood was a *really* long time ago." He handed the gift to her.

She was curious now; he could see it in her eyes. And he felt his cheeks warming, a little embarrassed now; he didn't know what she was going to think.

When the cloth came off, revealing a small, old, slightly tattered sketchbook…purchased in her world…she frowned up at him.

"Apparently, when I was little, I thought I'd try my hand at drawing," he said. "I still do a lot of that, but now it's all diagrams and stuff like that. I'm mostly only artistic with the carving…"

He was definitely nervous now as she opened the cover.

"Wow, Will," she said, sucking in a breath. "These are good."

He wasn't sure how old he'd been when he'd drawn them, but it was in the first couple of years he'd been in Bristlecone…still at the elementary school. The whole sketchbook was filled with drawings of things he'd seen there…the trees, the shops, the cars… and quite a few pictures of the kids at school.

There were kids studying at desks, chattering as they ate lunch together, playing at recess. And there was one picture…the only colored picture in a sea of pencil drawings…of a little girl playing on a swing by herself, daydreaming, by the look in her soft gray eyes, her long auburn hair blowing back in the wind.

Those eyes looked up at him now with tears in them.

"Yeah." He nodded. "I did…even then, it seems."

This time she pulled him into her arms and kissed him, starting with the pink spots that were quickly fading from his cheeks, pooling instead into a warm glow deep inside his chest.

"I love you, William Rose. This is the best birthday present I've ever had. Not this," she said, touching the book gently before setting it down on the table, "although I love it very much, but *this*," she placed her hand over his heart, "*this* is the present I'm most grateful for. Thank you for trusting me with it."

"Thank you for giving me yours," he whispered, placing his hand over her heart, and then leaning in to kiss her on the lips.

They held each other for a long time, just hugging, gently swaying back and forth, William's heart overflowing with tenderness for her. But finally, she yawned.

They both chuckled, and he kissed her on the nose. "You should at least sit down," he said.

"Okay," she agreed, heading toward her couch. He intended to follow her, but almost immediately, she stood up again, light pink filling her cheeks.

"What is it?"

"Nothing." But the pink was growing darker.

"What, love?"

Her cheeks were decidedly red now, but she giggled under her breath, relaxing him. "It's just... As soon as I sat down, I realized how much I want to be out of this stupid dress."

He looked down at the soft folds of the material, unable to stop himself from reaching to take some of the fabric of the skirt in his hand. "I don't know if I'd call it stupid..."

She rolled her eyes.

"So go change. You should go to bed anyway; you've got to be exhausted."

"Yeah... the problem is I can't get out of it myself." She turned her back to him, showing off an impressive line of tiny, intricate buttons. "And I'm sure Mia and Linnea are already both asleep."

"It's lucky for you I know how to operate a button. Otherwise, you'd have to sleep in this thing." He understood her blush now; warmth crept up his own neck as he reached for the top button. The heat rose higher as his unbuttoning revealed the lacy top of the cream-colored slip she wore underneath the dress.

His breath caught, and she twisted her head to look at him. "This is dangerous," she whispered.

"Very." He ran his hand across the silky lace, and then up her also-silky neck. Buttons forgotten, she turned to face him, and his lips found hers.

He was thankful that she had the wherewithal to pull away from him a few minutes later…because he wasn't sure he'd have been able to. "Sorry."

She raised an eyebrow, her expression teasing, not angry. "Are you?"

"Only because I want to do this right. At this particular moment, I'm wishing we were already married, and that I could have this job permanently." She kept her arms around his neck as he worked on the remaining buttons behind her.

"I wish that right now, too. It's going to be hard to wait."

He closed his eyes. Yes, traveling with her all the way to Philotheum like this was going to be next to impossible. As he stood there, trying to re-regulate his breathing, another course of action occurred to him. "Maybe we shouldn't wait."

"What do you mean?" She frowned. "We talked about this, I thought…"

"We did," he said quickly. "That's not what I mean… I meant, maybe we shouldn't wait to get married."

"We're leaving in a couple of days, Will. We can't just get married." There was a catch in her voice that he didn't understand…like something had just clicked, and she wasn't telling him.

"We can't have a big wedding, no…though all things considered we probably will still have to have a big, public ceremony sometime."

"So, what, like a small private ceremony here, and then we'd already be married when we go?"

"Why not?"

"Do people do things like that here?"

"Sure. It's not standard practice in my family, obviously, but these are not standard circumstances, either."

"Would your parents be okay with it?"

He walked around her and started working on the buttons again. "Quinn, I love my parents, and I know you do, too. And your parents…your mom, at least, is really starting to grow on me. But we're not talking about our parents here."

He reached the last button and, then, still talking, made his way across the room to retrieve her dressing gown from its hook in her bathroom. "I want to be respectful to our parents, of course, but you and I are both adults, and we're talking about marriage. This is about what's best for us…not them."

She slipped her arms out of the dress and into the robe, tying it around herself before he helped her step the rest of the way out of the skirt. "When did you turn into such a grown up?" She slumped down onto the couch, clearly relieved to be free from the heavy dress. He laid it carefully over the back of a chair before sitting down next to her.

"I am technically ten times older than you," he teased. "Since I grew up in this world."

"I don't know. You spent quite a bit of time in mine. It's possible now that Thomas and Linnea are older than you are. Maybe we should ask them."

He chuckled. "I'm sure we'll hear their opinions on the subject in the morning. Right now, I'm more interested in yours."

"Well, we are going to get married anyway."

"I hope so."

"We are, Will. I'm not wavering on that. I'm just trying to process a lot of things right now."

"I know, love." He scooted closer to her on the couch, and took her hand in his. "I'm sorry. It's been a long day. I should let you sleep."

"I'm wide awake now."

"So am I." He wasn't sure he'd ever been more awake.

"It would make some things easier."

"We could be sure to have your mom here, for one thing."

Her eyes widened, and he immediately felt bad…she obviously hadn't thought about that…that if they waited and were married after they arrived in Philotheum, there was a good chance her family *wouldn't* be able to be there. "My mom is leaving in three days. There's no way we could plan a wedding in three days."

"My mother could probably put together a wedding in three hours if she had to, Quinn. I'm not worried about that. If you want," he said, softly stroking her hand, "we could make this ceremony more like one in your world. Do all the traditional things you'd do there. I don't know what all of them are, but I'm sure we could find a way. My mother is a good planner; you can just tell her what you want. The hardest part of the whole thing will be finding someone to perform the ceremony on such short notice."

She chuckled once under her breath.

"What?"

"I don't think that part will be a problem."

"Why?"

"Alvin tonight…I didn't know what he was hinting about, but he pulled me aside and told me that he'd be nearby for the next couple of days, in case we needed his *services*. Now I don't know whether to laugh or cry."

"Laughing is usually best, I think."

She smiled. "Okay. So we get married sometime in the next three days, then."

He pulled her hand up to his lips and kissed her ring. "That sounds good to me."

Taking his hand in hers, she pulled it to her cheek. He ran his thumb against her cheekbone, smiling when it warmed to a light pink.

She tucked herself up under his other arm. "It's going to be awfully hard to be ready to say good-bye and leave everyone so quickly."

He wrapped his other arm around her, too. "Would that part be any easier if we had a hundred moons to prepare? Of course, I always imagined there would be more time…that our wedding would be a little more traditional and celebratory… but that's not what matters to me. I'm leaving the places where I grew up, sure, but I'm not leaving *home*, Quinn. You're coming with me."

"Don't make me cry. I still have makeup on."

He chuckled, and leaned in to kiss her nose. "You would be beautiful even if there were black streaks running down your face. But I don't want you to cry."

William was reliving some of his memories of laughing with Quinn as he walked down the hall to his room. One in particular…the memory of their first kiss in Ellen's basement…actually had him smiling, even though the situation had been very stressful at the time.

"Do you always smile like that when you're coming back from my daughter's room in the middle of the night?" Megan's voice made him nearly jump out of his skin.

"What? No! Megan, it's not like that…" he stammered, blanching.

She raised an eyebrow, but as he finally caught his breath, he realized that she didn't look angry. In fact, she was almost smiling.

"Really, Megan," he said, a little calmer, "I would never disrespect Quinn like that."

"I know," she said. "Or at least I hope I do. I heard the two of you come back up here just a little while ago. What's up with all the late-night secrecy?"

The change in his expression must have been obvious, because hers immediately registered concern. "What, William?"

"Would you like some tea?"

She frowned. "Is that all you do around here? Drink tea in the common room?"

"Twice a day, at least." He chuckled. "It's just what we do. People in your world watch television if they can't sleep, or if they're bored in the afternoon. We don't have television. We have tea."

"The stove's been cold for a long time."

He shrugged, walking into the common room. Once he reached the kitchen area, he opened one of the cabinets, and pulled out his electric kettle. "I used to keep this in my room," he said, as Megan settled herself on one of the stools, "it was sort of my own private thing from Bristlecone. I have trouble sleeping sometimes…or sometimes I'm just up all night working on some research project. But after Thomas told me he found Quinn in here one night, lighting the stove by herself, I moved it in here."

"She's always had dreams that wake her up. Even when she was tiny."

"I know. That's why I didn't want her to have to do all that work and wait half an hour for a cup of tea."

Megan smiled. There was a soft look in her eyes now. "You really love her, don't you?"

"I do." Something about this conversation was causing a thick feeling in the back of his throat. He busied himself getting out two mugs and a container of tea.

"You know, last time I was here…the only other time I was here…there wasn't any electricity."

"That was a project that took my father and Nathaniel a number of cycles. We didn't have it here at the castle until I was about ten. It's still not even close to what you're used to in your world. But most of the homes in the capital city at least have lighting now, and it's slowly spreading to more outlying villages. It will take a long time for us to reach the point of appliances much beyond that, besides the few Nathaniel or I have brought across, anyway. Our light bulbs are made by hand." He chuckled.

"Most of our world doesn't have even what we have here. Once we're at the castle in Philotheum, I suppose I'll have to get up in the middle of the night and build fires for Quinn's tea."

"You do realize that she would probably be offended if she heard you implying that she's not perfectly capable of building a fire herself."

He smiled. So Megan *did* know her daughter. "Good point. I may just have to keep her company while she works."

"Maybe she won't have the dreams anymore."

He sighed, looking into her eyes as he slid a steaming mug across the counter to her. "Maybe. I'm sure she'd appreciate it if she didn't. But my father and my oldest brother both have them, too. I think it may just be a firstborn thing. Did Samuel have them as well?"

"Yes." Megan was quiet for a moment, stirring her tea. "So is all of this really true…Samuel was supposed to be the king, and now that leaves Quinn to be the queen?"

"Yes, that's all true."

"Does that mean you'll be the king?"

"It does."

"Would you be offended if I said I didn't think you were the type?"

He laughed. "No. I think I'd have to say that's awfully accurate for someone who's known me for as short a time as you have."

"I gave you a really terrible first impression of myself, didn't I?"

"Well, to be fair, my *first* impression of you was as just one of the teachers at the school. I thought you seemed nice enough."

"And, knowing what you know now, do you really think I didn't notice you then? That I haven't always? I knew who you were, William. And I had *no* idea why Charlotte and Stephen would be sending you to live in Bristlecone with Nathaniel. Really, I could only think of one reason they'd do something like that."

"You thought they wanted your daughter."

"Was I wrong?"

"They never told me anything about it. I never knew anything about her...other than what I saw at school."

"I know. I know all of it. And I'm trying, for her sake, to understand it. I am sorry for how you saw me behave. I know it wasn't rational; I know I could have handled it better. And I know it's going to take time for you to trust me...the fact that you don't yet, well, in a strange way it actually makes this more bearable. I know I'm leaving her with someone who loves her as much as I do."

"I promise I'll take care of her always."

"Thank you."

"I meant it when I said you can come and visit as often as you want, and for as long as you want."

"Provided there's not still a war going on and I'm not risking being captured... I still don't know what I'm going to tell everyone about where Quinn has gone."

He nodded; this was going to be a complicated topic, especially as neither William nor Nathaniel would be returning either. Nathaniel had decided it was time for him to return permanently to Philotheum as well.

"As close to the truth as you can manage is usually best," he said. "Tell everyone that Nathaniel is actually Quinn's uncle, and she had an opportunity to travel with him."

Megan nodded. "Something like that, I suppose." She stared down at her hands, which were wrapped around her mug, and she sighed. "My husband, Jeff, has been wanting us to be able to move for a long time. He's coming back from Afghanistan soon. He's been offered another contract in Atlanta. It would start almost immediately if he took it, but it would be for three years. We've been arguing over it, really. He wants to take it, and for us to go down there with him. Whatever you think of me keeping Quinn from Nathaniel and your family…I kept my promise. I never tried to take her out of Bristlecone."

William swallowed hard. "It would be unfair of us to ask you to stay close to the gate so we could visit easily."

"Are you going to be close enough to the gate on this side for that to happen, anyway?"

"No. The castle in Philotheum is nearly five days' travel from here."

Megan nodded. "That's what I thought."

"Have you told Quinn about any of this?"

"Not yet. The plan was to try to enjoy as much of the time we have as possible, remember?"

"I recall something like that."

She rolled her eyes, reminding him instantly of Quinn. "I was planning on speaking to her tomorrow, if I can ever find some time alone with her."

"What are you going to tell your husband?"

"The truth. He's my husband. I've never lied to him about who Quinn's father was, or any of this. Not that I'm sure he *believes* all of it, but I did tell him."

William blinked. "You told him? Just like that?"

"Yes. Back when we were first dating, even. He's an engineer, you know. Kind of a geeky guy…he's always read a lot. He might have been more impressed with my story if it had involved dragons, but he still proposed after I'd told him. I wouldn't have married someone I had to keep a secret from."

"You kept it from your daughter."

"Jeff was never completely supportive of that. But she was a child. It was my job to protect her. That's a huge burden, you know, keeping that kind of secret from most people. I'm mad at myself now for dragging Annie and Owen into it. What happens when they go to school after this and tell their friends what they did during their break?"

"I don't think Owen *will* tell anyone. And Annie is still so little that everyone will think she's just telling stories."

"And I'm supposed to support *that*? Let my four-year-old think that people don't believe her when she tells the truth? That, right there, is the weight I never wanted to put on Quinn's shoulders when she was a little girl. Her life would never have been normal. And that would have been my fault."

"It wouldn't have been all your fault, Mom." William and Megan both looked up in surprise to see Quinn standing in the doorway, wrapped in her long robe, her thick auburn hair falling everywhere. William reached into the cabinet below him for another mug as she came to the counter. "Some of it might have been your fault, in a way, but doesn't there come a point where it's just the truth? Where we both have to accept that my life was never going to be normal?"

Megan brushed some of Quinn's hair back from her face. "How about we just both accept that I messed up big time, and I'm sorry? That I'm not perfect, but I love you more than my own life, and all I really ever wanted was for you to be happy and loved."

A Celebration

"ARE YOU NERVOUS?" Linnea asked.

"About getting married? Would you think I was crazy if I told you I'm not?"

"No. I would just take it as one more sign that you're doing the right thing."

"You know, Nay, I really think I am."

"I think you are, too. And for the record…William's not nervous about it either. I already asked."

"Of course you did."

"Well, I should clarify; he's not nervous about the wedding."

"Just about living with me for the rest of his life?"

Linnea snorted, pausing in her copious application of blush to Quinn's cheeks. "Hardly. It's not like he could find anyone else who'd put up with him."

Quinn aimed a half-hearted swipe at her friend, which Linnea easily ducked. "He's a good guy. You'd think you'd be more loyal to your brother."

"I've got lots of brothers. William's not the one I'd marry even if he wasn't my brother. He's too moody. I'm happy he found you, though," she added quickly, seeing Quinn's glare. "He's been less moody with you around, anyway. You're good for him."

"I think he's good for me, too."

"Yeah, you two are made for each other and all of that mushy stuff."

Quinn reached for Linnea's hand. "You're going to find yours, too, Nay."

"I know, I know. Not like you're any help. You could have at least given me enough notice to find a date for your wedding."

"It's a small ceremony and a lunch in the dining room. It's not exactly a date-worthy occasion."

"Well, then I'm going to start hunting now for someone to take to your coronation."

"Let's take it one step at a time."

Linnea sighed. "Close your eyes so I can do your eye shadow. I'm going to miss having William bring me back this kind."

"I'm sure we can figure something out… so, what *is* William nervous about?"

Linnea gave her a meaningful look. Quinn frowned, but then blushed as she understood. "He did *not* tell you he's nervous about that."

"He didn't have to."

This time Quinn's swipe wasn't half-hearted.

"What? You can't tell me you're not nervous, too."

"That is none of your business, Nay."

"Oh, come on. You're my sister now. And this quite definitely falls into sister territory."

"Speaking of sisters, when is Rebecca bringing my mom in here?"

"And she almost sinks the diversion into the ten-point goal, but the goalkeeper manages to bump it back with just the tips of her fingers."

"Seriously, Linnea."

"All right. I'm sorry. I shouldn't joke. I mostly just wanted to make sure you're okay, and that you know you can always talk to me. I'll be a nervous wreck the morning of my wedding, I think."

Quinn cocked her head to the side, trying to organize her response, though she earned an exasperated sigh from Linnea, who was shading her eyebrows with an eyebrow pencil. "I don't know. It's not like that, really. I mean, yeah, I'm sort of nervous… and I'm sure it will probably be worse later…if we ever actually *get* time alone tonight…but… it's William. Maybe if I was marrying someone I didn't really know, or I didn't trust the way I trust him, it would be different. But I'm not. I'm marrying him. It will all work out."

"All right. Now I'm jealous. Why did you let me bring this up again?"

"Um, because I couldn't stop you?"

Linnea set the last of the make-up brushes back on the counter just as there was a knock on the bedroom door. "Can we come in?" Rebecca called, though she was already inside.

Quinn stepped out of the bathroom as they entered…Rebecca leading Megan, and both of them followed by Mia, who had a long, white dress folded over her arm.

The dress had been a special project for Charlotte's personal seamstress and a couple of assistants over the last two days. White wedding dresses weren't a custom here in Eirentheos. She had tried insisting to Charlotte that it wasn't necessary…that she would be happy with something simple in the style of this world, but the queen was adamant about making this as special for Quinn as she could in the limited time she had to put it together.

And she had to admit it was a beautiful dress, exactly what she would have wanted, if she'd had any idea what that would be. It was simple, a perfectly fitted short-sleeved bodice with a delicately scooped neckline that skimmed just under her pendant. The back and sleeves were overlaid with lace, in a way that was pretty, but not over the top, and it had a long, flowing skirt that flared out a little, but wasn't too "poofy".

When they slipped it over her head, and she saw herself in the mirror, she gasped and shivered…she actually looked like a bride.

Megan was dressed already…Rebecca had been taking care of her all morning. "You look beautiful, Mom."

"You do, Megan," Linnea said. "You don't look nearly old enough to be the mother of the bride."

Quinn shot her a look…it didn't seem like a good idea to be bringing up the age thing right now…but Megan, for once, didn't take issue with it. She just smiled. "Thank you, Linnea. Are you going to change so I can see the Maid of Honor dress?"

"Absolutely. It's the only time I'm ever going to get to be one. I plan on enjoying it for as long as possible." Wedding attendants weren't part of the tradition here either, but Linnea and Thomas had jumped at the chance to participate. Linnea, who didn't often get emotional about anything, had actually cried when Quinn explained the role to her.

While Rebecca assisted Linnea with getting her dress on, Megan and Mia turned to Quinn. When Mia started fastening the buttons on the back, Quinn felt warmth flow into her cheeks at the memory of the other night.

"Are you getting excited?" Megan asked. "Or nervous?"

"Both. Even though the ceremony isn't really going to be anything big."

"It really doesn't matter if there are five people or five hundred, sweetheart. The ceremony is never the part that's big."

"I know."

"Your father and I had a very small wedding, you know."

Quinn shook her head. She'd never asked about her parents' wedding. She'd been at her mother's second wedding, been the flower girl, actually. While it hadn't been the kind of huge affair that

Simon's wedding here had been, it had been a big party, with lots of friends, and lots of Jeff's family.

"It was only your father and I, and Nathaniel and Maggie. We had it outside in a little park. We'd asked a friend of Maggie's father, who was a pastor, to perform the ceremony. But he never showed up. Instead, this strange old man came…it startled the heck out of Samuel, who seemed to know him. But he was nice."

"Alvin," Quinn whispered. She didn't know whether to be awed or horrified.

"Yes, that was his name. How did you know that?"

"You'll see him again downstairs. He's marrying me and William."

Megan was silent for several seconds, and then she shook her head. "At this point, I almost feel like I should have seen that coming."

Quinn was calm right up until she found herself alone with Nathaniel in a little room to the side of the ballroom. Then, her palms turned damp, and she could feel her heartbeat in her throat.

For the last two days, Charlotte, Rebecca, and Linnea had been ceaseless in their questions about wedding traditions in Quinn's world. Now, it appeared that they'd taken everything Quinn and Megan had told them, and replicated it as best they could in the ballroom. Although the door was closed to keep the scene a surprise for Quinn, when it had swung open for a few seconds to let her mom and Linnea out, she had caught a glimpse of chairs gathered on two sides of a carpeted aisle, leading up to a white, flower-covered arch, and she could hear the soft music coming from a small radio William had once brought back as a present for his brother Daniel.

"They're an unstoppable force," Nathaniel said, following her gaze.

"It feels like it's too much."

"Which is exactly the opposite of the truth, you know. You're going to be a queen."

She shook her head. "But I'm not yet. Besides, you don't know what's going to happen when I get to Philotheum."

A dark shadow crossed Nathaniel's face. This was the part they weren't talking about…the fact that this could all still go horribly wrong. After everything he'd told them, after they'd based their entire plan on his words, Jonathan had disappeared. Stephen had gone to speak with him the morning after the dinner party, and found his room empty, nothing left behind, as if he'd never been there.

Now, they didn't know what to believe, or what he would do. After hours of discussions and arguments, though, they'd decided that the course of action should be the same…Quinn must travel to Philotheum. If they waited, the fighting was only going to escalate. Tensions in the castle were high as it was…Linnea had been under constant guard ever since Jonathan had disappeared. Ben shadowed her every step if she was outside of the family's private quarters.

Even this wedding ceremony was as far under wraps as they could keep it, with only close family invited, and a few trusted servants assisting with the preparations and work. She knew Charlotte was still hoping they'd be able to have a "proper" ceremony sometime later.

"Well, future queen or not, you are my niece, and this is your wedding, and as such, it could never be as much as you deserve." He blinked hard several times, enough to make her wonder if he was tearing up a little.

"And I know I said this when you asked, Quinn… but being asked to give you away is the greatest honor I've had in my life. This tradition alone is almost enough to make me feel grateful that you grew up in Bristlecone."

Hot moisture pricked at the corners of her eyes, and she swallowed hard, unable to speak right away.

"Of course, I wish that Samuel were here to do it instead, and I know you're probably wishing Jeff was here..."

She shook her head, reaching for his hand, trying to keep her voice steady. "I love you, Uncle Nathaniel."

"I love you too."

Just as he kissed the top of her head, the music changed.

The rest of the preparations for the ceremony were as traditional and simple as they were beautiful. Nathaniel led Quinn behind the guests and toward the short aisle; the chairs were occupied mostly by William's family and the very few members of hers. Despite his ongoing uncertainty about her, Charles and his family sat on the "bride's" side of the aisle, in the row behind Ellen, Henry, Andrew, and Natalie. Quinn could see his daughter, Gianna, the other potential heir, sitting quietly next to her mother, Thea.

She had met the young girl two days ago, and liked her immediately. Gianna had been playing happily with William's sisters and Annie; unaffected by the serious atmosphere that hung over the adults. Whatever hopes or plans Charles may have pinned on his daughter, he hadn't burdened the child with them, and realizing that fact had given Quinn more respect for him.

She didn't have much time to focus on the guests, though. As soon as she reached the entrance of the aisle, she looked up. William was standing beneath the arch wearing a black tuxedo, and the biggest grin she had ever seen. Thomas stood just behind William's shoulder, in traditional Eirenthean formalwear, and Linnea, looking beautiful in her flowing purple dress, was on the other side, leaving a second space in the middle for when Quinn reached the altar.

Behind the arch was Alvin, dressed in a floor-length white robe, his blue eyes sparkling with his smile.

A row of tiny flower girls knelt on purple rugs on either side of the arch. They'd showered the aisle with so many flowers that Quinn's dress stirred up a small storm of white and red rose petals as she walked, causing the sweet fragrance to rise up and waft over everything. Charlotte had originally objected to her youngest daughters participating, saying that Annie should have the honor by herself, but it had been Annie who wouldn't hear of it…she wasn't going to do anything her new friends couldn't do, too.

Annie did stand right at the edge of the arch on Quinn's side, her lacy white dress a perfect contrast to Owen's black tux next to her. For a fraction of a second, as she saw them standing there, she nearly forgot her promise to herself that she wasn't going to think about saying good-bye to them. She was only going to cherish the fact of them being here, celebrating this day with her.

As she and Nathaniel reached the end of the aisle, she looked back up at William. There was elation in his eyes, triumph, even, but also something more. A flicker of sadness, of deep understanding, of not only having seen Quinn's mixed emotions a moment ago, but of being right there with her, his heart right in step with hers. And, *oh* how she loved him right then.

Alvin stepped forward and asked a question of Nathaniel that she didn't hear. She turned and was kissed by her mother, and then by Nathaniel, and then she turned to face William again.

As soon as William took her hands in his, she *knew*…knew in a deeper way than she'd realized, even when she'd said yes, even as they'd planned this event. It was going to be hard to say good-bye to the family and the world she knew. But this was right. This was her home now. William was her family.

She'd heard the wedding vows a hundred times before, but was surprised to discover how much it meant to say them to William, to hear them from him. There were even two rings on Owen's little pillow. William carefully untied the white satin strings and whispered a thank you to the ring bearer before taking Quinn's hand and slipping the band up next to the first one, while Owen beamed up at them proudly. Then she took the second ring, a band of silver inlaid with a gold stripe, and pushed it onto his ring finger.

William's smile took her breath away.

"You may kiss the bride."

There was a low chuckle in the audience at the unfamiliar line, but Quinn didn't care. For a moment, everything disappeared except William, who pulled her into his arms and kissed her…softly, but with an edge of something more, a promise to be fulfilled later.

"Beloved family and friends, may I present to you the eminent couple, Princess Quinn and Prince William Rose." William pulled her hand to his lips as they waved at their families, who were standing now, clapping and cheering.

Thomas and Linnea headed down the aisle first, and then Quinn and William followed, though they didn't make it far before they were swallowed in a sea of hugs, kisses, well-wishes, and even a few tears.

Quinn was dancing with Owen when she felt a tap on her shoulder. "The two of you look like you're having a grand time. Might I join you?"

"Uh, sure," Quinn said, opening their little circle to admit Alvin.

"I've noticed people often use that word, 'sure', when they're anything but. Are you unsure about me, Princess Quinn?"

She didn't know how to begin answering that question, but he didn't wait for an answer, anyway. Instead, he turned his bright gaze on Owen. "What about you, Sir Owen? Are you having a good time at your sister's wedding?"

Owen was staring up at Alvin with the widest eyes she had ever seen, like he was looking at a ghost. After several long seconds, he finally blinked. "I didn't think you were real," he said.

A cold, creeping sensation crawled down Quinn's spine.

Alvin smiled indulgently. "Of course I'm real. I've always been real."

"You were in my dreams."

As the first wave of the creeping cold settled at the base of Quinn's back, a second one began at her neck. She stared up at Alvin.

"Close your mouth, Princess. You'll have half the people in this room intruding on our conversation if you keep looking at me like Owen said I'd tried to *eat* him in his sleep, rather than merely visiting him, the way I have with you. Surely you didn't think you were the only one."

"But Owen is not even from this world!"

"Neither are you."

"You know what I mean."

"I understand your words, yes, but I don't see what it has to do with anything. You must have realized by now that I am not tied to one world or the other."

"I don't even know what to say to that."

"It's not necessary for you to say anything, dear one. I was merely stating a fact I assumed you already knew. But perhaps you didn't. I have been wrong before."

Quinn wasn't so sure he had. There was a part of her, in the back of her mind, that knew he was right…she had realized that. She had just never thought he would have communicated with Owen in *his* dreams as well. Or maybe she had... This was too much to think about right now.

"Well, then, since you seem to know so much about traveling between the worlds, perhaps you can tell me if my family will be able to cross back over tonight. Or did Jonathan really manage to destroy the bridge with his fire?" Her tone wasn't exactly polite, but she didn't care.

The issue of whether her Mom and Owen and Annie would even be able to return home had been haunting all of them, though they'd avoided speaking about it. Stephen had said there was no sense worrying about it until they went to see it and try it for themselves. The gate was scheduled to open again at sunset.

There was a small part of Quinn that knew she hadn't allowed herself to think about it because she was *hoping* the gate wouldn't be open, or that they would still be unable to access it because of the fire. She wasn't ready for her family to leave tonight.

Megan hadn't been sure she wanted to try the bridge on this opening, but with the heightened danger, and the fact that Quinn and William would be leaving for Philotheum anyway, they'd all agreed that if her family *could* get home today, then they should.

"The bridge still stands, Princess. As the guards King Stephen has sent to check on it will tell you later this afternoon. In any case, the operation of the gate is not terribly dependent on whether the bridge is intact, as the gate in your world would tend to indicate."

"What *is* it dependent on, then?"

"Magnetism, mostly."

"Excuse me?"

"Magnets. Now, I know you've heard of those."

"I don't know what they have to do with the gate."

"Did you think the gate was magic?"

She opened her mouth and closed it again. Truthfully, she sort of had thought that.

"Well, it isn't magic. Simple science, really. At certain times, these two worlds are lined up in just such a way that two powerful magnets, one on each side, can weaken the magnetic field between them, and allow someone to pass through."

"And someone just figured that out?" William had come to stand with them. He put his arm around Quinn's waist, and then his other hand on Owen's shoulder.

Quinn looked around the room. Everyone else was engaged in conversations. Nobody looked the least bit interested in their little group…or if they were, they were politely ignoring them.

"Yes, of course someone 'just figured it out'. The difficulty level is somewhere below using magnets in electrical currents. Finding a location where it would work was another story. The first passage had to be in a place where there was both a place where the fields aligned and there was already a naturally occurring magnet on the other side. Humans are inventive, though. They managed it. Some by accident, even." Alvin chuckled, his eyes lighting up.

"The *first* passage? So there is more than one?"

"Yes. Most of them are now long forgotten. And several of those who discovered this world by accident never realized what they'd done. Or that it would even have been possible to go back. After a while, this was simply where their lives were. They settled in, had children, lived, died, and that was it."

"So Quinn's world existed first."

"Was inhabitedby humans first, yes. This world has only had people for a thousand cycles or so…perhaps a bit longer; it's been awhile since I did the math…but it's quite young in that way compared to the world where Quinn was raised."

William nodded. "But the gate we use…that one wasn't an accident, was it?"

"No. That one was built on purpose. Not everyone traveled here by accident, and not everyone forgot. The gate you've been using was built by a young man who was very curious and scientific-minded…rather like you, Prince William. He studied how a naturally occurring gate worked, and thought he had it figured out. He dug up a piece of the magnetic rock under one of the gates, and then traveled to a place where he predicted another weak spot…a place in the Colorado mountains that is now known as Bristlecone, and he buried the rock there. Planted it might be a more appropriate term. Planted two pinecones with it; I never learned why.

"He was right, though. It worked."

"Why have you never told anyone this?"

Alvin smiled kindly. "I'm not much in the habit of telling people things they don't need to know. What you figure out on your own is yours to do with as you wish, but most of the hidden knowledge in this…in any…world is only meant to be understood by those who do the work to discover it."

"Then why are you telling us this now?" Quinn asked. "What difference does it make…why do we 'need to know'?"

"Now, the answer to *that* question, should you truly desire it, is for you to obtain, Princess."

"There must be a reason, Alvin. Something you want me to do with this information."

"All I've done is told you a story, Princess. As for what you do with it…that choice is yours. In any case, I believe I've shared with you enough that you can set aside your fears that your family will be unable to return home, and you can enjoy your wedding day. My heart is overflowing with joy that the two of you have found each other, and I am looking forward to many, many cycles of watching your relationship bloom. Thank you, Prince and Princess, for allowing me to share your precious day.

"Now, Sir Owen, it has truly been a pleasure meeting you in person. I can only hope we have the opportunity to do it again sometime."

Owen nodded, blinking up at Alvin with a rather serious expression. "Then what are the bridges for?"

Alvin smiled. "Keeping your feet out of the water." He winked as he squeezed Owen's shoulder, then took Quinn's hand in his and kissed the back of it before turning and walking away. When she looked for him again, only a few minutes later, he was nowhere to be found.

The wedding celebration lasted much of the afternoon, though the dancing tapered off as the crowd grew smaller. Charles and his family were the first to drift back to their quarters, followed by Ellen and

Henry. Quinn noticed that Maxwell and his girlfriend, Catherine, disappeared early on, too.

Eventually it was mostly only Quinn's and William's immediate families sitting around small tables and chatting, nibbling at the buffet, and playing games. Jacob and Essie, the only cousins who had traveled in for the ceremony, had settled in for the duration. Essie, newly pregnant, had discovered a new camaraderie with new moms Rebecca and Natalie. The three of them were huddled around a table, babies Quinn and Aiden asleep in arms.

As she watched, Simon's wife, Evelyn, drifted by and was immediately pulled in to the group. She had been suspecting that Evelyn was already expecting as well.

Simon had already found Jacob, Andrew, and Howard in another corner, talking and laughing. Simon had his little sister Hannah in his arms, and kept blowing bubbles on her tummy. Quinn imagined that these young families would be spending a lot of time together in the future.

The dance floor had been confiscated by the children, who were running back and forth, sliding around on the smooth marble, and making up their own dances. Thomas and Mia had spent a lot of time over there with them, and William had snuck in a dance or two with Annie and his little sisters, but most of the "grownups" were more interested in quieter activities.

There was an unspoken feeling in the atmosphere of the ballroom, a sense that they were all trying to soak up as much of this time together as they could, savoring the way things were right this minute, before everything changed.

The feeling in the room was bittersweet, full of love and celebration, but also a little melancholy. Quinn wasn't the only one about to permanently leave her home. Even the weather seemed to understand their mood. Shortly after the ceremony, dark gray clouds had filled the skies outside. Soon, enormous raindrops had begun splattering against the floor-to-ceiling windows and the glass doors that led to the patio, creating a symphony that overpowered the music inside.

Now, great puddles had formed on the stones outside, and the giant fountain in the middle of the patio was overflowing, each tier pouring down a bigger waterfall than the last. Every few minutes, distant thunder would rumble through the sky, but the lightning remained high in the clouds.

When Emma came and tugged on William's arm for "just *one* more round of Hokey Pokey" Quinn, who had already reached her limit on the game, drifted to the door and stood there watching the rain for several minutes.

It struck her then, as she watched both the rain, and the people behind her from their reflections in the glass, that someday, when she discovered that she was carrying William's child, they'd be far away in Philotheum, away from both of their families. No Rebecca or Evelyn to turn to for advice. No Linnea to giggle with at night.

"How can something so beautiful be so gloomy at the same time?"

She turned to see Thomas standing right behind her.

"I was just thinking that. It looks so sad out there right now, but it's such good news that it's finally raining."

"Hopefully it will rain long enough to finally put the fire all the way out," he said. "We need the water. Sorry that it had to be on your wedding day, though."

"I don't know. It seems kind of... fitting somehow. We're inside, anyway. Hopefully it will let up later...when it's time for Marcus and Ben to take my family to the bridge."

He reached for her shoulder, squeezing it gently, and leaned in to kiss her on the forehead. "I don't think I've had the chance yet to tell you how beautiful you look today. Nearly brought tears to my eyes when I saw you. And the look on William's face..."

"Where would I be without your flattery, Thomas?"

"Flattery? Did you not look in a mirror before you came down here, sweet sister?"

She rolled her eyes. "I did look in a mirror, and it's still flattery. But I like the sound of the word sister."

"Me too, sweetheart." He grabbed her and pulled her into a tight hug. "I like it a whole lot."

"I'm going to miss you."

He shrugged. "You're not going that far. And I'm not that easy to get rid of. Dance with me?"

"To the Hokey Pokey on repeat?"

He chuckled. "Why not? I'm only going to get one chance to dance with my new sister on her wedding day. I don't care what song it is…in fact, I wouldn't care if there was no music at all." He didn't wait for a response before taking her hand and holding it up to twirl her around.

"Hey, get your own girl," William said, several minutes later when the song had finally changed.

"I was only keeping her safe for your return," Thomas said, grinning. "Now that you're back, she's all yours." He leaned down and kissed her forehead again, and then gave her another hug before spinning her back to William's waiting arms. "I don't think I could be any happier for you two."

After several happy hours that Quinn and William spent mostly with Megan, alternating Annie and Owen between their laps, it was finally time to bring things to a close. Most of the dishes had been cleared from the long buffet table when Stephen rang a spoon against his glass, and offered one more congratulatory toast to Quinn and William. Then he and Charlotte walked across the room and hugged them both.

"It's so wonderful to welcome you to our family officially, Quinn."

"Thank you, Stephen. It means a lot to me to hear you say that."

"I mean every word."

Charlotte had tears in her eyes as she kissed Quinn on the cheek.

"Thank you for everything, Charlotte," Quinn whispered. "It was a beautiful day."

"It wasn't nearly as much as I wanted for the two of you."

"But it was more than enough, Mother. We both appreciate it more than you could ever know."

And then, at last, it was time for the part they'd been dreading. Quinn and William made their way to a secluded back hallway. Megan, Owen, and Annie, had changed from their fancy outfits into sturdy, rain-proof clothing. The few items they'd brought, and the many more they'd been gifted, had already been carried out to the saddlebags by Ben and Marcus, who would be accompanying them to the gate.

There wasn't anything to say; they'd said everything they could over the last couple of days. More words now would only make this harder. They just held each other tightly for as long as they could. William kept his hand on Quinn's shoulder as they both knelt down in front of Annie to give her the necklace they'd had made for her, a replica of the pendants she and William wore, only Annie's was half silver and half gold, and bore the symbol that connected their two kingdoms, the one that matched their Friends of Philip tattoos. On the back of her pendant were the words, *Love you forever Princess Annie.*

Owen's gift had been more practical, and was already tucked in a watertight bag and packed away in one of the saddlebags. It was a set of Eirenthean schoolbooks, a bit advanced for his age, but appropriate for Owen, that he had become obsessed with during his days in the castle. William had slipped a couple of his personal books in there as well, though Quinn didn't know what those ones were.

She'd also written each of them, Owen, Annie, and her mother, long letters, filled with her favorite memories of each of them, and telling them how much she loved them. Linnea had helped her bind each one into a little book, and Thomas and William had worked with her to stamp designs on soft sheets of leather that they'd then sewn over the pages.

All too soon, Ben appeared in the corridor behind them. He nodded, and after one last hug, Megan took Annie's and Owen's hands and they followed him outside.

"There's a reason," Linnea said, appearing in the hallway behind them, "that it's traditional for the married couple to leave the building and *go somewhere else*, at a predetermined time."

"So they can get away from their annoying little sisters?"

"Funny, Will. Are you really planning on staying down here the whole night? I know it's sad, but it isn't like you're never going to see them again, and people do actually leave their families when they get married."

"You're right, Linnea," Quinn said, swallowing back the last of the thick feeling in her throat, and blinking several times. "This is what we planned on."

"Good." Linnea smiled brightly, though it didn't reach *all* the way to her eyes, and Quinn had never appreciated her friend quite so much as she did now. As hard as this was, it was done now, her family was gone, and there were other things she needed to focus on…starting with her first night with William as her… she almost couldn't even think the word yet…*husband.*

"Let's go." Without waiting for a response, Linnea turned and headed back up the hallway.

William smiled, and she realized his cheeks were a little pink, too. When he took her hand, a little electric current raced up her arm, and it took her a second to catch her breath.

She smiled shyly back up at him, and he bent down to kiss her cheek before they followed Linnea.

"Where *are* we going, anyway?" Quinn asked when they reached the main staircase, suddenly thinking about how awkward it would be to head back to one of their bedrooms, where they'd be surrounded by his family.

Linnea's answering smile was a little smug. "Just follow me."

She led them up the stairs, but didn't turn at the entrance to the family's quarters. Instead, she headed for a different hallway, where there were guest suites for visiting dignitaries. Unfamiliar warmth blossomed underneath the surface of Quinn's skin, and she heard William begin to breathe just a little faster.

Linnea stopped just outside the door of a room Quinn had never been inside, and turned to them.

"Congratulations, both of you. I love you so much." She hugged William tightly, before turning to Quinn. "Do you need anything before I go?" she whispered. "Help with this?" She fingered the soft material of Quinn's gown.

The soft warmth that had been slowly building burst suddenly into a roaring flame. "I… I think I can manage," she stuttered, knowing her cheeks were probably shining brightly enough to guide a plane in for a landing.

Linnea, to her credit, only nodded and hugged her before turning and disappearing down the hall.

She'd barely turned the corner when William let out a giant snicker. A second later, they were both laughing so hard that tears were running down their cheeks and Quinn was gasping for air. He tried to turn the knob to let them into the room, but his laughter shook him so badly that it took several attempts before he finally got it open. Once he did, they both practically fell into the room; William landed against the back of the door as he closed it, his chest still heaving.

"Aren't you supposed… to carry… me across the threshold?" Quinn asked when she'd finally calmed enough to sort of talk.

William raised an eyebrow. "Aren't I supposed to *what?*"

"Carry me through the door."

"Why? Is that a tradition in your world?"

"You never watched any romantic movies while you were there?"

"No. You're not really serious, are you?"

She nodded.

William eyed the door dubiously. "I am not going back out there. What if somebody comes down the hall?"

Her eyes widened.

"If it's really important to you, I could like, pick you up and throw you on the couch or something."

That was all it took to start the giggles going again.

William reached to pull her into his arms, and she held her head against his chest, listening to the glorious, deep sound that kept time with her own. Slowly, they sobered, and she became aware of another sound in his chest…the heavy, rapid pounding of his heart. Her mood changed instantly.

William must have felt the shift, must have been right there with her, because he reached down with his finger and tipped her chin up until her lips met his. The kiss started out gentle and sweet, but it quickly turned into something more, something deeper. Instinctively, her hands went up to help him shrug out of the jacket of his tuxedo, and as soon as his hands were free, they reached around to the top button of her dress.

AN INTERRUPTION

QUINN WOKE WITH A start; her heart racing though she wasn't sure why. The room was quiet and dark. She'd fallen asleep with her head on William's chest; his breaths were as deep and even as hers were shallow and erratic. As soon as she lifted her head to sit up, though, he stirred, and his eyes opened.

"Hey, beautiful," he said, pulling himself up next to her. His hand was warm on her back as he leaned in to kiss her temple. She could almost hear him frown as he registered the irregular pattern of her breathing. "What's wrong? Why are you awake?"

"I don't know. I just woke up like this, feeling like something's wrong. But nothing is."

"Everything's fine, love." He ran the back of his finger down the side of her face and then he kissed her, first on her forehead, then her cheek, and finally moving to her lips, planting a soft kiss there before pulling back to look at her again. "Better than fine, I'd say."

She blushed, remembering the night before, how strange it had been as they'd walked into the bedroom together, her heart beating like a hummingbird at the sight of the large bed and the huge vases of flowers on the night tables on either side.

They'd both stopped at the same time, with the sudden realization that this was real, they'd actually gotten married…and neither one of them knew what they were doing.

She'd been standing there in her long slip, him still in his pants, with his dress shirt mostly unbuttoned, both of them blushing and awkward. Then they'd started giggling again.

His thumb traced the warm spot on her cheek now, and, though surely he couldn't see it in the dark room, he kissed it again, while she put her arms around his neck.

He kissed her lips again, running his hand down her face, to her shoulder and then to her back, but his hand stopped halfway down, and he pulled back a little. "Your heart is going a million miles a minute, Quinn. And I don't think it's from me."

She sighed. "No, it isn't. I'm sorry. I don't know what's going on. I just feel really weird. Anxious."

He moved away from her slightly, and a second later she heard a soft click, which was immediately followed by the room filling with blinding light. In truth, it was only a soft bedside lamp, but for a few tense seconds, it felt like he'd turned on the sun. "Sorry."

"S'okay." She blinked, and put her hand over her eyes. He stretched his hand toward her forehead, even though his lips had just been there.

"I'm not sick, Will. It was probably just a nightmare that I don't remember or something."

"It's okay. Whatever it was, I'm here." His fingers still went searching for the pulse at her wrist, and she rolled her eyes.

"Really, I'm fine." She pulled his hand away from her wrist, though she held on to it. "I promise." He wrapped his other arm around her and pulled her against his chest, stroking her back for a long time. Finally, her heart rate slowed, and she relaxed against him, feeling more normal.

"Do you want to try to go back to sleep?" he asked, his breath warm against her temple.

She shook her head. "I'm wide awake now. What time is it?"

He glanced around the room. The bedroom of the guest suite they were in was well-appointed, from the fresh flowers on the bedside tables, and the candles in crystal holders on the mantel, but there was no clock in here. "Dark? Unless those are the best curtains in the castle."

"Do *you* want to go back to sleep?"

He shook his head. "Are you hungry?"

Sometime late in the evening, when they'd finally stopped to check out the rest of their surroundings, William had discovered a note that Thomas had slipped under the door of the sitting room, letting them know that Ben and Marcus had returned, and Quinn's family was safely through the gate. It had also mentioned that there was dinner outside the door when they wanted it.

He'd opened the door for long enough to bring in the large silver tray filled with plates of sandwiches and fruit on a bed of ice.

Much care had been taken in the preparation of this little suite for them…for the only honeymoon they were likely to get anytime soon. The armoire had been stocked with several changes of clothes for each of them, and the bathroom shelves held all of their personal items. They'd even found bathrobes for each of them hanging on hooks behind the door.

It had made Quinn feel a little strange to see all of their things side-by-side like that, sharing space…a heady mixture of excitement and nervousness that this was real. They were actually married. And now he was here, with her, in bed.

"Quinn? Do you want some food?"

In truth, she *was* a little hungry, but it wasn't really food that she wanted right now. She almost told him what she did want, but discovered quickly that she was still a little too shy to come out and say something like that. So instead, she nodded.

William took her hand to help her off the bed, but before he led her out to the sitting room, he leaned in close to her ear. "We'll get better at this," he said, giving her the peculiar sensation that he'd read her thoughts. "We have the rest of our lives." And the way he smiled at her right then told her that he hadn't read her thoughts at all…he was having the same ones.

It was a long time before they made it to the sitting room.

Later, William was standing at the little buffet table, putting more glasberries on Quinn's plate when there was a sudden loud pounding on the door. Quinn leapt from the couch like she'd been shocked, and William dropped the plate, shattering it, sending shards of glass and green berries everywhere.

He looked at Quinn, alarm on his face. "Who is it?" he called.

"It's Thomas. I'm sorry, but can you open the door?"

William glanced down at himself, and then at Quinn…checking to make sure they were both covered, she supposed…before crossing the room in three quick steps and turning the lock…the feature in this room they'd both been the most impressed with.

"What's going on Thomas?" he asked.

"Linnea isn't in here, is she?"

"What? No. Why would she be?"

Even as William spoke, Quinn's insides quickened and froze into hard, black ice. "How long has she been missing?"

Thomas entered the room, and she noted immediately that he was dressed in regular clothes, but his hair was messy, and still bore traces of whatever he'd used to style it for the ceremony yesterday. He hadn't showered. And from the looks of the dark circles under his eyes and his sunken in cheeks, he hadn't slept, either.

"I don't know," he said, running his hand through his hair…that was what had mussed it up so badly. "Mother noticed it late last night when she went to say goodnight to her. I thought she'd gone to bed early or something. I can't even remember the last time I saw her. Not since the ceremony, I don't think."

"You didn't see her after she walked us up here?"

"No. And as far as we can tell, nobody else has, either."

The sitting room did have a clock on the mantel. Quinn saw William look at it at the same time she did. "It's almost six in the morning!" he nearly shouted. "And you're just telling us now?"

"Not…uh…*disturbing* the two of you was sort of a priority," Thomas said. "They didn't want me to come in here even now. Mother is highly distraught about taking the only peaceful night it looks like you might get, but I knew you'd be even more upset if I waited any longer."

"All right. We'll get dressed and meet you…"

"In Father's office. The little ones are still sleeping. We don't want them to know yet."

William nodded.

"I'm really sorry for bothering you."

"We'd rather know, Thomas," Quinn said, suddenly more than a little freaked out about waking up the way she had a little while ago. What did it mean?

"You okay?" William asked, after he closed the door behind Thomas and turned back to her.

"No." Her hands were shaking furiously, and she wasn't sure that she wasn't going to throw up. "Are you?"

"No."

William walked into the bedroom and pulled open the armoire, throwing clothes toward the bed without really looking at them, while Quinn headed for the bathroom. "Wasn't Ben supposed to be guarding her?" she asked.

"I'm guessing she disappeared while he and Marcus were going to the gate with your family," he said. "That was just a seriously overprotective precaution, anyway. She was *inside* the castle, for the love of roses. There's not somewhere *safer.*"

Quinn knew he was right. She also knew that the other questions that were floating around her brain, like were they *sure* they'd searched everywhere in the castle, were ridiculous. They'd never have come to William and Quinn if they weren't sure this was really an emergency.

In under five minutes, they were both dressed and back in the sitting room. William paused before he opened the door. "I'm sorry," he said. "This is not how I imagined our wedding night."

"I think at this point, it would be a little disingenuous to be surprised," Quinn said, wrapping her arms around his waist. "In any case… I thought the first part was pretty good."

"Just pretty good?" he asked, mock chagrin on his face.

"Hmm… maybe more like earth-shattering?"

He cocked his head to the side, looking up thoughtfully. "I can live with earth-shattering. Even if we're not technically on Earth."

"Fine, Deusterros-shattering, then," she said, trying out the name she'd only recently learned, after she'd realized that Eirentheos and Philotheum didn't make up the whole of this world.

He grinned and leaned down to kiss her one more time.

Quinn's transformation was complete before they even reached his father's office. Upstairs, with him, she'd been so… soft, somehow, blushing and uncertain… so warm, and so beautiful.

Now, she was still beautiful, of course, but there was nothing soft about her at all. As they'd walked…*dashed*…through the corridors, she had pulled her hair up behind her, fastening it with an elastic band she must have slipped on her wrist while she was putting on the linen pants and shirt, and the thick, cream-colored sweater. The drafty hallways were a little chilly this morning; he wondered if it was still raining.

The crowd in his father's office was small and distressed. His mother and father were there, along with Simon, Thomas, Marcus,

Ben and Nathaniel. William was shocked at how distraught Ben looked; he was nearly tempted to cross the room and give the guard…usually such a stoic…a hug.

"I'm so sorry!" Charlotte burst out, as soon as they entered the room. "I *told* him not to go and bother you yet."

"It's all right, Charlotte," Quinn said. "We would rather know."

"Did he wake you?"

His father shot his mother a look that he didn't quite understand, until a second later when Quinn stumbled over the answer. "Uh, no. We were... awake."

Heat flashed all the way to his toes, and he saw that pink had already spread down Quinn's skin.

Either nobody else in the room caught the innuendo, or they were all polite enough to ignore it.

Quinn cleared her throat. "So Linnea has been missing possibly since late yesterday afternoon, right after the wedding."

"Yes."

"So, clearly, someone took her."

"We know there's no way she would have left to go anywhere on her own."

William nodded. Linnea had a defiant streak, and he knew she occasionally felt a little claustrophobic about the restrictions that she'd been living under recently, but he remembered the haunted look she'd carried when Thomas was missing. No, Linnea would never do that to them. Not even for a few hours. She would have at least told Thomas if she was sneaking off somewhere.

"And the suspects are pretty much everyone who's not in this room."

"We can probably clear the children," Thomas said, without a trace of humor.

"I don't have any reason to suspect any of the guards who are Friends of Philip, all of whom were immediately accounted for and who are now conducting searches of the castle and the grounds, and questioning the other guards who were on duty," Stephen said. "All of our visitors from Philotheum were also found in their rooms asleep when we began the search. They seem as concerned and upset as we are."

"Does Tolliver ever come up with something more inventive than kidnapping and fires?"

William put his hand on her arm, stroking it softly with his thumb. "Do armies in your world ever get tired of bombs and guns? Fighting is about being effective, not creative."

"In any case, we've always known that Linnea was who Tolliver was really after, if he could somehow get her across the border and to the castle… I will be deploying additional troops to the border today," Stephen said. "For the time being, we will hold off on actually sending troops in to Philotheum, but if I get any indication that Linnea has crossed the border, then that will change."

William swallowed hard.

"So what can we do?" Quinn asked. "How do we start searching for Linnea?"

"At first light, we will attempt to locate Zylia and send her searching so that we can follow. But they may have a lead of over twelve hours on us and with the rain…"

"What can *I* do?" Her voice was a little more forceful this time, her hands clenching and unclenching repeatedly.

"You can do nothing Quinn. At least nothing to directly search for Linnea. In a few hours, you will begin your journey to Philotheum. You're our best hope for ending this thing. Ellen and Charles are already packing. Henry is going with you, but Thea and her children will be staying with us."

Marcus stepped forward from his position behind Stephen's desk. "Ben and I will be also traveling with you. As we've discussed before, we need to be able to protect you, but still keep our group as small as possible to avoid notice. We also need to leave some trustworthy guards here at the castle. As tonight's events have more than demonstrated, we can't take for granted our trust of *anyone*."

Quinn's gaze swung back to Stephen. "You're sending your two most trusted guards with *me*, when you need them here…when they could be searching for Linnea?"

His father took a step toward her. "Marcus is not *my* guard, Quinn. He never has been."

She frowned.

Marcus cleared his throat. "Since the beginning, Princess, my family has held a special position. It is a task that belonged to my father, and to his father before him. We guard the heir to the Philothean throne. My son and I intend to travel with you…to restore our family's honor, to return the new heir to her rightful place. My father never got over losing Samuel…he was eventually hung for treason when he dared to accuse Hector of the truth, of plotting to kill your father. As for me, I held out hope always that I would live to see you, to guard you, for my family to continue serving yours, as it was meant to be. Will you allow us the honor?"

Marcus and Ben both knelt in front of her then. The single tear that fell down her cheek was the only break in Quinn's composure during that meeting.

Rain

"REMIND ME NEVER TO go that long without riding, and then try something like this again," William said, coming up to where Quinn was leaning against a tree.

"I don't remember planning it that way this time," she reminded him.

"Are you holding up okay?" He glanced down toward her leg, which was a lot better after a week of healing, but he had only just taken out her stitches before they left.

"I'm fine."

"Liar."

"There's not really another option, is there? Besides, I spent all that time throwing knives and stuff in the practice arena. I'm in better shape for this than you are." She pushed playfully at his chest.

He raised an eyebrow as he captured her hand, pushing it out of the way so that he could move in close to her. "Is that right? I seem to remember keeping up some form of exercise lately..."

She giggled as he leaned in to kiss her, and she stretched her arms up around his neck, but then she remembered why they were out here, and her laughter stopped abruptly.

"What, love?"

"It just feels... wrong to be playing and smiling about anything when Linnea's missing."

He sighed. "I know it does."

"What if she's hurt or something?"

William closed his eyes. "We can't think like that, Quinn. Not that I'm not thinking the same things, but... she's probably safe, wherever she is. Unhappy, I'm sure, but Tolliver wants her so he can marry her. Whoever took her has to be under orders not to harm her."

"It feels so wrong to be leaving instead of searching for her."

"I know." He pulled her tight against his chest. "But this is the best thing we can do for her. We need to get to Philotheum, and see if we can get all of this sorted out, and then he won't *need* her."

"And what if we get there and Queen Sophia doesn't agree? What if she turns around and has us killed or something?"

"I'm sure we'll have a plan by the time we get there that doesn't have us just walking to our deaths." He tried to sound confident. "And you do realize, don't you, that Queen Sophia is your grandmother. That has to mean something."

"She has no way of knowing that, Will."

"Maybe not, but we can't think like that, Quinn. You have the exact same color hair she does. And from what I hear, you look very much like your father. Maybe she'll recognize you." *No*, she hadn't known that. She'd known her hair color was the same as her father's, but she had no idea that had come from his mother. She wondered who William had been talking to about her looking like her father. Those conversations hadn't included her.

"Yeah, maybe it will just be that easy," she said, placating him because she really didn't want to think too much about that right now.

"Do you want some dry clothes?" he asked, after a few minutes, running his hand against the damp material of her shirt.

"I was getting there." The first couple of hours they'd traveled away from the castle, it had still been drizzling. The slick riding coat she'd been wearing hadn't been enough to keep out all of the moisture.

About an hour ago, the sun had finally peeked through the heavy gray clouds, slowly warming them, though there was still a crisp fall chill in the air. They'd stopped now, in the secluded safety of a thickly wooded area, to rest and let the horses drink.

"Will! Quinn!" Nathaniel called from down by the river.

"Come on," William said, taking her hand. They hurried down to where the small group was huddling on a circle of rocks.

Ben handed each of them a sandwich before they sat down, and Quinn noted that he looked terrible. There were black circles under his eyes, and his complexion was ashen. She wanted to tell him that it wasn't his fault that nobody blamed him, but she had a feeling that he didn't want to hear it. Yesterday, at the wedding, Ben had asked Linnea to dance with him twice, and another time she'd seen him carrying two drinks toward a table far to the side of where most of the socializing was happening.

She was afraid his devastation now ran far deeper than feeling he'd failed in his duties, and she felt overwhelmingly guilty that Ben was here now, guarding her, rather than searching for Linnea.

"Marcus and I have been discussing the best plan for our route today. We'll rest for a little while longer here, and give everything a chance to dry out and warm up," Nathaniel said, nodding toward a small fire someone had built on the riverbank. "Then we're thinking we can make it to Cloud Valley before dinnertime."

"Are we actually going to stay in Cloud Valley? Is it safe if Eli knows?"

"Eli is a member of the Friends of Philip."

"What? Since when?"

"For a long time now," Marcus said. "Eli's father was one of my closest friends, and a personal guard of King Jonathan's."

"So he's from Philotheum?"

Nathaniel nodded. "Eli's clinic is one of the places we've been sending refugees as we find them. Cloud Valley is secluded and quiet; many people don't even know the town exists. The people there are loyal to our history and the united crowns. It's been a safe haven."

"Does Eli know who you are?"

"Yes. He is one of the few people who do. He doesn't know who you are, though I think we need to tell him. We're going to need the support of more Friends of Philip to get to that castle."

"How are we going to get across the border?" That task had been difficult the last time they'd done it, before they were at full-blown war.

"It's a good question," Marcus said. "But it's not one we're facing today. It's still another day and a half of solid traveling before we reach the place where we're going to try."

Quinn nodded; she knew they were taking a very long way around. The capitol city of Philotheum was in nearly the opposite direction from the way they'd been traveling. But if they'd tried to travel straight there…taken the route they'd gone the last time they'd made a journey like this…they would have had to go straight through the center of the fighting, and eventually they'd have crossed main thoroughfares in Philotheum.

"Okay, then," she said. "Cloud Valley by nightfall."

For a little while after their break, the weather was perfect for traveling. Sunny, but not hot, and the overnight moisture had brought out the vibrant colors in everything. This was William's favorite time of year. A few leaves had started changing from green to yellow, but only enough to give a splash of color to the landscape; most of the leaves still clung firmly to their branches.

But the best part of many of the trees was the fruit. The smell of ripe apples, pylinas, and peaches permeated the air as the sun evaporated the rainwater on the heavy limbs of the fruit trees. In many places, the crop was so plentiful that overripe fruit covered the ground below, and the birds, small animals, and honeybees were feasting.

"What are you thinking about?" Quinn asked, letting Dusk fall back a bit so she was even with him.

"Nothing, really. Why?"

"I don't know. You just had this look on your face, like you were thinking about something good and I could use a little good right now."

"Oh" He smiled. Determined to be strong for Quinn, and not let his own anxiety get the better of him, he had been forcing himself to pay attention to the scenery and focus his mind on pleasant thoughts. It had worked, he guessed. He'd lapsed into daydreaming when she caught him. "I was thinking about you, actually. About us."

"What about us?"

"About how different this trip would be if this was a real honeymoon. If we were out here enjoying the fall, just us."

"Hmm..." She looked around. "I could get behind an idea like that. What would we do?"

He smiled, taking note of the playful tone in her voice. "We could pack a picnic, maybe race the horses on the way out to the middle of nowhere, pick all the fruit we wanted, go for a swim, set up a blanket under a tree…"

She closed her eyes, trusting completely in her control over and relationship with Dusk as she allowed herself a moment inside his daydream. Even dressed in plain, rugged traveling clothes, with her hair braided tightly and tucked under a heavy, wide-brimmed hat, she took his breath away. And it struck him, then, that she was his *wife*. He was going to be able to catch glimpses of her like this for the rest of his life.

An irritated sound from behind them was an instant and unwelcome reminder that he and Quinn weren't alone at all. William's stomach sank as Charles' horse suddenly sped and went around them, not slowing again until Charles was well ahead of the group.

Quinn's eyes were open now, and they widened as she watched. "What was *that* about?"

He shrugged. "I wish I knew what his problem was."

She glanced around them. Most of the group was ahead of them, and she slowed a little, falling further back from Nathaniel. William matched her pace. Only Ben was behind them, and he was too far to hear anything they were saying.

"Do you think it's really that he wants his daughter to be the queen?"

"I don't know. I asked Nathaniel about it the other night, after that meeting where Charles was so… whatever he was. But Nathaniel doesn't think that's what it is. I guess Charles has always been very protective of his family, and he wasn't happy about bringing Gianna to the castle, even."

Just then, something wet landed on his hand. He looked down, frowning. There was a big drop of water on the back of his hand. He looked up to see where it had come from, and another one hit his cheek.

"It's raining," Quinn said, and they both looked up at the sky.

Where only moments before, the sky had been clear and blue, it was now filling with thick, gray clouds. As they watched, the sun disappeared, and the air around them grew cool. Quinn grabbed for her hat as a sudden breeze nearly blew it off.

A few seconds later, the scattered drops multiplied, and the rain began in earnest. Within five minutes, it was coming down so hard that William could barely see Quinn, though she was only a few feet away from him. Ahead of them, Marcus rode off the trail into a thick stand of trees. Everyone quickly followed.

Even the thick foliage offered little protection from the downpour as Marcus led them to the highest ground he could find. As soon as they found a place where most of the water was running downhill, rather than collecting, the men went to work. Within moments, they'd erected one tent.

"Get inside, Princess Quinn!" Ben shouted, using his body to shield the entrance from the downpour as he held the flap open for her.

She shook her head. "How can I help?"

Ben looked stricken. "Please, Quinn." William's heart pounded as he noted that Ben was too upset to bother with the formalities.

Nathaniel's voice was suddenly right in William's ear. "Take care of that," he said. "Get her in there. She doesn't understand, and you have got to help her."

William felt Charles' steely gaze boring into him as he dropped the edge of the second tent they nearly had standing. He crossed the short distance and grabbed Quinn by the elbow, nearly pulling her around Ben and into the tent, both of them landing on the floor. The flap snapped shut, and William could feel the structure vibrate as Ben tied some of the bindings.

"What in the *hell*, Will?" Quinn shouted, jerking her elbow away from him.

"I'm sorry," he said. "But you were about to make Ben have a stroke."

"How?"

"By not getting into the tent."

"Excuse me? I was just trying to help, to work the same as everyone else."

William took a deep breath. "I know you were," he said quietly. "But that's the part you need to understand. You're not the same as everyone else."

"Why? Because I'm a girl?"

"No, Quinn. Because you're the heir to the throne. If this whole adventure goes the way it's supposed to, you're going to be the *queen*.

It is Ben and Marcus' whole job to protect you. They don't need you to help them put up tents, they need you inside where they know you're safe so they can concentrate on what they're doing."

He could see that she was trying to listen, but that she wasn't *hearing* him yet. "And if I wasn't a girl…if I was the potential *king*, they wouldn't let me help?"

He closed his eyes for a second, trying to figure out how to make her understand this without making her more defensive. "Honestly? I'm sure the fact that you're a girl freaks them out a little more, makes them even more protective, *but,*" he held up his hand, silently begging her to let him finish, "if my father was out here, he would not be putting up tents. He would be inside one so that his guards could feel like they were doing their job…so that they could duck inside their own shelters as soon as they have them up, and not have to check up on him…and he would be inside making decisions about what's going to happen next."

She scooted back a few feet from him, as far as she could go in the small space, her gaze dropping to the floor. "That's what I'm supposed to be doing, isn't it? Running this show?"

He swallowed hard; he could have left that last sentence out for the time being. "Not all by yourself. You're supposed to have help. That's *why* Marcus is here."

She looked at him, raising one eyebrow.

"Yeah, Quinn. That is kind of what you're supposed to be doing. Judging from the look on Charles' face a minute ago, I have a feeling that this might be at least part of his problem."

The tent flap shook again, and then opened. First Ben, and then Marcus appeared in the opening, toting the saddlebags from Skittles and Dusk. They stacked them neatly close to the wall of the tent, making sure to not lean them against the material.

"Do you need help setting anything up, Princess?" Ben asked, and William couldn't tell from his expression what kind of answer he was hoping for.

"No, we can handle it from here, but thank you," Quinn said. "Are the tents set up for everyone now?"

"Yes."

"Well done. It looks like our best bet is to stay under shelter until this passes. Can we make sure there is food in all the tents, in case this keeps us here overnight?"

"There are provisions in every bag," Marcus said.

"Good. The two of you should take shelter now. We can talk more when this lets up."

"Very well, milady. Thank you."

William could hear them closing the entrance tightly after they exited, and he felt the tent move again as someone pulled hard on the lines securing it to the ground.

"Was that better?" Quinn asked, her voice small and wary.

"Hey," he said softly, crawling over to her. "You're learning on the job here. Nobody expects you to be perfect at it already."

"Charles does."

"I don't know what he expects, Quinn, but he's going to have to have some patience."

"He's not going to be the only one who expects the leader of a kingdom to know what she's doing." She buried her face in her hands.

"And you will. You're going to be good at this, love. Just take the lessons as they come. Today's lesson was to listen when your guards ask you to get inside."

"Point taken." She reached for the buttons on her soaking-wet shirt. William crawled over to the bag where their clothing was packed, grateful once again for the meticulous Mia who had tied everything neatly into bundles and covered them with waterproofed cloth. He dug out the small bundle of towels, and then searched until he found dry clothes for both of them. He carried them back to her. "Here, let me help you with that," he said, tugging on her sleeve.

She was quiet as they worked together to get them both out of their wet clothes and into dry ones, and once he crawled just a few feet away again, he wouldn't have been able to hear her over the pounding rain if she had spoken. He took out a length of thin rope and tried to rig a makeshift clothesline while she laid out the bedrolls. Both pairs of riding boots were hopelessly soaked, but he dried the outsides the best he could before stuffing some washcloths inside, hoping they'd absorb at least most of the moisture.

When they finally had everything arranged as best they could, he joined her over on the blankets, sitting down next to her, and wrapping one arm around her waist.

"Don't ever do that to me again," she said.

"What?" he asked, jerking his arm back.

Her eyes widened. "I didn't mean *that*." She took his arm and put it back where it had been, though this time she kept her hand over his.

Relieved, he smiled and kissed her forehead. "What, then?"

"Grab me like you did outside the tent. Order me around in front of them. Obviously, they're already having enough trouble taking me seriously. I can't... You can't undermine me like that."

He couldn't stop the small chuckle that escaped.

"You think that's funny?"

"No, I don't actually. I just... It's good to hear you like this. You amaze me sometimes, Quinn…most of the time. I know you think you're not doing a good job at this, but you are getting it so fast. You're a true royal firstborn…it pours out of you all by itself sometimes. And you're right. I can't do anything like that in front of people ever again. I'm sorry."

She shook her head. "You were only trying to help. I'm going to need your help learning this stuff. The customs, the etiquette, what I should let other people do, and what I should do myself."

"I'll help with what I can. I'm afraid you married the wrong one for some of it. They should have worked harder to set you up with

Thomas…or at least one of my brothers who actually grew up in the castle. I've always been exempt from half the rules myself."

"You think Thomas would have actually been able to get me into the tent and listening to him a few minutes ago?"

He frowned.

"First of all, Will, you're the one that I want." She turned and put her hand on his cheek. "I love Thomas…I love all of your brothers…but you're the only one I would have ever considered marrying."

He smiled, and brought her hand to his lips. "I know. I was just teasing you."

"Good. Second of all, you underestimate yourself. Thomas can talk to anyone…he charms everyone, gets them to talk to him, they'll share their secrets while he listens. But you... People *listen* to you. You don't speak as often, but if you suggest something, people do it, including me, usually. I know you're taking on a lot and that you would do it all just for me... but I don't think it's just because of me. I think that in the end, you're going to find that you're in your right place, too."

He smiled. "I wish I was as sure about me as I am about you… but I kind of like the place I'm in right now."

She followed his gaze around the small tent, this little world with just the two of them, the rain pounding down so hard that nobody could possibly hear anything outside the tent, and she smiled back.

VISITORS

IT WAS THE SILENCE that woke her. That and the soft yellow light that was starting to color the eastern wall of the tent. She opened her eyes without moving; William's arm was across her chest, heavy and warm. For several minutes she watched him sleep. He looked so relaxed, peaceful…she wondered if she ever looked like that, even when she was asleep. She was sure she hadn't lately.

His eyes were still closed when she felt his thumb slowly stroking her shoulder. After several minutes, he opened them and smiled. "Morning."

"Hey."

He kissed her gently, before pulling them both up and out of the blankets. "When did the rain stop?"

"It couldn't have been very long ago," she said, stretching and shaking her head. "Every time I woke up during the night it was still pouring."

He frowned, probably at her admission that she hadn't slept well, but then he nodded, already crawling across the tent for their clothes. There wasn't going to be time to dawdle, whether she'd slept or not. She dressed quickly in the heavy brown pants and tan shirt he handed her.

"Don't forget this," he said, pointing to the leather sheath that concealed a small dagger.

"We're in the middle of the woods. I'm just going to talk to Marcus."

"Exactly. We're in the middle of the woods, in an area that is unfamiliar to us, and you're going to talk to Marcus…who would be upset if you didn't have it. This is where you practice being the leader and listening to your guards."

"Right." She stretched out her leg so he could lift the bottom of her pants and secure the leather straps to her calf.

"I'll get everything in here packed and ready while you go talk to him," he said.

"Okay."

"Hey," he called, as she started unfastening the bindings of the door.

She turned to look at him.

"You can do this."

"I guess we'll find out."

He stopped what he was doing and came over to her. "You can, Quinn. But I'll be right here if you need me."

"Thank you."

He took her hand and pulled it up to his lips. "I love you."

She leaned in close and kissed him. "Can't I just stay in here and snuggle with you?"

"I would like nothing better, but…"

She sighed. "I know. I love you, too."

Outside, she was relieved to find that only Marcus was up, stoking a small fire. He looked up as she approached him. "Would you like some tea, Princess?"

"Yes, thank you."

He nodded, and set about pulling the small kettle from the coals while she sat down on a tarp-covered log that he'd pulled close to the fire circle.

Just as she was sitting down, she thought she heard a sound…maybe a twig snapping or something a few yards away from them. At first, she thought she might have imagined it, but Marcus stood and looked around, scanning the whole area for several seconds before he went back to his task.

Quinn listened again for a minute before she decided to speak. "Marcus?"

"Yes, Princess?"

"Is there a title I should be calling you, other than just Marcus?"

His smile was warm, almost fatherly, and she immediately felt more comfortable.

"No, milady, just Marcus."

"I know the titles and formalities are important to you, and I'm doing my best to try and get used to it, but this is a learning process for me."

"You're doing just fine."

"Thank you. I know there are a lot of things I'm getting wrong." She paused, debating whether to bring up something that had occurred to her during the night…not knowing if the mere question would upset him. *No,* she told herself…*you have to learn to be in charge. That means you deal with your concerns.* "But I've actually been wondering a bit about everyone calling me 'Princess'."

"What about it?" Ben's voice startled her…she hadn't even heard him coming up behind her. He must have been what had made the noise earlier.

"*That,*" she said. "The fact that we don't know who might be out here, who might overhear us at any time. Is it really safe to be calling me anything that might give away information we don't really want to be sharing?"

"She's right, Father," Ben said, coming to kneel beside the fire. When Marcus finished pouring water from the kettle into two metal mugs, Ben reached for a nearby water container to refill it.

"Yes. It's a very good point, milady," Marcus said. "Be careful with this now; it's hot." He stretched across the circle to set a steaming metal mug on the ground in front of her. Carrying a cup of his own, he retreated to a large rock. "What are you suggesting we call you, then?"

"Just Quinn would be fine with me, at least while we're traveling."

Both men looked uncomfortable. "How about Lady Quinn?" Ben asked. "It's an appropriate title for a guest of the castle or even a lesser princess, which you would be anyway by virtue of your marriage to Prince William."

"I can live with that."

"Fair enough, Lady Quinn," Ben said, the edges of his mouth almost quirking up into a smile.

Out of the corner of her eye, she caught sight of William exiting their tent. He smiled, but walked in the opposite direction from them, into the thick trees. Very soon, she was going to have to take a similar trip, but she could wait a bit longer. "What is the status of everything after last night's storm?" she asked. "Was anything damaged?"

"No, there's been no damage, milady. At least not to anything other than our progress at traveling."

She nodded. "We should get back on the trail as soon as possible this morning. How far are we from Cloud Valley now?"

"Not far enough." This time the voice that was much too close to her ear was unfamiliar. Her blood ran cold as Marcus and Ben rose instantly, both pulling swords from the sheaths that hung on their belts.

A scream caught in her throat as a hand wrapped around her upper arm, but Ben was fast. She wasn't sure how he got around the fire so quickly…he might have stepped over it…but an instant later she was behind him, away from the man who had grabbed her. She backed up quickly until she was sandwiched between Ben and Marcus.

The fair-haired man on the other side of the fire circle was well-built and imposing; the sharply shaved edges of his close-cropped beard somehow made him even more intimidating. But although the firm lines of his muscles were visible through his linen shirt, his stance and the inelegant hold he had on the hilt of his sword betrayed his lack of training and skill. He was no match for either Marcus or Ben.

Or he wouldn't have been, by himself. A movement in the trees behind the man alerted her to the fact that he wasn't alone. She surreptitiously nudged Ben with her elbow. His head didn't move, but she saw his eyes sweep the perimeter of their campsite.

"Five," he breathed.

How Marcus could communicate without moving or changing his expression at all, she would never know, but she saw him acknowledge the information.

Suddenly the weight of the leather sheath on her leg was comforting, as was the knowledge that she'd have no problem hitting her mark at this distance if she needed to…not that she wanted to. She couldn't stop staring at the man; something about him was familiar, although she had no idea why. She was almost certain she didn't know him.

"What are you doing here?" the man asked, at the same time she heard one of the tents rustling and someone stepping out. She didn't look to see who it was.

"We're just passing through," Marcus said, his voice completely level. "Who are you?"

The man shook his head. "You first."

"Weston Cook." Everyone turned at the sound of Nathaniel's voice. Two of the men in the trees moved forward, drawing knives;

she noted with relief that the man who'd tried to grab her was the only one who had a sword.

Nathaniel stepped away from his tent and walked down toward the fire. He moved casually, seeming relaxed, but she saw the wariness in his eyes. He nodded at Marcus and Ben, and then stepped toward the man.

"Doctor Rose?" The man frowned, looking carefully at all of them.

"Yes, it's me."

"What are you doing out here? What is all of this?"

"These are my friends; we were on our way to Eli's clinic in Cloud Valley last night when we got caught in a rainstorm. We don't mean harm to you. Could you and your friends put away your weapons?"

The man…Weston Cook…relaxed his hold on the hilt of his sword, but didn't let go. Now that she had a name, she realized that the man was, indeed, familiar to her. His daughter…*Katie*, she thought her name was, had been treated in the Cloud Valley clinic for shadeweed poisoning the last time Quinn had visited there.

William must have been waiting in the trees for an opportunity to move in safely, because he came running into the clearing just then, coming to stand right next to her. "Mister Cook?"

Weston turned to look at him. "Prince William?"

"Yes, it's me. How is your little girl…Katie, right?"

The man relaxed a little more, taking a step closer. None of the others came out of the trees, though. "Yes, that's right. She is doing well…no thanks to whoever is planting shadeweed around these parts and trying to poison our children."

"Well, it isn't us, Weston, if that's what you're thinking, though I don't blame all of you for being concerned when you find intruders out here. We want nothing more than to put a stop to it ourselves." Nathaniel said.

"But that's not why you're here, is it? You didn't come out here to put a stop to it."

"Directly? No. We have reason to believe that the source of the poisoning is coming from Philotheum."

The man's eyes narrowed. "We know it is, or at least some of us do. Though there are some who believe someone in the kingdom is doing it to our own citizens."

"I think that's what Hector and Tolliver want us to believe."

"What we don't understand is why Stephen isn't doing anything about this situation in Philotheum."

"He is, Weston. He's closed the borders."

"And what is that accomplishing, except preventing some of us from traveling and being with our families? And escalating a battle between our kingdoms? He could end this and restore peace."

"What do you want to see happen, Weston? The king hand off his daughter to Tolliver…give in to Hector's demands?"

"It would solve the problem."

"Would it?" Quinn asked, fighting back her anger at his callous statement. "Do you really think that would be the end of Tolliver, if he thought Stephen was so weak?"

"Who are you?" Weston asked.

"Lady Quinn," she said. "We met once before, when I visited the clinic in Cloud Valley with Prince William and Nathaniel."

The sound of a snapping twig distracted her, and she looked over in time to see two more people stepping out of the trees, a man and a woman.

"Lady Quinn?" the woman said.

Quinn looked at her. She was a young woman, maybe a few years older than Quinn herself. She had light brown hair and brown eyes. Her clothes and demeanor suggested that being in the woods and carrying a weapon like the knife at her belt wasn't new to her. The way the man's body moved with hers told her that they were a couple.

The man, actually, was much more muscular, and moved with more skill than Weston. She wondered why Weston was the spokesman for their group, when there were clearly members who were more qualified.

"Do I know you?" Quinn asked.

"We've never met," the woman answered. "But I know who you are. My name is Eloise Bennett, and this is my husband, Gene. We have a son, Elliott. He is being cared for right now by Gene's brother. I believe you met him."

Quinn sucked in a breath. "About seven cycles old?"

"Yes. My sister-in-law tells me you saved his life, pulling him out of that tree house…that you even injured yourself in the process."

"I don't know if it was that big of a deal, Mrs. Bennett…"

"Eloise, please. I've been hoping ever since I heard that I would have the chance to meet you. I don't have the words to tell you how grateful I am…we both are," she said, looking at her husband, who nodded.

"We think it's a big deal," Gene said.

She looked at him. "Your sister-in-law told me that you two were in Philotheum…"

"We were. We've only recently returned."

"Why?" she asked, more than a little suspicious. "What were you doing there? Are you *from* Philotheum?"

Eloise glanced at her husband, and then over at Weston. He shook his head, but the woman shrugged, almost defiantly before reaching up to the collar of her shirt and drawing it back.

She heard Marcus' sharp intake of breath when the tattoo came into view. "You're taking a very big risk showing us that."

Weston's hand was on his sword again.

"I know I am," Eloise said. "But something tells me we can trust you." Her eyes were on Quinn again. "I take it you all know what this means?"

"We do," said Quinn. "All of you?"

The look that Weston shot her could have withered a tree, but Eloise nodded.

"You hid it well," Quinn said, looking at Weston, "with all your talk of compromising with Hector."

"Hiding it is the point," he spat, his gaze still on Eloise. "I guess now is the time to really hope it's true that Stephen is sympathetic to our cause?"

"He is more than sympathetic," Nathaniel said, pulling back his own collar. "Stephen is a Friend of Philip, as well."

Weston put his hand in the air and waved. The two other people who'd been hiding in the trees stepped out; both of them were men, one maybe Simon's age, and another who appeared to be closer to Nathaniel's.

"All of *you*?" Weston asked. Marcus, Quinn, William, and Ben all pulled back their collars.

"So does Stephen have a plan, then? Some direction we may be able to take?"

"He does," Quinn said. "Maybe you should all come sit down and we can explain."

RESPONSIBLE

"SHOULD YOU BE DOING that?" Mia's voice surprised Thomas enough that he nearly dropped the sword he'd been practicing with.

He turned to face her. "I have to do something to keep my mind occupied. Might as well be this, in case I ever get my hands on the person who took Linnea."

Mia's eyes widened. His younger brother, Josh, who had been practicing with him, walked away from them, suddenly busying himself organizing the weapons along the far wall of the gymnasium.

"You wouldn't actually hurt someone, would you, Thomas?"

"Would I want to? No. But if I had to, Mia…"

She sighed. "I know, Thomas. That wasn't what I meant, anyway. I meant, should you be flinging a sword around so soon, with this?" She placed her hand over his chest. Even through both his shirt and the thick bandage, her touch made him flinch. She dropped her hand instantly.

"I don't have time to be sensitive about it, Mia. I knew what I was getting into."

Yesterday, after Linnea had been taken, and Quinn and William were preparing to leave, Thomas had gone to his father. He'd been willing to compromise before on waiting until his sixteenth birthday to join the Friends of Philip, but he wasn't anymore.

To his relief, his father hadn't objected at all; the only difficulty had been the close timing. It wasn't an ideal time to be recovering from the painful procedure, but he was determined that it wasn't going to slow him down.

"Yes, you did," Mia answered, "but it's only been half a cycle for me…I still remember what it was like." She put her hand over her chest, where her tattoo was.

"I'm fine, Mia," he said, kissing her on the nose. "I would be more fine if I was out searching for Linnea, but I understand why it's better for me to stay here right now."

"Have you had any news?"

"No. It would have been difficult with the rain last night, but I'm hoping sometime soon."

With the connection between his bird and William's, Thomas was best equipped to maintain the lines of communication between the castle and William's group. William's move to Philotheum was going to be a challenging transition for the birds. Eventually, he was sure, one of them was going to be short a companion bird…probably him…the birds would be likely to both follow their offspring to Philotheum.

For now, though, they seemed to be tolerating the traveling. Thomas had the large doors to the gymnasium open, listening for the birds. He expected Aelwyn to come sometime soon with an update from the travelers. Most of the other seeker birds in the castle were busy tracking Linnea's bird, Zylia, to see if she could find her master.

Thomas's bird, Sirian, though, was being kept at the castle in case they had a message to send in a hurry.

"I hope so, too," Mia said. "Will you let me know if you hear anything?"

"Of course."

She nodded. "I need to get back to the children. But I wanted to come and check on you."

"Thanks," Thomas said, pulling her into his arms and kissing her. As he pulled back, he caught a glimpse of something through the doorway that stopped him short. "I'll see you in a little while?"

"Lunch in an hour. I'll have some sent up to the common room. For you too, Josh," she said. Thomas hadn't even realized his little brother was still in the room.

"Josh, have you seen Maxwell today?" Thomas asked, after Mia left.

"No. I'm not sure I remember the last time I saw him, actually. Why?"

"No reason. Can you watch for Raeyan or Aelwyn for me for a while?"

"Sure."

Leaving Josh behind in the gymnasium, Thomas ran back into the castle and dashed up the stairs. He reached Maxwell's room just in time to see his brother touching the doorknob.

"Where in the hell have you been, Max?" he spat. "Everyone is frantic with worry, William and Quinn are on their way to Philotheum in the middle of a splicing war, and you're what? Off with your girlfriend?"

Max pushed the door open and held his hand out, gesturing Thomas inside.

Once they were in, Thomas noticed that his brother didn't look right. His face was drawn and he looked like he hadn't slept in days. Of course, they probably all looked like that right now.

"Seriously, Max, what is the matter with you?"

Maxwell closed his eyes, putting his hand on his forehead. "Thomas… I think I've made a big mistake."

"Aside from the obvious, you mean? Abandoning your family when something like this is going on? Look, I know you haven't agreed with all of Father's decisions, and that you're upset you weren't told about Quinn, but *this*?"

Max looked stricken. "I know, Thomas. I'm sorry. I was so stupid…"

A sick feeling settled in Thomas's stomach. "What's going on?"

"You know Catherine and I have been getting closer lately…"

"I know you've been spending a lot of time with her."

"I should have realized it… should have noticed. I liked her, Thomas, or I thought I did… we had our issues, but she understood my frustrations with what was going on, and she understood how I felt. I should have noticed, paid attention. She'd been asking so many questions lately…never all at the same time of course, but a few at a time…about Quinn and William, about what's going on between Eirentheos and Philotheum… about the castle."

All of the blood drained from Thomas's face. "Max… no."

"Yeah, I think so. I realized last night that I hadn't heard from her since right after the wedding, that she left early, said her brother was coming to pick her up… and all of the pieces started coming together. I went this morning, rode out to her family's home, and they're gone. Nobody is there. And it doesn't look like they're coming back."

"Max, we have to go. We have to tell Father, tell Simon and Luke."

Luke Willoughby, Mia's father, was their father's head guard, now that Marcus had gone. They had all left the castle early this morning to follow up on some leads about where Linnea might have been taken.

"I already sent a message; I don't know what to do until they get back."

Quinn was the first one to see the bird circling overhead as they rode.

"It's Sirian," she called, and Marcus, who was leading the group, immediately stopped.

"It's too soon for Aelwyn to have gotten a message to the castle and Sirian to have gotten here already," William said. "Maybe they've heard something."

"It's my brother Thomas's bird," he said, addressing the newcomers in their group as he dismounted and made his way to where Sirian had landed gracefully a few feet away from them. The bird held out his leg so that William could open the silver canister.

"What is it?" Nathaniel asked, climbing down and walking over to him.

Quinn, too, dismounted from Dusk when she saw the alarmed expression on William's face.

"They think they know who might have taken Linnea," he said, handing the note to Nathaniel.

Everyone was off of their horses now.

"Who?" Marcus said.

"The family of Maxwell's new companion, Catherine Whittier."

"Whittier?" Gene said, a strained sound in his voice. "Is her father Edmund Whittier?"

"I'm not sure," William said, "but that sounds right. Why?"

"Their family and Hector's go way back. His father was from Dovelnia, and shortly after Jonathan's death, Hector brought them over to Philotheum. Edmund's father, Callum, has been the head councilman of our village for many cycles."

"You don't like him," Quinn said, judging the expression on his face.

"He's one of the reasons that we left two cycles ago with Elliott and brought him here to live with my brother. I'd heard rumors that his son had gone to Eirentheos, but I never knew if it was true. Nobody could imagine why he would want to. Hector has rewarded the Whittier family quite well for their loyalty to him. They've recently expanded their estate by another fifty acres."

"Well now you know why. Because his granddaughter was consorting with the Eirenthean royal family."

"It isn't good news," Gene said. "That family has influence everywhere. They could have taken Linnea anywhere…could get her across the border undetected."

"So what do we do?" Quinn asked.

"We don't fool around with trusting people like Stephen has done," Charles cut in suddenly. "We don't stop in Cloud Valley and give your position away to even more potential people. We get you to the castle as quickly as possible, and we end this."

She frowned. "Eli in Cloud Valley is a Friend of Philip. Can't we use all the help we can get right now?"

"I trust Eli," Nathaniel said.

"Isn't all of this trusting everyone what has us in this mess?" Charles said. "Mother trusted Hector. Stephen trusted some girl to come into his castle to see his son…"

Charles' words made sense, Quinn knew. It didn't feel right, but he wasn't wrong, *was he?* All of this had been caused by trusting the wrong people. And Charles already had enough problems with her.

She nodded. "Fine. We won't go to Cloud Valley. We'll send a message with Sirian, letting Stephen know what we know about the Whittiers. Maybe it will help them know where to start looking. And we will keep traveling."

Nathaniel gave her a strained look, but she ignored it. They'd only planned on stopping in Cloud Valley for the night anyway, and the night was over. They should keep traveling.

"Gene, will you please write down anything you know that might be important about the Whittiers that we can include in our message?"

"Tired?" William asked, as he helped Quinn down from Dusk when they finally stopped for the evening.

"I'm ready to be done riding." She slid down into his arms and wrapped her arms around his waist.

"Did you sleep at all last night?" He'd been thinking about it as they rode…she'd mentioned waking up during the night, but he'd never gotten the chance to ask her about it.

"A little."

"Dreams again?"

"I don't think so. Just regular trouble sleeping. If any of this is regular." He pulled her closer to him, leaning down to kiss her forehead.

"Lady Quinn, Prince William?" They both turned to see Ben standing a few feet away from them. "May I take care of your horses for you?"

William paused, looking to Quinn, waiting to let her handle the request. She started to shake her head to object, and he squeezed her hand gently, a reminder.

"Yes, Ben, we'd appreciate that. Thank you," she said.

When Ben was a few feet away, William leaned in close to her ear. "Perfect."

She sighed. "It still doesn't feel right. We're not at the castle. I should be pulling my weight."

"You *are* love; it just looks different now."

"What is it supposed to look like, then? Me standing around watching while other people do my work? There aren't any decisions to make right now. Should I walk around and supervise, tell people what to do?"

He sighed. "No, I think what you're doing is fine. Actually…" he put his lips near her ear again, "I think everyone is trying to make as much effort as they can to give us some time alone. We did just get married." He twined his fingers with hers, and brought both of their hands up to his lips, kissing her fingers.

She smiled, resting her head against his shoulder. "I suppose that's true." A moment later, though, she looked up at him and frowned. "You think *maybe* that's what everyone is doing, or you heard someone say something about it?"

He grimaced. "I heard someone say something."

"*Who?*"

"Ellen. She was talking to Henry and Charles. They didn't realize how close I was to them."

She closed her eyes. "I guess I shouldn't have hoped that we'd avoid being teased if we were away from Thomas and Linnea."

William swallowed hard. There'd been no hint of teasing in the conversation he'd overheard between Quinn's aunt and uncles. If anything, it had been one of the more serious conversations he'd ever been privy to.

His reaction didn't slip by her. "What aren't you telling me?"

"I'm not specifically *not* telling you something. It just didn't come up…until now…that I heard them talking about us."

"What did they say?" Her voice was suspicious now.

He looked around. Everyone was working…setting up tents, unsaddling horses, digging into saddlebags for food. Nobody seemed to be paying any attention to them, but it wasn't as private as this conversation should be, either. "Do you have your knife on you?" he asked.

Her eyes widened. "Constantly now. Why?"

"I just thought maybe we could go for a little walk. It's probably an excessive precaution, but…"

"But that's where we are right now," she finished for him. "Do you have yours?"

"So, what did they say that has you too freaked out about my reaction to tell me where they can see me?" she asked, when they'd walked a little way into the woods.

"I'm not freaked out. I just thought we could use some privacy."

"Liar. How bad was it?"

"It wasn't *bad*… it was just… heavy." He stopped walking, and leaned against a tree, reaching his hand out toward her. "You and I haven't really talked about the biggest issue here…the prophecy."

She looked down at the ground, kicking at a rock with her boot. "No, we haven't."

"I get why we haven't," he said, pulling gently at her hand so that she had to take a step closer to him. "Between the two of us, it wasn't an issue. It's not why I asked you to marry me, and I know it's not why you said yes. But here we are. We're married now, and the prophecy is still there, and it does mean something to other people."

"I don't even know if I believe in the prophecy."

"I don't know if I do either. But I don't think it matters. If it's real…we could fulfill it. If it's not real, which it probably isn't… our marriage is still pretty significant politically, Quinn. We're still bringing together the crowns of Philotheum and Eirentheos. And that is huge to a lot of people. Including the people who are on this journey with us."

"So they want to see us looking like we just got married."

"Something like that."

"Do they think we're faking it…this is just a marriage of convenience?"

He looked to the sky for a moment, trying to come up with the best way to answer her question, but there just *wasn't* an easy way. "I don't think it would bother them if that's what it was, love, so long as…" Warmth flooded up his neck.

"So long as *what*, Will?"

"So long as we produce an heir."

Quinn coughed and took a step backward. "Is that what they were talking about today?"

"Yes."

"An *heir*. Like, a baby."

"That's typically what it means, yes."

"What, *now*?"

"I think they're willing to wait nine moons."

"We've been married for two days."

"I know."

"Us getting married and 'fulfilling the prophecy' isn't enough for them? They want a baby, too?"

He took a deep breath. "You have to look at it from their point of view, Quinn. If we go through all of this, fight this battle, stop Tolliver's bid for the throne…having someone to pass the throne to, to keep the line going…that's going to be a big deal."

She closed her eyes for a long moment, and finally nodded. "I get it. I told you before, I *do* want children. I just wasn't thinking about it *now*, that's all. And it seems like you're saying that everyone's over there hoping we're busy making a baby right now."

William couldn't help the chuckle that escaped. "I don't think anyone is going to come looking for us, if that's what you're asking."

She shot him a dark look. "I wasn't asking."

"You did ask what they were talking about. And I told you."

"You're right. I'm sorry…I shouldn't take it out on you. I just…this is a *lot*."

"Want to turn around now and go back to the gate? Go back to high school and worry about failing your World History class?"

"Is it bad that that's sort of tempting right now?" She took a few steps away from him and sank down on a low tree stump.

"No. That sounds like a pretty normal reaction." He crossed over to her; there was nothing else to sit on, but he didn't care. He sat down on the ground in front of her stump, pulling his knees up to his chest, and setting his hands on her knees. "Are you serious? Because it's not too late."

She sighed. "No. I'm not serious, Will. I made this decision, and I'm not going to change it. I guess I just have to expect that some things are going to hit me like this…this is why everyone wanted me to take my time, isn't it?"

"This, and a thousand other reasons, love. You're not just changing your address."

She smiled, placing her hands over his. "I should have seen this one coming, shouldn't I?"

He shrugged.

"I mean, I know we're married…not that I've gotten used to that…but the thought of having a baby just wasn't even on my radar yet."

He held her hands, running his thumb around her wedding band. "At the risk of pointing out the obvious, I could remind you that we haven't exactly been doing anything to prevent that from happening."

Her cheeks instantly turned a glowing shade of red. "Does it make me the biggest idiot in the world that I didn't even consider that?"

"I don't know. It's not like I said anything to you, either."

"Would you be okay with it?" she asked. "If I did get pregnant?"

"Okay with it isn't the right way to put it." He looked into her eyes. "This world is so different from the one where you grew up, Quinn. Sometimes I forget how different. It's not even a question here, you know. We try to find ways to space children out sometimes, but most people aren't big on preventing them from coming at all. Babies are good. Every child here is considered a gift from the Maker.

"I wouldn't be *okay* with it if you were pregnant…I would be excited, wondering whether my child was going to be strong and beautiful like her mother, or quiet like me. I'd be sleeping with my hand on your stomach, hoping one night he'd wake me up with his tiny kicks…" He pulled on her hands, bringing her down onto his lap.

"I know this is strange and new and scary for you. I know it's all coming so fast. But we'll deal with it. I'm trying not to freak you out with every crazy detail you haven't thought of… but I probably should have brought this one up before you had to deal with it like this."

"I'd have probably had at least a minor melt-down no matter how you brought it up," she said, smiling and wrapping her arms around his neck.

"Hey, we have a deal, remember? Either one of us is allowed to freak out whenever we need to…just not both of us at the same time. So, you worry about ruling a kingdom, and I'll worry about the babies."

It worked; she laughed. "Have I told you lately that I love you, Will?"

"Hearing that from the most incredible girl in two worlds could seriously over-inflate my ego you know, but I'll take it." He kissed her.

"Seems like it would be a shame to waste all of this privacy," she said, looking around them.

"Then we'd better not."

FEAR

QUINN DIDN'T GET A chance to speak with Nathaniel alone until the next afternoon. After several hours of traveling through thickly wooded areas, away from any kind of road, Marcus had finally brought them to a stop. There was a place near here where they'd been hoping to be able to cross the border without detection. Marcus and Ben had gone to check it out, leaving the rest of them in a sheltered area.

The run-in with the Friends of Philip the day before had grown their group; Eloise and Gene Bennett had decided to travel back to Philotheum with them and help how they could. This morning, Aelwyn had carried a message to Gene's brother with a letter to little Elliott from his parents.

"We want to be proud of the Philotheum we bring him back to," Gene had told Quinn when they'd spoken to her about their decision. "You've shown us already that you care enough about people to risk yourself. We want to see the throne restored to your family."

The others, Weston Cook, and the other couple who'd been with them, the Evans', had stayed behind.

Nathaniel was crouched by a small stream, refilling water pouches when Quinn approached him. "Can I talk to you?" she asked.

Nathaniel stood immediately, closing the top of one of the pouches. "Of course."

"Are you mad at me?"

"Why would I be mad at you?"

"It's just… yesterday, when I agreed with Charles that we wouldn't stop in Cloud Valley…it seemed like you weren't happy about that. And we've never really had a chance to talk since then."

"We haven't talked because things have been busy, Quinn. I'll be honest…I didn't agree with Charles about not trusting Eli enough to stop over in Cloud Valley, but I understand why you would make that call."

"You think Charles was wrong."

Nathaniel sighed. "I understand where he was coming from. I understand why he doesn't think we should trust anyone. I know he thinks Stephen has been wrong to trust the people he's trusted. But for me, yes, I think my brother is wrong in withholding trust from the people who have earned it."

"Even though it's incredibly dangerous right now? Look what happened with Linnea."

Nathaniel looked at her thoughtfully. "Do you think Stephen was wrong to allow his son to bring his girlfriend into the castle?"

"It didn't turn out very well."

"Is that Stephen's fault?"

She paused. "It's not his fault, exactly, but he could have prevented it."

"Do you know that?"

"What do you mean? If Catherine hadn't been allowed into the castle, her family wouldn't have been able to kidnap Linnea."

"Not as easily, maybe. Maybe not in the same way, but if they were determined enough to do it, they probably still could have. In the meantime, Stephen might have done real damage to his relationship with his son."

"So what, are you saying we should just trust everyone and cross our fingers that they won't murder us in our sleep?" she snapped.

Nathaniel's eyebrows rose into his hairline. "Really, Princess?"

Heat flooded her face; she didn't even know where that tone in her voice had come from. "Sorry."

"Good." He nodded. "Because, queen or no, Quinn, I won't put up with that. You have enough of an uphill battle getting people to take you seriously without adding acting like a spoiled brat to the list."

She took a deep breath, swallowing back the sudden nauseated feeling. "You're right, Nathaniel. I'm sorry. I shouldn't have spoken to you like that."

He put his hand on her shoulder and squeezed it gently. "It's easy for me to forget that you're only seventeen, and that in your world, seventeen is much younger than it is here."

She closed her eyes for a long moment, steadying herself. "It doesn't matter how old I am, Nathaniel. I don't have any room for excuses."

His gray eyes were kind as he looked at her. "You have some room with me, but you're right. Your every move, every action, every *word* is being watched carefully by others. It's a lot of pressure. I'm not angry with you, but I am going to let you know when you cross a line."

"I need you to."

"Yeah, you do." He smiled and leaned down to kiss the top of her head.

She wrapped her arms around his neck and hugged him. "Thank you, Uncle Nathaniel."

"I'm here for you. You know that, right? I'm sorry that I haven't always been, but I am here now."

"I know."

"Anyway, you were asking me about trusting people…I don't know what all the right answers are, Quinn, and I know that times are scary. But I will tell you what I believe."

She nodded.

"I believe that most of the great evil in the world happens not at the hands of malice, but of fear. Because good people, the ones who would do the right thing, don't do it, out of that fear. Maxwell wasn't wrong to trust Catherine Whittier. She was wrong to betray that trust. Stephen didn't do the wrong thing when he trusted his son's judgment.

"What would happen if Stephen really became mistrustful and fearful of everyone in his castle and his kingdom? You know who's afraid of everyone and everything? My stepfather. And he's raised his son, Tolliver, in that fear. It's turned them into people who live believing that they need to crush everyone before they, themselves, get crushed. Fear is like a weed in a garden. Once you allow it to take root, it spreads, replicating itself, until, eventually, it chokes out all the other life there. Trust, love, kindness…none of those things can ever really bloom in a garden of fear."

"But sometimes there's actually something to be afraid of."

"There's *always* something to really be afraid of. Sharks are real, Quinn. You have to be reasonable…you don't go swimming in shark-infested water with an open cut…but you don't kill all of the sharks in the ocean, either. And you don't avoid the ocean. You don't spend your whole life never learning to swim or sail or surf just because sharks exist and sometimes they bite."

"And you don't rule a kingdom never trusting anyone just because some people aren't trustworthy."

He nodded. "Mistrust breeds untrustworthiness. Fear breeds malice. Trust breeds peace and hope. If Stephen had treated Maxwell as if he were untrustworthy because of the *possibility* he was making an unwise decision, where would their relationship be now? Would Max have gone to him when he did figure out the truth? Or might he have decided that since his father didn't trust him anyway, he might as well go along with the people who did?"

She closed her eyes. "And when we didn't go to Cloud Valley, we were telling Eli that we don't trust him."

"We were turning away from good, letting ourselves be controlled by fear. Cloud Valley is a village that has consistently been a safe haven for Philothean refugees…the ones who truly needed help. The people there have opened their doors and their hearts to everyone in need. There are more Friends of Philip there than anywhere else I know. And, in a way, we just punished them for the actions of others. We turned away from good, in favor of honoring evil by giving it power over us."

"That's not what I was trying to do. I was just trying to keep us safe."

"I know that. I told you I understood your decision. I'm just telling you the other part to consider; asking you to think about where you might be allowing weeds to grow instead of planting roses."

"Again with the roses and the weeds."

He shrugged. "It's a family story."

She nodded. Of course it was. Of course Alvin would show her visions of that in her dreams without ever offering an explanation.

"You did the same thing you know, Nathaniel, when you didn't want me to go help at the emergency clinic during the fire. You wanted me to stay safe instead of doing the right thing."

"If I ever tell you I'm perfect, Quinn, feel free to remind me about all the ways I'm not. It's not easy. It's even harder when you're making decisions about people you love. I'm doing the best I can. *You're* doing the best you can."

She nodded again, looking down at the ground. "I'm trying."

"I know."

They were quiet for several minutes before she finally looked back up at him. "People surf in Eirentheos?"

He rolled his eyes. "Yes, actually…we don't call it that, but yes. But that wasn't my point."

"I know. That just caught my attention. I guess I never thought… Do people ski here, too?"

"Cross-country, in some places where the winter gets very snowy. More for travel than for sport."

"Quinn! Nathaniel!" William came walking up to them. "Marcus and Ben are back. Marcus would like to speak to everyone."

"Okay," Nathaniel said. "Let's go."

William frowned, watching Nathaniel walk back toward the group. "Is everything okay?" he asked.

"Yeah, everything's fine," she answered. "Just a lot of stuff for me to think about. But I suppose if I'm going to be the queen of a kingdom, I'd better get used to that."

William nodded, leaning down to kiss her on the forehead.

"We have a problem," Marcus said, once everyone had gathered. "There are soldiers patrolling the area by the border. As far as we can tell, there aren't any on this side, but we saw two across the river."

"Why are they here? There's nothing around here. No villages, no people, nothing."

"Nothing except the last place we can get horses across the river for more than a full day's travel."

"So we're going to lose two whole days finding another spot," Quinn said.

"At least. The terrain gets more challenging here," Nathaniel said. "We're getting into the mountains."

Quinn frowned, she hadn't seen any mountains.

"They look like tree-covered hills compared to where you're from," William said quietly in her ear, "but they're mountains."

"We don't really have another option, do we?"

"We could risk it with the soldiers," Marcus said. "It didn't seem to be a large regiment. Maybe we could avoid them."

She shook her head. "Too dangerous. We don't know how many there might be behind them. And we don't know who's leading them."

"There are a few places we could probably get across the river on foot without drawing much attention to ourselves, but we'd never get the horses and all of the supplies with us."

"What is our plan for after we're across?" Quinn asked.

"There's a safe house in a village not far from where we are now," Ellen said. "Maybe another hour of traveling. It's a property owned by a cousin of ours, Brian Miller, who has managed to keep his involvement in the resistance quiet, and Tolliver has left him alone. I'm not even sure he remembers, or cares about Brian's family since, in his mind, they're not important royals. If we can get there, Brian can connect us with a way to get to the castle; we can make a plan, and find the support we need."

"Can we afford to take…what, probably three days or more to get there?" Quinn asked.

"We may not have a choice," Marcus answered. "But every moment that Linnea is missing is time we're losing."

Quinn nodded, trying to think. She looked at Ellen. "How long would it take us to reach your cousin's house on foot?"

"*Our* cousin," Ellen corrected. "He's the son of my mother's brother."

"Our cousin's house, then. If we didn't have horses, how long would it take us to get there from the border?"

"Well, the next place we could cross the river is probably two hours on foot from here. From there to the Miller Estate…maybe a few hours, less than half a day" Marcus answered, studying a map he'd laid out on a rock.

"Do you know where it is?" she asked.

"Yes. I've known Brian Miller for a long time, and have been there before." When Quinn frowned, he looked at her. "The Friends of Philip has been my life for many cycles, Princess. The Miller Estate has long been one of our greatest assets. Brian's parents cut off most of their contact with the Philothean castle right after Jonathan died, and their whole family has worked quietly since then. It was a very smart move…Hector has no idea of the threat they pose to him."

"Or he *didn't*, anyway," Ellen said. "I don't think we can take anything for granted now. Our mother has certainly remained in touch with them."

"Okay." Quinn nodded. "So what if we consider a third option…some of us crossing the border on foot and heading to the Miller Estate, while everyone else takes the horses and supplies around the long way?"

"It's risky," Marcus said. "We may have trouble getting back together."

"All of the options are risky," she answered. "I just don't think we have the time to wait."

CROSSING THE BORDER

"I'M SO SORRY, FATHER. I don't know what I was thinking, I should have never…"

"I know, Max. You never meant for this to happen. It isn't your fault…you aren't the one who took her."

"I just didn't think…"

"None of us ever want to think something like that, son. That someone we trust could betray us like that."

"The thing is, I don't think I allowed that to happen because I trusted her, Father. I think it happened because I didn't trust you."

Stephen sighed, sinking down onto a chair across from his second-born son. "Maybe that's my fault. I kept a lot of information from you, and there were a lot of things you didn't understand about why I was making the decisions I was."

"You had good reasons."

Stephen nodded, looking Maxwell in the eyes. "I did have good reasons."

"I know that now."

"Perhaps it's my fault, and I should have communicated with you more, Max. Or perhaps I've given you reason to doubt my judgment?"

"I don't know, Father. I know I felt left out. I couldn't understand why William would be allowed in meetings I wasn't."

"What would have happened if I had shared Quinn's identity with you earlier than I did, Maxwell? If you'd been aware of it before we knew how willing Gavin was to betray us?"

The sudden widening of his son's eyes told Stephen everything he needed to know. Maxwell had always had a greater desire to impress people than his other sons. He'd always been competitive with his cousins when it came to sports, and girls, and one-upmanship. The mortification he saw, though, told him that he didn't need to lecture Maxwell about it. He'd gotten the point.

"How much information does Catherine Whittier have?" he asked instead.

"I've been trying to remember. She was so subtle. Everything just came out in regular conversation."

"Does she know who Quinn is?" This was the one that terrified Stephen the most.

"No. She obviously knows that William and Quinn are married, though. Which is bad enough. You should have never allowed me to invite her."

"I trusted you, Maxwell. And, in any case, you would have told her that anyway."

Max's face went gray. "I still don't see how she could have gotten Linnea out of the castle."

"I don't know that either, although I can think of a few possibilities. I'm not going to focus on that, however. The fact is that she, and whoever was helping her, did. When…*when*…Linnea returns, we can ask her." His voice broke on the end of the sentence, and he had to rest his forehead on his hands for a moment. His little girl…

"What can I do, Father? Will you allow me to help in the search?"

"No, Maxwell. I need you here at the castle, waiting for news. And right now, I want you to take some time and think. Think about every conversation you had with her, every question she asked, every single detail you might have told her, even if it seems small and insignificant. We need to know what they know about us."

"Yes, Father."

"This is what you call a place we can get across?" Quinn asked, looking down the steep gorge.

"There's a ledge, just there," Ben said, pointing. "We can walk along it until we reach that slope, where those trees are. From there, it'll be slow going, but we can get down to the water. It's mostly shallow there, and not moving fast enough to sweep us away."

She stared down at the small waves breaking against the rocks. "Are you sure?"

"It isn't going to be easy," Marcus said. "But there's good cover here, and we can do it."

"We're just not going to be dry by the time we get to the other side," William said.

"All right, then," she said, looking up at the afternoon sun. "I guess we'd better get to it, then, if we want to have a chance at drying off before sundown."

Marcus and Ben led the way down the ridge. It was only the five of them now; Nathaniel followed her and William. Dangerous as it was, Quinn still felt this was better than waiting until all of them could cross together with the horses. So, yesterday after much discussion, the five of them had packed as much as they could onto their backs and headed to this spot.

They'd spent a long night camping outside, not wanting to cross the river in the darkness.

It had been an interesting debate, deciding who should come. Charles had wanted to, had almost insisted, but in the end he hadn't wanted to be separated from Thea, and they just couldn't send that many on foot, when they were leaving so many horses and supplies behind.

Part of Quinn was relieved at being away from Charles for a while, but there was another part of her that worried about what the consequences would be if anything important happened, and Charles didn't get to be part of the decision. She'd been picking up on his intense need to know things and to be in the middle of them. More than once, he'd spent several minutes asking questions about every detail of a small decision, only to agree at the end with what had already been decided.

She was actually starting to suspect that his biggest problem with her…aside from the fact that he really didn't trust her to know what to do or how to do it…was simply that he'd been left out of anything having to do with her, including being informed of her very existence. William hadn't been so sure when she'd explained her theory to him, but the more she got to know Charles, the more she thought this was right.

She did know that to take the crown and bring peace back to Philotheum, she was going to need his support, and anything that could, even potentially, complicate that made her nervous.

The walk down the ridge was treacherous, but not as difficult as she'd been worried about; it was more time-consuming than anything. Their careful climbing down to the riverbank took over an hour.

Once they were finally at the bottom and standing at the edge of the river, she could see that Marcus had been right; the water didn't look especially deep or dangerous here…though she knew from experience that the appearance of a current could be deceiving. She had been twelve the summer she'd ventured out into a river that looked calmer than it actually was. If her stepfather Jeff hadn't looked up from his fishing line at the right moment…

"Climb on my back, Princess." Marcus' voice brought her thoughts back into sharp focus.

"What?" she said, suddenly noting that Ben was holding his father's backpack, and that Marcus had his hands extended behind him. "I can cross just like everyone else."

She looked to William for support, but he only shrugged. "I don't see any reason for you to have to get wet."

"I can't let you carry me, Marcus. It just doesn't seem right."

"Then I will," William said, shedding his backpack. "Get on, Quinn."

His voice was light, but she heard the undertone. There was nothing to win here, but there was plenty to lose.

"I'll carry your pack, Princess," Ben said, reaching to help her remove it.

"And I've got yours, Prince William."

Her face was red as she climbed onto William's back, but she tried not to show her chagrin.

"Sorry," she whispered into his ear as he hooked his arms under her knees.

He shook his head slightly, reaching up with one hand to gently squeeze her wrist as he waded into the water. He shuddered at the sudden cold, and she tightened her arms around him. "You did want me to carry you across the threshold," he said. "I thought maybe a princess deserved something a little bigger."

"You're lucky I love you."

"I couldn't agree more; even if you are the most stubborn person I've ever met."

The trek through the water was almost uneventful, except for one time when William's foot slipped against a rock, almost sending them both tumbling into the water, but Ben, who was walking right beside them, caught his arm and steadied him.

She still felt bad when they reached the other side and she was the only one who was dry. Everyone else was soaked, all the way up past their knees.

Although all four of the men were dripping, water sloshing out of their boots, Marcus didn't think they could afford the time to stop and dry out if they were going to reach the Miller Estate before nightfall. Quinn reluctantly agreed, and they climbed up out of the riverbank and continued their journey through the thick woods almost immediately.

William caught her hand as they walked, and leaned down to kiss her hair. "It will get easier," he promised.

She shook her head. "I'll get better at it, probably, but I don't think it's ever going to be easy to just expect people to step in and do things for me."

He squeezed her hand.

"You're right about one thing," she said.

"What's that?"

"I'm lucky you love me."

He looked at her. "I very much do, Quinn."

"Would you still love me even if I *don't* get used to it; if at some point I freak out on everyone for treating me like such a girl?"

William's laugh was loud enough that everyone turned and looked at them. They all turned back around quickly, though, when William gave them a shy, half-embarrassed look. Quinn got the feeling they were trying to give her and William privacy. Part of her appreciated that, but there was another part that found it even more embarrassing.

"Can I point out one thing to you?" William asked, once everyone was ignoring them again.

She raised an eyebrow.

"You are a girl."

"So what? That means I can't do the same work as everyone else? That I have to be carried around?"

He sighed, looking at her. "Quinn, you know how everyone is being patient with you, because you're new at this, and you don't really know how to behave in every situation, or what to do?"

She swallowed. "Yes."

"Is there any chance you could give the rest of us some of that same consideration? We don't know what we're doing, either. We've never had a firstborn daughter become queen."

She nodded, thinking. "So do you just really believe that because I'm a girl, I'm weaker somehow? I need protection from things?"

"It's not exactly like that."

"Then what's it like? I'm not trying to argue, Will, but I don't understand."

He looked up at the sky, clearly deep in thought. She had to tap his shoulder to point out that they were approaching a fallen log they needed to navigate around. "Thank you," he said, chuckling.

"So, help me understand, please," she said, when they were on solid footing again.

"I think part of the problem here is that we're coming at this from different places. In our world...or at least in Eirentheos...while it's true that we've always been led by men, there's never been a divide like I think there is in your world, Quinn. I did study history there...which is an advantage I suppose you haven't had about this world. If you would have *passed* history here," he teased.

She jabbed him in the ribs with her elbow. "I didn't *always* do badly in history. I was a little distracted, you know."

"I know." He reached for her hand again, twining his fingers in hers. "Anyway, it was always so strange to me, to learn about the history in your world. How women weren't allowed to make decisions, or own property. How, in a lot of ways, they've had to fight *against* men just to have the same kind of life."

"And you're saying it's better here?"

He shrugged. "It's not perfect here…you've seen that. You got an up-close view of how Tolliver sees women. But maybe you haven't seen enough of the other side. My father rules the kingdom, sure, but he rarely makes a decision he hasn't talked to my mother about, gotten her input on. And, often, she's the one who came up with the idea in the first place. And everyone knows that, expects it. And if something happened to my father, my mother would have all of the power."

"Just like Sophia really does in Philotheum."

"Exactly. And outside of actually being the king, which is passed in a certain way through families, women in Eirentheos…and Philotheum, for that matter, can have the same jobs, and have the same rights as men do. Look at Essie and Jacob…she runs that clinic every bit as much as he does. Lily does more than Graeme. Back in their village in Philotheum, Lily was more influential in their council than Graeme was."

"I haven't seen any guards or soldiers who are women, Will."

He paused for a moment. "I suppose that's true. There aren't many."

"Are there some?"

"A few, actually. But they're certainly not the majority, and I can see how it looks to you. Women are *allowed* to be soldiers and guards, here. If they want to do that, they can. They're paid and treated the same, too."

"Oh."

"It's just different here, love. It's different than you're thinking it is, coming from where you've been."

"Well, nobody carried you across the river, and you're just as royal as I am."

He chuckled. "So hang us, Quinn. Your husband and your uncle, who both love you very much, and a couple of guards…who are growing rather fond of you as well, I suspect…wanted you to be warm and dry. And we were capable of making it happen, and there was no good reason not to. Is that really a terrible crime?"

"No."

"Sometime, I'll let you carry me across a river, if it will make you feel better, okay?"

She looked up at him dubiously. He was nearly a full head taller than she was. "Point taken."

He smiled.

"Husband…" she said, after a few more minutes of walking. "That sounds so strange, but I like it."

His grin was huge. "I like it, too. I especially like that it means you have to put up with me doing things like being chivalrous and taking care of you whether you *need* me to or not."

"Is that what it's called, chivalry?"

He kissed her hand again. "That's what it's called."

"All right. I suppose I can learn to deal with the chivalry. But if you start undermining my decisions, or treating me like I'm not perfectly capable of doing things for myself, I still reserve the right to freak out on you."

"Good. I hope you do." He pulled her hand up to his lips and gently kissed her knuckles.

"You hope I freak out?"

"I hope you always tell me what you're feeling, and that we work things out when we have issues. I have plenty of moments where I need you to knock some sense into me, too. I really love the way we can talk, Quinn. I like that we can question and challenge each other. I never want us to stop that, okay?"

"Okay."

"Besides," he teased, "I really like what happens after."

She giggled, feeling her face warm. "I do, too."

He paused just long enough to kiss her behind her ear. "I love you."

"I love you, Will."

They hadn't taken more than twenty steps in silence when Quinn suddenly stopped and froze in place, nearly making William fall with the abrupt motion. She stared into the trees to the side of them in disbelief.

"Nice catch, Princess."

The new voice halted everyone else in their tracks, too. Marcus and Ben had their swords drawn before their feet even stopped moving.

"Easy now," Jonathan said, holding his hands up in front of him. "You can come and take my weapon, if you'd like."

Marcus and Ben hesitated, but Nathaniel didn't. He walked right up to his younger brother, and reached for his belt. Jonathan kept his hands in the air the whole time Nathaniel was unfastening it.

"Now the knife," Nathaniel said.

Jonathan nodded down toward his right leg. Nathaniel took that weapon too, pausing to check Jonathan's other leg before carrying the blades back to where the rest of them were standing.

Quinn didn't look away from Jonathan to see what Marcus and Ben were doing, but she could tell they were searching the surrounding area with their eyes, looking for more people.

"What are you doing here?" Nathaniel spat, once he was a safe distance away.

"Looking for you. Well, for Princess Quinn and Prince William, specifically, but I'm happy to see the rest of you, as well."

"How did you find us?"

Jonathan let out a low whistle, and a moment later, a bird flew down from the treetops, landing a few feet in front of him. She was beautiful, almost pure white except for the midnight-black feathers on the tips of her wings and right at her neck.

"Your niece," he said, glancing once at Quinn before turning his gaze back to Nathaniel, "has a gorgeous little seeker who is not yet quite experienced enough to be subtle and remain hidden while he travels. Avriel here had the chance to become acquainted with that bird before we left Stephen's castle."

Quinn thought she was going to be sick. William's arm curled automatically around her shoulders, steadying her. "Does that mean Tolliver knows where we are as well?"

"No, Princess. Fortunately for you, neither my father nor my half-brother ever quite developed the knack of training a companion bird. They're both convinced, of course, that the birds that flew away from them were defective or sabotaged somehow. But I think we can all agree that seeker birds are simply too intelligent for that."

"Why are you here, Jonathan?" Quinn asked. "Kidnapping me once wasn't enough?"

Jonathan's face grew very serious. "I'm not here to kidnap you, Princess. But I am very much hoping that you'll consent to coming with me…all of you of course," he added, when Marcus and Ben moved to raise their swords.

Quinn frowned. She couldn't read his expression well at all. He looked sincere, but she'd chosen to trust him before, and then he'd run off again, with no explanation. And now he'd ambushed them in the woods. "Come with you *where?*"

"To meet my mother."

"You're in luck," Nathaniel said. "Because that's where we're headed. You should know that…it was your advice, wasn't it, that we bring Princess Quinn back to Mother at the castle?"

"I was very much hoping that's what you would be doing, yes."

"If you were hoping so much to see us, why did you leave the way you did, taking off in the middle of the night?" Quinn asked.

"What did you expect me to do? Wait around there for someone to figure out where I was and report it to my father and Tolliver?"

"Didn't they already know?" Nathaniel said, unable to keep the irritation out of his voice. "Aren't they the ones who sent you to Eirentheos in the first place, to spy on us?"

Jonathan's gray eyes were icy. "You'd do well to remember that some of us have been fighting this battle from the inside for the last twenty-odd cycles, Nathaniel. Not hiding out enjoying life in another kingdom…or another *world*."

He walked toward them now, seemingly oblivious to the fact that Marcus and Ben's swords were all the way up now. "You don't have any idea how difficult it is to constantly hide your real intentions, to fight against someone while making sure they still trust you."

"And how do we know that's not what you're doing to *us*, right now?" Quinn asked.

Jonathan looked back at her. "You don't, Princess. I've told you that already. You don't have one reason to trust me. But you should understand that you don't have a better option. You're not going to get to my mother without me."

"And how are you so sure about that?"

Jonathan raised an eyebrow. "Two guards, two princes, and a princess. How were you planning on getting inside the castle? Don't answer that, because it doesn't matter anyway. My mother isn't at the castle."

"Where is she?" Nathaniel demanded.

"She is staying at the Miller Estate."

Quinn blinked. "That's where we're headed."

Jonathan nodded. "I wondered as much, when I caught wind of the direction you were traveling. And that's when I became desperate to find you."

"Why?"

"Because, if you continue to the Miller Estate alone, you're walking into a trap that is going to get you killed."

"I thought you said nobody else knew we were here."

"They don't. But they would if you got anywhere near the Millers'. You see, because *some* of us can be subtle and keep a secret, Hector and Tolliver have no idea that the Millers are members of the Friends of Philip. We've used that to our advantage. Enough so that Tolliver decided to hide my mother there and have his new…*bride* brought to her."

"Linnea is at the Miller Estate? Now?" William's arm tightened almost uncomfortably around Quinn as he spoke.

"Yes. She arrived yesterday afternoon…she's fine, from what I hear. Upset, I'm sure."

"You haven't seen her?"

"No, I haven't. As I said, I would prefer that it wasn't common knowledge that I was at Rosewood Castle recently. I'm assuming that Princess Linnea is aware that I was?"

Quinn nodded.

"There's enough of a risk she'll mention it to someone who shouldn't know without actually seeing me. We're balancing on a very precarious edge here. Ideally, we need to get Linnea out of there, and returned to Eirentheos, before Hector and Tolliver realize that I'm working against them."

"You don't think it's possible they've realized that already?"

Marcus' voice almost startled Quinn. It was the first time he'd spoken in the conversation, and she had grown used to his silent presence.

Jonathan's eyes grew wide when he turned to study Marcus for the first time. "Marcus Westbrook? Is that you?"

"I'm surprised you remember, Prince Jonathan."

"Yours would be a difficult face to forget, Marcus. You still look the same as you did when I was a boy."

Marcus chuckled. "You're a flatterer, Jonathan. But then, you always were."

"I'd always hoped you were still alive somewhere. There was a part of me that always knew you must be…and the same for my brother." He looked at Nathaniel. "You've been missed more than you know."

"Have you told Mother, then? That I'm alive?" Though so subtle it would have been hard to catch if you weren't listening closely, Nathaniel's voice caught on the last part of his question. Quinn was overcome with a sudden impulse to hug him.

"I spoke with her yesterday morning. She knows about you…but not about Quinn," he added quickly, anticipating their question. "Sharing the news about you, Nathaniel, was emotional enough, and she's always held out some small hope that you might not actually have died. Keeping this secret is a big enough challenge. She needs to *see* you, Quinn, safe in front of her, before we can risk telling her."

"How do you think she's going to react to finding out about me?" Quinn asked, and William's hand tightened on hers…he knew this was one of the things she worried most about.

"She'll be pleased, I think, Princess. But as I've said, we have to handle this very carefully. She must find out about you before Tolliver does."

"And before Tolliver forces Linnea to marry him."

"Yes, that, too."

"Is Tolliver at the Miller Estate?"

"He wasn't when I left. I don't know when he's planning on arriving…I try to communicate with my half-brother as little as possible. But whether Tolliver is there or not, we're not going to be able to just walk onto the grounds of the estate. There are soldiers everywhere."

"Are you including yourself in that *we*?" Quinn asked. "Because I don't understand why *you* can't just go back to the estate by yourself."

"I am including myself, yes. I don't intend to go back to my mother without a solution to this problem…without *you*."

"Is that all I am…a 'solution to your problem'?"

"I've only just met you, Quinn. I don't know anything about you except that you're my brother's daughter and you apparently grew up in an alternate world. So, yes, I'm going to have to learn a little more about you before you're anything except a means to keep Tolliver off the throne."

She knew better, but still his words irked her a little. "How do you know I'd be any better a ruler than he would?"

To her surprise, Jonathan's mouth broke into a huge grin. "I didn't…until just now. Yes, Princess, I think you'll do just fine. Now, where's the rest of your group?"

Quinn raised an eyebrow.

"Well, I know you didn't walk all the way out here by yourselves, just the five of you. Where are the horses? Where are Ellen and Charles, and whoever else was traveling with you for that matter?"

Nobody answered him for a long moment.

"All right, then," Jonathan said. "I'll walk away for a few moments…go tend to my horse or something while you decide whether you're going to trust me or capture me and try to do it your own way. The only option you *don't* have is getting rid of me. Just shout when you're ready for me to come back." And with that, he turned and disappeared into the trees.

"Well, he did leave his weapons here," Marcus said, nodding toward the sword and knife that were lying on the ground.

Nathaniel reached down to pick up the knife, running his fingers over the floral design on the sheath. "He could have ten more back there somewhere. And fifty soldiers."

"What would be the point of that?" Quinn asked. "Why wouldn't they have ambushed us already?"

Nathaniel sighed. "I don't know what his motivations are, Quinn. All I know is that the first thing he did when he got into Eirentheos was kidnap you. That makes his motives a little suspect to me."

"Do you have a better option?" she asked. "We let fear of him win, and *then* what do we do?"

Her barb hit its mark; Nathaniel looked chagrined. "That is what I'm doing, isn't it?"

Quinn shrugged. "It's a little harder to tell when you're making real decisions than it is when you're discussing the hypothetical, I think."

"Do *you* trust him, Quinn?"

She closed her eyes, drawing in several deep breaths while she thought, while she tried to sort emotions from facts, but finally she opened her eyes and nodded. "Yes, I do. Or at least, I'm willing to try."

Nathaniel stared at her for several seconds before he sighed. "Okay. All right. We'll go with him. But can I at least keep his weapons?"

William chuckled, but Quinn shook her head. "No. If we're going to listen to him, we need to show him we trust him. Besides…if he doesn't actually have more weapons somewhere else anyway…an unarmed person could be a liability if we run into any trouble. He's more useful if he has them. And I'm guessing that Jonathan is better with swords and knives than you are, Nathaniel."

DREAMS

STEPHEN OPENED THE BEDROOM door quietly, not wanting to disturb the baby if Charlotte was putting her down for her morning nap. When he saw her leaning over the cradle, he was even more careful as he closed the door behind him.

Charlotte still heard him, though. She straightened and turned to watch him cross the room to her. Coming up behind her, he wrapped his arms around her waist, and bent down to kiss her neck. Her hand lifted automatically to his cheek, a habit borne of twenty-five cycles of marriage, one that made him feel complete.

Together, they stared at the tiny girl in the carved wooden cradle, the beautiful, sturdy little bed that had held each of their thirteen children. Hannah's dark curls splayed out against the white sheet on the soft mattress, looking so much like Linnea's, although, in her infancy, Linnea's curls had always had Thomas's fingers wrapped up in them as they slept in this cradle.

"We think we know where she is," Stephen whispered in Charlotte's ear.

She turned to him in surprise, taking his hand and leading him out of the bedroom and into the sitting room of their apartment. "Where?"

"Nathaniel's bird arrived just a little while ago. Apparently, he's discovered that Linnea has been taken to the Miller Estate in Philotheum."

Charlotte frowned. "I don't think I even know who that is."

"Brian Miller is related to the Philothean royal family…a third-cousin, maybe. Nathaniel obviously didn't send a lot of details with the letter, but the estate is outside of Casprian."

"Why did they take her there?"

"I don't know. But now we know where she is. It'll take a while to get anyone there, but at least now we have a direction."

"She could be long gone by the time anyone gets there."

"Or Nathaniel's information could be wrong, and she might not be there at all. But it's all we have. Maybe this will be the break we need to get her back."

Charlotte nodded. "Is Nathaniel headed there as well?"

"I would guess that he is, but of course he wouldn't include that information in a letter that could be intercepted. He did say that everyone is all right."

"Good." Charlotte sighed, sinking down onto a couch. "So we can divert at least one regiment to the Miller Estate, then."

"Yes…" He sat down beside her, taking her hand in his. "I was actually going to send a regiment from here… with Luke Willoughby."

"Oh?"

"She's our daughter. I want her brought back by someone I trust."

Charlotte nodded, studying him with her too-observant eyes. She noticed everything. "You're thinking of going as well, aren't you, Stephen?"

"I was going to speak to you about it first."

"It's a little dangerous."

"Yes, it is… but I can't ask my men to take a risk for my child that I'm not willing to."

"No. And it makes more sense anyway. Nobody will stop you at the border, and everyone will be safer with you there."

"I'll be fine, Charlotte."

"I know. But we have a deal, Stephen…I allow you to do what you need to do without complaining, and you allow me to worry about you until you're back safe with me."

"Yes, that was our deal." He pulled her closer to him, kissing her on the cheek. "Not that I'd deny such a beautiful queen much of anything."

"All this time later, and you still think you can get your way with flattery."

"Can't I?" he asked with mock chagrin.

"I am helpless in the wake of your charm, Stephen."

He smiled, burying his face in her neck, and holding her tight. "Are you holding up okay with all of this?" he asked, after a few minutes.

She shrugged. "As well as possible. At least we know she's probably safe."

"Yes. She's no good to him if she's injured."

Charlotte nodded, but her lower lip trembled just a little. Stephen pulled her closer to him again. "I know."

She shook her head. "It's not even just that… it's… this whole thing with Linnea has really made me realize what we just did to Quinn's mother. It's nearly the same, isn't it? We stole her daughter to marry our son, for political gain. We couldn't promise Megan she would be safe, either."

Stephen swallowed hard. "William isn't Tolliver."

"And Linnea isn't in another world that we can't even always travel to."

"I know, Charlotte. We've discussed this so often, but it doesn't get any easier. We're all going to be paying for Samuel's choices for the rest of our lives. But Megan more than anyone."

"And Quinn, and her siblings, and the man who raised her as his daughter."

"That's why it had to be her choice. And we did let her make it. We didn't force her hand."

"No, we just made sure we helped her along, made sure we influenced her enough that she wanted to."

"Do you really believe that, Charlotte? Do you really believe she's a lovesick girl who is only here because of William?"

She looked down at the floor. "No. That doesn't sound right."

"That's because it isn't, sweetheart. It's true we might have crossed a line, sending William to her world to go to school with her…but I don't think that's the only thing that brought her here. And I don't believe it was truly our influence that brought her here…that brought her home."

"We're not that good, are we?" she said, smirking up at him.

"No." He brought her hand up to his lips, and kissed her gently on the palm. "We can accomplish many things together, you and I…but we're still not *that* powerful. Quinn is here because she was supposed to be, and because she made the choice to be. It's just very difficult for those who have to live with the consequences."

She must have heard the catch in his voice, because she looked up at him in concern. "Have you still been having the same dreams?"

He closed his eyes, unable to look her in the eyes as he nodded. "I don't understand why, or what it means, but I keep seeing the same thing."

"Quinn being unable to get back through the gate."

"Yes. *Nobody* being able to go through."

"If that really happened…"

"I know, sweetheart. I don't want to think about it, either. We've always known that using the gate was dangerous, but for

Quinn not to be able to use it now would be devastating. Let's hope this is one of those times that the dream is a symbol, and not really the way things are going to happen."

"You know," Will whispered, "I never spent much time imagining my honeymoon, but if I had, I don't think it would have been like this."

Quinn giggled and snuggled closer to him. No, sleeping outside for the second chilly night in a row, with very little privacy, wasn't how she would have imagined her honeymoon, either. "Tonight *is* a little better than last night," she said.

"That's true." Tonight, at least, they had a couple of small fires and a tarp shielding them from the light breeze, courtesy of the supplies Jonathan had been carrying. They were even sharing a blanket, which at the moment was wrapped around both of them as he leaned against a fallen tree, and she leaned on his chest, both of their legs stretched out toward the little fire Ben had built just for them.

Quinn's hands had twitched as Ben had carefully cleared the area under the tarp for them, carefully sweeping away every last rock and twig, and then carefully using the tarp and some large sticks to build a neat little shelter.

Finally, she'd gone to help Nathaniel and William set up the rest of the camp…a short distance away from the shelter for her and William. Everyone was still very serious about the idea of giving the two of them whatever privacy they could. She wasn't sure if she would ever get over being embarrassed by that.

Marcus had gone with Jonathan to scope out the perimeter of the Miller Estate, half an hour away from their campsite. They'd all been wary of sending Jonathan off alone with one of their guards, but

Quinn had decided that it was time to put it on the line. If they were going to trust Jonathan, then they needed to really trust him.

And they'd both returned safely, less than three hours later, with the news that they were fairly certain Tolliver hadn't yet arrived at the estate, but that the area was quite heavily guarded, and they'd had to be careful even getting close to the property.

Over a warm dinner of fresh roasted vegetables, also thanks to Jonathan, they'd discussed their plans. Quinn thought they should just go ahead and try to get her and Nathaniel into the estate to see Queen Sophia. Jonathan was wary. He was afraid of doing it with no military backup, in case things went badly with the soldiers outside, or Tolliver arrived too soon.

For now, they'd compromised. They'd sent birds off with messages to both Stephen and Charles, telling them as much as they could about the situation without giving themselves away. And now, they waited. Camped out in one of the most rural parts of Philotheum, away from any village, a place where smoke likely wouldn't be investigated, so long as they kept it to a minimum. Nobody would expect anyone to be out here.

"Are you warm enough?" William asked, wrapping the blanket more securely around the front of her.

She nodded, still staring into the flickering flames of the fire. "I'm rather comfortable at the moment, actually."

"Me too," he agreed, kissing her just behind her ear. His hand found the bottom of her shirt and slid inside, soft and warm as it rested against her belly, making her shiver from something very different than the cold.

"You know," she said, finding his hand with hers, and twisting her fingers with his. "I could probably imagine worse honeymoons than this one."

"Really? You can imagine something worse than sleeping on the ground, and other people being around constantly, and worrying about being attacked by an army at any moment?"

"Sure. I can imagine having to face any one of those things without you. Anywhere I am with you is going to be our honeymoon, Will. Forever."

"Forever sounds good to me, love."

She didn't understand how she'd gotten there, but she knew exactly where she was. The stone bridge stretched across the river in front of her. The shadows from the surrounding trees were long and wide; it was nearly dusk.

Suddenly, she realized she wasn't alone. There was a man on the bottom step of the bridge. His hair was an unusual shade of gray, almost true silver, though there were light brown strands that snaked through at odd intervals. His neatly trimmed beard and mustache were the same strange color.

She'd never seen him before; nothing was familiar about him at all, and yet she knew who he was.

She sucked in a breath as Hector made his way up the steps of the bridge, just as the sun began to sink below the horizon.

Her blood ran cold when he disappeared, taking the sun with him and plunging the whole world into darkness.

In the next instant, it was light again, but the scene was different. Although it was dusk, just as it had been before, the grass under her feet was newly covered with frost. As she looked down, uncomprehending, she realized there was no grass at all. The entire ground was covered with dandelions, mostly withered and frozen under the frost, except for one.

A perfect dandelion bloomed at the foot of the bridge, the largest one she'd ever seen. As she watched, its pristine yellow petals changed, in slow motion, to the familiar white seed-bearing tufts.

She wanted to run, to pull it, to throw her body over it to prevent what she knew was about to happen, but her feet wouldn't move. It was as if she, too, were frozen to the ground.

She could do nothing when the wind began to blow, to lift the seed heads up and off the plant, diffusing them everywhere, until the air was filled with thousands of them, blowing in every direction.

Still frozen, she stared in shock as Hector reappeared, but this time, his hands weren't empty, and he wasn't alone.

Right behind Hector were three police officers. She couldn't see all of their faces, but she recognized instantly the one she could. Louis Chavez, her best friend Abigail's older brother was just behind Hector, his gun drawn.

For a moment, she thought the weapon was pointed at her, but then she realized it was aimed just over her left shoulder, and as she turned, she saw Stephen standing there, reaching toward her. And then the gun went off.

"Quinn! Quinn! Wake up, love, please, Quinn!"

She struggled in William's arms as she slowly came to consciousness. Her heart was racing, and tears streamed down her face. She heard herself yelling, but she couldn't understand the words, or what was going on.

"Quinn, love, I've got you, I'm right here. Shh…" William pulled her tight to his chest and held her there, rocking her and smoothing her hair back until finally, finally, she stopped struggling and opened her eyes.

He held her for several more minutes, while her breathing calmed and she fully woke.

"You scared me, baby. What was that?" he asked, pressing his lips against her temple.

For a moment, she didn't even know, but as she opened her mouth to tell him she couldn't remember what the dream had been about, it all came rushing back, slamming into her with the force of a freight train. "It's Hector, Will. He knows about the gate. He knows, and he's going to use it."

"How would it be possible?" Nathaniel said; both anger and fear were thick in his voice…William had never actually seen him this angry. "I thought you said you didn't tell Hector or Tolliver what you learned about the gate."

"I didn't. I didn't tell *anyone*, least of all either of them."

"Then *how* Jonathan? Because I am about to seriously regret trusting you at all." He'd already taken Jonathan's weapons again.

"It was only a dream, Nathaniel. It might not mean anything."

William shook his head. Quinn's hands were still trembling, and she'd been awake for a good half hour now. He still had her wrapped in a blanket in his lap, with his arms around her…the fact that she was allowing him to do that in front of people told him this was more than one of her ordinary nightmares. "This is serious," he said.

"Does she have these kinds of dreams often or something?" Jonathan asked.

"Yes. It's a trait of royal firstborns," Nathaniel said.

"Well, you'll have to forgive me," Jonathan said pointedly. "I haven't grown up with the privilege of knowing any." He shot Nathaniel a look that almost made William feel guilty. "Are the dreams always an accurate portrayal of the future?"

"No." Quinn sat up now, finally shrugging the blanket off, and pulling away from him. "I never know what they are, exactly. Sometimes they do show something that's going to happen, but other times, they're just to warn me about something, or to help me decide something."

"So this could still mean nothing," Jonathan said. "I know my stepfather has some idea that a gate between worlds might exist, but there isn't any way he knows exactly where one is, or when it opens. *I* don't even know how it works; I couldn't have told him."

"I don't think it means nothing," Quinn said. "Something about this… It was more powerful than it usually is. Obviously it's not a literal interpretation of the future, but it isn't nothing. I think we need to consider the possibility that Hector really does know about the gate, and that he intends on using it…possibly the next time it opens."

"That would be very, very bad," William said. A shudder ran through Quinn's entire body, and he leaned up to put his arms around her again.

Jonathan frowned. "Do you think he would really be able to find the support there to accomplish his goals here?"

"No," Nathaniel said. "Hector is not in any way prepared for what he would encounter on the other side of that gate. If he went there with the intention of finding someone to assist him in his miserable excuse for a war…"

"He'd probably find himself on a seventy-two-hour mental health hold," William finished.

"The problem isn't that Hector would find something there that would help him," Nathaniel said. "Although, if he did somehow manage to bring back a gun…" He sighed. "There is no easy way for me to explain the differences between the two worlds, but the risk of the people of that world discovering this one…it's worse than anything you could possibly imagine, Jonathan. They have weapons you've never dreamed of. The smallest army from there could destroy all of us, both of our kingdoms, *all* of the kingdoms in Deusterros, before we even knew what was happening."

Jonathan's jaw dropped. "Why would they do that? Nobody here has threatened or harmed anyone from that world."

"It wouldn't be about that," Quinn said quietly. "It would be about discovering a world where people live ten times as long…yes, that's true, Jonathan. Ten days here in Deusterros equals only one day on Earth, in the world where I was born. And compared to that world, this is a world that's clean and beautiful and probably full of resources that are valuable to the governments of that world."

"But it isn't theirs!" Jonathan was aghast. Marcus' and Ben's eyes were as wide as William had ever seen them. Though they were two of the very few guards who knew about the world he and Nathaniel had been visiting, they'd been told very little about it.

"It doesn't matter. It's so unprotected here. We wouldn't stand a chance." William heard something in Quinn's voice now that he'd never heard before. Although she had decided to stay here and claim her throne, this was the first time he'd ever heard the note of ownership in her voice …the loyalty to this world over the one where she'd been born.

"Is it really so terrible there that they would want to come and steal what we have?"

Quinn shrugged. "It would take me a hundred cycles to explain it, unless you've experienced it. It just…isn't about that."

Nathaniel shook his head. "It's not actually that different than Hector trying to take a kingdom that doesn't belong to him. It's enough to understand that there are people in that world who are the same. Only they have much better weapons, and resources that we don't have. And they would win."

"We can't let that happen," Marcus said.

Nathaniel's complexion had gone gray. "No. We can't even risk the *possibility* of it happening."

"Can we stop Hector?"

Jonathan shrugged. "I don't know where he is, or how he's planning on getting to the gate in Eirentheos, if he even is. I can say with certainty that he is capable of it. Worse, I can tell you that if Hector really does know about it, he is not the only one. He'll have shared the information with his oracle, and possibly the king of Dovelnia as well."

Quinn's whole body started trembling. William reached to take her hand, praying that the motion would steady her, reassure her, although he, too, was feeling pretty hopeless.

When Quinn spoke, her voice was so quiet they had to strain to hear her. "We have to close the gate," she said. "We have to disable it so that nobody can use it."

Everyone was silent as they absorbed the impact of that statement. A sick heaviness filled William's stomach, and he could feel that Quinn's hand had grown cold and clammy.

This was a decision that would affect her more than anyone. Sure, he and Nathaniel had enjoyed the access they'd had to the other world, and his kingdom had benefitted in many ways from the things they'd learned there. And there had been many more things they'd hoped to learn, supplies they'd wanted to bring back, even a few personal possessions that had been left at the house he and Nathaniel had shared.

But his family was here. Quinn was here. He would get to keep everything that truly meant anything to him. But Quinn… He couldn't even think about what she would have to sacrifice to make this decision. Couldn't think about Megan, Annie…*Owen*.

She'd never even had the chance to say good-bye to her friends, or to Jeff, the man she'd always known as her father.

He wanted to pull her into his arms and hold her tight, but he was afraid she wouldn't like how that appeared…that it might make her feel weak when she needed most to be strong. So he just held her hand and stood there beside her.

Jonathan was the first to speak. "How? I already tried burning it down. It's a stone bridge, and it still worked after that, did it not?"

"It did," Quinn said. "I don't think we can close off the gate by destroying the bridge."

"Then is it even possible to close it?"

"Yes, I think it is," she said. "But I don't know exactly how, and I don't think it will be easy, but we have to try. We have to get back to the gate before Hector does. The sooner the better, because it could take us days to figure out how to close it."

"When is the gate supposed to open again?" Jonathan asked.

"Four more days," Nathaniel said. "I've just done the math several times. It will be open again four evenings from now."

"Well, this changes everything, then," Marcus said. "We don't have time to wait for Charles, or for anyone else. We have to try to get Linnea from the Miller Estate ourselves. Today."

THE MILLER ESTATE

"ISN'T IT TOO DANGEROUS to try to take Quinn into the estate itself?" William asked, as they walked. "She's the one person we can't afford to lose."

"We can't afford to lose anyone," Quinn said, taking his hand and squeezing it. She understood what he was doing, and she loved him for it. She was having plenty of trouble thinking about allowing *him* to take part in this, but there wasn't going to be a choice. "But it doesn't matter. We're not just sending someone in to try and get Linnea."

"That would never work, anyway," Jonathan said, stopping and turning around to face them. His horse snorted at the sudden interruption. The animal was already irritated at their slow pace; Jonathan had been walking alongside the horse all morning, holding its lead.

"We'd never get her out of the Miller Estate unchallenged. And the chances that we would win…it's not even worth attempting. We'd put Linnea in more danger. Our goal now is to get Quinn *in* to see my mother. And it would be best if you were with her, Prince William."

"How do we know this isn't just a trap?" Nathaniel asked. "A way to get all of us inside?"

A swell of irritation rose in Quinn's chest, and she snapped. "Enough, Nathaniel! I understand that you're worried…we all are. But this wasn't even Jonathan's idea. He was willing to wait for backup from Charles and Stephen. This is because of me, because of what *I* dreamed. Jonathan has had plenty of opportunity already to betray us. He could have had us killed in our sleep last night. He could have us surrounded with Philothean guards right now.

"Yes, he kidnapped me, before he knew who I was, when he was looking for answers. He's your brother, and during this whole thing here, he's given us no real reason not to trust him."

Nathaniel sighed. "You're right. I'm sorry. Jonathan, I'm sorry."

"I can't say I blame you, Nathaniel," he said, shrugging. "I never did apologize to you…to any of you…for taking Quinn. And for taking your family. I'm sure that distressed you, and is very good reason for all of you not to trust me. I haven't had the resources that you have, though. I've lived with and dealt with Hector and Tolliver all of my life…and if I hadn't, you all would stand no chance right now. I hate to point out the obvious, but…whatever your reservations might be, Nathaniel…you don't have a better option right now."

"Or any other option at all," Quinn said. "So how do you propose we do this thing?"

"We'll come up on the perimeter of the property in about ten minutes. If we can keep to the trees and get as close in to the main house as possible, I know where my mother is staying. The important thing is to get inside without being detained by any guards or soldiers. Brian Miller and his family are Friends of Philip…they'll fight, if they have something to fight *for*. Right now, they are avoiding getting into a fight with Tolliver's men…they don't want to give up their loyalties until it is necessary. Quinn will be worth the fight…if my mother recognizes her as the heir."

Quinn's heart thudded in her chest, and her palms were suddenly damp. "This is all on me."

"Get used to that, Princess. Quickly."

They'd only walked for about five more minutes when Jonathan stopped suddenly. "Be silent," he hissed through his teeth, and they all froze.

Quinn heard it almost immediately. Footsteps and low talking from at least two people, but possibly more, only about ten yards to their left.

Marcus and Ben were around her so quickly that she didn't even see them move. Even William pulled out his knife.

They all held their breath and listened. The footsteps continued, but didn't come any closer. Once they had faded away, Marcus nodded, and they all continued walking, but with much more care, and making as little noise as possible.

When they crested a hill and caught a glimpse of a sprawling stone-and-wood house, Jonathan stopped and tied his horse to a tree.

"There will be guards everywhere," Jonathan said, under his breath. "And some regular soldiers, too. Some of that is standard, with the queen in residence, but even more will be special details because this is where they've brought Linnea, and Tolliver is coming…if he's not already there. Many of them won't even know about Linnea."

"Where will they be holding her?"

Jonathan shook his head. "I don't know. It's only a house…a big house, but also pretty ordinary. There is a basement under one of the wings, but Tolliver and his guards wouldn't know about it."

"Is anyone *in* the basement?" Quinn asked. Underneath Ellen's house on her estate, the basement served as a hiding place for fugitives who belonged to the Friends of Philip.

"Probably, though that isn't our concern. Anyone there will be safe, so long as they're not discovered. We're trying to get to that wing back there." he pointed to a long section on the opposite side of the house from where they were standing. "That's where the guest quarters are, and where my mother is staying. There's a back entrance."

"We just have to get through it without getting caught?" Quinn asked.

"Without getting caught by one of Tolliver's soldiers. The good news is, all the members of the Miller family are Friends of Philip…and so are their personal guards."

"The bad news is there are lots of soldiers here who aren't?"

"Yes, Princess. If you reveal your tattoo to the right guard, it could save us all; but if the wrong person sees it, you could lose your life."

"Great. Glad we've cleared that up." She couldn't resist flashing a thumbs-up sign at him. William snickered under his breath, but the effort was lost on Jonathan…the motion didn't mean anything to him. "Let's go."

"It's always the little things," William whispered as they walked, and she remembered a conversation they'd had back when they'd first started courting, before they'd even made their courtship official.

She'd asked him if he had ever gotten used to spending so much time in a world that was so different from his own, and he'd told her that it had been easier than he'd expected getting used to the big things…like school, and cars, and television. What had always been harder were the "little things"…the small habits and customs that were so ingrained that nobody ever even remembered to tell you about them, like which hand to shake with when you were meeting someone new, the slang terms for things, the "right" way to eat certain foods.

In third grade, he'd told her, his class had earned a pizza party for some special occasion, and he'd embarrassed himself by asking for a fork. The whole ordeal had been made even worse when he'd finally held his slice and taken a bite of it, only to discover that he didn't even like it. Tomatoes weren't native to his world, and he'd never tasted anything like the thick red sauce under the cheese.

He squeezed her hand now, and she squeezed back gratefully. She knew how lucky she was to have found him…the one man who could really understand both parts of her life, and how strange this transition was for her.

Of course, it wasn't *always* the little things, and she was steeling herself right now to face one big thing William couldn't relate to at all. She was about to meet her grandmother who didn't even know she existed. She hadn't had much time to process that before, but it was the biggest thing on her mind now. What was Queen Sophia going to think of her? Would she believe her? Accept her as the heir to the throne?

Everything…the decision she'd made, the journey they were on, turning her back on the world she'd been born in, leaving her family behind…it could all be for naught, if Sophia didn't accept her as her granddaughter.

She glanced up at Nathaniel, and she saw the apprehension on his face, too. He was about to see his mother for the first time since he was a young teenager. His mother who had believed all this time that he was dead.

She reached up now and squeezed Nathaniel's shoulder. For a moment, he covered her hand with his, and gave her an understanding smile.

And then they were there.

Somehow, they'd walked all the way around the property, hidden in the safety of the trees, without catching the attention of any soldiers. They could see the door to the guest wing now, only a short distance away, across a wide, open space.

A single guard patrolled near the door.

"Thank the Maker," Jonathan whispered.

"What?" Quinn asked, looking up at him.

"I know him. He's a Friend of Philip. I'm going to go talk to him."

And before she could stop him, Jonathan was gone, walking across the wide lawn, and then chatting casually with the large, armed man.

Her stomach felt like it was folding in on itself, forming a solid mass. She was waiting for it all to go horribly wrong…for more guards to come around the corner, for Jonathan to betray them…she didn't know how it was going to happen, but she could feel that it was.

For the first time ever, she found herself following the example she had seen William set so very many times, and she whispered a prayer to the Maker, asking for their safety, asking for the courage to do what she needed to do.

And then Jonathan held his arm in the air and waved them over.

In what felt like the very next instant, Jonathan was ushering them into the sitting area of a large, well-appointed guest room. "This is where I was staying," he said. "Wait here and I'll be back in a few minutes."

Quinn, William, and Nathaniel all stared at each other, none of them sure what they were supposed to do. Just standing there was uncomfortable, but sitting down was awkward, too.

Marcus and Ben walked to a far corner of the room, and took up sentry positions, obviously trying to be as unobtrusive as possible.

William had just wrapped his arms around Quinn's waist, and had his lips by her ear, about to whisper something that she was sure was meant to be calming, when, without fanfare, the door swung open.

Quinn gasped at the same time the woman standing there did. There was no question about who she was. They'd traveled all this way to see her. And her hair, pinned up on top of her head, was the same warm auburn as Quinn's.

But that didn't account for the fact that Quinn recognized her. There was no way she'd ever met this woman, no chance she could have ever really seen her, and yet, somehow she knew she had. Perhaps in one of her dreams.

The way Queen Sophia was staring made Quinn think for a moment that maybe she, too, was staring at a vision from her dreams.

But then, she realized that her grandmother wasn't looking at her at all.

"Nathaniel… it's really you…" Sophia's voice was barely more than a whisper as she crossed the room to her son. She paused there, her hands twitching as if she was fighting the urge to reach out and touch him.

"Yes, Mother. It's me." Nathaniel's eyes were actually damp, and he took her trembling hands in his.

The moment that passed between Nathaniel and Sophia then was so tender and personal that Quinn almost felt like she was intruding by watching it, but she couldn't pull her eyes away.

So this was the woman who had somehow raised both men like her father and Nathaniel, and a man like Tolliver. Quinn wanted to understand that, and as she watched the scene unfold in front of her, she thought she caught a glimpse of at least some of it.

Tears were streaming down Sophia's face by the time Jonathan put his hand under her elbow, and carefully led her to one of the couches, handing her a handkerchief before sitting down next to her. After a long moment, she finally looked up, seeming to notice for the first time that there were other people in the room.

Looking first at William, she frowned. "You must be one of Stephen and Charlotte's sons, but I'm afraid I don't know which one."

William smiled kindly, bending down as he stepped closer to her. "I'm William, their fourth born."

"And those are your guards?" she asked, tilting her head back toward the corner. Innocent as the motion was, it let Quinn know that Sophia wasn't quite as unobservant as she seemed.

"Fourth born. Just like Nathaniel," she said, nodding.

"Yes, Mother," Nathaniel's voice was tentative. "William is a healer, like I am. He and I have been very close since he was young."

"So you've been living in Eirentheos all this time?"

"Mostly."

"And everyone kept this from me? Stephen knew? Everyone knew?"

"Calm down, Mother," Jonathan said, resting his hand on her shoulder. "It wouldn't have been safe for you to know. If Hector had found out…"

Sophia took a deep breath, staring at her lap and smoothing out invisible wrinkles in her dress. "You're right. You're right. I'm sorry." She looked back up at Nathaniel.

"And so, William, son of Stephen, may I ask what you are doing here? Has Stephen finally decided to lend his support? To help me find some way to avoid handing the throne over to my youngest son? To keep my husband from ruining our kingdoms?"

Quinn felt dizzy as the rest of them exchanged wary looks.

"Mother," Jonathan said, very softly, "we have more to tell you."

"So you're my granddaughter," Sophia said, studying Quinn intently. She held both Quinn's and Samuel's pendants in her hand, and was rubbing the etched surface of Samuel's with her thumb. "I can see it; you certainly look the part. Those are Samuel's eyes."

She looked at Nathaniel. "Why would he have done this? Why didn't he just come back when he was an adult?"

Nathaniel sighed. "I'm afraid I don't know all of the reasons, Mother. He was afraid…for himself, for Quinn, for his wife, who didn't even know who he really was."

"How is that possible? Surely everyone in Eirentheos…"

"It doesn't matter how, Mother. It's the truth." He opened the backpack he'd been carrying, and pulled out an envelope, handing it to Sophia so she could examine the certificate inside, the one from Quinn's Naming Ceremony, signed by Alvin. "Quinn only just learned who she is about a moon ago."

"And now you've pushed her into a marriage, so that she can fulfill the prophecy?"

"No." Quinn was careful not to shout, but her voice was firm. "My marriage to William had nothing to do with the prophecy."

"Other than the fact that it conveniently fulfills it?" Again, there was that tiny spark in Sophia's eyes.

"That was rather fortunate," Quinn agreed.

"Quite. Not that it matters. You're married now…however that came to be. Are you with child?"

A flash burn raced across Quinn's cheeks. "We've only been married six days."

Sophia raised an eyebrow, but continued speaking. "And you're standing here telling me that you're prepared to take your birthright, to take my place as queen."

Quinn swallowed hard. "Yes."

Sophia nodded. "This should have been different, I suppose. I should have known you existed, for one. I should have been prepared to meet you, and greet you properly and get to know you a little bit… but that isn't where we are. So, for today, I'm going to have to say that I've been praying for an answer…any answer that would keep the throne away from Hector and Tolliver, and you'll do."

SOPHIA

SHE'D DO. Quinn didn't know what she'd expected, but hearing her long-lost grandmother tell her "she'd do" hadn't quite been it. She supposed it was better than rejection.

She was still reeling from that response, trying to figure out what exactly it meant, when Sophia turned to Jonathan. "Go and speak to Hadrian. Have the girl brought to me, please. I don't care what he has to say about it."

"Yes, Mother." Jonathan stood and walked toward the door. When he reached it, though, he turned around with a strange look on his face. "Has it been like this the whole time?"

They all looked. Although he'd not yet grasped the knob, the door was ajar, just slightly.

Sophia frowned. "I thought you closed it all the way."

"I did."

She shrugged. "These old houses…sometimes you can't be sure. This is a private, secured hallway in any case. I'm sure it's fine."

Once Jonathan was gone, the silence was awkward. They all stared at each other for what felt like a very long time.

Quinn finally decided to speak. "So you believe me? That I'm your granddaughter and the heir to the throne?"

"Do you have some reason to lie to me that I don't know about? If someone was simply trying to usurp the throne, I suspect they'd have sent me a boy. Though it would have been hard to find one that looked as much like Samuel as you do. And harder still to find one that Stephen would have allowed one of his children to marry."

"I suppose that's true."

"Yes, it's true. Besides, you still have a difficult road ahead of you. I doubt my husband or my son will give up very easily."

"Or at all." The new voice startled them all as the door swung all the way open.

The first thing Quinn saw was Linnea, which confused her, because it wasn't Linnea's voice she'd heard, it was… Adrenaline rushed through her veins as she realized that Tolliver was just behind Linnea, and he had one arm around her chest, and he was pointing a dagger at her throat.

"I hate to intrude on your lovely little meeting here, but I think there are a few things you haven't considered." Slamming the door closed with his foot, Tolliver strode purposefully into the room, pushing Linnea in front of him.

Linnea looked terrified, her arms dangling by her sides, although her eyes scanned the room, taking in her surroundings. After a brief glance at Quinn, William, and Nathaniel, Linnea's eyes locked on something to the far side of the room, and she made a small grabbing motion with one hand.

Quinn didn't dare follow Linnea's gaze. Marcus and Ben were over there, but the way Tolliver was standing, she didn't think he'd seen them.

"I don't know who you are," Tolliver said, looking right at Quinn. "Or why Stephen thinks he can get away with tricking my mother out of my throne, but if you don't pack up and head back to wherever it is you're from, I will kill her."

"How will you fulfill the prophecy if you do?" Quinn asked.

Tolliver looked stunned, but only for a second. "I won't. I'll come up with some other way. I'm sure that killing Stephen's daughter will make him angry enough to really fight. Perhaps then my father can bring in some real forces from Dovelnia to defend our borders."

"And what will that accomplish, Tolliver?" She didn't care about the answer, wasn't even sure what she was asking. Her only goal right then was to keep him talking, keep him focused on her. Ben and Marcus had managed to creep around the outside of the room.

"What business is it of yours? All you need to know is that if you don't leave here now, I really will kill the girl. And I don't think you want that." He pressed the tip of the knife into Linnea's neck just enough to draw blood.

"Will you let her go if I leave?"

"I won't kill her. I'll still need her to fulfill the prophecy then, but I assure you, she'll be treated as a proper princess of Philotheum, as my *wife*."

Suddenly, Tolliver gasped in pain. As he did, Linnea reached up with her left hand and grabbed his knife, pulling it away from her neck. Somehow, she twisted around, out of his grasp, and pointed it at his chest.

Only then did Quinn see the quickly growing bloodstain on the leg of Tolliver's pants. It took a second to realize the source…the small dagger embedded in his thigh.

Marcus and Ben were both behind him with lightning speed. Ben took the knife from Linnea, and held it at Tolliver's neck himself while Marcus grabbed his hands and held them behind his back. Then, Ben moved to the side so Marcus could force Tolliver down onto the ground.

"Quick, I need something to tie his hands with."

Everyone looked around for a few seconds, seeing nothing. William finally unbuckled his belt, and handed it to Marcus, before grabbing his sister, and pulling her back toward the couch.

That was when Quinn realized that Linnea was bleeding, too. There was a trail of blood on the carpet, dripping from her hand where she'd grabbed the blade of Tolliver's knife.

Just then, Jonathan appeared again in the doorway with two guards behind him. He blinked when he saw the scene. "Well, I guess you took care of it." Turning to the two guards, he said, "Take him, please. He's under arrest."

"Please," Tolliver spat, though he was still being pinned to the ground by Marcus. "You can't arrest me. I'm the heir to the throne." He looked at Sophia. "Mother, don't be ridiculous. You need to end this before my father finds out."

Sophia sighed. "I will always wonder how much of your sense of entitlement is my fault, Tolliver. Somewhere along the line, I should have managed to teach you that I'm the one you really needed to answer to. You're right about me needing to end it, however." Squaring her shoulders, she looked right at the two guards. "Arrest him. Make sure his injuries are treated, but don't let him go anywhere."

"Don't move him yet!" Nathaniel said, stepping in front of the guards, and kneeling down next to Tolliver.

"Nathaniel…" Williams's voice was strained.

Quinn turned, looking toward where she'd heard William's voice, but she saw Linnea first and gasped. There was a lot more blood on Linnea's hand than there had been a minute ago. A dark red stain was spreading across her shirt. There was also a trickle running down the side of her neck. William was already over there, kneeling in front of the couch where she was sitting…he was the one who had taken the hem of Linnea's skirt and wrapped her hand in it as best he could.

Nathaniel looked at William. "I have some supplies in my bag," he said. "Quinn, can you hand me my backpack? I need to get Tolliver's injury stable before he bleeds out."

"Like you would care," Tolliver said, acid in his voice. But there was sweat beading on his forehead, and he was starting to look pale.

There was a *lot* more blood under Tolliver now; forming a pool on the carpet by his leg.

"Whatever else I am, Tolliver, I'm not someone who's going to sit by while my brother dies when I could have done something."

"Brother? What are you talking about?" Tolliver looked frantically between Nathaniel and Sophia. "What is he talking about?"

"Nathaniel is your brother."

"No, my brother Nathaniel died when I was young. Just like Samuel."

"Samuel didn't die, either," Sophia said. "At least not when you were a child. He lived long enough to produce an heir. Quinn is his daughter."

"That's impossible."

"No," Nathaniel said, "what's impossible is you staying conscious much longer with that hole in your leg. I think she hit an artery."

"Well, maybe if you took the damn knife out! I'd do it myself, but I'm a bit indisposed."

"And it's a good thing you are," Nathaniel said, unzipping the bag Quinn had handed him. "If you pulled that thing out right now, you'd bleed to death right here. And as much as, right now, I think I wouldn't mind watching that, I'm sure later on, it will be more satisfying to know you're watching Quinn sit on the throne from your prison cell."

"Nathaniel!" The shock in Sophia's voice matched Quinn's own feelings. She couldn't believe she'd heard Nathaniel say that…not that she disagreed with him, but still…

"Don't tell me there's not at least a part of you that feels the same way right now, Mother. He *kidnapped* Linnea, and was going to force her to marry him. The last time he met Quinn, he nearly attacked her…his own *niece*."

"I didn't know that." Tolliver said. There was still derision in his voice, but it was weaker now. He'd gone pale white; the cloth Nathaniel was tying around the knife was already turning red.

"It doesn't matter what you knew," Nathaniel said through his teeth. "You're a miserable excuse for a human being for even trying it. And you deserve what's coming to you. But right now, I'm going to save your life so I can make sure you get it."

He looked up at Jonathan. "Is there somewhere we can take him…with a table, maybe? And are there supplies here of any kind?"

Jonathan nodded. "These two will take him for you. I will speak to Brian about whether there are any supplies…for both of you."

The two guards, under Nathaniel's direction, carefully lifted Tolliver and headed toward the door.

As Quinn picked up William's backpack to carry it to him, she heard Jonathan talking quietly with Sophia.

"Come on, Mother. Let's let them take care of this." Quinn glanced at her grandmother and saw that she'd gone almost as white as Tolliver, and her hands were shaking.

"Are we safe here?" Quinn asked Jonathan, as he helped Sophia to her feet.

"Yes." Sophia answered. "As safe as you would be anywhere, now that we know where Tolliver is."

"Where is Hector?"

"I don't know where my husband is, Quinn, but I know he wasn't traveling in this direction any time soon. Jonathan will ask some more guards from the Friends of Philip to stand outside the door for you, if it will make you feel safer. Perhaps we can talk later, after I've had a chance to rest."

"We can keep watch in the hallway as well," Marcus said, looking a little green himself. The carpet did look a bit like a murder scene. "Ben?"

Ben was in the middle of scooping Linnea into his arms to carry her into the adjoining bedroom. "I'll stay inside and guard here…if that's all right?" He was looking at Linnea as he asked.

Linnea gave a weak shrug. "That's up to you."

Marcus closed the door tightly behind him. Quinn followed

William, Ben, and Linnea into the bedroom, although a not-small part of her would have gladly gone with Marcus into the hallway.

"I am going to ruin that," Linnea said, as Ben tried to set her gently down on the soft white comforter. Quinn darted in front of them, and Ben lifted Linnea back up a little, so Quinn could pull the blankets off.

"Are there any towels anywhere?" Quinn asked.

Ben looked around helplessly. "I don't see anything in here. I can go ask someone to bring us some."

William nodded. "Water would be great, too. The biggest pitcher or basin you can find." He was digging through his backpack, pulling out everything that resembled a piece of cloth or a medical supply. Quinn was relieved to see him take out his leather bag and set it on the bed.

Ben hurried out of the room.

"So, how bad is it?" Linnea asked.

William looked up from the supplies he was organizing and ran his finger down the side of his sister's cheek. "That had to have been the most amazing thing I've ever seen in my life, Nay. I am stunned, and so proud of you."

And that was when it hit Quinn, so hard that the realization made her knees go weak, and she had to sit down on the bed beside Linnea. That had all just really happened. And Linnea was here, right in front of them. Safe...*mostly, anyway.*

She couldn't stop herself from pulling Linnea into her arms...injuries and blood notwithstanding, she needed to touch her, to feel that she was real.

"That's not what I asked," Linnea said, once she and Quinn had finally let each other go, and Quinn had helped her lie back against the pillows. "How badly did I damage myself?"

"Well," William said, sitting down beside her and unwrapping the strip of cloth he'd tied around her hand. "You are definitely going to be seeing the wrong end of a needle for the first time. But I think it's going to be okay."

Quinn rubbed Linnea's shoulder.

"Is it going to hurt?"

"Doesn't it already?"

"It's starting to. It didn't really when it happened. Is that weird?"

"No. It was a sharp knife, and you had a lot of adrenaline in your system. It's a clean cut...you probably didn't feel much of anything. It's deep, but not so bad. Stitches will fix it. Same with the cut on your neck. Fortunately, I do have most of what I need here. Part of me thought it was stupid to carry this stuff across the river instead of just sending it with Skittles, but now I'm glad I did."

Linnea nodded, though her lower lip trembled a little, and the color had drained from her face.

William frowned, reaching up to feel her forehead. Quinn watched as he took longer than necessary, running his hand across her forehead, then down the sides of her face with supreme care. She thought she saw tears in the corners of his eyes as he took the wrist of Linnea's uninjured right hand and felt for her pulse.

"I think you might be in a little bit of shock," William said to her. "Honestly, I think we might all be. I'm going to get you fixed up, though, and then we can rest and figure things out."

He rubbed at his eyes with the sleeve of his shirt before reaching back into his bag, and Quinn had to swallow back a lump in her throat.

"Here," William said, tossing a small, plastic bottle to Quinn. It took her several seconds to figure out what it was...a bottle of hand sanitizer, from her world. She didn't know why, but she almost felt like crying as she used some of it to clean her hands.

"Okay, sweetheart, I'm going to get started numbing up your hand here in a second," William said.

Linnea's eyes grew wide. "I can't believe I did this to myself," she said.

"Enough." William's voice was more serious than Quinn had ever heard it. "You didn't do *anything* to yourself. You were a hero in there. And right at this moment, I'm wishing Nathaniel would have let Tolliver bleed to death from that awesome move of yours. *You* are going to be fine. I can fix this."

"The numbing medicine is the worst part," Quinn said, echoing what Thomas had told her the first time she'd gotten stitches. "It stings for a minute. But then you won't even feel the stitches."

"Tell me I didn't give you too much of a bad time when you were scared of a needle," Linnea said.

"You did, but I'm not much for revenge," William said, smiling, though it didn't reach all the way to his puffy red eyes. "Besides, I never earned my cuts the way you earned yours. It'll be over in a minute. You just look at Quinn, and not at me. I need you to just relax and breathe, okay?"

Linnea nodded. Quinn scooted closer to her on the bed and faced her, holding her uninjured hand.

"Okay, Nay. Take a deep breath in, and then blow it out through your mouth. Big pinch."

"Ow." Linnea's hand clenched Quinn's tightly. "Okay, Will, I'm sorry I ever teased you."

"Don't be. It was probably funny." Though his eyes never left what he was doing, he used his free hand to rub gently at her upper arm.

There was a soft knock on the open bedroom door, and Quinn looked over to see Ben standing there, holding a large stack of towels.

"How is she?" he asked, with obvious worry in his voice.

"She's going to be fine," William said. "It's just a couple of cuts. The one on her hand is going to keep her from grabbing another knife any time soon, but she'll be okay."

Ben didn't look convinced. "Are you sure?"

"I'm fine," Linnea said. "You don't have to talk about me like I'm not here. I'm here."

That made Ben smile. "I'm sorry. I should have known better. Can I come in? I've got these, and there's a basin of water on the table out here."

Linnea shrugged. "It's not very exciting. Come on in if you want."

William leaned close to her ear. "Are you sure, Nay? I still have to do the one on your neck."

She grimaced, but nodded. "Ben, you're fairly warned that you might see me cry or something else ridiculous if you do stay."

Ben's eyes widened and he darted to her side. Quinn moved out of the way. "Does it hurt?" he asked, kneeling next to her.

"Yes."

"I'm sorry. You hurt Tolliver a lot worse than he got you, though. That was incredible."

"Thanks for trusting me and giving me that knife," she whispered. "That was you, too."

"I'm surprised I could even think, seeing him with you, like that… I just…"

Quinn raised an eyebrow at Will; she'd never seen Ben like this. Or Linnea actually. William shrugged and gave her a half-smile. "I kind of like it," he mouthed.

Quinn did, too. Ben and Linnea… yes, she definitely liked the idea.

"Okay Nay, ready to finish this up?"

"No. But go ahead."

"Can I hold your hand?" Ben asked.

"I don't know. I might really feel like a weakling…needing my hand held for a couple of stitches if I'm surrounded by three people who have a Friends of Philip tattoo."

"My father had to hold my hand when they did my tattoo," Ben said quietly. "And I'm supposed to be a big tough guard. And that was my choice, and that wasn't as bad as what just happened to you. Even you, strong Princess Linnea, are allowed to fall apart sometimes and let other people take care of you."

Linnea bit her lip and nodded, a single tear rolling down her cheek.

William wiped his sister's tear away with his thumb. "Even if you don't think you need it, Linnea, we all really need to take care of you right now, okay?"

"Okay." She held out her hand toward Ben.

A NIGHT AT THE MILLER ESTATE

WILLIAM HAD FINISHED working on Linnea, and they were all just sitting around her on the bed, when there was a knock on the door out in the main room.

None of them moved to answer it, but after a moment, Marcus appeared in the bedroom doorway. "Is everything all right?"

Quinn put her fingers to her lips and climbed gently off the bed...Linnea had been about to doze off.

But her efforts failed. "I'm fine," Linnea called out, just as Quinn reached Marcus.

Marcus raised an eyebrow, but Quinn sighed and nodded. "She's okay. She just needs to rest."

"Okay. There's someone out here I want you to meet." He tilted his head behind him, and Quinn could now see there was someone standing out there. A man, a few cycles older than Marcus, perhaps, with salt-and-pepper coloring his neatly trimmed hair and beard. "You, too, William and Ben."

"Princess Quinn, it is a profound honor," Brian Miller said, lowering his head, after Marcus had introduced her.

She flushed, and started to tell him the gesture was unnecessary, but William's hand on her elbow reminded her quickly that she was supposed to accept such deference.

"I'm sorry for barging into your home the way we did," she said instead. "We're all very grateful for your hospitality."

"My home is open to you at any time, Princess," he said, pulling back his collar to reveal the symbol that she'd already known was there. "You are certainly more welcome here than our other, uninvited, *guest*. Anything you need here, anything I might be able to provide, if you don't see it, you need only to ask."

"Thank you. I take it this means you know who I am?"

"Yes, Princess. Your grandmother and your uncle have explained it to me. I'll admit that I've never been so shocked in my life, but also never so filled with relief and hope. You are the true heir, and your marriage to Prince William will fulfill the prophecy. This is wonderful news, indeed."

"Thank you," she said. "I was afraid this news would be difficult for people to accept."

"It might be for some," Brian agreed. "For those who have been influenced by Hector and Tolliver, for those who gave up the hope and the fight in exchange for promises of favor under the new regime, it will be a challenge.

"But I think you underestimate the power of tradition and of your family in particular...and how we feel about the connection of the crowns. Over the past twenty cycles, we've seen our relationship with Eirentheos slipping slowly away, carrying our friends and families further from us. You, Princess, may just be able to give that back to us."

"I certainly hope so. Thank you for being one of the first to give me that chance."

"Anything, Princess. And I must apologize to you that my home was not a safe haven for you when you first arrived. I never imagined that keeping the secret of my loyalties *too* well would result in my home being seen as a hiding place for that…" He shook his head.

"I'm so sorry. Please tell me that Princess Linnea hasn't suffered any permanent damage. It was only a few hours ago that I realized they'd brought her here as a prisoner, and I nearly lost my mind. I couldn't believe even Tolliver would stoop so low."

"Are there members of the Friends of Philip hiding here, then?"

"Yes. About twenty-five who are known to Tolliver's troops. More, of course, that they're unaware of."

Quinn's eyes widened. "So many?"

"Yes. Until recently, many were coming here so we could help them get across the border into Eirentheos. Queen Sophia has done much for the cause in the last half-cycle or so." He sighed.

"It doesn't matter now. We're done hiding. It had already been decided when we realized Linnea was here. We were going to get her back home safely, whatever we had to do. I'm actually glad you all arrived when you did. Otherwise, you might have walked in to the middle of a battle. Tolliver's troops are being removed from my home as we speak."

Quinn blinked. "Are you telling me there's a battle going on, here, right now?"

"Yes, although I suppose it isn't much of a fight. Soldiers or no… the only advantage they ever had over us was that we were trying to keep this safe house hidden."

"We were traveling with more people," she said, suddenly alarmed. "They were on their way here as well."

"Yes, Prince Jonathan spoke to me about Prince Charles and Princess Ellen, and the others with them. Prince Jonathan has sent them a message with his bird, and a small contingent is heading out to look for them and escort them back safely."

"Okay, good," she said, breathing again. William put his arm around her shoulders. "Do you know how Tolliver is doing?"

"I don't particularly *care* Princess, but when I checked in with Prince Nathaniel, he said he thought he'd be all right. There were two other healers here at the estate, and they went to help him as well."

"All right."

"In the meantime," he said, eyeing the bloodstained floor, "I imagine you are all tired and hungry, and would probably like to get cleaned up. I am having some rooms prepared for you."

An hour later, Quinn, William, and Linnea found themselves alone in a much larger suite.

"Is this place as big as the castle, or something?" Quinn asked, looking around at the expansive sitting room. It was very nice, featuring several couches and a fire crackling in the large stone fireplace.

William nodded, rubbing her shoulders. "Well, maybe not quite as big, but these old estates owned by royal families are pretty impressive sometimes."

"Right. The Millers are related to me somehow?"

"I think so," William said. "But I'm not exactly sure how, probably distant cousins or something."

"Yeah, Queen Sophia said they were cousins," Linnea said. "But not how."

William and Quinn both looked at her. "You spoke with Sophia before this afternoon?" Quinn asked.

"Yes. They brought me to her first. We've been talking for the past two days. Tolliver wanted his mother to get to know his bride, you know." She shuddered and sank down onto one of the couches, being careful of her bandaged hand.

"Was she really going to let that happen?"

"I don't know, Quinn. She wasn't happy about it, but she didn't really see any other options. I almost told her about you yesterday.

Tolliver only arrived here a little while before you did. If I'd had the chance to talk to her before he was dragging me in front of all of you at knifepoint, I probably would have told her today."

"I would have been okay with that, Nay. Anything that might have helped you." She sat down next to Linnea on the couch, and William went to kneel in front of both of them. He was so grateful to have Linnea safe in front of him, he would have been okay with anything.

"How did it happen?" he asked. "How did Catherine get you out of the castle?"

"You found out who it was?"

"Yes. Maxwell figured it out somehow. Don't even get me started on how angry I am about all of that."

"I don't think he knew, Will. I mean, I never really liked her, either, but I don't think he had any idea that she was just tricking him the whole time. I thought she was kind of... well, anyway, still, I didn't think she was the kind of person who would do this."

"What did she do? How did she pull it off?"

Quinn gave him a look, and he realized how insensitive he was being. "Sorry, Nay. You don't have to talk about it if you're not ready to," he said.

"No, it's okay," she said. "It was simple really. She just found me in the hallway, after I took you two up to your room... She started being all nice to me, and then she asked if I wanted to meet her brothers, since I never had. Said they were driving her father's new carriage. I didn't really want to, but she was Maxwell's companion, and I thought I should be nice."

Tears started forming in her eyes, and William sat down next to her on the opposite side of Quinn, and they both put their arms around her, holding her tightly.

"I can't even really remember what happened after that. We went out the front door...I saw one of her brothers waiting outside of the carriage, even though it was raining...and the next thing I knew, there was a pillowcase over my head, and I was on the floor of the carriage, and it was moving. Someone's hand was over my mouth…" Her shoulders started shaking.

"Shh, Nay," William said, his heart rising into his throat. "You don't have to tell us anything else, sweetheart. It's all over now. You're safe; we've got you."

William didn't hear him enter the room, but when he looked up from where his head was buried against his sister's shoulder, he saw Nathaniel standing there, watching them…all three of them huddled together on the couch, a shuddering mass of tears and hugs.

William wiped his face on his sleeve before waving his uncle in, and Nathaniel dropped to his knees in front of them and put his arms around them all.

Sometime later, William looked up again and saw Quinn watching him. Her tears were dry now, leaving grimy streaks down her cheeks, and he realized for the first time just how dirty they all were. Quinn was the only one of the three of them with no blood on her clothes. Nathaniel looked like a scene from a horror movie…not that William had ever watched one, but Thomas had, on the computer when he'd visited, and William had seen a little bit of it.

"They said there was water for baths, right? I'd do just about anything for a bath right now."

Quinn nodded toward several large pots sitting near the fireplace. "I don't know if we're supposed to climb in those, or what."

Nathaniel chuckled. "There's probably a bathtub in one of those rooms," he said, pointing toward the doors that led off of the main sitting room. "It'll even have a drain through the floor, and a water pump from the well, but that water will be *cold*. The water over there is for warming over the fire, and then we can mix it in the tubs. We can ask some servants for help."

Quinn shook her head, and he knew how she felt. He didn't want to see any more strangers right now either.

He and Nathaniel hefted one of the heavy pots up and onto the hook over the fire, and then they all explored the rest of the apartment.

Nathaniel had been right, in addition to two bedrooms, there was a bathroom with working pumps both at the sink and by the enormous cast iron bathtub.

Quinn went with Linnea into the bathroom first. The anesthetic William had used earlier was starting to wear off, and they all wanted to get her cleaned up and in clean clothes for bed before she was really hurting.

While the girls were in the bathroom, there was a knock on the door, and when Nathaniel opened it, two servants carried in large trays of food. One of the servants, a strong young man, was upset he hadn't come early enough to warm the bathwater for them, but William assured him they were fine. Still, he insisted on hanging the second bucket for them and refilling the empty one.

"Are you going to go and check on Tolliver again tonight?" William asked, once the servant had left.

Nathaniel shook his head, shrugging out of his bloodstained shirt, and into a soft linen one that had been left on a chair in the corner of the room. "If I never see that man again, it will be too soon. There are other healers; they can take care of him."

"They don't have the knowledge you do."

"Is Tolliver entitled to the knowledge I gained because I had to run away to another world to avoid actually being killed by my own stepfather or half-brother?"

"No. I don't disagree with you, Nathaniel. I just… I know who you are, and I wanted to make sure you'd thought it through. I don't care who he is…you saved his life already, and that's more than he deserves. I'll never be more proud of anyone than I am of Linnea right now…and I hate violence."

Nathaniel smiled. "She was wonderful. And nobody's ever deserved that as much as Tolliver did. Even while I was pulling that knife out of his leg, he was still making comments…thinks he's going to get back at all of us. He said a couple of things about both Quinn and Linnea that made me want to shove that thing in further."

William's eyes widened. "What did he say?"

"You don't need to hear it, William. But I did go and share it with my mother, and I plan on sharing it with Stephen, as well. Tolliver won't be seeing the light of day again. I don't care what Hector has to say about it."

"Do you think Hector really is going to try to go through the gate?"

"I don't know. It's not worth taking the chance. We have to let Stephen know what has to be done. How bad is Linnea? Would she be all right traveling, if we could find a way to get her back home?"

"She'll be all right. I think she'd be okay to travel tomorrow if she needed to, though the day after would be better. She's going to be hurting tonight."

Nathaniel nodded. "I didn't have a lot of morphine, but I saved a dose for her. She deserves it more than Tolliver does."

"Agreed."

Nathaniel paused for several seconds. When he spoke again, his voice was hesitant. "Does Quinn really know some way to close the gate?"

"Sort of. Alvin told us both about it at our wedding…how the gate works."

"Really?"

"Yeah. There's some kind of magnet buried in the ground on either side. Then, when the two worlds are lined up just right, the magnets weaken the magnetic field between them. But if either magnet is missing, then the gate doesn't work."

"So we have to find the magnet."

"Right, but I don't have any idea how."

"Or if it's even possible."

"I hope it's possible," William sighed. "If Jonathan is right, and Hector really has told more people about the gate, then it's not going to be enough to just stop him. Our world could be in danger forever."

"Do you think Quinn is really going to be okay with that? With closing the gate?"

"No, she's not. How could she be? Her family is over there, Nathaniel. I don't know if *I'm* going to be okay with it."

"Okay with what?" Quinn's voice startled both of them; they turned to see her coming out of the bathroom.

"Is Linnea all right?" Nathaniel asked.

William could tell that she saw right through the quick change of subject, but that she decided not to pursue it…he knew she'd ask him later.

"Yes, she's just finishing getting dressed. I was just coming to get a hairbrush." Quinn sighed. "She says she's completely fine, but I think she's still pretty shaken up. I was thinking maybe…" she looked at William hesitantly, "maybe I should sleep with her tonight?"

He didn't have any idea why she would be worried about asking him something like that, and he was about to tell her that, of course, she should stay close to Linnea tonight, when the bathroom door, which had been barely cracked, came flying open, and his sister stalked into the room.

"I. Am. Fine." Linnea said. "You two have had a bed to sleep in together for exactly one night since you got married. I am not going to be the reason you're separated tonight."

"Nay," William said softly, walking over to her. "Quinn and I are going to be married for a very long time. Neither one of us is worried about a few hard nights."

Linnea closed her eyes. "Can we compromise? How about I sleep on the couch, and everyone can keep an eye on me as much as they want to?"

"How about this, Linnea," Nathaniel said, "you sleep in that bedroom there, on a bed where you can actually be comfortable, and

I sleep on the couch, where I can hear you if you need anything at all?"

Linnea raised her eyebrows at William and Quinn. "Satisfied?"

"All right, Nay," William said, sighing to himself. He'd never in his wildest dreams imagined himself on this side of an argument. "So long as you eat a good dinner, and then you let me give you some medicine that will help with the pain and make you sleepy…I'll agree to that."

"Fine."

Nathaniel took his bath while the rest of them ate and got Linnea into bed. When Quinn and William came back out of Linnea's room, Nathaniel looked up at them. "I'm going to go speak with Marcus and Ben before I go to bed. Maybe see if I can find Jonathan, as well. I'll be back in an hour or so." And he disappeared into the hallway.

Quinn watched him go. "Well, that was subtle."

"Better than Linnea, who practically gave us a checklist for what she expects us to do."

Quinn giggled. "She did not."

The look he gave her made her giggle again, and he wrapped his arms around her. "It's nice to hear you laughing."

"You wouldn't think that would be possible after a day like today."

"I don't know. What's so bad about today? The meeting with your grandmother went… well, it was interesting, but I'd say the outcome was good. We got to watch Linnea stab Tolliver…that's a decent day in anyone's book, I think."

"William!"

"Well, it was. He deserved much worse, and I'm not going to feel bad that he got what he did."

Although it surprised her a little, Quinn didn't feel even a little bit bad about Tolliver, either. She knew he wouldn't have hesitated to do it to Linnea…to any of them if they were standing in the way of what he wanted. Still, all of their problems hadn't been solved by Tolliver's arrest…or even by Sophia's acknowledgement of Quinn as the heir.

"We still have to deal with Hector, you know."

He kissed her on the forehead. "One day's problems at a time, love. Much of Hector's power is gone if he doesn't have Tolliver. And he doesn't have Tolliver…or Linnea. Today was a good day."

"That's not the only reason I'm worried about Hector."

"I know it isn't. Do you want to talk about that right now?"

No, she didn't. She didn't even want to think about that right now. William was right…one day's problems at a time. She shook her head.

"Okay." He kissed her again, and then stepped away from her toward the bathroom. "It looks like Nathaniel already put fresh hot water in the tub; that was nice of him."

She followed him in there; the steam coming off the water already felt good just standing next to it. "That definitely looks better than washing in a cold river."

He nodded. "Much better. Do you want to go first?"

"I'm not the one with blood on my clothes."

"You make it sound like I'm covered in it or something. It's just a little bit on my pants. I changed my shirt. I washed my hands and face. I can wait a little longer. And besides, I think I had more sleep than you last night. You should go first so you can relax after."

But standing here with him, in this warm, steamy little room, she suddenly wasn't tired at all. In fact, looking at the huge bathtub gave her an idea…but she wasn't sure she could say it out loud.

"Why are you blushing?"

Oh, no… she definitely was not brave enough to ask him this… was she? She felt her face getting hotter and hotter. She swallowed hard, pulling herself together. It was William, her *husband*, she could do this. "I was just thinking how much easier it would be if we didn't have to heat water and fill the tub again after this…"

He looked back and forth between her and the tub, and then a grin spread across his face, reaching all the way up to his beautiful gray eyes, lit up with his love for her. *Yes… her husband.*

"I like the way you think, Mrs. Rose."

MORE DECISIONS

"HOW'S THE BREAKFAST?" JONATHAN asked, walking into the sitting room.

"Better than dried meat and stale bread," William said, scooping up another bite of eggs.

Quinn had to agree…though they'd had a little more than that while they were traveling, it hadn't been as nice as this by half.

"Did you sleep well?" The question sounded like it was directed toward everyone, but Jonathan was looking at Quinn.

"Yes, I did, actually, thank you," she said. For the first time in a long time, this was true. William had awakened before her this morning, and she couldn't remember being up at all during the night or having any disturbing dreams.

"And Princess Linnea, how are you feeling?"

"Sore, but all right."

"Excellent. Because I've just heard that someone is riding up…someone I'm sure will be anxious to see all of you. I'll be right back."

She frowned as he went back out the door. "That was…*strange*. Do you think it's Charles and Ellen already?"

"They should be arriving any time now, actually, but then why wouldn't he just tell us? And why would he say some*one* instead of naming them? Who else even knows we're here?"

"I don't know," Marcus said warily, standing and going to get his sword. Ben quickly followed.

Quinn, too, was on the verge of questioning her decision to trust Jonathan when the door opened again, and Stephen walked in.

She nearly fell off her chair in relief.

At first, he didn't have eyes for anyone except Linnea. His gaze zeroed in on his daughter the second he entered the room, and he went straight to her, lifting her from her chair and into his arms.

Until she winced at his tight grip, it was clear he hadn't even noticed her bandages. When he did, he gasped and quickly let her go, stepping back to look at her fully. "What happened? Who did this to you? Was it *Tolliver*?" Stephen's whole face and neck were red with his anger.

"Yes, Stephen, it was," Jonathan said, his voice apologetic. "But he's been arrested now. He's being held until he recovers enough to be transferred back to the capital."

"Perhaps you should send him back to *my* capital," Stephen said through his teeth.

"I'm sure that's probably open for discussion" Jonathan didn't quite manage to disguise his grin.

"What is he *recovering* from that he can't be moved today?"

Jonathan raised an eyebrow at the rest of them.

After Nathaniel and William explained what had happened, Stephen pulled Linnea back into his arms…a little more gently this time. "That's my girl," he said, close to her ear. "I'm proud of you."

They hugged for a long time, pausing briefly so that Stephen could hug the rest of them…he even embraced Marcus and Ben, thanking them for what they'd done, but when Stephen sat down at the table to speak to everyone, he pulled Linnea's chair next to his, and kept his arm around her while she leaned up against his chest.

"How did you get here so quickly?" Nathaniel asked.

"After I got your note that you thought Linnea was here yesterday morning, we left within a few hours…it's just me, Luke Willoughby and a couple of other guards. We rode hard through most of the night…I'm sure the horses aren't very appreciative."

Stephen looked at Jonathan. "This place was easier to get into than we expected…we were afraid it might be a fight."

Jonathan nodded. "Yesterday, it would have been. Much has changed with the arrest of Tolliver. The troops that were here with him are regrouping somewhere, I think. Perhaps they're trying to get into contact with Hector. Nobody seems to have heard from him or knows where he is."

"That sounds dangerous. Does he have any troops with him?"

"I don't know." Jonathan's eyes flicked to Quinn. "We're afraid the danger might be a little more serious than that."

As soon as Stephen's eyes met hers, Quinn knew that he knew. She tried, unsuccessfully, to keep her voice from shaking when she asked her question. "Did you have a dream, too?"

He didn't look away from her, though she could see that it took effort on his part. "Yes, I did."

She swallowed. "You think it's a real threat."

"I think you know the answer to that. Using the gate has always been dangerous, and none of us have been as careful about it as we should have been."

"I still don't understand how Hector could have found out about it," Jonathan said.

"It doesn't matter how. Nothing matters at all except keeping him from using it." Stephen's expression was grim. "And we have very few options for doing that. We can't station troops around it without being prepared to tell them why…and now is not the time to be giving that information to more people."

"No," Quinn said, "I already know. I've already been through all of this in my mind, over and over. We have to try to close the gate;

we have to prevent Hector…and anyone else he may have told…from ever using it. And, no, I'm not okay with that and I probably never will be, but it doesn't matter, because the alternative is even worse. So, I don't want to talk anymore about how it will affect me, or what it means. I think I know how to close it, and we just need to do it."

William reached for her hand, and…for just a fraction of a second…she didn't want it. She yanked her hand away, out of his reach, but then just as quickly put it back, and allowed him to hold it tightly.

"Okay," Stephen said, after several silent, strained minutes. "So you tell me everything you know about closing it, and we will send a message to Simon, Maxwell, and Thomas today. Hopefully they can start trying to get it figured out. Our horses need a rest after that ride, and so do the rest of us, I think, but we can leave to take Linnea back to the castle tomorrow morning, and if we hurry, we'll still make it back a day or so before the gate is scheduled to open again."

The look on Ben's face as they talked about Linnea leaving nearly broke Quinn's heart, and she saw Linnea glance sadly up at him, too. *Oops*…she doubted the two of them had meant for *that* to happen.

There was a knock on the door then, and when Jonathan opened it, they saw the young man who'd attended them last night. "Sorry to bother you, Prince Jonathan," he said, "but Prince Charles and Princess Ellen have just arrived, and I was told you wanted to be notified as soon as they were brought in."

"Yes, I did. Thank you very much, Zavier. Are they in the house now?"

"Yes. Mr. Miller asked that they be shown to their accommodations, and that their horses be taken care of. Would you like me to take you to them?"

"Please. And some of the supplies the horses are carrying belong to our guests here. Can you please ask someone to sort that out and bring them in here?"

When there was another knock on the door less than an hour later, William expected that it would be Charles and Ellen, or perhaps Jonathan, giving them more information about what was going on. But, instead, his father opened the door to find Queen Sophia standing there, by herself.

"Stephen," she said, coming in and allowing him to close the door behind her. "It's been a long time...too long."

"Indeed it has, Sophia. Although I must say, you're looking as beautiful as ever."

"Your wife may still allow you to get away with that, Stephen, but I've had too much experience with insincere flattery to believe it anymore."

William felt a lump in his throat at the queen's words. She was, in fact, still very lovely. And she deserved more than a man like Hector who had made her feel this way.

His father, too, had sadness in his eyes as he regarded Sophia, and he shook his head gently. "In my eyes, you'll always be the lovely, loving mother of my dearest friend...the way you were when Jonathan was alive. The two of you were one of the happiest couples I'd ever seen. Even as a teenage boy, I knew that."

"We were the happiest couple I knew. Until I saw you and your Charlotte."

"Well, Charlotte's a special case."

"Indeed she is. And now I already see it between your son and my granddaughter. I suppose something of the magic has survived."

Stephen smiled over at William; he was sitting on the couch, still with his arm around Quinn's shoulders. They'd all just been chatting before Sophia arrived. "More of the magic than you think, Sophia. It's all still here, if only you'll take hold of it."

Sophia nodded. "It's been too long, Stephen; I've missed all of you. I'm sorry things have gotten to this point between our kingdoms. I know much of that is my fault. I trusted the wrong person."

"No, Sophia. It isn't your fault for trusting him. He betrayed a very valuable gift you gave him. Although you could, perhaps, have asked for help when you first realized the truth…back when it would have been much easier to fix things. Before so many things were lost."

"Until my dying day, I will regret that I didn't…that I allowed things to get this far."

"It's a waste of time to focus on what we regret, Sophia. I would like to do what I can to help you move forward…to move all of us past this, and to right the wrongs we are able to."

"Yes, well, I have been discussing things with Jonathan, and I've even had a chance to speak with Charles and Ellen…imagine, all of my children are under one roof again…even Samuel, in a way," she glanced at Quinn. "It's unfortunate that my youngest is here under arrest, but those are the choices he made. And he is going to have to live with them, for the rest of his life." Her shoulders shook a little as she spoke, and Stephen reached out his hand to steady her.

"Thank you." She cleared her throat. "Our discussions have led me to this conclusion. I don't know where Hector is, but I need to assume my rightful role and get rid of him before Quinn will be safe here in Philotheum, and we can proceed. I have the necessary troops at my disposal and the support of the Friends of Philip as well."

"Of course, you always have the support of Eirentheos. We may even be able to help locate Hector."

"We'll take whatever assistance we can get. I am going to ask my children…including Nathaniel…to accompany me back to the castle and help me build the support of our people for Quinn's coronation…as both the rightful heir, and the one who has fulfilled the prophecy through her marriage to your son.

"For now," she said, turning to Quinn, "I've decided you both should return to Eirentheos. I am planning on releasing knowledge of your existence to our people, and you will be safer there until we've located Hector."

Quinn's eyes were wide, and William thought he knew why. There was certainly no guarantee that she would be safer from Hector in Eirentheos…well, not safer from *him* personally, anyway. Her grandmother was right in that Quinn might be less a target of Hector's troops, if she were safe in the castle in Eirentheos. He rubbed her shoulder.

"Also," Sophia continued, "we need to do things the proper, public way. You must have a public wedding ceremony, in Eirentheos, so that everyone is aware of your marriage, and of what it means to our kingdoms. I will attend that wedding, with all of my children, in approximately one moon's time, provided Hector has been caught. Once the wedding has been accomplished, we can move forward with bringing you back to Philotheum for your coronation."

Quinn's jaw was practically on her chest.

"Close your mouth, Princess. You will soon be a queen."

Though she still seemed speechless, Quinn did as she was told, sitting up straighter on the couch, too.

"In the meantime, of course, the private wedding that was already performed will still be considered the real date of your marriage. I am sorry to have missed it." With those words, Sophia turned and headed toward the door. Her hand was on the knob to turn it, when she suddenly whirled around and walked back toward Quinn.

Sophia knelt down in front of her, surprisingly gentle after the fervor of her speech. "And thank you, precious child. I don't yet know you as well as I wish I did, but I do see what you've done here, and the sacrifice you've chosen to make to right the wrong that occurred when your father left Philotheum. We'll work this out, and then you'll come to be with me, and perhaps you just might be the cornerstone on which we begin to rebuild our family."

She then turned to William. "You're brave, Prince William, getting yourself into this. Thank you for loving her enough to stand beside her…beside all of us. And welcome."

Sophia bent down and kissed Quinn on the top of her head, but she didn't wait for a reaction or a response before she really did leave.

Nathaniel let out a low whistle as the door closed behind his mother. "I haven't seen her like that since I was four cycles old. I've never forgotten it though."

"I think it's a good thing," Stephen said.

"As do I."

William didn't know her well enough to be sure, but he did think it was a definite improvement over the woman they'd seen yesterday, who'd looked like a strong wind would knock her over.

They sat there for several minutes, all of them in a sort of dazed silence. Linnea was the first one to break it. "A big wedding will be fun."

Everyone chuckled…everyone except Quinn. She had grown very still and quiet beside him. He looked down at her. "Excuse me," she said. And she stood and walked quickly into the bedroom he'd shared with her the night before.

They all looked at each other again. His father stood up. "I think I'd like to go check on all of the horses. It sounds like yours have all arrived here as well. Anyone want to come with me?"

It was almost comical how quickly everyone was out of the room, leaving William standing there. His father paused in the doorway. "Do you have your coin?"

He nodded. "It's in my backpack in the other room."

His father smiled gently, reaching into his pocket. "Always in your pocket, son. Here." He pulled his hand out and held it over William's, dropping a small coin into it. "We'll stay out of your way for a while."

After his father left, William approached the bedroom door. Inside the bedroom, Quinn was sitting on the bed, leaning up against the headboard, her knees pulled to her chest.

"Please, Will," she said, as he was closing the door behind him, "I just need a little bit of time alone."

He didn't leave, though. He just slowly approached the bed and stood at the foot of it, flipping the little coin between his fingers as he spoke. "There aren't many requests I wouldn't grant you, Quinn…except you asking me to leave you when you're upset."

"I'm not upset. I just… need some time to think."

He raised an eyebrow at her.

She looked up at the ceiling. "If I am, it's my problem. I have to deal with this, Will."

He ignored her defensive position, and walked around to the side of the bed, kicking off his boots.

"I mean it, Will." Her voice was starting to sound scratchy.

"I know you do." He climbed onto the bed, and sat with his legs crossed right in front of her. "I know. But I mean this more."

She looked at him.

He held the little coin between his fingers. "After we told my parents we were getting married, they pulled me aside one evening. They brought me into their room, and sat me down, and gave me this…well, one like it, anyway. This is my father's, since I didn't have mine in my pocket like I'm supposed to."

"What is it?"

"It's just a coin. It's nothing special…it's not even money. But it's a reminder." He handed it to her and watched as she examined it, studying both sides.

"Is that a thorn?" she asked, showing him the etching on one side.

"It is. And it's a dandelion seed on the other side."

"Again with that…" she said, and he smiled. "What is it supposed to be a reminder of?"

"To never run away from each other in a fight…to stay until we've worked it out."

"We're not fighting."

"I know. You and I don't fight…at least not so far. But we both have a tendency to do this…to withdraw when we get upset, and think that everything is only our own problem."

"Sometimes it is."

"No, love. It never is. It never will be. You're my wife. For the rest of my life, everything that worries you or upsets you or hurts you…it does me, too. Even if the only way it affects me is that it makes *you* sad. Even if the only thing I can do about it is be there for you."

He took the coin back, and held the side with the dandelion seed up to her. "Dandelions represent the easy way. You pick up a dandelion and it's so soft, and it's so easy and even fun sometimes to blow the seeds everywhere. And you don't even realize what you're doing. Nothing happens right then, except you get a pretty little show in the breeze. It's not until later, sometimes a long time later, that you look out in your garden and realize what you did."

He put his hand on her knee. "It's easy, love, to pull back, to hide in yourself, to run and say you're just taking some time, to keep all of your emotions inside, maybe even to think you're protecting me from something. It would be easier still for me to let you do that. To watch you blow those dandelion seeds everywhere, and pretend it won't damage anything. To pretend we won't wake up one summer morning to discover we've allowed a huge patch of weeds to grow between us, opening up cracks in the foundation of our marriage."

Her lower lip trembled, and he saw her bite down on it, but he didn't stop. He flipped the coin over, and rubbed his thumb against the etching of the thorn. "Thorns, on the other hand… they're not easy. They hurt. They make you want to give up on the whole plant sometimes. But if you don't give up, love, if you fight through it, allow yourself to be hurt…the result is beautiful and strong. And it will last forever if you care for it."

Tears dripped down her cheeks now, and he reached to wipe them with his thumbs. "You're my rose, Quinn. And I choose the pain, sometimes. I choose to fight it out, even when it would be easier to withdraw. I choose to love you, even when you're feeling unlovable. You can't get rid of me…I'm not going anywhere; I don't care how many thorns you aim at me."

Now she was crying in earnest, and he felt tears starting to flow down his own cheeks, but he didn't care. He wasn't going to be embarrassed about that with her, or let her feel that way with him. He just pulled her to his chest and held her tight, running his fingers through her hair and rocking her.

When she finally stopped, she looked up at him. "I love you, Will."

He kissed her on the forehead. "Good. That's the point of all of this, isn't it? I love you so much, Quinn. And I will do whatever it takes to make sure you know that, every day for the rest of our life together."

"That's one big advantage of choosing this world, isn't it?"

"What?"

"That our life together will be so much longer than it would have been in my… in my *other* world."

"That's definitely an advantage in my mind, love."

He held her for several more minutes, waiting until she was completely calm before asking his question.

"Are you sure about this decision, Quinn? I'm sure we could find another way."

She shook her head. "I've played that game before, William…too much, and for too long. Not making a decision, avoiding a decision, halfway making a decision…those are all decisions, too. Only when you do those things, you let the situation control you, instead of the other way around."

He sighed, nodding, knowing she was right.

"I'm not happy about it. It's not the decision I *want* to make. But it's the right one. I can't have it both ways. We have to find that magnet and close the gate."

"Maybe…"

"Yes, maybe," she said. "Maybe lots of things, someday down the road. But I can't go into this halfway, trying to make a someday work out, Will. *You* can hold on to some of that for me, think of the maybe somedays, that maybe in a cycle or two we can open it again, or we can find another gate somewhere else…

"But I can't think about that right now. Because *maybe* it will never be safe to open it again, or we'll try and we won't be able to. I have to have my eyes open, and make this decision for real. I have to know I'm closing that gate with my family on the other side, and that might mean never seeing them again."

"Okay," he said, though inside his heart was breaking for her…for both of them. "I'm here for that, too."

"Okay." She opened his hand and picked up the coin again. "I think I need one of these."

DUSK

THE TRIP BACK TO Eirentheos was different than the trip to Philotheum. They were leaving Charles and Ellen behind, but the absence they felt most was Nathaniel's.

They rode in silence much of the time, pushing the horses as hard as they reasonably could, hoping to make it to Eirentheos with a full day to spare before the gate opened. Their travel time would hopefully be reduced greatly by the escort they had gotten to the Philothean border, and their ability to travel on main roads.

Early in the morning, before they'd left, Stephen's bird had returned with a message from Simon. He, Maxwell, and Thomas, along with a couple of others who knew about the gate planned to begin searching the area today looking for a magnet...though none of them knew exactly what it would look like or where it would be buried.

"At least you'll have a chance to say good-bye properly and take the things you need when you go to Philotheum for real now," Linnea said, riding up beside Quinn and interrupting her thoughts.

It took a minute for Quinn to understand what her friend...her sister, now...had said. "I suppose you're right. It does feel like sort of a reprieve…getting to go home for a while first. And it's true that we never really got to tell everyone good-bye."

Linnea gave her an odd look, but didn't say anything else. Maybe it was over her calling Eirentheos "home"…but that's what the castle there was to her, now. The only home she was going to be able to go to for a long time maybe. She wondered how long it would take before the castle in Philotheum felt like anywhere she belonged.

"I'm pretty impressed with your one-handed riding skills," she said, changing the subject a little. "Are you holding up okay?"

"I'm going to use up William's supply of those pills from your world, but I'm all right. I don't know what he's going to do when those run out and he can't go…" Linnea stopped suddenly, and looked up at Quinn. "Sorry."

"It's okay, Nay. It's not like we can avoid making any mention of it forever. Earth was a big part of William's life, too, and he learned a lot of things there. The topic will come up."

"What topic?" William asked, edging Skittles up closer to them.

"Of me using up all of your medicine," Linnea said.

William shrugged. "We had more of it here than we could probably really use before it expires. I've been studying it, too. I can make a liquid version that works almost the same, but without the benefit of chemicals that make it taste better without making it spoil easily… it's something that's best left for home or a clinic, not for traveling."

Linnea raised an eyebrow. "Really, Quinn? You listen to him when he talks like this? I don't even understand what he's saying."

"As opposed to someone who talks horses, fishing, and weapons?" William said, a little pointedly.

Linnea's cheeks glowed red. "Kind of a low blow isn't that, Will?" she said, glancing back behind them where Ben was riding. "It's not like anything can even happen there."

"Why couldn't it?" Quinn asked.

"He's going to Philotheum, probably in a little over a moon."

"Philotheum, Nay," William said. "Not Earth. And I'm going to Philotheum to be with Quinn."

"Yes, but you're of age."

"You will be by then, too." Quinn said.

Linnea blinked. "My parents would never…"

"Of course they would, Linnea." William said. "It's not as easy as falling for someone who's going to stay in the kingdom, but… this is between you and Ben, not anyone else. A moon is plenty of time to see if the two of you want to pursue something."

The color hadn't yet faded from Linnea's cheeks. "I don't even know if he's…"

"Oh, he is. Trust me on that one." Quinn said, grinning.

Linnea looked at William. "Uh, yeah, Nay. No question," he said.

They all glanced back at Ben…he was watching them, too. Linnea turned even redder when Quinn waved him up.

She shot Linnea a sly grin. "Sometimes," she said, when only Linnea could hear her, "it's not so bad to listen to someone talk about weapons or horses…or medicine. Honestly, when someone is trying to talk to you about those things, the important thing they're *always* saying is that they care enough about what you think to try to share themselves with you."

They made it back to Eirentheos the next afternoon…Quinn would never know how Stephen had managed to travel that far in less time.

Despite the fact that they were all exhausted, they sent Linnea ahead to the castle with most of the guards, and Stephen, Ben, Marcus, Quinn, and William went straight to the gate.

Quinn spotted Thomas there almost immediately. "Have you found anything?" she asked, riding up and dismounting right next to him.

Thomas grinned and held his hand out to steady her as she stumbled, before wrapping her in an enormous hug. "Hello to you, too, Princess. Until we got your message last night, I'd thought it was going to be much longer until I saw your beautiful face again."

"Hey, hands off my wife." William came up behind them, his wide smile erasing any chance of seriousness in his tone.

"She's my sister now, too. You can't keep her *all* to yourself."

"I can try."

"But you won't succeed. I'm too good at what I do." As soon as Thomas had let go of Quinn, he had William wrapped in a tight hug, too. "Eight days, and I already didn't know what to do with myself without you," Thomas said. "I'm glad it was only a practice run, and we have a little while before it's real."

"I think you speak for all of us."

"Where's Linnea?" Thomas asked, looking around at everyone else who was dismounting and searching out Simon and Maxwell, who were down closer to the riverbank with shovels.

"Headed back to the castle. She's not up for digging just yet."

Thomas's eyes widened. "Why? What happened to her?"

Quinn looked at William…*right*, the messages they'd sent hadn't told the whole story.

"It's a long story, T. But she's *fine*. Really, she's okay." William set his hand on his brother's shoulder. "Actually…you'll want to hear the story, but I'll let her tell it when we get back to the castle."

"If you're sure she's all right."

William nodded, but the lighthearted mood of reunion was gone now. Thomas looked around them.

"So far we haven't found anything. Not that we even know what we're looking for, which would help, but there's nothing out here that looks anything like a magnet, or even like an unusual rock. I know you couldn't say a lot in the messages with the birds…is there anything else you know about it that you haven't told us?"

Quinn shook her head. "No. Not anything."

Thomas looked at her intently for a moment. "Quinn… you're not really trying to permanently close the gate, are you?"

She felt William's hand on her shoulder immediately. "Yes, Thomas, she is. But the whys and hows and all of it are something we can discuss later, okay?"

"Of course. So, you're sure this magnet is here somewhere?"

"Yes. At least, according to Alvin, it is."

"And that's all we know."

"Yes. It's not very helpful, is it?"

Thomas shook his head. "But whatever it is…wherever it is, we've got just over a day to find it before the next time the gate opens. Are you sure Hector is actually going to show up here tomorrow?"

"No, but he could. He could probably show up anytime, for that matter." William said.

"All right then. There are some extra shovels in that wagon over there."

By late the following afternoon, Quinn didn't think she'd ever been so exhausted or so discouraged. The gate would be opening in less than an hour, and they hadn't found anything. They'd dug up nearly the entire riverbank…even crossing the bridge and digging on the other side, and still they hadn't found anything.

Nobody even knew if they were digging deep enough.

She didn't understand it. Why would she see what she'd seen in her dream, and then be unable to do anything about it. Part of her kept looking around for Alvin to show up suddenly and just tell them where to find the magnet, but so far they were out here alone.

Stephen had sent several patrols out around the area, looking for anything unusual, any sign that Hector or his troops were around, but they hadn't found anything, either.

Pausing for a moment to rest her aching arms, she looked out at the river. Early evening sunlight bounced off the fast-flowing waves, creating a warm, golden effect. The weather had heated back up again the last couple of days. Though not quite as bad as it had been a few moons ago, William had told her that this time of year still saw plenty of hot days. Everything was ten times longer here…even the seasons.

The seasons. "Will?" she called suddenly.

He stopped digging and looked over at her.

"Is the water level in the river always this high?"

"No. In the colder moons, it drops much lower than this. It practically turns into a stream…*oh.*"

"Yeah."

Despair washed over her as they stopped and looked at the river. The golden waves suddenly looked a lot less peaceful. *The magnet could be anywhere.* It could be buried out there, under several feet of quickly-moving water.

"*Why*, Will? Why would Alvin tell us about this, why would I have this dream…your father have this dream, if there was nothing we could do about it? If we were just going to waste our time coming out here and digging up half the riverbank, all just to watch it happen anyway? I don't understand."

Even now, the sun was beginning to dip below the tops of the trees. She picked up her shovel and threw it, hard. It landed with a clatter against a large rock…one they'd already tested with a magnet. It was just a rock, like every other rock on the riverbank.

Marcus came running at the noise. He looked over at the shovel, and then back and forth between William and Quinn, and then he glanced up at the sky, which was growing less blue and more purple with every passing minute. She'd overestimated how much time they had left. Wishful thinking, probably.

"We should get you home, Princess," he said gently. "We should get all of you back. It's not going to be safe to have you out here."

She started to nod, ready to concede, but a sudden movement at the corner of her vision told her they were already too late.

He didn't look exactly the same as he had in her dream. He was older than the man she'd seen in her vision…the strange silver now dominated his hair, and his beard and mustache were overgrown and dirty. He must have been hiding in the trees somewhere near here for days.

Perhaps he'd tried the gate every evening, not knowing exactly when it would open. But the look in Hector's eyes now told her that he knew this was the night.

Quinn, William, and Marcus were standing between him and the bridge, and everyone else was rushing over. But they were unlikely to stop him. He had a gun.

"That's right, Princess," Hector said, correctly reading the expression on her face. "You'd better tell your friends to step aside before they find out firsthand what I can do with this thing." He pointed the gun at each of them in turn, finally landing on Quinn and keeping it aimed at her head.

Marcus looked at her in shock, but she nodded. "Move out of his way," she said. Her voice was barely above a whisper, but she knew they all heard her.

She didn't understand it, didn't know how this could have happened, but she knew that if they challenged him, someone she cared about would likely die. Or she would. Maybe she was going to anyway…Hector certainly wouldn't want her to live.

Hector stayed where he was, with the weapon aimed at Quinn, until the line had parted far enough that he could walk through without anyone getting to him. When he did move, it was with an arrogant confidence that started Quinn's frozen blood bubbling deep inside of her.

Maxwell must have felt the same way, because when Hector was halfway up the steps, he made a run for it, trying to grab him.

Quinn watched in horror as Hector turned, aimed, and then a sickening crack filled the air.

Max fell back, and for a few seconds, the world stopped entirely, until he stood back up again; the shot had gone wide. Very wide.

"He hasn't fired that thing in many cycles," Marcus whispered, loud enough for only Quinn and William to hear. "I doubt he has very many bullets, either."

It would have been a hopeful thought, if only it wasn't already too late. Hector was at the top of the bridge, about to take the step that would make him vanish.

Except it didn't.

It was fully dusk now. The gate should have been open. But Hector's next step didn't take him anywhere. He kept going, but he only reached the end of the bridge. Looking confused now, he turned and walked back. But no matter what he tried, he remained standing where they could see him.

He pointed the gun at Quinn again. "What did you do?" he asked.

"I didn't do anything."

"You're the one who was born there…Samuel's little brat. You weren't ever supposed to come here. Samuel never even told you about this gate…he couldn't have. You're the one who did this. What did you do?"

And that's when she knew. Knew where he'd gotten the gun. *He hasn't fired that thing in many cycles, Marcus had said. Many cycles.* He hadn't found out about the gate just recently from Tolliver. He'd known all along.

"You killed my father."

"And now I'm going to kill you."

But he never got the chance. She'd taken the knife out of her belt as soon as he'd aimed that gun at her. He was still fumbling with the gun…he hadn't re-cocked it after the last shot…when two blades hit him, almost simultaneously, one in the chest, and one in his neck, knocking him instantly to the ground.

The gun clattered to the stone floor of the bridge as Quinn looked around, trying to figure out who had thrown the second knife.

"It was me," Marcus said. "Stay here."

Marcus, Ben, and Luke ran up the steps of the bridge while the rest of them stood there. Quinn started shaking. First it was just her hands, but then it quickly spread up her arms, and to the rest of her body. At the first click of her teeth, William grabbed her and pulled her against him, holding her tightly. But the shaking didn't stop.

When Luke yelled, "He's dead," her whole body felt like it had turned to ice.

AFTER

WHEN QUINN WOKE LATER, she knew where she was…in the bedroom in the castle she'd been sharing with William…but she had no idea how she'd gotten there.

"Hey, love." William's hand was on her the second she moved; he must have just been sitting next to her on the bed, watching her the whole time.

"Hi." She smiled weakly. "What am I doing here?"

"We brought you back in the wagon," he said. "I gave you some valoris seed…I'm sorry, but I was worried. You were pretty shaken."

"Well I just…" She didn't want to say the words, didn't even want to think them. She closed her eyes for a second while he rubbed her arm reassuringly until she could speak. "I just *killed* somebody, William."

He pulled her up and into his arms. "Maybe. Marcus says he doesn't know which knife did what…and we don't know which injury actually killed him."

Quinn held herself back far enough to give him a look.

"He had a *gun* pointed at you, Quinn. He may or may not have actually been able to shoot you with it, but he sure wasn't going to hesitate to try. He killed your father, and had your grandfather killed…maybe he even did that one himself; we may never know. But he should have been hanged for those crimes in the first place.”

“Well, I wish he would have been.”

“Me too, love. Me too.”

She sat there for several minutes, reveling in the comfort and safety of his arms before she spoke again. “What happened with the gate?”

He shrugged. “I have no idea. Simon and Max both tried again to use it, several times. They even tried throwing things through it, all the way up until it was completely dark. And it never worked. It was like it didn’t even open.”

“Do you think we found the magnet and we didn’t even know it?”

“I don’t know. I don’t think so…even if we did, we didn’t *take* it anywhere.”

“So strange,” she said.

“Yes, it is.” He kissed her forehead. “Are you hungry? I’d like to see you get some food in you after that.”

She nodded. “We should probably go see the rest of your family…”

“*Our* family.”

“…*Our* family. I’m sure everyone’s worried.”

“They are. Thomas and Linnea are probably still pacing the hallway outside the apartment. You and Linnea can swap hero stories now.”

She shivered. “That didn’t feel heroic.”

He kissed her on the nose. “I think that means it really was.”

The next moon…Quinn was surprised the day she discovered herself calling it that automatically…was the most bittersweet time she’d ever spent in Eirentheos.

There was a general tone of celebration in the air everywhere. Hector's death and Tolliver's arrest had put a stop to the hostilities between the kingdoms…mostly. The border was opened again, and people were free to travel and be with their friends and families. Quinn was thrilled the day Eloise and Gene Bennett appeared at the castle with their son, Elliott, requesting an audience with her and William.

Not everyone was happy, of course, and they still heard reports of fighting inside Philotheum, as those who enjoyed power under Hector and Tolliver tried desperately to hold onto it. The queen's troops and the Friends of Philip quashed it as quickly as they could, but it was likely to continue for some time.

There were many in Eirentheos who had been badly scarred by the shadeweed incidents as well, who weren't happy about the open border, who lodged complaints with Stephen. It was going to be a long time before everything was fully back to the way it should be.

Quinn knew she would have much to learn when she took over leadership of Philotheum. One of the first things she did was ask Marcus to be her top advisor.

About a week after they'd arrived back in Eirentheos, they were surprised when Nathaniel appeared. He'd told Sophia that he was needed more in Eirentheos, to assist with the wedding preparations, to check in with the clinics he'd started, and to be with Quinn and William.

While they were happy he was there, and grateful for his help, he did spend much of his time away from the castle…especially on trips to Cloud Valley.

It was Thomas who clued them in to the reason for that. "You know he's thinking about asking Cammie Winthrop to court him officially," he said one day at lunch.

Quinn nearly dropped her glass of milk, causing Josh, who was sitting next to her, to snicker, and after she steadied the glass, she elbowed him in the ribs.

"Hey!" Josh said. "Aren't you supposed to be all dignified or something?"

"Queens reserve the right to put their little brothers in their proper places when necessary," she said, giggling before turning back to Thomas. "Cammie Winthrop, the widow?"

Thomas nodded. "With the three little kids… you remember them?"

"Of course." Quinn would have a hard time forgetting little Tallie and Caleb, whom she and Thomas had spent a night caring for in their house while their mother stayed at the Cloud Valley clinic. Her oldest child, David, had been a victim of the first round of shadeweed poisoning. "How do you know he's courting her?"

"These are the kind of things I know. I'm just that good."

"He's scary," Mia agreed, and Thomas kissed her on the cheek.

Things were warming up nicely between Linnea and Ben as well, and on the night they held a big celebration for Thomas and Linnea's sixteenth birthday…and Linnea's coming of age…Ben presented her with a courtship bracelet. It looked like Linnea might be joining them in Philotheum before too much more time had passed.

The day after the party, Linnea joined the Friends of Philip. Quinn was holding her hand when they received the news that the absence of both Hector and Tolliver from the capitol had delayed all executions in Philotheum, and that the queen was releasing all prisoners who had been jailed for treason against Hector's false rule. Dorian and James Blackwelder sent personal messages to Quinn and Thomas.

And Quinn and William got to relax and have a much nicer honeymoon. Although their afternoons and evenings were usually busy with family and preparations for their wedding and real move to Philotheum, the nights and mornings were just for the two of them.

They stayed together in the little apartment, keeping late hours and waking up late, too, ready to enjoy long, leisurely breakfasts from the trays that appeared outside their door.

Every night, Quinn would fall asleep in William's arms, thinking it wasn't possible for anyone to be more in love than she already was, but then she'd wake in the morning and discover that, somehow, she loved him even more.

The dark shadow that hung over all of it, of course, was the gate. Learning that Hector had known about the gate for a long time…and that it was almost certain he would have told others…terrified all of them.

Quinn knew that she'd made the right decision, that the gate had to be closed, that it would be safer for everyone if it never opened again. But still, the night that the gate was scheduled to open again, but didn't, was a difficult one.

"The worst part, I think," she told William that night when they were in bed, "is that my family doesn't even know yet. It's only been two days for them. They probably won't even try to come and visit until the summer. There hasn't even been a school day since we left…nobody will even know that we're both gone…and I never even got to say good-bye."

He held her for a long time before he spoke. "Maybe it's easier this way, love…for your friends at least. There's nothing you could have ever told Abigail or Zander that they would have accepted. It would have been another argument, and another bad memory."

"What are they going to think?"

"Your family… if we can really never go back, it will always hurt, Quinn. They'll miss you, we'll miss them. Your friends…" he sighed. "Your friends will be upset and talk about it for a few weeks, maybe a couple of months. But they'll believe your mother that you went away to live with your father's family. And they'll do what teenagers do in your world. They'll move on, go to college, get married…"

"Yeah, I suppose." She leaned back against him, playing with his fingers, twirling his wedding band around. "I still would like to know how we actually closed the gate…if what we did is permanent."

William cleared his throat. "I'm not sure *we* did anything."

"What do you mean? Do you think someone got there before us?"

He shook his head. "Not on our side, anyway."

"What?"

"Do you remember who else was standing with us when Alvin told us about the gate…when he gave us a very specific clue about how to find the magnet on the Bristlecone side…that it was buried with two pinecones?"

She thought about it for a second, and then gasped. "Owen."

He nodded. "Alvin never actually said the magnet on our side even could be found. He never said someone put it there on purpose. It could just be a magnetized piece of the earth itself, under the riverbed. But the one on the other side *was* buried on purpose. And, I've spent a lot of time on that riverbank, Quinn. There is a tree, maybe a few yards away from the bridge itself. A huge, really old pine tree, with two trunks wrapped around each other…like two trees were once planted in exactly the same spot."

Had her heart actually stopped beating? It felt like it. "But why would Owen…?"

"He said he has dreams sometimes, just like you do, love. He even knew who Alvin was. Maybe he had the same dream you did, or a similar one, and he knew what he had to do."

"Then why would he show me what he showed me… why put me through all of that, when Owen was the only one who could do something about it, anyway?"

"I only have theories, love. I don't know the real reasons. But if I had to guess, I would think that maybe it was important that closing the gate was a decision you had to come to yourself, for you to be all right with it. Maybe you needed to understand *why* it had to happen. And maybe it was to make sure we were at the gate when we needed to be to catch Hector."

She sighed. "Maybe."

"Either way, all I really know is that I'm sorry. I'm sorry you had to make the decision. I'm sorry that Sophia gave Hector power that she shouldn't have. I'm sorry that your father left and chose to marry and have a child in another world. I'm sorry that nobody put a stop to any of this before you. I'm proud of you for doing it. For being brave enough to put your kingdom and this world first, even though you had to pay the price for it. And I'm sorry for what it's costing you."

She wiped away her tears with the handkerchief he handed her. "I couldn't have done any of this without you, Will."

"Yes, you could have. I think you would have, all of it, whether I was around or not… but it's definitely better together. I'm honored, love, that you would allow me to stand beside you."

On the night before their "public" wedding, she finally decided to tell him. It had been six weeks since their real wedding, and he'd known for two. They'd bathed and changed into their pajamas, and she was standing there at the edge of the bed with her hair wrapped in a towel, comb in her hand, a shy look on her face and pink flooding her cheeks.

"Talk to me, love," he said, walking to her and pulling off the towel. He rubbed the ends of her hair the rest of the way dry and then took the comb from her.

She was quiet for several more seconds, as he began combing out one long strand at a time. Her fingers twitched nervously when she finally spoke. "I'm late, Will."

Further into their marriage…the second, third, and fourth times she would tell him this, he would tease her, ask what she was late for, and if she needed help finding her shoes again, but not this time.

This time, he could tell she was too nervous. He'd told her he would be happy when the day came, but perhaps she was still too unsure about how he would react. Or maybe she was unsure how she even felt about it herself.

So this time, he dropped the comb onto the bed and turned her around. He wrapped his arms around her waist and planted a soft kiss on her nose. "That," he said, "is truly the most beautiful thing I have ever heard in my life."

"What will people think?"

He smiled. She still didn't get it…still hadn't lived in this world long enough for it to be part of the way she thought. "They'll be ecstatic, Quinn. Everyone will. You're carrying the heir, love," he put his hand over her belly, which, though it would still be flat for several more weeks, seemed to be surrounded with an almost magical aura, "the future king or queen of Philotheum. Our child. I love him already. Or her…I don't care which it is." He bent down and kissed her there.

"But our wedding isn't until tomorrow. People can do math."

"It's not a secret that this wedding is only for show, Quinn. Everyone knows we're already really married. The news has spread through both kingdoms that we've fulfilled the prophecy. Relax, okay? Celebrate with me." He kissed her neck.

She swatted him playfully. "Don't tell me you're going to get all gushy and start picking out nursery furniture before I'm even showing."

"Oh, I am. Believe me. If you won't join me, I'm sure Linnea will."

She swatted him again, but this time she was giggling, and he pushed her down onto the bed, kissing her everywhere, making her giggle more.

"I'm going to do this until you're actually happy about it," he warned, kissing her belly again.

"All right, already, I give," she said, when she was laughing so hard that her cheeks had turned a bright, rosy red, and they were both out of breath. "I'm happy."

THE END

OTHER BOOKS BY BREEANA PUTTROFF

The Dusk Gate Chronicles
The continued adventures of the Rose family in
Eirentheos and Philotheum

Rumpelstiltskin's Daughter
A new take on an old fairy tale

COMING SOON
The Gatekeepers
An all-new adventure featuring some familiar characters

Visit www.BreeanaPuttroff.net to find out more!

www.ingramcontent.com/pod-product-compliance
Lightning Source LLC
Chambersburg PA
CBHW031617180726

48284CB00005B/1587